LOVE UNDISGUISED

THREE PREVIOUSLY PUBLISHED REGENCY NOVELLAS

GRACE BURROWES

AUTHOR'S NOTE

Author's Note

The novellas in this volume share several characteristics. First, they are all rompin' fun little happily ever afters—but you knew that. Second, they all originally appeared in novella trios I published with writin' buddies Susanna Ives and Emily Greenwood. Third, each of my stories has to do with lovers who must see past one another's disguises and assumed identities. Fourth, to get to that happily ever after, the protagonists must ask themselves: But who am I, really, and who can I become if I allow this wonderful love into my life?

What a marvelous question. I hope you enjoy the answers!

The Governess and Norse God originally appeared in **Marquesses at the Masquerade.**

His Grace of Lesser Puddlebury originally appeared in **Dukes in Disguise**.

Duchess in the Wild originally appeared in **Duchesses in Disguise**.

THE GOVERNESS AND THE NORSE GOD

Previously published in
Marquesses at the Masquerade

CHAPTER ONE

"You'll make all the other Vikings jealous, Papa, for you look splendidly savage."

Darien St. Ives, Marquess of Tyne, looked—and felt—a proper fool strutting about the nursery in trews, crossed garters, linen tunic, and fur cape.

"My choices were a highwayman, of which there will be dozens, a Titan, which would necessitate indecent attire, or this."

"My papa is the best Viking ever," Sylvie declared with the limitless loyalty of a seven-year-old. "Your longboat would be the longest, and the monasteries you sacked would be reduced to... to... mere reticules."

It's not that kind of sacking. Miss Fletcher, the girls' governess, had instructed Tyne on the inappropriateness of correcting Sylvie's word choices when the child was trying to be gracious. He knelt and scooped up his daughter, the only plunder worth capturing in the nursery.

"You think I cut a dash?"

Sylvie squeezed him about the neck. "The ladies will swoon at the sight of you. When you brandish your long sword, your enemies will tremble with mortal dread."

The ladies would swoon with boredom. Tyne's weapon of choice was a sharpened pencil most days, his shield an abacus. Solitude was his preferred fortress and the mathematical error his sworn foe. For a settled widower, the vast reaches of the marquessate's estate ledger books were adventure enough.

"Papa, you forgot to shave."

This worried the girl. She was easily worried, having lost her mother at the age of four and not having found Miss Fletcher until six months ago. The intervening two and a half years had been a succession of failures in the governess department, for which Tyne blamed himself.

As heir to a marquessate, he'd had governors and tutors from the age of three. The lot of them had been priggish, sedentary, and forever spouting rules.

Miss Fletcher was about as sedentary as a lightning bolt, though she spouted rules—at her employer.

You shall tuck Sylvie in on the nights that you are home.

You shall kiss both girls on the forehead before departing on the evenings you go out.

You shall recall their birthdays, and you shall most especially note the anniversary of their mother's death with a family outing to some location their mother enjoyed.

You shall resume socializing, so your daughters know that life moves on and they need not surrender to grief forever.

You shall bestow on your daughters the occasional bouquet of flowers, for how are the young ladies to know what to expect of a gentleman if their own papa doesn't comport himself as one?

For a small woman, Miss Fletcher had an endless store of commands and warnings. By the time she'd arrived, Tyne had been grateful for anybody who brought a sense of competence and order to his children's lives, and her approach had borne fruit.

Sylvie hadn't had a nightmare for months. Amanda was playing the pianoforte again.

"I did not shave," Tyne informed his daughter, "because Vikings were a rough lot. I'm trying to be authentic to my role."

Sylvie's solemn gaze said she was considering whether this excuse would wash. "You need a name, Papa. Vikings had grand names."

Oh, right. Sven Forkbeard. Harold Battleax. Ivan Bignose. All quite barbaric. "If I had an eye patch, I could be Tyne One-Eye."

"Not Tyne," she said, wiggling out of his grasp. "Then everybody would know who you are."

Lately, Tyne himself had felt a sense of his identity fading. He was the marquess, of course. He voted his seat in Parliament, he dined at his clubs, he made the occasional speech in the Lords regarding economic matters. At Yuletide, planting, and harvest, he opened the ancestral hall to the neighbors and tenants.

The year was a succession of predictable moves, like an old-fashioned court dance: Holidays in the country, remove to Town. Opening of Parliament, beginning of Lent. Polite invitations during the Season to make up the numbers, waltzes with wallflowers.

A restful lot, the wallflowers. He liked them and envied them their anonymity.

Then came grouse season, which he usually spent at the family seat, pretending to tramp about with a fowling piece on his shoulder, while searching for a place out of the wet to read for a few hours.

Harvest, the opening Hunt Ball, the holidays in the country... All the while, his daughters grew taller and more articulate. His estates prospered, and he... He missed Josephine, though he hadn't known his marchioness all that well.

"You should be Thor," Sylvie decided. "You need a hammer."

"How shall I waltz while carrying a hammer at Lord Boxhaven's masquerade?"

"You set the hammer down, Papa, just as you'd set down a cup of punch. Or you could hang it from your belt."

An untoward image came to mind of Thor's hammer swinging from Tyne's belt and smacking a dancing partner in an unmentionable location. This was what came of wearing crossed garters and a fur cape.

"To bed with you, darling Sylvie," he said, picking her up again and carrying her into her bedroom. "Miss Fletcher will not tolerate even a Norse god keeping you up past your bedtime."

The nursery maid rose from the rocking chair next to the hearth and ducked a curtsey.

"Doesn't Papa look dashing, Helms?"

"Very dashing, Miss Sylvie." The woman was likely twice Tyne's age and silently laughing at him. Perhaps he did need a hammer.

"Sweet dreams, Sylvie," he said, kissing her forehead. "If I see any unicorns, I'll capture one for you."

"I want a blue one," Sylvie said, scooting beneath her covers. "With a sparkling purple horn."

How could this fanciful child be his offspring? "Blue with a purple horn, of course."

"*Sparkling* purple, Papa."

"Your wish," he said, making her the sort of court bow that always earned him a smile. "Now say your prayers and go to sleep, or Miss Fletcher will hurl thunderbolts at us."

He escaped the nursery to the music of Sylvie's giggles. He had bid good night to Amanda before donning this outlandish costume. She'd grown too big to cuddle or carry about. She was acquiring the knack of a rational argument, which too few people practiced on a marquess.

Soon, she'd put up her hair.

Soon after that, Tyne's hair would sport some gray at the temples. Life was passing him by, which ought not to be possible when he was wealthy, titled, in great good health, and content in every particular.

Thirty-three was hardly ancient.

Perhaps he'd stop by the livery and find himself a convincingly stout mallet to carry about the ballroom. Anything to put off attending the masquerade for even an additional five minutes.

"HE'S GONE," Lady Amanda said, watching the coach pull away from the front drive two stories below.

She was thirteen years old, too young to have her own sitting room, but Lucy Fletcher had found the marquess to be a creature of habit rather than convention. When he gave an order—such as "Move my older daughter into her own bedroom."—he was in the *habit* of being obeyed. The largest bedroom on the nursery floor other than Lucy's had a sitting room; *ergo,* into that bedroom, Lady Amanda had been moved.

"But where is Papa off to?" Amanda murmured, letting the curtain at the window drop.

Lucy had no idea what events graced Lord Tyne's social schedule for the evening, but Amanda was at the age where adults fascinated her in a way they didn't interest younger children. To little Lady Sylvie, the marquess was simply Papa. He had sweets in his pocket or a scold to deliver. His other adult obligations were mysterious, vaguely annoying details to Sylvie.

Amanda, by contrast, was intrigued with her father's adult responsibilities.

What *was* a marquess, historically speaking?

What did the House of Lords *do* all evening that Papa had to be there so late?

Why did that simper-y Mrs. Holymere wiggle her fingers like that at Papa in the park?

Lucy knew exactly why the pretty widow wiggled her fingers— and her hips—at the marquess. He was too good-looking, too titled, too wealthy, and—worst of all—too decent not to gain the notice of some wiggly widow in the very near future.

So Lucy would do for the girls what she could while she was governess here, little though that might be.

"We can hope your father is enjoying a social outing," Lucy said. *For a change.* If Lord Tyne were one-tenth as attuned to polite society as he was to the politics of the realm, he'd have four engagements each night.

"How will I be invited to tea dances if Papa has no social connections?" Amanda asked, flouncing onto the sofa. "I won't have any callers, I won't be granted vouchers to Almack's."

"You'd best prepare yourself for holy orders," Lucy said. "Start memorizing the New Testament, because you will need the comfort of all four Evangelists in your endless spinsterhood."

Amanda's chin came up in a gesture reminiscent of her father. "I'll go to tea dances when I'm fourteen. I'm thirteen now."

Lucy took the place beside her, because this great eagerness to grow up, to be treated as a young lady, was normal. For a marquess's daughter to be normal, rather than hopelessly spoiled or regularly hysterical, was rare in Lucy's experience.

"You are thirteen years and three months," Lucy said. "Give your Papa some time to find his bearings. He is not a man prone to precipitous action. Your aunts have many connections."

Amanda made a face, such as Sylvie made when somebody forgot to sprinkle cinnamon on her porridge. "The aunties have babies. I'm never having babies. Aunt Eleanor says children ruin a woman's figure."

Amanda had only the merest beginnings of a figure, thank heavens. "Your aunt is approaching her fourth confinement. She is entitled to be testy. Will you read tonight?"

"You can't teach me more card games?"

Of course Amanda would ask that tonight. "I'm fatigued, Amanda. Perhaps another time. If the weather's fine tomorrow and your lessons go well, we can picnic in the park."

"With Syl-vie," Amanda said, martyrdom oozing from all three syllables. "I am the elder by six years, but I never go anywhere without her. I can't wait to put up my hair."

"Find a book, write to a cousin, experiment at your vanity with your combs and hair ribbons." Lucy half-hugged Amanda and rose. "I'll see you tomorrow."

"Good night, Miss Fletcher." Amanda remained on the tufted sofa, a precocious child left all alone for yet another evening.

Lucy knew how that felt. "Would you care to join your father some morning for an early outing in the park?"

Amanda had grown two inches over the winter, which meant she'd become too tall for her pony. His lordship had grumbled when Lucy had pointed out that the hems of Lady Amanda's habit nearly dragged on the ground, but he'd also come home the next day leading a dainty gray mare named Snowdrop.

"An early outing?" Amanda twiddled the gold tassel of a purple velvet pillow. "How early?"

"Dawn, when the mist is rising from the Serpentine, and the day is full of possibilities. All the fashionable gentlemen and not a few ladies ride at dawn."

Amanda set aside the pillow and crossed to her vanity. "Sylvie will never get up that early."

To be included in a family outing, she would. "She'd need a nap if she managed to waken at dawn."

Amanda pulled the black ribbon from her right braid. "She hates taking naps."

"While I love a refreshing respite in the middle of the afternoon. Those being in short supply, I'll bid you good night."

Before Amanda could ask for help arranging her hair, choosing a book, or deciding on a poem to memorize, Lucy slipped out the door. The hour was early by fashionable standards, but for a governess who had to change into a costume and find her way to a masquerade ball, time was of the essence.

THE MASQUERADE WAS BECOMING NOISY, the inevitable result of polite society donning masks and then partaking of the mayhem passing for mine host's lemon punch. In the ballroom itself, Lord Boxhaven's mama and grandmama would prevent outright debauchery, but in the garden shadows and unused parlors, mischief would abound.

Under the minstrels' gallery, a centurion leered down the bodice of a shepherdess in the manner of centurions from time immemorial. A portly satyr danced by with his arms about Good Queen Bess. The lady's skirts would likely keep her horned partner from living down to the potential of his costume on the very dance floor.

Tyne silently promised himself escape in fifteen minutes.

"Good evening, sir," drawled a voice to Tyne's right. "What a fine figure of a Norseman you make."

Ye gods. Lady Artemnesia Chalfont was nicknamed Lady Amnesia, so predictable was her habit of leaving a reticule, glove, or fan behind at a social call. She'd retrieve the item at the time of her choosing, and she always selected a moment when the bachelor sons of the household were on hand to play Find the Glove at my lady's direction.

"My thanks for your compliment," Tyne said, bowing. "I gather Roman legend inspired your own ensemble." She was Diana, aptly enough. She'd hunted Tyne for the past two Seasons, though she didn't appear to recognize him now. "I believe I saw a centurion patrolling beneath the minstrels' gallery."

The dance floor was full of the usual assortment of highwaymen, Rob Roys, a Louis Quinze with his Madame de Pompadour, and Greek goddesses. Couldn't have a masquerade without a few dozen bow-wielding ladies waltzing about in their dressing gowns.

Tyne was the only Thor so far. Thank heavens he'd bothered with a half-mask, or Lady Artemnesia would have started plaguing him the moment he'd arrived.

"Come now," Lady Artemnesia said, smacking his arm with a closed fan. "Should I trouble myself with a mere centurion when I can instead pass the time with a *god?*"

The centurion put his hand on the shepherdess's shoulder, and she sidled out from under his grasp. Because he didn't remove his paw from her person, the strap of her gown was briefly pushed off her shoulder and drooped down her arm. She reassembled her bodice, her mouth compressed in a line.

"Perhaps the centurion is free to dance," Tyne said, holding up the sledgehammer he'd rested headfirst against his boot. "I'm rather encumbered by my accoutrements."

"What a mighty hammer that is."

Seven more minutes, and Tyne would have outlasted his personal endurance record at a masquerade.

"Blasted thing is heavy," he said. "Puts a crimp in even a god's waltzing."

What sort of shepherdess carried a spear rather than a crook? And what *was* that upon her head? The young lady besieged by a Roman army of one had positioned her spear in her right hand, the same side upon which Maximus Gloriosus stood. His hand was back on her shoulder, his thumb brushing over her bare flesh in a most familiar manner.

"You will excuse me," Tyne said. "I believe I've spotted my partner for the next set."

"But you said you weren't dancing."

Tyne bowed and propped his sledgehammer on his shoulder. "I'm not." He sauntered along the edge of the ballroom, earning some stares. The sledgehammer was a lovely touch, quite authentic. Perhaps he'd start a fashion for carrying sledgehammers rather than sword-canes on Bond Street.

"Excuse me," Tyne said, bowing to the spear-wielding shepherdess with the bizarre millinery. "I believe my dance is coming up."

Gloriosus glowered at him. "The Valkyrie isn't dancing. She told me so herself. I'm sitting out with her."

Behind her half-mask, the lady's blue eyes flashed perdition to presuming soldiers. "I said I was not free to dance *with you*, sir. I suggest you find somebody who is."

Gloriosus was the Honorable Captain Dinwiddie Dunstable, an earl's younger son who had apparently suffered a few blows to the head in the course of his military career. He was as stupid as he was indolent, and he stood much too close to the lady's spear for his continued good health.

Tyne offered his arm. "Madam Valkyrie."

She shoved her spear at Gloriosus. "You may have this, to fend off all the women doubtless waiting to importune you for a turn on the dance floor."

She was a compact little creature, her hair pinned back under some winged copper contraption that might have been concocted of spare kitchenware. Her mask obscured her eyes and half of her nose, and her complexion was English-lady pale.

"We needn't dance," Tyne said, leading her in the direction of the gallery. "I've grown fond of striding about with a sledgehammer on my shoulder. If I set my hammer aside in this company, somebody's likely to steal it, and then I'd lose my magical powers."

"A guest at this gathering would steal a sledgehammer?"

"A guest, a footman, a maid. Some of the extra staff hired for a social gathering can be less than exemplary. It's a fine tool and the property of a god, after all. No telling what imps or fairies might yearn to wrest it from me."

She peered up at him, as if visual inspection might reveal how much of the punch Tyne had imbibed. "It's a hammer, sir. A handle and a weight, for smacking things."

"Like most well-made tools, this hammer has probably been handed down from father to son to nephew. One replaces the head, the other replaces the handle, and yet, it's the heirloom hammer, carrying a craftsman's share of pride from one generation to the next. I call that magic, and I'm a god, so you mustn't gainsay me. A pouting god is an unpredictable creature."

He found them a cushioned bench beneath a burned-out sconce. The guests strolling the garden were doubtless enjoying more of nature's delights than Tyne would consider decent, while the gallery was both quieter and cooler than the ballroom. A fine place to spend the three or four minutes remaining of his penance with...

How embarrassing. He could not place the Valkyrie's voice,

though she sounded familiar. Educated, of course, and not particularly regional.

"We could dance if you insist," he said. "I'll secret my hammer behind an arras."

"Thank you, no. My personal Praetorian Guard might think himself welcome to renew his attentions. Is that all people do at these affairs? Leer and flirt and swill punch?"

"I'm told this is called socializing among the English."

She stretched her feet out before her. "I'm English, rather than who I appear to be. You must forgive my lack of familiarity with masked balls."

She wore sturdy half-boots instead of dancing slippers. The Valkyrie were known to be unsentimental ladies, though half-boots were astonishingly practical.

"Isn't that rather the point of a masquerade?" Tyne asked. "To be somebody else for a short time, to impersonate a more daring, dashing creature than one is in truth?"

"I'm impersonating a friend," she said. "Somebody I went to school with. She asked me to attend, wearing this costume, so she might for once stay home and rest. I am not deceived, though. She wanted me to have an adventurous evening. I'm ready to fly back to Valhalla, if this is society's idea of an enjoyable evening."

The Valkyrie were also honest, apparently.

"I have a suggestion," Tyne said, rising. "Like the conscientious, plundering Viking that I am, why don't I make a pass through the buffet? The least you're owed is some sustenance before you give up on your adventure."

"I'll guard your hammer," she replied. "I love fruit and cheese above all combinations."

Tyne rested the long handle of his hammer against the side of the bench. Because the sconce was unlit, he couldn't see his companion in detail, but he could *hear* that she was smiling.

So was he. "I'm to watch for a blue unicorn with a purple sparkly horn. No other breed will do. Guard my hammer well, Madam Valkyrie."

He strode off, wondering if the single cup of punch he'd sampled had addled his wits. He was about to set a new record for his appearance at one of Boxhaven's masquerade balls. Sylvie would be proud of him, and Amanda would think him quite silly.

Though, as to that, he hadn't even confessed to Amanda where he'd be spending his evening. And poor Madam Valkyrie. The notion that anybody could meet with adventure at a venue as tedious as a masquerade ball was absurd. Tyne could locate strawberries, though, and oranges, and stewed apples.

But what on earth could he find to *discuss* with the lady while they consumed their victuals?

～

"FRUIT AND CHEESE," Thor said, passing Lucy a plate. "Also some ham, for I imagine all that flying you Valkyries do from battlefield to battlefield is hungry work."

He settled beside her on the bench, the furniture creaking under his weight. He was blond and Viking-sized, and the cape swirling about his shoulders and hint of golden beard on his cheeks gave him a dashing air.

Lucy took the plate, which was heaped high with food. "I can't possibly eat all of this."

"That's the idea," he replied, bumping her with his shoulder. "You eat as much as you like, and I'll deal with the rest. English plates are too small for a man of my northern appetites."

"Melon," Lucy said, picking up a silver fork. "I lose my wits in the presence of fresh melon."

"Your adventurous spirit has been rewarded. What else would make this evening enjoyable?"

"Peace and quiet, though this cheese is scrumptious." Blue veins, pungent flavor, creamy texture. The perfect complement to the melon.

Thor used his fingers to pop a rolled-up slice of ham into his mouth. "You sound weary, Madam Valkyrie."

His earlier comment, about flying from battlefield to battlefield, was more apt than he knew. Lucy's specialty was children who'd lost a parent. Even the aristocracy boasted a sad abundance of the half-orphaned. Wealthy parents might not take much notice of their offspring, but the children noticed when a parent died.

The agencies that placed governesses knew Lucy dealt well with such families, and thus she'd landed in Lord Tyne's household.

"I don't typically keep such late hours," she said, spearing a strawberry. "I'll pay for this tomorrow."

"Try sitting in Parliament. Why the wheels of government can only turn after dark has ever confounded me. I've a theory that most men have a quiet dread of the ballrooms and dinner parties, and Parliament schedules its debates and committee meetings the better to spare its members the social venues."

Lord Tyne seemed to thrive on his parliamentary obligations, though he also struck Lucy as a man in want of sleep most of the time.

"What would you rather be doing?" she asked. Perhaps Thor was an MP, though at this gathering, a titled lord was more likely.

He considered another rolled-up slice of ham. "I'm watching for stray unicorns. The work is hardly exciting, but you meet all the best people."

Was he *flirting?* "And you get to carry a very fine hammer about all evening."

"A consummation devoutly to be wished."

They ate the fruit and cheese—Lucy took a single slice of ham— in companionable quiet. "Take the last strawberry," and "Should have found you a spoon for the apples," the extent of the conversa- tion. Marianne wouldn't understand how this qualified as an adventure for Lucy—sharing a plate with a strange god—but Lucy was enjoying herself, mostly.

"Do you read much Shakespeare?" she asked.

Thor set the empty plate on the floor to the side of the bench. "I'm a literate Englishman, so I'm supposed to say yes. The truth is, I haven't had time to read for pleasure in years. Now, I'm called upon to read to my children occasionally, and they seem to like that. If I have a choice between brushing up on *Romeo and Juliet*, or spending an hour in the nursery, I've lately chosen the nursery."

He was married. This revelation should not have disappointed Lucy—she'd be back in her own bed in little more than an hour—but his marital status reminded her that this was a masquerade. He wasn't Thor, she wasn't in search of an adventure, or a *unicorn*.

"*Romeo and Juliet* isn't exactly light reading," Lucy said. "You're better off enjoying the company of your own children rather than reading about somebody else's doomed offspring." She'd never liked the tragedies, particularly tragedies that left the stage littered with dead adolescents. "Your children will thank you one day for reading to them."

He relaxed back against the wall, stretching long legs before him. "Have you children, that you can offer me such an assurance?"

"I had a papa. He read to us."

"I'm sorry for your loss." Those quiet words, spoken not by a bantering deity, but by a very human man who was himself a father, nudged Lucy's mood in a sad direction.

"Papa was a god," she said. "Jovial, wise, bigger than life, kinder than the angels. He knew what to say, he knew when to say nothing. I miss him."

Which was why she grasped the world of a grieving child.

"I miss my wife," Thor said. "Trite words, and we had a trite marriage. We'd known each other since childhood, had always expected to marry one another. We suited wonderfully, and yet, we barely knew each other. There's nothing trite about grief, particularly when bewilderment and guilt get into the mix." He laid his hammer across his lap. "My apologies for burdening you with such conversation. Loneliness makes fools of us."

Why couldn't Lord Tyne be this insightful? He was a good man, an honorable man, but sometimes, Lucy wanted to shake him. Perhaps his lordship needed some enchanted creature to kiss him, to waken him from his parliamentary bills and estate ledgers.

The wiggly widows would allow Tyne to stay lost in his politics and accounting, and that would not be a happy ending for Lucy's employer.

"What would help?" Lucy asked. "What would ease your grief and rekindle your joie de vivre?"

He lifted his hammer and considered the battered weight that made it an effective tool. "Joie de vivre is in short supply at Valhalla. As you doubtless know, we go in more for gory sagas, epic wrestling matches, and kidnapping maidens who don't belong to us."

He had a very nice smile, though Lucy wished he wasn't wearing a half-mask. She'd like to see his eyes more clearly. His voice was that of any well-educated Englishman, much like Lord Tyne's voice, but Thor's conversation included humor and honest emotion.

"The wrestling matches sound interesting," Lucy said as a satyr galloped past with a giggling nymph in tow. The gamboling couple apparently hadn't noticed Lucy and Thor sitting in the shadows, for the nymph allowed herself to be caught, then pressed against the wall for a protracted kiss. The sight should have been ridiculous—the satyr's horns sat askew on his head, the nymph's golden wig was similarly disarranged—but the sheer glee of the undertaking made Lucy cross.

The nymph wiggled free, gave the satyr a smack on the bum, then darted off down the gallery. "Ye gods and little fishes," Thor said, rising and shouldering his hammer. "I do believe it's time I kidnapped a maiden."

He took Lucy by the hand and led her off into the shadows.

CHAPTER TWO

What consenting adults got up to was no business of Tyne's, but he'd be damned if he'd be made to watch an orgy.

"I apologize for that... that... scene," he said, ducking out of the gallery and into the corridor that would take them to the front of the house. "I've overstayed my tolerance for the evening's entertainments. I will find your escort and take my leave of you."

He didn't want to. The lady was easy to talk to and sensible. Miss Fletcher, who answered to the same proportions as Madam Valkyrie, though with fewer curves, was also sensible. So why did Tyne feel as if he had to mentally prepare for every interaction with his children's governess?

"Are we in a hurry, sir?"

"A tearing hurry. Outside the purview of the chaperones in the ballroom, first the wigs fall off, and then clothing starts flying in all directions. I should have known better, but one loses track of time. Why otherwise rational human beings, who will nod to one another cordially in the churchyard, must comport themselves like—"

The Valkyrie planted her booted feet and brought Tyne to a halt.

"You are not responsible for their folly, and I'm hardly an innocent maiden to be shocked by kisses and flirtation."

Tyne peered at her, but the damned masks made interpreting an expression futile. "I was shocked. Some kisses are meant to be private."

"I was affronted, but mostly I was amused." She linked her arm with Tyne's. "If we're to find my escort, he's the only monk in the crowd."

The monk was Jeremy Benton, Lord Luddington, heir to an earldom. The Valkyrie moved in good company, though Luddington was a flirting fool.

"I expect Brother Monk will be among the last to leave. Shall I escort you home?" The offer was out in all its well-meant, bold impropriety before Tyne could call it back. Down the corridor, glass shattered and a roar went up from the crowd in the cardroom.

"I'll need my cloak," Madam Valkyrie said. "I can't parade across London looking like this."

"Not without your spear, you can't," Tyne said. "Take my cloak. What it lacks in fashion, it makes up for in warmth." He draped the fur cape about the Valkyrie's shoulders and fastened the frogs. The cloak reached nearly to the floor on her, which would afford her both warmth and modesty.

A laughing footman ran past—full tilt—with two shepherdesses in pursuit.

"Time to leave," Tyne said, offering his arm. "I believe that was Lord Malmsey impersonating a footman."

"Interesting strategy. I should at least tell Brother Monk that I've found another escort."

Tyne tripped the next escapee from the ballroom—a man dressed as a jockey—by the simple expedient of tangling the man's boots in the handle of the sledgehammer.

"Find the monk and tell him the Valkyrie is being escorted home by a trustworthy friend."

"I say, is that—?"

Tyne hefted his sledgehammer across his shoulders, like a pugilist stretching with an oaken staff. "Find him now, please."

The jockey saluted with his riding crop. "Will do, guv."

Tyne took the lady's hand, lest some marauding pirate carry her off, and led her through the front door. The night air was brisk, the drive lined with waiting coaches and lounging linkboys.

"We'll wait half an hour for my coachman to get through this tangle," Tyne said. "Do you live far from here?"

Her hand was warm in his. Valkyries were apparently no more inclined to wear gloves than Norse gods were. The familiarity of clasped hands inspired in Tyne a mixture of awkwardness and pleasure. He hadn't held hands with a lady since he and Josephine had courted. He had forgotten the comfortable friendliness of joining hands. He stood beneath the wavering torches, telling himself to turn loose of his companion and trying to summon his coach forward with a wish.

He wasn't a leering centurion or a frisky monk, and yet, dropping the lady's hand would seem more gauche than pretending he was at ease with the presumption.

"I live not far from here," Madam Valkyrie said. "We could walk the distance by the time your coach arrives."

"Fine notion. Lead on, if you please."

"You're sure it's no bother?"

How he wished she'd take off that dratted mask, but then he'd have to remove his own mask and reveal himself to be not a god, but rather, a shy marquess toting a sledgehammer through Mayfair.

"No bother at all, though I need a name for you. In my mind, you're Madam Valkyrie, which conjures images of strapping shield-maidens and longboats with bedsheets flapping from their rigging."

"You have a vivid imagination, Thor."

"If I am Thor, perhaps you could be Freya?"

"A goddess. That will serve."

They reached the foot of the drive, and Freya turned left, in the direction of Tyne's neighborhood. This was coincidence, of course, not good luck, fate, or divine providence. Certainly not a sign from on high, or Valhalla, or anywhere else of any import. Nonetheless, in the lowly region of Tyne's breeding organs, notice had been taken that he was in proximity to a female of marriageable age and interesting temperament.

"What made you decide to be a Valkyrie tonight?"

"I didn't. I'm impersonating a friend, and she chose to be a Valkyrie. Why are you Thor?"

"The costume was simple. The cloak you're wearing was sent to me by a cousin in Saint Petersburg. Crossed garters are a matter of some purloined harness, and the sledgehammer is borrowed. Add an old shirt and some worn chamois breeches and riding boots, and you have a god."

Also a surprisingly comfortable ensemble. No cravat half-choking a fellow, no sleeve buttons at his wrists, no waistcoat that must lie just so under his exquisitely tailored evening coat. Perhaps wardrobe alone explained why the Vikings were such a cheerful lot.

"This thing on my head," Freya said. "I feel as if I'm wearing a copper pot on my hair. It's beastly uncomfortable."

That Tyne should enjoy rare liberty from the tyranny of his tailor while Freya suffered seemed unfair.

"Let's have it off, shall we? Whatever stewpot gave up its life to become your helm won't be missed if it should end up in yonder bushes."

"Please," she said, dropping Tyne's hand. "The dratted thing pinches behind my ears." She tried to lift the helmet off, but some bolt or other caught in the collar of her cloak.

"Let me," Tyne said, moving behind her. He explored along the edge of the cape's collar with his fingers—gently and thoroughly—finding warm skin and soft tresses in addition to fur snagged on a joint in the metal. He ripped the fur and lifted the helmet. Calling upon long-dormant cricket skills, he tossed the helmet up and used his trusty sledgehammer to bat it off into the darkened square beside the walkway.

The helmet landed with a *clonk* many yards away.

"Better," Freya said. "My thanks."

She'd wrapped a scarf about her hair, like a turban, so Tyne was deprived of even hair color as a hint to her identity. She made no move to take his hand, but rather, twined her arm through his in proper escort fashion.

Well, drat. What was a god to do? Tyne had not the first clue how to comport himself with a goddess, but a gentleman made pleasant conversation with a lady.

"You mentioned that your papa read to you. Have you any favorite tales?"

"I loved the myths and legends, the stories with fantastical beasts and clever maidens. Improving sermons put me to sleep, and fables, with their thinly disguised moralizing, bored me."

"A woman of particular tastes." Miss Fletcher was such a female. Tyne had the odd thought that she'd be pleased with him for this night's version of socializing. "Do you still love the fantastical stories?"

She was silent until they reached a corner. "No, I do not. The heroic feats and strange lands are fine entertainment, but one grows up. The amazing accomplishments become dealing with disappointment, finding meaningful employment, and learning the uncharted terrain of adult responsibility."

She sounded so sad, so resolute.

"I had a tutor once," Tyne said, "who claimed that no great problem was ever solved without creativity and courage. The fables and legends can help us be courageous and creative. Perhaps you should resume their study."

He'd like to give her a book of fables or a compendium of the world's mythologies.

Or a kiss. Perhaps he should whack himself on the noggin with his borrowed sledgehammer.

"An interesting notion," she said. "What of you? Do you love to reread certain books? Know classical tales you can recite almost by heart?"

"Wordsworth's poetry is still wafting about in the dungeons of my memory, and I was quite fond—"

Freya stumbled on an uneven brick and pitched against Tyne. "I beg your pardon."

"Steady on," Tyne said, slipping an arm about her waist. She had a lovely figure, and he didn't turn loose of her until she had clearly regained her balance. "How much farther? I can summon a hackney if you're growing fatigued."

"I'm managing." She sounded as if she was uncertain where she'd left her abode. They were only two streets up from Tyne's town house, a delightful coincidence, in his estimation.

He resumed walking, his pace slower. "Will you think me unbearably forward if I ask whether a particular swain has caught your fancy?"

Now, he was grateful for his mask, though he wished he could read Freya's expression. This late in the evening, the neighborhood was only half conscientious about keeping terrace lamps lit.

"My affections are not engaged," Freya said. "I admire... a man, but he's much taken up with affairs of state, and my esteem is that of a distant acquaintance only. I suspect I would like him, given a chance to know him better, though I don't see that chance befalling me."

Her affections were not engaged. That was good. As for the rest of it...

"I'm sure he's a decent sort," Tyne said, "but he sounds as if he'd bore you silly before the conclusion of the first set. Best look elsewhere for a man worth your attention."

She turned at the corner, onto a street where not even half the porch lamps were lit. Tyne didn't know his neighbors well, and he certainly wasn't acquainted with the families on this street—not yet. "How can you form an opinion of a man whom I myself don't know that well?"

"Because he's an idiot," Tyne said. "A goddess admires him from afar, and he takes no notice. Trust me on this, for I am a god, and the workings of the mortal male are well known to me." He was a fool, but a fool who was enjoying his evening for the first time in... years?

"Do you fancy a particular lady?"

They'd reached a portion of the street where not a single household had bothered to light a lamp. This was providential, because some admissions were more easily made under cover of darkness.

"I notice my share of women," he said. "And those ladies are lovely, and sweet, and could easily become dear, but because I never had to learn the art of romantic persuasion, I know not how to make my interest apparent. I know not, in fact, if my interest qualifies as genuine liking, loneliness, or the base urge that motivates a great deal of male foolishness."

Or something of all three.

"You won't learn the answer to that conundrum if you simply watch the ladies waltz by on the arms of other men," Freya replied. "You can't expect them to divine your thoughts by magic."

Miss Fletcher would have offered that sort of observation, and she would have been right. Again.

"Is this where you live?" Tyne asked, for she'd brought them to a halt before a house from which not a single light shone.

"My friend bides here."

Tyne took a moment to count how many houses lay between the closest door and the corner. "You advise me to make my feelings known," he said. "In the manner of a plundering Norseman, I'll do just that. I'd like to kiss you, if you'd be comfortable allowing me such a liberty on a deserted street at a quiet hour. I've enjoyed your company very much, Freya, and—"

She mounted the steps that led to the covered porch, where the darkness was dense indeed. Tyne followed, and she passed him what could only be her mask.

"Your plundering needs work, sir. Allow me to demonstrate."

She plucked off his mask and tossed it aside, then braced herself with a grip on Tyne's shoulder, cupped his cheek with her free hand, and kissed him.

SO THIS WAS ADVENTURE, to stroll down a darkened street with a strange gentleman, discussing highly personal subjects and wishing the night could go on forever.

In the company of her tall escort, Lucy felt daring, bold, and oddly safe. With Thor, she wasn't simply a governess owed the courtesies shown to a member of a marquess's staff, she was a female to be protected against all perils.

The greatest peril had become her own curiosity.

Not the long-dormant curiosity of the eager girl. Lucy had weathered that risk with a dashing infantry captain named Giles Throckmorton III. She'd hoped for passion of mythic proportions and reaped only rumpled clothing, awkwardness, and some anxious days. Three weeks later she'd received a nigh-illegible letter from Giles releasing her from any obligation arising from "that dear, brief friendship."

For months, she'd pined and paced and considered writing back to him, protesting that she would wait, she could be patient, and they'd had more than friendship. Except... they hadn't *even* had a friendship. They'd had a foolish, awkward moment. She had burned his letter years ago, when she'd learned that Giles had married a Portuguese lady and was growing grapes and raising children with her on the banks of the Douro.

The curiosity that gripped Lucy now was more dangerous for being more mature. Thor raised philosophical questions: How much of Lucy's yearning for male companionship was simply loneliness? She attributed loneliness to the Marquess of Tyne, but perhaps it belonged to her as well.

Did his lordship even sense that he'd caught her interest, and what if he had? Was he politely ignoring her, for Tyne was unrelentingly polite? Was Lucy willing to embark on that trite convention of bad judgment, an affair with her employer?

This conversation with Thor would stay with her long after she'd bid him good night, and later—under bright sunshine—she'd consider the conundrums he'd raised. Now, she'd send him on his way with a kiss.

He was tall enough that Lucy had to go up on her toes to kiss him. He accommodated her by bending his head and taking her in his arms. The handle of his hammer hit the porch rug with a soft thump, and Lucy got a whiff of bay rum before she learned the true meaning of the verb *to plunder*.

Thor's strength was evident in the security of his embrace. He knew how to hold a woman, how to bring her body against his in a manner that offered shelter as well as intimacy. He was no green recruit to the ranks of manhood, but rather, a seasoned campaigner who could conquer by negotiation.

Lucy pressed her lips to his and half missed her target, getting the corner of his mouth, which kicked up in a smile. He corrected her aim by settling his lips over hers—*I'm here, you see?*—a greeting and then a tease with his tongue.

He tasted of cinnamon, from the stewed apples, and patience which was all him. Lucy gradually understood that she was being invited to explore as he did, his fingers tracing over her features and his tongue acquainting her with his mouth.

She had fallen for the army captain's clumsy charms, even knowing her soldier was more enthusiastic than skilled.

Thor was skilled enough to hide his enthusiasm, to build Lucy's interest instead. By the time she rested her forehead against his chest, she was hot and disoriented, and in no doubt that she was desired by a god.

Who is he? His shirt was of the finest linen. His scent up close included the sweet smoke of beeswax candles. He came from means, he was well educated, and unlike Lucy, he had the leisure to regularly mingle with the fancy and the frivolous.

His hand wandered her back, while Lucy tried to gather her wits and mostly failed.

"We must part," he said, "for the hour grows late, and lingering in London's night shadows is never well advised. May I see you again?"

He wasn't asking to pay a call on her, and that was just as well, for his lordship's housekeeper had been quite clear that Lucy was not to encourage the notice of any followers.

"That might not be wise." Though it would be adventurous and—with him—passionate.

Thor turned loose of her and picked up his hammer. "Wasn't it you who said I must make my sentiments known, madam? You who encouraged me to speak of my feelings lest opportunity be lost forever? I'm honestly a dull fellow. I'll not be snatching you away to my mountain hall or plying you with mead until you're lost to all sense. I'd thought another quiet stroll might appeal, or an ice at Gunter's."

Lord Tyne took his daughters to Gunter's, one of few pubic venues in London where the genders were free to mix socially. If Tyne should get wind that Lucy was meeting with a gentleman, he'd be curious, at least.

"The Lovers' Walk," she said. "Vauxhall, a fortnight hence at eleven of the clock. I'll wear your cape."

"A fortnight?" Clearly, he'd hoped to see Lucy sooner, and that gratified more than it should.

"If either of us should fail to appear, we'll know that a single encounter will have to suffice. One of those charming young ladies might return your interest, and I might engage the notice of my busy, distant gentleman."

Though, how likely was that, when Lucy had bided under his lordship's nose for months, and he'd done little more than hand her out of carriages and ask her to pass the teapot?

A linkboy trotted past, the lamplight giving an instant's illumination to an aquiline profile and hair curling with the evening damp.

"We are to be prudent deities," Thor said. "That ought to be a contradiction in terms."

She liked him. Liked his lively mind, his subtle humor, his skillful kisses. If nothing else, this evening had proved that she could like a man and that there was more to passion than she'd known with her randy captain.

"I will be a prudent, impatient goddess for the next two weeks," she said. "On that thought, I shall bid you good night."

Lucy had chosen this house because a pair of widowed sisters lived here. They would neither hear a conversation on their porch, nor spare the expense of candles kept lit through the night. They would assuredly keep their front door locked, however, and thus sending Thor on his way was imperative.

He leaned down to kiss Lucy's cheek. "Eleven of the clock, Vauxhall. Two weeks. Until then, I'll see you in my dreams."

He strode off into the darkness, pausing only to scoop up his mask. She watched him go, waited another ten minutes, then found her mask and hurried down the walkway toward home.

"DO MY EYES DECEIVE, or is the Marquess of Tyne making a social call upon me?" Lord Luddington asked, ambling to the sideboard. "Hair of the dog or tea?" He lifted the glass stopper from a decanter and let it clink back into place.

"Neither," Tyne replied, "though of course you should dose yourself with whatever medicinal will ease your present ailment. I trust you kept late hours last night, as usual?"

Luddington had been the sole monk at the previous evening's bacchanal. Sole, but hardly solitary.

He pushed sandy-blond hair from his eyes and poured himself a tot of brandy. "The ladies at the masquerade were much in want of company, and my charitable nature had to oblige them. I didn't see you there, but then, how can the blandishments of a masked ball compare with parliamentary bills regarding turnpike watermen?"

"Without those watermen—"

Luddington held up a hand. "Please, Tyne, no politics. I truly did overexert myself last night. The ladies were all agog about some chap who'd decked himself out as Thor. You never heard so much twittering and cooing about the size of a man's hammer before, and nothing would do but they must compare... well, the night was *long*, so to speak."

Tyne had already returned the sledgehammer to the stable. "Thor, you say? Not very original."

"What would you know about originality? He had the hammer, the fur cape, the trews, the whole bit. Strode about the ballroom with his shirt half unbuttoned and sent the ladies into quite a stir. I reckon he went back to Valhalla with some toothsome shepherdess, for nobody knows who he was."

"A good-sized fellow?"

Luddington peered at Tyne over the rim of his glass. "A bit taller than you, more broad-shouldered. More the strapping specimen, less the scholarly politician."

Insult warred with amusement, though Tyne had time for neither. Miss Fletcher had requested an interview with him before supper, and Tyne dared not be late.

"You doubtless escorted a lady to the festivities. What did she make of the Norseman?"

Tyne posed the question while peering out the window to the garden behind the house. Daffodils were making an effort, and the tulips weren't far behind. He waited, his back turned to his host, and hoped for a name.

"The plaguey female ran off. Some tipsy jockey told me she'd departed the premises with a woodsman or a barbarian of some sort, and my sister will tear a strip off my backside, for I didn't see any woodsmen. Saw plenty of pillaging and sacking as the evening wore on, not that I'm complaining."

"Your sister dislikes woodsmen?"

Luddington downed half his drink, then refilled his glass. "You don't know Marianne. She entrusted some friend of hers to me, an acquaintance from finishing school, and then I lost her. Marianne frowns on brothers who lose her friends. *I* frown on me for losing her friend."

"Then Marianne ought not to send her friends to masquerades, where the entire point of the evening is to lose one's identity. You don't know the name of the female whom you lost?"

Tyne had little acquaintance with Marianne Benton, though she'd made her come out a good ten years ago. If she was Freya's contemporary, then Freya was a mature woman, a point that weighed in favor of keeping Tyne's next appointment with her.

"I wasn't supposed to know who she was," Luddington said. "I prefer not to be burdened with a lady's secrets—or a shepherdess's—for even Boxhaven's masquerades are not monuments to strict propriety. Next time he holds one, you should go, Tyne. Do you good to get out and socialize with a friendly nymph or two."

Luddington gave him a bored look that suggested Tyne's secret was being kept—for now.

"I'll bear your suggestion in mind, though a hammer strikes me as a particularly inane fashion accessory when a gentleman's usual purpose is to stand up with the wallflowers. Good day, Luddington, and next year, consider escorting a Valkyrie instead of a shepherdess. I'll leave you to your hair of the dog and show myself out."

Luddington gestured elegantly with his glass, spilling not a drop. "A pleasure, Tyne. As always."

Tyne made his way home, his steps taking him past the house where he'd kissed his goddess the night before. He'd been up early out of habit and taken a morning stroll through the back alleys of the neighborhood, pausing to inquire at the mews regarding the sixth house from the corner.

A pair of devout older widows dwelled there—both stable boys had agreed. The ladies kept a pony cart for trips to Hounslow, where one of them had a son who was a schoolteacher. No young lady had ever bided with them, and the son was unmarried.

Freya, in other words, had lied. Tyne did not care for dishonesty, but a lady was entitled to her privacy when a masked man asked for kisses in the dark. He hadn't exactly been forthcoming himself.

Her demeanor had suggested she'd have little patience with a dull marquess who could spend fifteen minutes debating which waistcoat to wear for a speech fewer than a dozen men would hear.

He set aside thoughts of Freya, for another forthright female awaited Tyne in the family parlor, one whom he was equally unlikely to impress with his speeches, ledgers, and politics.

"Miss Fletcher, good day."

She set aside her book and rose. "Your lordship." The light in her eye suggested a battle was about to be joined, and Tyne barely refrained from smiling in anticipation.

CHAPTER THREE

The scent of England was always Giles Throckmorton's first impression of home: briny and brisk regardless of the weather, with an undertone of ancient geology, as if the stony hills ringing Portsmouth lent an aged, unchanging bedrock to even the smell of the place.

The languages he heard along the docks and in the coaching inn's common were mostly English, with smatterings of French, other Continental tongues, and the occasional American accent. The variety would have been still greater in Portugal, for that nation had made seafaring even more a part of its soul than England had.

"Good to be home again?" Giles's brother, John, asked, stepping down from a smart traveling coach in the inn yard.

"Always good to be home, but it's beastly cold here."

John clapped him on the back. "This is a fine spring day, nearly hot, but every time you come home, you complain of the cold. Portugal has made you soft."

Portugal had made Giles desperate.

He returned to England yearly, mostly to get away from his children, also to gain a respite from the alternating work and worry of the vineyard. He'd learned enough of the winemaker's trade to realize wealth was accumulated over decades, if not generations.

Worries accumulated overnight.

"How are matters in Portugal?" John asked as Giles's trunks were loaded onto the back of the coach.

John was being tactful, but then, John was a diplomat, always haring off to some treaty negotiation or conference.

"Matters in Portugal are difficult. The twins grow in mischievous tendencies as well as height, and the younger two follow the example of their elders. Without Catalina to mind the domestic concerns, I'm hard put to give the vineyards the attention they're due."

"You were married to the lady for years. Of course you still miss her."

Giles missed Catalina's ability to charm her father and brothers into assisting with the vineyard. He missed her management of the nursery and the household, however mercurial that management had been. He'd loved and admired his wife, and loved and admired the notion of building a vineyard empire with her.

But more than a year after her passing, there was also much —*much*—Giles did not miss about her. The guilt of that admission was tempered by the notion that if the boot had been on the other foot, Catalina would likely have felt the same about him.

"Do you like your wife, John?"

John pretended to study how the groom secured a trunk to the boot. "I like Agnes exceedingly, more with each passing year. We are friends first and spouses as a result of that friendship. Agnes understands me, and I very much value her counsel and affection."

Catalina's counsel had often been delivered at high volume and to the accompaniment of shattered porcelain. Her affections had become rare after the birth at long last of a daughter. Had Catalina not perished of a lung fever, the marriage would doubtless have found firmer footing as the children matured.

Giles had assured himself of that happy prognostication often in the early days of widowerhood. For the past few months, he'd taken

to assuring himself that an English wife, one inured to the tribula-
tions of the nursery and happy to improve her station even at the cost
of journeying to a foreign land, would solve many of his troubles.

"Agnes will be so pleased to see you," John said as a fresh team
was put to. "We very nearly dropped in on you after our last jaunt to
Gibraltar."

"I would have been delighted to receive you." A lie, that. Without
Catalina to nip at the house servants' heels, the staff did the bare
minimum in terms of cleaning and maintenance. The harvest last
year had been disappointing, and competition in the port market was
fierce.

Giles was determined to take an English bride back to the chaos
he'd left behind in Portugal, and his efforts in that regard would start
with Miss Lucy Fletcher. The lady had cause to recall him fondly—
very fondly, in fact. He'd paint a romantic picture of his fiefdom in
Portugal, play a few bars of the grieving widower's lament, and take
Miss Fletcher away from the drudgery of her life as a governess in the
household of some stodgy old marquess.

Giles was even handsomer than he'd been as a youth. Lucy was
doubtless plainer than ever, and sweeping her off her feet would be
the work of a few weeks' courtship.

MISS FLETCHER HAD INSISTED that she and Tyne dispense
with the bow-and-curtsey ritual. Tyne had wanted to object—a
gentleman extended courtesy to everyone, not only to the people he
sought to impress—but she'd pointed out that he did not bow to the
housekeeper and would feel ridiculous doing so.

"You asked for a moment of my time," Tyne said. "I trust Sylvie
and Amanda are well?" This was all Tyne knew to do with her—
discuss the girls, be polite, keep his questions to himself. Freya's
comments came back to him, though: How was a woman to know
Tyne esteemed her if he never gave voice to his sentiments?

Miss Fletcher was nothing if not tidy, though today her hair was arranged more softly about her face. Her dress was a high-waisted blue velvet several years out of fashion, and the color flattered her eyes. If he said as much, she'd likely box his ears with her book.

"Lady Sylvie and Lady Amanda are in good health, my lord. Both, however, could stand to improve their equestrian skills."

Tyne had ridden like a demon almost before he'd been breeched. He missed that—riding hell-bent at dawn, his brothers thundering along beside him. Josephine hadn't had much use for horses, or the stink, horsehair, and mud that inevitably resulted from time in their company.

"Did you or did you not," Tyne said, "recently scold me into buying Amanda a mare to replace the equine sloth she was previously riding? If she can ride a pony, she can ride anything."

"With the pony, she was on a lead line most of the time. A lady should be in command of her own mount."

Miss Fletcher wore a lovely scent, not one Tyne had noticed previously. Minty with a hint of flowers. "What were you reading?"

She edged to the left two steps, putting herself between Tyne and the discarded book. "I was merely browsing, awaiting your arrival."

He reached around her. Myths, Fables, and Ancient Legends of the North *by Roderick DeCoursy.*

"Are you in want of adventure, Miss Fletcher? Looking for an exciting tale or two?"

She took the book from him. "And if I am? Do you suppose because I am a governess that I don't enjoy a light dose of excitement from time to time? We can't all be devoted to ledgers and parliamentary committee meetings."

She was in fine form today, very much on her mettle. "Regardless of my boring proclivities, I will not subject my daughter to unnecessary risks. You are working up to a demand that I take the girls riding in the park."

Ah, he'd surprised her. She didn't retort until she'd turned to the shelves.

"Most children on this square are taken for regular outings in the park on horseback. My *request* would have been reasonable."

She was trying to reshelve her myths and fables, but the library had been arranged for Tyne's convenience, and she was petite, relative to him. He came up behind her, took the book from her, and slipped it onto the shelf above her head.

She turned, and abruptly, Tyne was improperly close to his daughters' governess. She regarded him steadily, neither affronted nor welcoming.

"What is that scent?" Tyne asked, leaning down for a whiff of her hair. "It's delightful."

She apparently found the toes of his boots fascinating. "Did you just pay me a compliment, my lord?"

He had the odd thought that she'd fit him much as Freya had were he to take her in his arms—which he was not about to do. He did, however, treat himself to another sniff of her fragrance.

"I did, and now that I know the heavens do not part, nor the end times arrive as a result, I might venture to pay you another. I'd take the girls riding, except I have no notion how well Amanda's mare would deal with such an outing."

He stepped back, though he wished he knew which myth or fable Miss Fletcher had been reading.

"Surely you bought a quiet mare for your daughter?"

"Shall we sit? I've been running all over Town today, and last night went later than planned."

Miss Fletcher had fixed notions about what constituted excessive familiarity between employer and governess. She joined the family for informal meals, always arriving and leaving with the girls. She attended services with them. If Tyne took the young ladies to call on family, Miss Fletcher did not go along.

And yet, the girls were blossoming in her care. Tyne had no doubt she would give her life for them, and surely her ferocious loyalty excused Tyne's vague fancies regarding a woman in his employ. He tugged the bell-pull and prepared to embark on a small adventure of his own.

"You're ringing for tea?" she asked.

"Am I to starve for the sake of your etiquette, Miss Fletcher? Supper is hours away, and I'm peckish. Perhaps you could stand some sustenance yourself."

She looked tired to him, as if an afternoon spent curled up with that blasted book wouldn't have gone amiss. She perched on the edge of the sofa, like a sparrow lighting on an unfamiliar windowsill. Had some loss or heartache made her so careful with social boundaries? The idea explained much, including a love of fairy tales masked by a brisk lack of sentimentality.

"A cup of tea while we discuss an outing for the girls would be permissible," she said.

"Two cups," Tyne replied. "They're quite small. If Englishmen were sensible, they'd drink their ale from tea cups and their tea from tankards. We'd all get more done that way, and the streets would be safer."

"Back to Lady Amanda's mare, if you don't mind, sir."

Tyne did mind, but he was nothing if not persistent. Freya had been right—fate would not hand him a marchioness and the girls a step-mama. He hoped his Valkyrie kept their appointment in two weeks, mostly so he could thank her for inspiring his determination where Miss Fletcher was concerned.

"You refer to my daughter's lovely mare," Tyne said, "whom the auctioneer assured me could canter from one moonbeam to the next, never putting a hoof wrong. I'm not of a size to ride the mare myself, else I'd take her out the first few times. If she should shy at the sight of water or prove unruly in traffic, Amanda will take a fall, and matters will deteriorate apace."

"Can't the grooms take her out?"

"My grooms disdain to ride aside, and Snowball is a lady's mount."

"Snowdrop, my lord."

"Mudbank, for all I care. I propose that you take out the mare, Miss Fletcher. I will ride with you, so the horse can accustom herself to the company of my gelding. If all goes smoothly after several trial rides, Amanda can join me for a hack."

A fine plan, so of course Miss Fletcher was scowling. She didn't pinch up like a vexed schoolteacher, but her brow developed one charming furrow, and her lips—she had a pretty mouth—firmed.

"My habit is hardly fashionable, my lord."

"But you do have one, and you have neglected your adventuring sorely. Ride out with me, Miss Fletcher, and call it an adventure."

A tap on the door saved Tyne from elaborating on that bouncer. No lady had considered any time in his company adventurous, with the possible exception of Freya. The first footman wheeled in the tea trolley, and Tyne waved him off.

"Miss Fletcher, would you be so good as to pour out?"

Her scowl faded as the dawn chased away the night, to be replaced by a soft, amused smile.

"Never let it be said I allowed you to starve, my lord. Have a seat. You prefer your tea with neither milk nor sugar, if I recall."

That she'd noticed this detail pleased him, thus proving that he was addled. "You are correct, while you prefer yours with both."

Her smile became a grin, and she fixed Tyne's tea exactly as he preferred it.

LUCY WAS lucky to get on a horse once a month, if Marianne wanted to hack out on Lucy's half day. The outings invariably left her sore and frustrated.

Sore, because she didn't ride often enough to condition her muscles to the exertion.

Frustrated, because as a girl growing up in Hampshire, she'd ridden almost every day when the weather had been fine. The weather this morning was very fine indeed, though brisk enough that the horses would be lively.

The prospect of starting her day with a gallop in the park had her in a happy mood, despite her out-of-date riding habit, despite the early hour.

"Up you go," Lord Tyne said when Lucy had been ready to lead the mare over to the ladies' mounting block.

His lordship looked fixed on the task of assisting Lucy into the saddle, and she was in too good spirits to argue with him. His grasp around the ankle of her boot was secure, and when he hoisted her into the saddle, she got an impression of considerable—and surprising —strength.

She took up the reins as his lordship arranged her skirts over her boots, a courtesy her brothers had never shown her.

"Thank you," Lucy said. "If you could—"

He was already taking the girth up one hole. "The stirrup is the correct length?"

"Yes, my lord."

He walked around to face the mare. "Behave, madam, else it shall go badly for you."

So stern! For an instant, Lucy thought his warning was for her. Then the marquess stroked his gloved hand gently over the mare's neck, giving the horse's ear an affectionate scratch. "Miss Fletcher tolerates no disrespect," he went on, "and any high spirits must be expressed within the confines of ladylike good cheer."

Ah—he was teasing. He was teasing *Lucy*, for one could not tease a horse.

"Walk on, Snowdrop," she said. "An entire park awaits our pleasure. If his lordship thinks to interfere with our enjoyment, it will go badly for him."

His lordship swung into the saddle without benefit of a mounting block and walked his gelding alongside the mare.

"We'll start slowly," he said as the horses clip-clopped down the alley, "because you ladies have not kept company before. Attila, stop flirting."

The gelding, a substantial black with a flowing mane, whisked his tail.

"He's a good lad," Tyne said. "Up to my weight, calm in the face of London's many terrors, but he's shamelessly spoiled for treats. About the mare, he cares not at all. For the slice of apple in your pocket, he'll be your personal servant."

"I brought carrots."

"Carrots might earn you an offer of eternal devotion. Where did you learn to ride?"

As they navigated the deserted streets of Mayfair at dawn, Lucy saw a new side to her employer. He was an attentive escort, pleasant company even, asking her one polite question after another and listening to her answers.

Actually listening, to the story of how she came to be able to write with either hand.

"I was determined not to fall behind my brothers in my school-work, and yet, my wrist was broken, not sprained. I had to learn to write with my left hand or suffer the torments known only to younger sisters with very bright older siblings."

"You were allowed to climb trees?" his lordship asked as the horses walked through the gates to the park.

"If one is to invite one's dolls to tea in the treehouse, one had best be a good climber. Shall we let the horses stretch their legs? Snow-drop has been a pattern card of equine deportment."

Attila, on the other hand, was prancing, apparently ready for a gallop.

"Let's trot to the first bend in the Serpentine and then find room for a more athletic pace."

Tyne was being careful with her, giving her and the mare a chance to become cordial. Attila was having none of it and all but cantered in place as Lucy cued Snowdrop into a ladylike trot. A few other riders were up and about, but today was Thursday. Most everybody of note had likely been at Almack's late the previous evening. They would miss this glorious morning in this gorgeous park.

Attila had taken to adding the occasional buck to his progress, which his lordship rode with the same equanimity he showed toward parliamentary frustrations, feuding footmen, and cross little girls. Truly, not much disconcerted Lord Tyne, a quality Lucy hadn't much appreciated in recent months.

"This way," Lucy called, turning Snowdrop onto a straight stretch of bridle path. "Tallyho!" She urged the mare into a canter, and joy welled, for the horse covered the ground in a beautiful, smooth gait.

Tyne let Attila stretch into a canter as well, and the gelding soon overtook the mare, though Snowdrop refused to be baited. She kept to the same relaxed, elegant pace, and every care and woe Lucy had brought with her into the saddle was soon cast away.

When the horses came down to the walk, Lucy was winded, while Tyne had plenty of breath to scold his horse.

"You, sir, are a naughty boy. You wanted to show off for the ladies, though how you expect to gain anybody's respect by bucking and heaving yourself about in such an undignified manner beggars all comprehension. You should be ashamed of yourself, and"—the gelding began to prance—"anticipate the cut direct from Miss Snowdrift if you ever attempt to stand up with her again."

Tyne's chiding tone was offset by an easy pat to Attila's shoulder.

"Do you always talk to your horse, my lord?"

"Is there a proper English equestrian who doesn't?"

"No," Lucy replied, "and the conversation is invariably witty and charming."

"Do you imply that I could be witty and charming, Miss Fletcher?"

Despite his bantering tone, Lucy suspected the question held some hint of genuine curiosity. "I dare to imply that very possibility, my lord." He was also an athlete, with natural ease in the saddle, strength, skill, and fitness Lucy would not have suspected based on the time he spent penning correspondence or drafting bills.

Another feature of his riding was tact. He reminded his horse to behave; he chided; he did not bully.

"I speak honestly when I say that you ride well, Miss Fletcher. We must get you into the saddle more often, because you clearly enjoy yourself there."

A governess did not expect such consideration. "I love to ride—really ride, not merely mince along on some doddering nag wearing a saddle. I sometimes forget that."

"Why is it," Tyne said, "the voice of duty can drown out all other worthy considerations? We must make an agreement, Miss Fletcher, to remind one another that an occasional gallop in the park, an afternoon with a good book, a picnic even, are all that makes the duty bearable sometimes."

The gelding snorted, the mare swished her tail. As the horses walked along beneath greening maples on a beautiful morning, Lucy realized once again that her employer was lonely and that part of his devotion to duty—like hers—was a means of coping with the loneliness.

"I will honor that pact," Lucy said, "though picnicking with two high-spirited children isn't exactly my idea of a treasured joy."

"Who said anything about dragging that pair along? I meant picnicking in the company of a congenial adult of the opposite sex. Perhaps even—one delights to contemplate the notion—reading to her on a blanket spread upon the soft spring grass, or sharing a glass of wine with her while she cools her bare feet in the summer shallows of an obliging brook."

Oh, how lucky that lady would be. Tyne had a beautiful reading voice, and his grip on a wineglass had the power to rivet Lucy's attention. She had discovered months ago the pleasure of sketching his lordship's hands, trying to capture their grace and masculine competence with pencil and paper.

As he tormented her with further descriptions of his summer

idyll, Lucy's imagination went further: What would Tyne's hands feel like *on her?*

"You are quiet, Miss Fletcher. Has the company grown tedious? Shall we have another gallop? And I do mean a gallop. You and Snow-moppet are fast friends now, and I know you want to see what she can do."

"One more run," Lucy said, "and then we must return to the house, for the children will be rising."

Lord Tyne aimed Attila back up the path they'd cantered over earlier. "The children have highly paid, highly competent nursery maids to attend them, a staff of four in the kitchen to feed them, and various other domestics to ensure there's no falling out of windows, climbing of trees, or other wild behavior. After you."

He gestured with his riding crop. Attila pretended to spook, and Snowdrop lifted easily from walk to canter and from thence to a tidy gallop.

Some of Lucy's joy in the outing had fled, because she was soon to reunite with her duties. She'd change out of her habit and into the drab attire of the governess, correct the children's manners at the breakfast table, and turn her attention to... irregular French verbs.

The mare seemed to share Lucy's diminished glee, for her gallop was less than exuberant by the time the path joined one of the park's larger thoroughfares. Lucy slowed Snowdrop in anticipation of that turn and realized the mare wasn't simply tiring, she was off stride.

"Miss Fletcher!" Lord Tyne called from three lengths back. "Something is amiss with your mount. She's favoring the right front, blast the luck."

He was out of the saddle in a smooth leap before Attila had come to a halt. The gelding stood obediently as Lord Tyne lifted Snowdrop's right front hoof.

"She's picked up a dratted stone. Why the bridle paths aren't strewn with straw, I shall never know." He produced a folding knife, flipped it open, and applied the tip to the offending stone. "Some lord or other ought to introduce a bill forbidding the use of gravel near bridle paths. The poor beast could have been seriously injured. Walk her a few paces, if you please."

He set down the mare's hoof and tucked the knife away.

Lucy directed Snowdrop across the grass rather than along the path. "She's not right," she said. "She's not lame, but she's not right."

Attila snatched a mouthful of grass, but otherwise stood like a sentry where Tyne had dismounted.

Tyne regarded the mare, his hands on his hips. "If this outing has caused Snow Princess to become lame, Amanda will ring a peal over my head that makes the bells of St. Paul's sound like a polite summons to the family parlor."

"I can walk," Lucy said. Though hiking through the streets of Mayfair with her riding skirts over her arm was hardly an appealing prospect.

"Nonsense," Lord Tyne replied. "You shall take Attila, and I will walk."

They'd left their groom loitering with the other grooms at the gates of the park. "I could take the groom's horse."

"James brought out an unruly ruffian by the name of Merlin for this outing. He'd run off with you for the sheer pleasure of giving me a fright. Damned beast should go to the knacker, but James is fond of him."

Tyne approached the mare and held up his arms. "Down you go, Miss Fletcher."

Lucy unhooked her knee from the horn, gathered up her skirts, and eased from the saddle, straight into Lord Tyne's arms.

TYNE HAD BEEN ready to curse aloud, to damn all lame horses, all pebbles, and all parliamentary bills for good measure, until Miss Fletcher slid into his embrace.

He'd been striving mightily to achieve a tone of harmless banter and failing at every turn. Miss Fletcher had made the requisite charming responses, but she didn't simper or flirt, she didn't offer any bold conversational gambits of her own. The sum of the morning's accomplishments had been to prove that she was a natural equestrian, and he was a failure as a flirt.

Fancy that.

Then Miss Fletcher slipped from the saddle on a soft slide of velvet and lace, and the fresh morning air became tinged with the fragrance of mint and possibility. She was warm from her exertions, and her arms rested on Tyne's biceps, while his hands remained about her waist.

"Your skirt," Tyne said, reaching behind her, "is caught on the billets. I'll have you free in no time."

The lady could not move, because she was pinned to the horse's side by her habit. The moment was theoretically dangerous and exactly the sort of mishap that inspired gentlemanly assistance with a lady's dismount in the first place.

Tyne eased the fold of velvet from between the lengths of leather, though his task required that he all but crush Miss Fletcher against the horse.

She didn't appear to mind. In fact, she might have leaned into him, and she certainly kept her hands on his arms. For a moment, she was embracing him while he fussed with yards of damned riding habit and tried not to let a particularly eager part of his anatomy become obviously inspired by her closeness.

Which was no use. He had to step back, lest public improprieties ensue.

"I can walk," Miss Fletcher said.

I very nearly cannot. "That won't be necessary. If you'd hold the mare's reins, I'll switch the saddles, and we'll be on our way shortly."

That exercise took enough of Tyne's concentration that he regained a measure of composure. Then, however, came the challenge of hoisting the lady onto Attila's back. Because the gelding was considerably taller than the mare, a simple hand around Miss Fletcher's ankle would not suffice.

"Step into my hands, and I'll boost you up," Tyne said. "Attila, you will stand like a perfect little scholar reciting his sums, unless you want to make the knacker's acquaintance before sundown."

Attila stood. Miss Fletcher gathered her skirts over her arm and lifted a dainty boot into Tyne's cupped hands. She scrambled aboard Tyne's horse and took up the reins, leaving Tyne to do further battle with the sea of velvet.

He tightened the girth a hole, took up the mare's reins, and sent Attila a warning glower. "You will walk, with all pretensions to dignity, horse. Set one hoof wrong with Miss Fletcher aboard, and you will never lay eyes on a carrot or apple again, not if you live to be thirty and win the Derby in three successive years."

"He's trembling with fear," Miss Fletcher said, patting the wretched beast. "A quaking mass of equine nerves, my lord. If you'll show the way, we shall summon all of our courage, put our complete trust in your leadership, and brave all the terrors awaiting us. Is that not what an adventure requires?"

Tyne's spirits lifted at the sight of her smile—for she was smiling at him, not at the stinking creature trying to impersonate a harmless lamb.

"As long as you're having an adventure, Miss Fletcher, my joy in the day is complete."

"As is mine."

That was ladylike banter, by God. In an entirely acceptable, though unmistakable, manner, she was bantering with her employer and possibly even flirting. Tyne tried not to smile the whole distance back to the house, and Attila came along, as docile as a perfect little scholar.

BECAUSE THE MARE was recovering from her stone bruise, Lucy was excused from riding out again with his lordship. In little more than a week, she'd face the choice of whether to keep her assignation with Thor, or let her single encounter with him fade into fond, if frustrating, memory. She had the odd notion that if she discussed her choice with the marquess, he'd offer her considered, disinterested advice, much as a true friend would.

But did she want to limit the marquess to the role of friend? He'd been *charming* on their dawn ride, attentive, considerate... very nearly swainly. He'd shared a longing to read to some lucky woman on a picnic blanket, to admire her bare feet...

"I find you once again among the fairy tales," Lord Tyne said, striding into the library on Saturday afternoon. "Where are the children?"

He was looking all too handsome, blond hair slightly disarranged, suggesting he'd been at his ledgers. His blue eyes were impatient and held a hint of mischief.

"Sylvie has taken it into her head that Amanda and I are too old to join the nursery tea parties, and Amanda has decided that sketching embroidery patterns does not require my assistance or the distraction of a younger sibling. That they are amusing themselves, and separately, is a good sign, my lord."

Tyne gestured to the other reading chair positioned before the hearth, and Lucy nodded her assent. He was so mannerly, so—

He plucked her book from her hand. "I knew it. Mr. DeCoursy has carried you off again. He will simply have to wait his turn today, for I'm intent on carrying you off as well."

Lord Tyne was mannerly *most of the time.* "I'm not exactly a sylph, your lordship, and I object to being hauled about."

"No, you do not, else you'd never have lasted a single waltz at the tea dances you were doubtless forced to attend. From my observation, too many fellows do little more than haul their partners about. Why the waltz hasn't been outlawed for the preservation of the ladies' toes is a mystery for the ages."

He wore no coat, which was unusual for him, and a trial for Lucy. She knew now how strong those arms were, how muscular his chest. She had become fascinated with his wrists—sketched them for an hour last night—and they were on view because he'd turned back his cuffs.

"Perhaps some obliging fellow of a parliamentary bent might draft a bill outlawing the waltz," Lucy said. "Do you happen to know an MP who could oblige?"

Tyne rose and shelved the book. "Why would I associate with such a prosy old dodderer when I can instead kidnap fair maidens and take them to Gunter's?"

Maidens, plural. "You'd like to take the girls out for an ice?"

"Not without you," he said, extending a hand to her. "If I take them by myself, I'm outnumbered. Any papa knows that's bad strategy. I also lack your ability to settle their squabbles with a calm word."

Lucy took his hand and rose, though she was capable of standing unassisted. She simply wanted to touch him and wanted him to touch her. The short time she'd spent in Thor's company had awakened some mischievous inclination in her, or made her loneliness—and her employer—harder to ignore.

"The girls squabble to get your attention," she said. "If they were boys, they'd resort to fisticuffs for the same reason."

"Some boys scrap for the pure joy of it. My younger brothers were always at each other, until Papa threatened to send one to Eton, one to Harrow, and one to Rugby."

His younger brothers had likely been trying to get *his* attention. "Did you scrap for the pure joy of it?" She'd pictured Lord Tyne as a quiet, dignified boy—or she had until they'd ridden out together.

"I was the oldest, and thus the largest. I had to let them come at me in twos or all at once to make the fight fair. You will think me quite the barbarian, but I did enjoy horseplay as a youth."

She smoothed her hand over his cravat, which was a half inch off center. "You scrap with the boys in the House of Lords now, don't you?"

His smile was downright piratical. "You've found me out. Let's mount a raid on Gunter's, shall we? A spot of pillaging lifts the spirits of any self-respecting barbarian."

Lucy took his arm, which was ridiculous, but so was fisticuffs for the joy of thrashing one's siblings, so was categorizing a barberry ice as plunder, and so was entertaining fanciful notions regarding one's employer.

"Perhaps we ought to take a blanket to spread beneath the maples," she said. "Raiding on such a lovely day might tire out your foot soldiers."

"Excellent notion," his lordship replied, pausing at the foot of the main stairs. "You will doubtless do a better job of ordering the infantry from their barracks. I'll meet you here in ten minutes."

He strode away with his characteristic energy, and Lucy watched his departure with uncharacteristic longing. Berkeley Square boasted no babbling brook into which she might dangle her bare feet, and his lordship simply wanted assistance with the children—not some sighing damsel for him to read poetry to.

What Lucy wanted was becoming increasingly unclear, though barberry ices were her favorite treat, and that was insight enough for the day.

CHAPTER FOUR

Tyne's habit had been to avoid imposing on Miss Fletcher's time unnecessarily. If he was taking the children to call on family, their governess could better use that hour to steal a nap, visit friends, or drop in on the lending library.

He'd apparently erred, for the children were much better behaved when Miss Fletcher was on hand to quell insurrections before they became outright revolts. The first attempted insurrection had come from Sylvie, who had wanted to bring along a platoon of dolls.

"You may bring one," Miss Fletcher had said. "Provided you and your doll of choice are back downstairs in the next five minutes."

The next sign of rebellion came from Amanda, who refused to sit next to a doll. Miss Fletcher solved that dilemma by placing herself beside Sylvie and Lady Higginbottom, the privileged doll of the day.

Amanda took her place beside Tyne on the backward-facing seat, which occasioned an outthrust tongue from Sylvie. Miss Fletcher pretended to be absorbed in retying her bonnet ribbons rather than remark Sylvie's rudeness or Amanda's return fire.

"You spend your entire day with these rag-mannered tatterdemalions, Miss Fletcher?" Tyne asked. "I marvel at your fortitude. What flavor of ice do tatterdemalions prefer?"

"What's a tatter... tatter the dandelion?" Sylvie asked.

"An unkempt, roguish vagabond," Miss Fletcher said.

"I want to be a tatter... a roguish vagabond when I grow up," Sylvie said. "Lady Higginbottom and I will be the scourges of the high toby too."

"Then you and your doll will be taken up by the sheriff," Amanda retorted, "and bound over for the assizes. If I'm lucky, you'll be sent to the Antipodes to serve out your days in hard labor."

"What manner of sister," Tyne observed, "would rather send her only sibling halfway around the world than join her in an adventure? I do wonder if such a sister should even share an ice with her family."

"Sorry, Syl," Amanda muttered.

"We wouldn't hold up *your* coach," Sylvie replied. "We'd brandy our pistols and protect you."

"Brandish," Amanda said, gesturing with her parasol. "Brandy is that nasty potion Papa keeps on the sideboard in his study. Brandy makes your throat burn and your nose run."

Miss Fletcher cast Tyne an admonitory glance: *Your adolescent daughter has sampled the brandy. You will not roar and carry on about it in front of Lady Sylvie or me.* Her gaze held sympathy and humor, and Tyne was reassured. He had sampled his papa's brandy at a much younger age than Amanda was now, and it had made his throat burn and his nose run too.

Another good sign, in other words, that Amanda was exhibiting normal youthful curiosity.

"We're here!" Sylvie shouted, bouncing on the seat. "Lady Higginbottom wants a lemon ice. I shall have maple."

"Elderflower," Amanda said as the coach came to a halt.

"Miss Fletcher? You might as well give me your order now."

"Barberry," she said. "Which treat would you like, my lord?"

The treat he longed for was a kiss from Miss Fletcher, which was all wrong. They were in a coach with two children and a doll, she'd done nothing other than smile at him, manage the children, and share a few moments bordering on the parental. In her plain straw bonnet, she was hardly alluring, and yet...

She was *his* Miss Fletcher, and he'd held her in his arms, and now his imagination was like a horse newly escaped from captivity.

"I'll want a nice, refreshing serving of patience," Tyne said, climbing from the coach. The children spilled forth, while Miss Fletcher made a more dignified exit. She perched on the step, her hand in Tyne's.

"Girls, you will mind your father, or there will be extra sums for all of next week."

"I like sums," Sylvie said. "So does Lady Higginbottom."

"Capital cities, then," Miss Fletcher said, making a graceful descent. "We are in a public venue, and our deportment reflects on the dignity of your papa's house. Best behavior, or his lordship won't be inspired to invite us out again."

Was she warning him to be on his best behavior?

Miss Fletcher shot him a wink and dropped his hand. "They'll try hard for about five minutes, but cakes and ices have never been known to settle children down."

Nor did winks settle down grown men. Tyne placed the order and took Sylvie's hand as they crossed the street to the grassy, shaded square, a groom carrying their treats. Miss Fletcher chose the spot under the maples for their blanket, and Tyne allowed himself one moment to wish that the children might have been gamboling away the afternoon with some obliging cousins out in Kent, while Tyne...

Gamboled away the afternoon with Miss Fletcher in a secluded meadow far, far from the Mayfair gossips. In little more than a week, he had to choose whether to keep his assignation with Freya, and the lonely, bored part of him that could be intrigued with a single kiss was inclined to do that.

The part of him that had daughters to raise, parliamentary bills to put forth, and a lovely governess underfoot wasn't inclined to pursue a fairy tale when the genuine article was already sharing his household.

The ices were consumed, and the children resumed bickering until Miss Fletcher suggested they entertain themselves with the ball she'd thought to bring along.

"Amanda will soon be too dignified to kick a ball about in the park," Miss Fletcher said. "She should enjoy playing with her sister while she still can."

"When the family removes to Tyne Hall this summer, we'll get up some cricket games with the cousins," Tyne said. "My sisters all play, and the best pitcher of the lot is my brother Detrick's oldest girl."

Another pair of girls joined in the game of kickball—Lord Amery's oldest and some cohort of hers with a deadly accurate left foot. Much yelling and argument about rules ensued, as it should when children played out of doors.

"When you remove to Tyne Hall, I ought to seek another post," Miss Fletcher said. "The girls are moving on from their mother's death, and you should find them a governess whom they won't associate as closely with their grief."

What the hell? Tyne had been lounging about on the blanket, propped on one elbow.

He sat up. "Your logic eludes me. The time of grief was more than two years ago, when their mother went to her eternal reward. Your tenure with the girls has been a period of improving spirits, better sleep, and a happier papa. Why should I now tear the children away from somebody who has brought them such boons?"

Miss Fletcher's gaze remained on the girls, who were trying to kick the ball straight at a dignified old maple, and—with the exception of the left-footed terror—mostly failing to hit their target.

"Are you a happier papa?" Miss Fletcher asked. "If you are happy enough to consider courting another marchioness, that's reason enough for me to seek a different post. I have overstepped with your children, because I knew they were without a mother's love. Your new wife will fill that role, and the children's loyalties would be torn if I stayed on."

"Good God, now you have me married to some woman I've never even courted. Have you been reading too many fairy tales, Miss Fletcher?"

"Perhaps—or not enough of them. Promise me you'll think on this, my lord. I can assist with the choice of a successor governess, if that's not getting above my station. There's no hurry, but you should give the notion some consideration."

Tyne considered *the notion* for two entire seconds and found it dreadful. "You have it all wrong, Miss Fletcher. One doesn't pike off as soon as the bonds of affection have been secured. I know not what experience put that ridiculous idea in your head, but you will only hurt the children if you leave us now. Amanda is facing the hardest years of a young lady's life, Sylvie will need a steady anchor as her sister makes her bow, and I won't have my daughters cast aside because your courage has failed you."

She untied her bonnet ribbons and would have retied them, except Tyne plucked her millinery from her grasp. Whatever losses had inspired her into a life in service were doubtless to blame for this harebrained plan to leave. She honored somebody's memory by remaining within earshot of grief, much as Tyne kept Josephine's portrait in the formal parlor.

"If we're to have a proper argument, madam, at least do me the courtesy of looking me in the eye while you threaten desertion."

"You need heirs," Miss Fletcher retorted, snatching the bonnet back. "Male heirs of your body. You're a marquess, need I remind you."

"If you think I can forget for one instant that I bear the responsibility for an old and respected title, you have been doing too many sums. Need I remind *you* that I have seven nephews thriving in my brothers' nurseries, which are heirs enough to secure any succession?"

Though sons would be lovely. Noisy, boisterous, little fellows who rode like hellions, tracked mud into the house, and drove their parents barmy.

"Where's Sylvie?" Miss Fletcher asked, scrambling to her feet. "I don't see Sylvie."

"She's deserted us," Tyne said, rising. "Gone off without giving notice."

"Badger me some other time, my lord. I don't see her anywhere." A thread of panic laced Miss Fletcher's voice. "I'm her governess and I've lost her in the middle of London. This is awful."

The panic was contagious, for Tyne had never before misplaced a daughter. "She can't have gone far," he said, invoking a calm he did not feel. "We'll find her. Steady on, Miss Fletcher. Let's talk to the other girls."

But neither Amanda nor her friends had seen Sylvie slip away, and though the square was small and plenty of people sat on benches or in coaches by the roadside, Sylvie was nowhere to be found.

HOW COULD Lord Tyne be calm, how could he think at all, when Sylvie was missing?

He was utterly composed. He dispatched the two grooms to work their way around the square, bench by bench, asking after Sylvie. Amanda and her friends did likewise with the children, while Lucy's heart hammered against her ribs and guilt hammered her conscience.

"She could have been snatched away," Lucy said, gaze upon the busy streets surrounding the square. "She could be lost, she might have been knocked witless by a passing carriage, and she's so little, nobody would even—"

"Miss Fletcher," Lord Tyne said, putting a hand on each of Lucy's shoulders. "This is not your fault, and we must look at the situation logically. Sylvie is a sensible child. She has had your example to guide her for quite some time, and she knows better than to dart into traffic. She will not take foolish risks, will not talk to unsavory people, and will not leave this area without us."

He took Lucy by the hand and led her back in the direction of the coach.

"Where are we going? We can't leave, not with—"

"We have searched the square, and unless Sylvie has learned to levitate straight up into the boughs, she's not here. We must check the coach and the coaches of acquaintances who happen to be enjoying the square. Thanks to you, Sylvie has many little friends, and she might even now be cadging another ice with one of them."

That... that made sense. Lucy's panic subsided the least bit. "I still feel responsible. She's a little girl, and I am her governess."

"While I am merely her father? You are being ridiculous. This outing was my suggestion, Sylvie is my daughter, and she will be fine, assuming she survives the scolding we'll give her."

His tone was cool, his grip on Lucy's hand steadying. His lordship inquired at three different coaches, and still no Sylvie, not even a sighting of a child who might be Sylvie.

"We need to look in one last place," his lordship said, escorting Lucy back across the street to Gunter's. "I should have started here, because I have every confidence that we'll find the prodigal and her accomplice slurping maple ices and looking entirely—"

"There you are!" Lucy said, dashing among the tables and wrapping Sylvie in a hug. "We looked everywhere for you, and I was so worried. Sylvie, you must *never* again give us such a fright."

Sylvie yet held her spoon—she was indeed enjoying another maple ice—while Mrs. Holymere looked on with tolerant amusement from the seat at Sylvie's elbow.

"I had to get Lady Higginbottom," Sylvie said when Lucy could stand to turn loose of her. "I forgot her, and I'm not supposed to be forgetful. Mrs. Holymere helped me cross the road and said we should wait for Papa to come fetch me." The girl looked uncertainly from her father to Lucy and then set aside her spoon to pick up her doll. "Am I in trouble?"

Mrs. Holymere beamed at the marquess. "Of course not, my dear. Looking after you for a few moments was my pleasure, and you really must not let this delicious ice go to waste. My lord, won't you join us? Lady Amanda is somewhere about too, isn't she? Perhaps the governess can take the child back to the square while we enjoy some adult conversation."

The governess. Mrs. Holymere turned her smile on Lucy, clearly expecting *the governess* to take Sylvie by the hand and disappear for so long as it pleased Mrs. Holymere to publicly flirt with the marquess.

Sylvie took Lucy's hand, and Lucy had picked up the half-eaten ice when Lord Tyne offered Mrs. Holymere a bow.

"While I thank you for aiding Lady Sylvie, I am not free at this moment to tarry. Good day." He plucked Sylvie up onto his hip, passed Lucy the spoon Sylvie had been using, and strode in the direction of the door.

Lucy offered the barest curtsey and marched after him.

The ride back to the house was taken up with Amanda chattering about Rose and Winnie, her kickball opponents, and Sylvie debating the merits of maple ices over those flavored with lemon. Happy, normal babbling about an enjoyable outing on a fine spring day.

When the coach pulled up in the mews, the girls scampered into the house. Lucy climbed out last, accepting Lord Tyne's hand to assist her to the ground.

"You are still upset," he said, keeping hold of her hand as the coach pulled away to the carriage house.

"I am furious."

"With Sylvie?"

Lucy shook her head, willing herself to remain civil, to keep to her place.

"With me?" Lord Tyne asked.

"You were wonderful. You kept your head, you didn't panic, you applied common sense and persistence, while I wanted to run up and down the walkways shouting Sylvie's name."

"That would have been my next step as well, having exhausted all other possibilities. If you're not wroth with me or Sylvie, then who has earned your ire?"

Standing this close to Lord Tyne was distracting, but not distracting enough. All over again, Lucy saw Mrs. Holymere's smirk, heard her dismissing *the governess*, the better to be seen sharing an ice with the marquess.

Lucy stalked the half-dozen paces across the alley and into the garden, Lord Tyne following. "I am furious, my lord, though I know I shouldn't be. I am furious at Mrs. Holymere for dragging an innocent child into her machinations, for pretending to be Sylvie's friend, for entirely disregarding the difficult position she put a little girl in. Was Sylvie to suffer a birching for the betterment of Mrs. Holymere's designs on you? Do you know how far back that would set the poor girl?

"Sylvie was trying to fetch her doll," Lucy went on, "which I have admonished her to remember to do over and over, and that woman, that manipulative, sly, flirting menace to the peace of the nursery, had the audacity—"

Lucy was pacing a circle around the smallest fountain in the garden and came smack up against his lordship.

"I'm sorry," she said. "I ought not to criticize my betters."

"Mrs. Holymere is not your better. If I had any doubt of that before today, I'm convinced of it now. You must calm yourself, Miss Fletcher. Sylvie is safe. She was at no time in danger, and a few reminders about keeping us apprised of her whereabouts are all the repercussions she should face."

"I am not calm," Lucy said. "This is why I should leave. I love those girls, and that is unpro— unprofessional of me." Her breath hitched, and she tried to turn away, but there was the marble sculpture of a laughing boy, his half-tipped urn eternally spilling into the pool at his feet.

Lord Tyne passed her his handkerchief, put his arms around her, and drew her close. "You aren't going anywhere, not at the moment.

Now, have a good cry—however one defines such an oxymoron—and then we must talk."

Lucy indulged her tears, because the comfort Lord Tyne offered was irresistible. To be held, to be cosseted, to be allowed for once to share an emotional burden... The relief was as exhausting as her worry over Sylvie had been. She never cried—almost never—but to think of Sylvie in harm's way, lost, alone, at the mercy of an unkind fate.... That was worth a few tears.

"My nose is probably red, and my cheeks are splotchy. Allow me some time to repair my toilette, and I'll be happy to—"

"Miss Fletcher... Lucy, if I may be so bold. I hope you know I would never trifle with the help?"

She took a seat on the nearest bench, because his lordship's reassurance was anything but cheering.

"Of course I know that, sir. You are all that is kind, and I'm simply overset."

He came down beside her. "With good reason. Sylvie gave us a fright, or rather that Holymere woman did. I knew her husband, so I attempt to be courteous to her, but my courtesies are at an end."

"You'll cut her?" Lucy liked that idea exceedingly.

"I will be merely civil, which is all the rebuke allowed to me as a gentleman. You are quite fond of the girls."

Hadn't Lucy said as much? "Which is why I should find another post now, my lord. I will grow more attached, and that cannot end well for anybody." The words hurt, but that pain was familiar, unlike the growing attachment Lucy felt for his lordship.

"And yet," he said, "I cannot abide the notion of you leaving us."

A sad silence went by. The garden was coming into its fragrant, colorful summer glory, but like the flowers blooming in such abundance, Lucy's time in Lord Tyne's household would soon be over. She nearly started weeping all over again, which made no sense.

A trip to Gunter's was not an adventure. A man who kept his head when a small child went missing was not a dashing flirt.

Lord Tyne was so much more than that. "We can speak further of this later, my lord. I am, as you say, not at my best."

He assisted Lucy to rise and stood staring down at her. Lucy could almost hear him rearranging mental chess pieces, hear him choosing the phrasing by which he might offer her a higher salary to remain in his employ. She did not want a higher salary—had no need of it, in fact.

"When we speak later," he said, "please consider that while I would never trifle with a woman in my employ, and your privacy is inviolable, and I am not keen on being trifled with myself, if you should ever be inclined to show me the sort of regard that—"

"Excuse me, my lord, Miss Fletcher." The first footman stood several yards up the garden walk. "I apologize for intruding, but the gentleman has been waiting for some time."

"What gentleman?" Lord Tyne asked.

Regardless of the gentleman's name, Lucy wished him to perdition. Whatever his lordship had planned to say mattered more to her than some gentleman pacing in the parlor.

"He's an acquaintance of Miss Fletcher's," the footman said. "Says he's an old friend, a Captain Giles Throckmorton, and he'd be very pleased if Miss Fletcher could spare him a few minutes of her time."

"MISS FLETCHER WAS wild with worry for you, Syl." Amanda had been worried too.

"Mrs. Holymere said I was to come with her, and I needed to fetch Lady Higginbottom." Sylvie situated her ladyship back among the other dolls on the nursery shelf. "I think Papa was angry with me."

Amanda flopped into the rocking chair where, when she'd been smaller than Sylvie, she'd climbed into her papa's lap and fallen asleep while he'd read to her. The memory made her sad now, which was silly.

"If Papa was angry with anybody, he was angry with Mrs. Holymere."

Sylvie took the other rocking chair, her feet not reaching the floor. "John Coachman calls her Mrs. Holy Terror. She smiles too much. I told her I'd already had an ice, and I'd helped Lady Hig finish hers too, but Mrs. Holymere insisted I stay with her to have another."

Mrs. Holymere's agenda had become clear to Amanda when the woman had called upon Papa several weeks ago, pretending to need his advice about how to manage her domestics. Amanda had every confidence Mrs. Holymere was a dab hand at managing her servants, her friends, and half the bachelors in Mayfair.

The housekeeper had said as much, and Cook and Mr. Drummond, the butler, had agreed with her.

"Mrs. Holymere wants to marry Papa," Amanda said. "Wants to add him to the staff she manages."

Sylvie set her chair rocking. "Papa is a lord. Nobody manages him but Good King George."

"Miss Fletcher manages him. She made him take us to Gunter's for ices, and now he has the knack of it on his own. She's the reason he sometimes brings us flowers, Syl, and before she came, you weren't even taking breakfast downstairs."

Sylvie's chair slowed. "I like breakfast downstairs. I like Miss Fletcher. So does Lady Hig, and Miss Twitlinger, and Her Grace of Dumpwhistle, and the Honorable Mr. Woddynod. Mr. Hamchop doesn't like anybody."

Amanda liked having Sylvie at the breakfast table. With a younger sister underfoot to get jam on the table napkins, mash up words, and speak too loudly, Amanda felt more at ease.

"Breakfast was awful before Miss Fletcher came. Papa hid behind the newspaper and forgot I was there."

"How could anybody forget you, Manda?"

The question was genuinely perplexed, and guilt rose again to upset Amanda's belly. "I forgot you, Syl. I was so busy trying to kick the ball at that tree, I didn't realize when you'd wandered off. I'm your older sister. I should have kept an eye on you."

Sylvie hopped out of her chair and went to the toy chest. "I waited until it was your turn to kick before I went to fetch Lady Hig. I didn't want anybody to know I'd forgotten her again."

"Do you ever get tired of playing with dolls, Syl?"

"Yes, but there's nobody else to play with, unless Miss Fletcher has me invite Rose or Jessica or Clementina or Daisy or Maude or Lizzie or—"

"Who does Miss Fletcher ever play with, Syl?"

"Grown-ups don't play. I can't find my tops."

Grown-ups did play. They played fancy dress-up and called it a masquerade. They played all manner of card games, and Papa had once said Parliament was a glorified cricket tournament.

"Mrs. Holymere wants to play with Papa."

Sylvie left off plundering the toy chest. "You said she wants to marry him. She told me that I have been too long without a mama, and Papa needs to do his duty by the session."

"The succession, the title. She meant we need brothers, though we have seven male cousins on the uncles' side. Mrs. Holymere wants to marry Papa so he can have sons with her."

"Will brothers play with me?"

Amanda crossed the room to fetch a pair of spinning tops from the mantel. "From what I understand, brothers are a little bit of a friend and mostly a bother. Miss Fletcher writes to her brothers often." Papa did not seem to bother the aunties, though he called upon them more often than they called upon him.

"Miss Fletcher has the most beautiful handwriting," Sylvie said. "I want to learn to write as she does, without getting ink all over my blotter."

Amanda had developed beautiful handwriting under Miss Fletcher's tutelage. She was also tackling her third Beethoven sonata and, according to Miss Fletcher, was already equal to any of Herr Mozart's challenges.

"Papa can do his duty by the succession without involving Mrs. Holymere," Amanda said.

"You found my tops!" Sylvie took the one painted with blue and white rings. "Let's have a race!"

They'd been playing this game forever, setting both tops spinning until one toppled, and the one still whirling was the winner. Amanda rolled back half the carpet, Sylvie plopped to the floor, and Amanda tried to do as Miss Fletcher had done on the blanket in Berkeley Square—fold gracefully to her knees, then shift to one hip, legs tucked aside.

That was harder than it looked, like most attempts to emulate Miss Fletcher.

"How is Papa to find me some brothers without marrying another lady?" Sylvie scrambled to her feet and fetched Lady Hig and Her Grace of Dumpwhistle—they had made their come outs together, after all.

"Papa could marry Miss Fletcher."

Sylvie whipped the string off her top and set it spinning on the smooth oak floor. "Miss Fletcher isn't rich or fancy."

"Papa's not fancy, and he likes Miss Fletcher a lot. They smile at each other when they think we're not looking."

Sylvie watched her top, still going at a great rate, more of a blue blur than a highly polished wooden toy.

"We have had a lot of governesses," Sylvie said. "Miss Fletcher laughs and hugs me, and she doesn't say I'm too old for my dolls."

"She makes Papa listen and makes him talk to us."

"He wishes us good night now. I like that, but how do we make sure they marry?"

"We tell Papa, and he proposes to Miss Fletcher, and they marry."

The top wobbled, then fell to its side, all momentum gone. "I don't think it's that simple, Manda. Wind your string, and we'll have our race."

"We'll talk to Papa and maybe to Miss Fletcher. We'll give them the benefit of our informed guidance."

Informed guidance, according to Miss Fletcher, was to be esteemed as highly as a pot of chocolate and fresh shortbread, but not quite as highly as heavenly intercession.

"I'll tell Papa that Lady Hig didn't like Mrs. Holymere *at all*. Start on the count of three."

Amanda counted with Sylvie, in the age-old nursery tradition, and then they let their tops fly.

Even though Sylvie was only a little girl, her complicity with Amanda's plan was a comfort. They would talk to Papa and to Miss Fletcher. Exactly how they'd go about that task without being able to consult either source of wisdom first was a puzzle.

Amanda enjoyed puzzles. She loved her papa and Miss Fletcher, thus she would find a way to give them the benefit of her guidance— and Sylvie's and even Lady Higginbottom's, if that was what she had to do to bring Papa and Miss Fletcher together.

CHAPTER FIVE

Giles Throckmorton had been handsome as a youth, and the years had only improved his looks. A young soldier had matured into a man with some character to his features, a subtle dash to his attire, and gravity in his gaze.

Lucy noted those developments impersonally, for Mr. Throckmorton's arrival had interrupted some sort of declaration from Lord Tyne—a declaration or a disclaimer. Lucy hadn't been sure if his lordship had been about to confess a *tendresse* for her or to warn her not to develop one for him.

A bit late for the warning. Any other employer would have blamed the governess when a child went missing. Lord Tyne had solved the problem, taken responsibility for it, and reassured Lucy most kindly afterward.

"Mr. Throckmorton." Lucy curtseyed. "Your call is unexpected."

He bowed. "You are ever tactful. I think what you mean is, my calling upon you is a great presumption. I had to come nonetheless."

"Lord Tyne will not turn me off for receiving an acquaintance from long ago," Lucy said. "Shall we be seated?"

Giles took the only wing chair—he'd been shown to the formal sitting room—and he looked quite at home there. The Portuguese sun had burnished his blond hair to gold, and the effect of the elements on his complexion was to make the blue of his eyes more vivid.

He wasn't as tall as Lord Tyne, not as muscular either.

"You look the same," Giles said, studying Lucy as if she were a portrait. "As pretty as ever."

He was up to something. Lucy had brothers, and those brothers had wives, and those wives kept her informed of every scrap of gossip from home. Giles regularly came back to England, and not once had he brought his children or his wife, not once had he called upon or asked about Lucy.

"Mr. Throckmorton, please don't take this as rudeness on my part, but your opinion of my appearance is of no interest to me. I am happily employed in a very respectable house, and I hope to remain in that blessed state for some time."

He smiled, and heavens, that smile had matured in Portugal as well. Giles had always had more charm than was fair, and he'd learned to add a dash of regret to his gaze, a soupçon of self-mockery that blended humility with amusement.

"You won't believe me, Lucy, but more than your affection, more than your lovely appearance, more than your humor, I've missed your common sense, and you are right: My opinion of your good looks is of no moment. I merely remark the obvious. How have you been keeping?"

A friend could ask that.

"I do very well, thank you. My work matters to me and allows me to use my gifts for the benefit of others." Flinging the reality of Lucy's situation at Giles's feet felt good. She hadn't married, hadn't taken any other lovers, but she'd made a good life for herself. "I trust your family thrives?"

"John is a natural-born diplomat. He sends you his regards, as do my sisters. They've kept me apprised of your situation, though I gather they haven't done the same for you in my case."

His sisters had never so much as sent Lucy a note after she'd removed to London.

"I did not feel I had the right to inquire after you." Lucy hadn't, in fact, spared Giles more than a passing thought since she'd come to Lord Tyne's household. "You wrote me the once, years and years ago, and I took your letter for a polite admonition not to spin fancies where you are concerned."

He rose and studied the portrait of the late marchioness that hung over the sideboard. "My children are all in good health, but perhaps you had not heard that I was widowed more than a year ago."

That explained the sadness in his gaze, the gravity where a high-spirited young man had been. "I am sorry for your loss, and I know your children must miss their mama terribly."

The thought of those children tugged at Lucy's heartstrings, and she even felt some genuine compassion for Giles. He'd been a young man going off to war, and Lucy's choices where he was concerned were her own responsibility.

"The children and I are a little lost." He sent Lucy an unreadable look. "Sometimes more than a little. I can be honest with you, Lucy. My marriage was not a bed of rose petals, and I know my wife had her frustrations where I was concerned, but we muddled along, and we loved our children."

"Of course you did. Tell me their names."

He resumed his place in the wing chair and spoke with fond exasperation about four small children clearly bereft of their mother's love. Somewhere in the discussion of the children, Lucy recalled that Giles had been her first love, if a very young woman's foolish fancies could be called love. He was a good man, and according him that honor allowed Lucy more compassion for her younger self too.

Giles was a father, older, wiser, and undoubtedly sadder. Lucy had been desperately upset over his only letter, but eventually, she'd seen that he'd done her a kindness. The war had gone on for years, and too many soldiers had never come home.

Waiting for him could have been so much futility ending in bereavement.

"Twins are always a challenge," she said. "I've noticed that if I make the effort to refer to them as individuals, using their names rather than simply calling them 'the twins,' or 'you two,' I have fewer problems. I've also noticed that always dressing them alike, in the manner of matched footmen on display, isn't wise."

Giles sat back as if startled. "I had never thought... I had never considered... But then, in the army, when the drill sergeants are dressing down the recruits, the sergeants refer to the lads in collective insults—'you lot,' 'you disgraces.' When they praise a man, they always single him out by name."

"It's a detail," Lucy said. "Probably of no significance at all."

"I doubt that, and yet, none of the nurses, tutors, and governesses I've employed ever once put forth these insights."

An odd moment went by, during which Lucy had the sense she was being reassessed, and that old affection—or whatever Giles had brought to this reunion—was being supplemented by new respect. The clock chimed the hour, and he stood. "Might I call on you again, Lucy? We haven't nearly begun to catch up. I have much to tell you about Portugal and about the business of making port. The land is beautiful in a way I can't describe, not as tame as dear England, and the people are wonderful."

"I am torn," Lucy said, rising. "While I am glad to know you prosper, and I wish you every joy, I do not want to create any mistaken impressions. I love my life here, Giles, and I love Lord Tyne's children. I am prospering too, in my way, and the terms of my employment do not contemplate that I will be socializing with many gentleman callers."

"I do believe I have just been given a preemptory spanking," he said. "I understand your situation, Lucy, but even a governess is entitled to meet an old friend on her half day."

Where was the harm in that suggestion? He'd go back to Portugal, and Lucy would be able to close the door on a youthful indiscretion that she'd never quite come to terms with.

"I can meet you for an ice at Gunter's on Tuesday at two of the clock. If I'm not there, assume my duties intervened, as they sometimes do."

Or she might have changed her mind, as she seldom did.

"I'll look forward to it," Giles said, bowing over her hand. When Lucy would have withdrawn her fingers from his grasp, he smoothed a caress to her knuckles, then kissed the back of her hand. No other gentleman had ever taken such a liberty—nobody except Giles, who apparently hadn't lost all of his youthful audacity.

Lucy snatched her hand back, ready to deliver a sound scold, but Giles strode to the door.

"Until Tuesday, Lucy. I'll be counting the hours."

TYNE MET Miss Fletcher's guest at the door, for Captain Throckmorton by rights ought to have called upon Tyne, then asked after Lucy. He ought, in fact, to have brought a mutual acquaintance to make introductions between host and caller too. That he hadn't observed those courtesies made the whole question of chaperoning the call awkward. The housekeeper was out for the afternoon, and the senior maid enjoyed her half day on Saturday.

Tyne took an interest in these details of the household schedule because Miss Fletcher had informed him months ago that he must. No lady of the house was on hand to maintain domestic order. The staff had to know somebody was in charge, otherwise slacking—a transgression sufficient to threaten the peace of the realm—might ensue.

"Captain Throckmorton, good day."

Throckmorton was a good-looking devil and several years younger than Tyne, damn the luck.

The captain bowed. "Do I have the pleasure of encountering Lord Tyne?"

"You do." A purely masculine pause ensued. Tyne took control of the figurative snorting and pawing by handing Throckmorton his hat. "Any friend of Miss Fletcher's will always be welcome under my roof, provided that friend comes in good faith. We *cherish* Miss Fletcher, and her happiness matters here."

Throckmorton apparently had little experience with parliamentary flag signals. What sounded like a pleasantry could be a threat, which Miss Fletcher's caller would understand the instant he misstepped.

"Lucy is an old and very dear friend," Throckmorton replied. "I've been remiss to let the connection lapse in recent years, but my regard for her is of long standing. I rejoice to know that her situation here is so comfortable."

Tyne all but shoved Throckmorton's walking stick against his chest. "She is *Miss Fletcher* to you."

"I beg your pardon. You are right, sir. Miss Fletcher."

Never had Tyne wanted so badly to smash his fist into another man's jaw, but Miss Fletcher would scold him about fisticuffs in the foyer, setting a bad example, and jeopardizing the decorum of a peer's household. She might even assign him a list of sums. The altercation would be worth the set-down, if she'd scold Throckmorton as well; but, alas, Tyne was the host.

Miss Fletcher had firm ideas of how hosts should behave.

Hosts should show a polite interest in every guest. "Will you be in England long, Mr. Throckmorton?" Tyne had consulted with Drummond, who as butler had gleaned that Throckmorton was visiting from his vineyards in Portugal and had known Miss Fletcher before deploying to Spain as a captain in Wellington's army.

Drummond was overdue for an increase in wages.

"I haven't decided how long I'll stay," Throckmorton said. "I'd forgotten how lovely the land of my birth is, and now that my children are once again in need of a mother, I'll likely be spending more time here."

Meaning Throckmorton was in need of a wife. "My condolences. All I can tell you is that the pain of losing a spouse fades, but the ache never entirely leaves you."

Throckmorton's expression of genteel sorrow faltered, suggesting he'd alluded to his widower status out of something other than paternal devotion to the children he'd abandoned hundreds of miles away.

He pulled on his gloves. "My thanks for that sage observation. Army life gives a man some perspective where death and loss are concerned, but your view is also appreciated."

How bloody gracious of him. "My years in Lower Canada afforded me the same perspective. The winter alone cost us many good soldiers." Tyne had served for only two years and mostly in peacetime. Papa had decreed that a man destined to help run an empire ought to see something besides sheep pastures and ballrooms before he sat in the Lords.

In the military, Tyne had become proficient in all manner of card games, perfected his aim with a rifle, and learned to tolerate cold the like of which no self-important grape farmer would ever encounter.

"I'll wish you good day," Throckmorton said, bowing. "Until next we meet, my lord."

"Until that happy occasion," Tyne said, signaling Drummond to open the door. "Should I not have the pleasure of encountering you again, safe and swift journey home when you rejoin your children."

Tyne summoned the same smile he used on junior MPs spouting radical notions. *Out you go, lad, and mind your manners around Miss Fletcher.*

Throckmorton had no choice but to accept his dismissal, and Drummond closed the door.

"Is Miss Fletcher to be at home to Mr. Throckmorton in future, sir?" Drummond asked.

If Tyne said yes, he was admitting into his home a potential

competitor for Miss Fletcher's services as a governess. A nursery full
of bereaved little souls in Portugal would call to her, as they should to
anybody with half a heart.

Throckmorton was also a competitor for her affections. His
posturing, his attempt to circumvent propriety, his use of informal
address... Tyne had every sympathy for a grieving widower, and no
patience at all for a manipulative bounder.

And yet, if Tyne said no, that Miss Fletcher was not at home if
Mr. Throckmorton called again, then Tyne was disrespecting the
lady's independence. After all she'd done for Tyne and his children,
she was owed, and she surely had earned, his respect.

"You must ask Miss Fletcher," Tyne said, "and inquire of her as
well whether our housekeeper ought to join any future calls that Mr.
Throckmorton pays on my household."

More than that, Tyne could not in good conscience do—not until
he'd completed the awkward conversation with Miss Fletcher that
Mr. Throckmorton's arrival had so inconveniently interrupted.

WE CHERISH MISS FLETCHER, and her happiness matters here.

Lord Tyne had spoken at sufficient volume that Lucy had heard
him in the formal parlor. Giles's half of the conversation had been
harder to discern, which was just as well. Eavesdroppers never heard
any good of themselves.

Though, to be *cherished*... His lordship did not posture for the
sake of impressing anybody, least of all a casual caller.

"I have seen Mr. Throckmorton out," the marquess said,
wandering into the formal parlor. "If you'd like a chaperone for any
future calls, please let the housekeeper know."

"Thank you."

He took the piano bench. "What are you thanking me for, Miss
Fletcher?"

Being yourself. "Being protective. Giles is an old, old friend, but I hadn't seen him for years. People can change over time."

His lordship spun around and opened the cover over the keys. "You call him Giles."

What mood is this? "I knew him when I was a girl, and before he left for Spain, we had something of a flirtation."

"Are you being delicate?"

"Yes." And euphemistic. *A mutual pawing* would have been a more accurate description. The thought made Lucy smile, which, where Giles was concerned, was a relief. What a pair of young nodcocks they'd been.

"You recall him fondly, in other words." His lordship began the slow movement from Beethoven's Piano Sonata No. 8 in C minor, often called *Pathétique.* The first theme was lyrical and lovely, and he played it at the flowing, calm tempo the composer had intended.

"Mr. Throckmorton would like me to recall him fondly." Lucy had come to this realization somewhere amid Giles's recitations regarding his children. Why was he making this effort now?

The marquess played on, and Lucy wished she might simply enjoy the music. Amanda got her musical talent from her papa apparently, and Sylvie showed signs of the same gift. Giles's visit had further disrupted an already unsettling day, though, and Lucy had questions for the marquess.

"How many children does he have?" his lordship asked.

"Mr. Throckmorton? Four, including a pair of twins."

"Twins." Twins, spoken in that tone, with that expression, suggested somebody had committed a dire offense. "Will you leave us to help him raise his twins, Miss Fletcher?"

The notion that Giles had been looking for a governess—an English governess experienced at dealing with grieving children—had only begun to form in Lucy's mind. If so, he'd have been better off approaching her in writing with an offer of a post instead of pretending to call on an old friend.

Much less presuming to kiss her hand, for pity's sake. "I haven't been offered that opportunity."

His lordship brought the music to a sweet, stately close rather than carry on to the more tempestuous, contrasting theme.

"I am confident that you will be offered that opportunity. If it's in your best interests to pursue such a post, then you should."

That was what a true friend ought to say, and what nobody ever had said to Lucy. "I thought you sought to keep my services, not toss me onto the first boat bound for Lisbon."

His lordship closed the cover over the keys. "You will be tempted, by the children in his nursery who are doubtless struggling for want of their mama's love, by the notion that an old friend deserves your loyalty at a trying time, and—we have always been honest with each other, have we not, Miss Fletcher?—by the excuse to leave a situation here which has come to mean much to you."

He rose, and Lucy thought he was finished expounding on her motivations, which he'd identified more clearly than she could have herself.

"What is wrong with being useful?" she asked.

Lord Tyne drew her to her feet and again kept hold of her hand. Unlike Giles, he wasn't flirting. Lucy wasn't sure exactly what his lordship was about. He didn't seem angry, exactly, but then again, when Sylvie had gone missing, he hadn't shown any sign of anxiety either.

"Being useful is a worthy goal," he said. "Compassion and service should figure prominently in any meaningful life, but what of joy? What of pleasure, dreams, hopes, and wishes? Children grow up, Miss Fletcher, and devoting yourself to their well-being while ignoring your own is a scheme that will leave you old and lonely. Fond memories are some compensation for decades of your life, but you deserve more than that."

Thor would have admonished her thus, and at that moment, Lord Tyne put Lucy in mind of her Norse god.

"What were you about to say to me in the garden, my lord?"

"In the—? Ah, that. I'm not sure those sentiments are relevant now. Perhaps after Captain Throckmorton has returned to the wonders of Portugal, I might recall what point I was trying to make."

I will kill Giles. "Whatever you have to say is of interest to me, sir. Your happiness matters to me too."

His brows rose. "A cheering revelation. I'll see you at dinner, Miss Fletcher." He leaned down to brush a kiss to her cheek and strode out, closing the door softly behind him.

CHAPTER SIX

Lucy heard not a word of Vicar's sermon, so preoccupied was she trying to sort out emotions, options, and innuendos.

Lord Tyne had kissed her cheek, which for him amounted to a bold declaration, but of what? Good wishes on a venture in Portugal? Support for Lucy's ability to choose a course? His attachment to her as a member of the household?

Something *more?*

She should ask him, she *meant* to ask him, except that he'd again become the remote, reticent man whom she'd met when she'd first joined his household. The children must have sensed his mood, for they didn't exchange a single whisper during the service.

After church, his lordship took the children for Sunday dinner at Lady Eleanor's house, leaving Lucy to begin and then tear up three different letters to her oldest brother's wife. What was Giles about? What had shifted in his lordship's regard for his children's governess?

And what was Lucy to do about Tuesday night's assignation with Thor?

About her Tuesday afternoon meeting with Giles?

The life of an adventuress is complicated. Freya would have known that. Lucy was making a fourth attempt at correspondence when she heard the jingle and clatter of the coach in the mews. Curiosity had her setting aside her pen and capping the ink, because the children hadn't been gone long enough to enjoy a Sunday meal with family.

"Manda is sick," Sylvie announced before Lucy had untied the child's bonnet ribbons. "Papa said I might get sick too, but when I asked him if he could get sick, he didn't answer me." Sylvie gave her father a half-hopeful, half-peevish look.

"Your father has a very strong constitution," Lucy said. "Illness befalls us all, but his lordship appears to enjoy great good health. Amanda, what's amiss?"

"Her throat hurts," his lordship replied. "She's congested, she aches. Every symptom of the blasted flu, in other words."

Illness terrified this household, and for good reason. The marchioness had been well one day and at death's door a fortnight later. The best physicians, the most fervent prayers, had been useless against the sickness that had befallen her.

Lucy put her hand against Amanda's forehead. "No sign of fever. Your eyes lack the characteristic shine of one battling influenza." She aimed a glower at the marquess. "Amanda has very likely caught a spring cold or taken some blooming flower into dislike. Come upstairs, and we'll cosset you with willow bark tea, lemon drops, and card games."

"I've sent for the physician," the marquess said, joining Lucy and her charges on the stair.

"I don't want to see a doctor," Amanda retorted. "I have a cold. You heard Miss Fletcher, Papa."

"A cold or a hay fever," Lucy said. "Neither one should inconvenience you for more than a few days. Sylvie, you will write a story to amuse your sister during her convalescence. Your lordship will inform the physician that his services are not needed, and I will see the patient settled in her bed."

Lucy put an arm around Amanda's shoulders—the girl was

growing so tall—and spared his lordship a quelling glance.

Steady on, sir. We've dealt with this before.

Sylvie had come down with chicken pox a month after Lucy joined the household, and Amanda had had colds in both spring and fall. Illnesses happened, and with good care and luck, most children recovered. The blow to a parent's confidence likely did permanent injury.

Lord Tyne paused at the top of the steps. "I don't see the harm in having Dr. Garner drop around—"

"Today is the Sabbath," Lucy said. "Leave the poor man one day of peace. Amanda has a sniffle, possibly a cold. She has no serious injury, no signs of infection, no fever. She will be well in no time."

Lucy continued with Amanda into the girl's bedroom, leaving Tyne and Sylvie holding hands at the end of the corridor. The picture they made, father and daughter, equally worried, equally brave, made Lucy's heart ache, but what they needed was her calm and good sense.

So, calm and sensible she would be.

"Are you truly ill, Amanda?" Lucy asked when the door was closed. The first time Amanda's courses had befallen her, she'd been practicing duets at the home of a cousin. Because Lucy had instructed the girl regarding contingencies, Amanda had known to plead a megrim and always have cloths in her reticule. She'd been returned posthaste to Lucy's care.

Lord Tyne had paced outside his daughter's bedroom for nearly an hour before Lucy had been able to explain the situation to him. His reaction had been relief rather than embarrassment. He'd observed that the late marchioness had been known to use the poppy on occasion to ease the same indisposition.

That conversation had given Lucy the first hint that his lordship not only worried for his children, he also loved them—desperately.

"I'm sick," Amanda said. "A cold, as you say. My head aches, my throat itches, and I sneezed three times in a row."

"Is that what had your papa summoning the physician?"

"Yes, but how can one not sneeze?"

"Into bed with you. Prepare to be spoiled and pampered out of your sneezes. We'll get you a pile of old handkerchiefs, because they are the softest, and some peppermint tea to help clear your head."

Amanda yawned. "Do I have to take the willow bark tea too?"

"That will ease your headache and any soreness of your limbs," Lucy said, starting on the hooks at the back of Amanda's dress. "Change into your nightgown, and I'll be back to redo your braids more loosely."

"Papa is worried." Amanda sounded more forlorn than anxious. "Will you stay with me? He'll fret, and then Sylvie will have nightmares, and it will all be my fault, because I sneezed."

Lucy hugged the girl. "Nobody can help sneezing, and of course I will stay with you." She kept the embrace brief, because Amanda had also inherited a certain dignity from her father.

Amanda hugged her back. "You won't leave us, will you?"

Oh, dear. Lucy stepped away. "I beg your pardon?"

"That man who called on you yesterday, the friend from your girlhood. Mr. Drummond told Cook that your caller is a widower living in an exotic land, and he might be trying to entice you away from us. I shouldn't like that, and Sylvie—"

"Will have nightmares," Lucy said. "All children have nightmares, Amanda, but nobody has offered me a post in a far-off land, so we needn't discuss this."

"Good."

Lucy fetched the book of Norse fairy tales and read to Amanda until the child dozed off. The evening was spent in the same manner, with a break to marvel over Sylvie's tale of Her Grace of Dumpwhistle's public altercation with Mr. Hamchop-who-doesn't-like-anybody. Several times, Lucy heard Amanda's bedroom door opening and closing. She didn't have to look up to know Lord Tyne was peeking in on his daughter—and fretting.

Lucy fell asleep in the chair beside Amanda's bed, the book of fairy tales in her lap. When Monday morning came, Lucy was in her own bed, with only a vague notion of how she'd arrived there.

She'd been carried in a pair of strong arms, laid gently on the mattress. Her slippers had been eased off, then she'd been covered with not one but two quilts. The fairy tales were on her bedside table, and her slippers were by the side of the bed.

She recalled a soft kiss to her forehead, and she recalled—with embarrassing clarity—returning that kiss with a desperately heartfelt embrace that she'd never wanted to end.

"FOR GOD'S SAKE, are you a horse or an overexcited puppy?"

Attila kicked out behind, hopped left, and propped on his back legs. Because Tyne had been up too late Sunday night worrying over Amanda, Attila hadn't left his stall since Friday. By Tuesday morning, the gelding was an unruly ball of unspent energy.

"Then let's run," Tyne said, aiming his horse at an empty stretch of bridle path. The park was more than three hundred acres all told, but none of the paths afforded the miles and miles of open country that Tyne and his mount needed to truly gallop off the fidgets.

This was all Miss Fletcher's fault. Tyne had thought to press a good-night kiss to her forehead, and mayhem had ensued. The happiest, most unexpected, inconvenient... She had lifted herself into his embrace and held him for a long, aching moment in the night shadows.

And then, her kiss, ye gods her kiss. As if he'd been slumbering in some fairytale castle of old, her kiss had wakened desire and determination in equal measure. Freya's parting gesture had been intriguing; Lucy Fletcher's sleepy passion was riveting. She'd held nothing back, had clung to him as if her dearest secret longings could be fulfilled only by him. Tyne had hung over her recumbent form, returning her passion and longing to do more... Except that lady had clearly been exhausted, and very likely she'd been kissing a phantasm from a dream.

I yearn to be the lover of her dreams and the man at her side when she wakens.

The emotions that had coursed through him as he'd shared that fervent embrace with her had been wonderful—joy, hope, desire, affection—and terrible—uncertainty, loss, despair. And while Tyne abhorred drama, that embrace had answered one question for him: He was very much alive, very much still human, and that was a good, if painful, gift.

In the morning, Miss Fletcher made no mention of what had passed between them the previous night. She hadn't so much as hesitated at the door of the breakfast parlor.

Perhaps she had no recollection of that heated embrace, but Tyne was haunted by it.

"That will do for now," he said, bringing Attila down to the walk. The horse's sides were heaving, but one short burst of speed wouldn't be enough for him, just as one heartfelt embrace wasn't enough for Tyne.

"But was she clinging to me, to some conjured shadow from her imagination, or to Throckmorton, may God rot him straight to the bottom of the River Douro?"

Tyne's mind was made up on one point: Two weeks ago, he'd kissed a stranger on a darkened front porch. The encounter had been sweet and unexpected. That passing delight could not in any way compare to the depth of his regard for Miss Fletcher. She had seen him and his children through many difficulties, from illness, to grief, to adolescent awkwardness.

"She's loyal, loving, resourceful, and she won't let me slack as a papa. I suspect she wouldn't let me slack as a husband either." *Or as a lover.*

Attila snorted.

"You're a gelding. Your opinion on the matter is uninformed."

Tyne set the horse to cantering back up the path and spent another half hour humoring his mount's high spirits. By the time the horse was clip-clopping up the alley to the mews, the creature was sweaty and docile, not a buck or a hop left in him.

"My attachment to Miss Fletcher is beyond doubt," Tyne concluded as the stable came into view. "But have I engaged her affections?"

Attila sighed, a big, horsey, side-heaving exhalation.

"You are telling me I'm making this too complicated, and as usual, you are right, my friend. I must risk losing the woman my children adore—the woman I adore—and plainly state my intentions. She'll either laugh and decamp to Portugal, or she'll become my marchioness."

For there could be no un-saying a declaration of intentions, no battling those words back into a sealed box, never to be recalled. No un-leaping over the precipice once honest emotions had been disclosed.

"Tomorrow," Tyne said, patting Attila's sweaty shoulder. "I'm expected at Eleanor's for dinner this evening, and choosing the proper words requires some thought. Freya might wait for me briefly tonight, but I suspect she's already come to her senses as well. A future isn't built on a single kiss, no matter how lovely or adventurous that kiss might be."

Tyne's logic was sound, his mind made up. Now all he needed were the right words and endless courage. He could forgive himself for forming an unreciprocated attachment, but his daughters would never pardon him for driving Miss Fletcher away to dratted Portugal.

AMANDA'S COLD had done as colds did and given her a passing inconvenience. By noon Tuesday, she was back to bickering with Sylvie, and Lucy was more than ready to pitch the pair of them into the garden fountain.

"I am going out this afternoon," she said, coming upon her charges by the garden fountain. "I suggest you ladies spend the hours between now and supper in neutral corners."

"What are neutered corners?" Sylvie asked.

"Neutral," Amanda said, punching the air. "Like when pugilists rest between rounds of a fight."

"What are pew... puganists?"

"Pugilists," Lucy said. "Combatants, bare-knuckle fighters. You and Amanda are cross with each other today, and I cannot bide here to referee your verbal sparring. I'll be back well before supper."

"Where are you going?" Sylvie asked.

"Don't be rude, Syl."

"I'm not being rude. I'm being curious. Miss Fletcher says a curious mind is a gift from God." *Miss Fletcher is sometimes an idiot.* "Sylvie, I have a few errands to see to, and that's what half days are for. If you truly wanted to impress me, the two of you might consider working on your duet."

Older and younger sister wore identical expressions of distaste.

"I'm off," Lucy said. "Behave, please."

"Yes, Miss Fletcher." They spoke in unison, and Lucy hurried through the garden gate. She turned to drape the latch string over the top and saw two girls, holding hands, regarding her departure with forlorn gazes.

A movement in an upstairs window caught her eye. Lord Tyne had pulled back the curtains in his study and stood at the window watching the tableau in the garden. Lucy waved to him—he'd been excruciatingly proper since Sunday night—and he nodded in response.

Lucy took that nod as acknowledgment that she and the marquess had unfinished business. He was having dinner with his sister's family tonight—thank heavens—and Lucy had matters to tidy up with Giles and with a certain Norse god. Then, by heaven, she and Lord Tyne would finish the discussion they'd begun in the garden on Saturday.

And—if she was brave and he was willing—they'd resume the kiss that had haunted her dreams since Monday morning.

As she made her way to Berkeley Square, Lucy gave up wondering what his lordship had been about to say and embarked on the fraught exercise of determining what *she* wanted to say. Instead, a list grew of admissions she was reluctant to make:

I have become that pathetic cliché, the governess in love with her employer.

I am still young enough to give him sons, truly I am. I hope.

One can be lonely in a house full of people.

I desire Lord Tyne. I want a future as his wife and as step-mother to Sylvie and Amanda.

All too soon, she was in front of Gunter's and approaching Giles, who lounged on a shaded bench across the street. He rose and tipped his hat as Lucy came up the walkway.

"My dear, lovely to see you."

I am not your dear. "Good day, Giles. Shall we order our ices?"

He offered his arm. "I suppose the proprieties require it."

Lucy's predilection for barberry-flavored treats required it. "What is your favorite flavor?"

"The offerings here are all so much cold sweetness," Giles said, patting her fingers. "Gunter's is an excuse to profit from a clientele that seeks to mingle with members of the opposite sex. Lemon will do for me."

Giles could be blunt. Lucy had forgotten that. He wasn't entirely wrong, but neither was he correct. "I bring the children here often, and I dearly hope amatory matters have not yet caught their fancy."

"So you're a nursemaid as well as a governess?"

Good gracious, he'd left his manners in Portugal. "Lord Tyne accompanied us on our last outing. Is he also a nursemaid?"

"He's something of a bore, if you ask me. Does he interrogate every person who calls upon you?"

"He did not interrogate you. Perhaps you'd best place our orders, Giles."

Except Giles hadn't asked her what flavor she wanted. He came back from the counter with two lemon ices and carried both across the street, then settled himself beside Lucy on a bench.

The moment put Lucy in mind of their youthful encounters. Giles had strutted about, making pronouncements that were supposed to paint him as a worldly, sophisticated man-about-town, while Lucy had wondered if her company meant anything to him. Then he'd turn up flirtatious just as she was about to leave him to his self-importance, and she'd—

"I have missed you, Lucy Fletcher." He drew his spoon from his mouth slowly, his lashes lowered.

Lucy used her spoon to swirl the letter T into the top of her ice. "Thank you. I have also thought of you over the years. Is there something in particular you want to discuss with me, Giles?"

A few people loitered around the square or strolled beneath the maples, but the conversation would not be overheard. Lucy wanted this appointment concluded, and she wanted her late-evening appointment with Thor over with as well...

If she even kept it. She was under no obligation to appear. What would be the point? She did still have his cloak—a beautiful article of clothing—and should return it to him. She didn't anticipate another kiss from a stranger with any joy, though, and she ought not to be haring about after dark on her own.

"You thought of me from time to time?" Giles replied. "I will content myself with that admission, because I know you were raised in a proper household. I also know that you've strayed, Lucy."

Lucy set aside her ice, which was too tart by half. "I *beg* your pardon?"

"Come now," Giles said, holding a spoonful of ice before Lucy's mouth, as if she required feeding like an infant. "We have a past, you and I. An intimate past. Surely that means something to a woman who in all these years has never married."

Lucy gently pushed his wrist aside. "It means we were very foolish, very long ago, also very lucky that our foolishness didn't have unfortunate repercussions. Giles, are you thinking to offer me a post as governess to your children?"

The lemon ice slipped from his spoon onto his thigh. "*What? As governess?*"

"Of course, as governess. I am a governess and a very good one. I'm particularly skilled with children who've lost a parent, and yours fit that sad description."

He tossed the remains of his ice to the grass beside the bench. "Lucy, you cannot think that I'd travel the ocean, call on you personally, and regale you with the details of my situation simply to offer you employment?"

"Of course not. You travel back to England to see your family, not to see me, but why else would you bother to call on me after sending me exactly one letter since the day you left for Spain?"

He regarded her with a pained expression, as if she'd made a weak jest. "I am attempting to embark on a proper courtship of you, Lucy. I know you regard yourself as in possession of experience no blushing bride ought to have, but of all men, I am the last to judge you for that. You'll like Portugal, and I know you love children, else you'd never have consigned yourself to a career caring for them."

Lucy had the sense she'd been thrust into some other woman's life, a poor creature expected to flatter and fawn over any male buffoon who made calf's eyes at her.

"Giles, at the regimental ball, you encouraged me to drink from your glass of punch, and you kept that glass refilled. I had never before, and have never since, been tipsy. I hold myself entirely responsible for my actions, but you are very fortunate that my brothers didn't get wind of your behavior. I can assure you, no gentleman has since doubted my good name."

He stared at the empty walkway. "Has any other gentleman paid you his addresses?"

This conversation had all the earmarks of one of Sylvie's grand dramas involving Her Grace of Dumpwhistle and Lady Higginbottom.

"I have attracted the respectful attention of the occasional gentle-man. More than that is no concern of yours. I consider you a friend from my girlhood, Giles, one who became a passing fancy on his way to war. I am unwilling to leave my present post to join you in Portugal on any terms."

Lucy refused to give him the comfort of the you-do-me-great-honor speech, because he hadn't done her any honor whatsoever. The nerve of him, showing up after years of silence, and all but proposing...

Giles used a handkerchief to dab at the damp spot on his breeches. "I will try to change your mind, Lucy. You must allow me that. I've been hasty, leaping to conclusions, making assumptions. We were fast friends when we were young, passionate lovers for too brief a time. I have four motherless children, including twins, and you love children."

As if twins were some sort of parental prize? As if he'd been the one to carry those twins or bring them forth into the world? "Giles, you must put this notion aside. I am content with my present post."

"But you are very nearly *in service*," he retorted, balling up his handkerchief after he'd succeeded only in spreading the stain. "Don't you long to have a household of your own? Children of your own? You once assured me you yearned to see foreign lands, sail the sea, and sample exotic cultures. You told me you longed to follow the drum because you were so infernally bored with England. Don't you long for those things still?"

Well, no. Once upon a time, what Giles offered would have been all Lucy had ever dreamed of. Once upon a time was for fairy tales.

"Giles, I have sufficient funds of my own. My parents saw to that, and my brothers have managed that money very competently. If I want to travel, I needn't marry to do so."

"You have *money*? And still you spend your days wiping the noses of other people's brats?"

Lucy rose lest she start laughing at his version of a governess's responsibilities. "I love children. Surely that concept isn't unheard of?"

"No," he said, rising. "Not at all unheard of. I see I have been precipitous and that your situation is not what I thought it to be. I refuse to give up, though, Lucy. What you need, what you deserve, is the proper wooing you should have had years ago. If I call on you again, you will receive me, won't you? For the sake of old friendship?"

She ought not. She ought to send him packing with a flea in his presumptuous ear, but widowers could be a desperate lot, and their dignity should never be avoidably slighted.

"Lord Tyne told you himself that I'm welcome to see old friends, but you mustn't entertain false hopes, Giles."

"No false hopes," he said, bowing. "But perhaps a few new hopes."

Lucy left the square with a new hope of her own: that Giles would sail back to Portugal with some other blushing bride at his side, and make that journey soon. His four children doubtless missed him desperately, though in recent years, Lucy had stopped missing him in any regard.

~

"WE WANT TO TALK TO YOU," Sylvie said.

Her expression was solemn, making her look much like her mother. Josephine had had an inherent gravity that Tyne hoped would not entirely overtake her daughters, not so soon.

"Do I mistake the matter," he asked, "or are we not in conversation already? Whose turn is it to select my cravat pin?"

"You are grown up," Sylvie said, advancing three more steps into Tyne's bedroom, all but dragging Amanda by the hand. "You can choose your own cravat pin, like I choose what dress to wear every day."

Miss Fletcher's handiwork at its subtle finest. Give the young ladies choices, she'd said, and they'll learn to exercise independent judgment.

"I haven't much sense of fashion," Tyne replied, "but you're correct. I am capable of making an adequate selection."

"The sapphire." Amanda dropped Sylvie's hand. "It brings out the blue in your eyes."

Tyne would have chosen something more subdued. "The sapphire it is, a gift from your dear mama, like the two of you."

"Mama would want you to be happy," Sylvie announced with such conviction that Tyne suspected it was a rehearsed conclusion, or one supplied by Amanda.

"I am happy." That approached telling his daughters a falsehood, though one kindly meant. Tyne was grateful for his life, he was abundantly blessed by good fortune, he was hopeful... But happiness had eluded him for a long time.

"Happy like when Mama was alive," Amanda said. "We think you should marry Miss Fletcher."

Pain stung Tyne's chest as he stabbed himself with his sapphire pin. "Blasted, dashed, deuced,"—Sylvie's eyes grew round—"perishing, dratted, infernal,"—Amanda was grinning—"accursed, wretched, *damn*."

"Papa said a bad word." Sylvie was ecstatic.

"He was overset," Amanda crowed, quietly. Tyne's daughters were ladies.

He assessed himself in the mirror. No blood, which was fortunate for his valet's nerves. "I am *not* in the least overset. I am ambushed by a pair of..."

They'd gone serious at his severe tone, watching him with the same wariness he used to feel toward his own children, before Lucy Fletcher had joined the household and made a family of them.

He knelt and opened his arms. "I've been waylaid by a pair of insightful young ladies who take my welfare very much to heart."

Sylvie barreled at him full tilt, while Amanda graciously

permitted herself to be hugged. Tyne reveled in their embrace, and to hell with wrinkled linen, being late for dinner, and admitting his aspirations to his children.

When he turned loose of his daughters, Sylvie went skipping around the room. "You have to woo Miss Fletcher, Papa. Bring her flowers and steal kisses."

"And give her chocolates," Amanda added with an earnest nod. "She liked the French chocolates."

At Amanda's urging, Tyne had given Miss Fletcher chocolates at Christmas, months ago. "Excellent suggestion. What else?"

"You should read to her," Sylvie said, tripping on the carpet fringe, then skipping in the opposite direction. "She always reads to me, and she loooooves books."

"Do you think she'd enjoy my rendition of Norse fables?"

"I think she'd enjoy your version of anything," Amanda said. "You're handsome, kind, and intelligent. Do you know how to kiss, Papa? The uncles might have some ideas how to go about it."

"Your mother took care of that aspect of my education." Bless her for all eternity.

"Then," Sylvie said, climbing the steps and bouncing onto Tyne's bed, "when you've brought Miss Fletcher chocolates, and read to her, and vowed your every lasting devotion, you ask her to marry you!"

Amanda sent her papa a grown-up smile: *everlasting*.

"Such a campaign will take time," he said. "You must not say anything to Miss Fletcher or to the staff. This will be a family undertaking. Are we clear?"

"Because," Sylvie said, leaping from the bed, "it's *personal*."

Tyne set the sapphire cravat pin back in his jewelry box. "Exactly. Very personal, and there's no guarantee I'll be successful."

"But you won't muck it up, will you, Papa?"

He chose another cravat pin, this one more subdued, also unlike any he'd seen in London ballrooms or house parties in the shires.

"If my objective is to ensure Miss Fletcher's happiness, then success is assured. My regard for her is such that I truly do want her happiness above all things, though my hope is that marriage to me will fulfill that aim."

"What's that?" Sylvie said, peering at his cravat pin.

"My lucky cravat pin," Tyne said. "This stone is very rare, coming from only one area of Derbyshire. It's called Blue John and found nowhere else in the world." The color was halfway between lavender and periwinkle, the stone a cross between marble and quartz, subtle rather than sparkly, and unique.

"Why is it lucky?" Sylvie asked, crowding in beside him at the vanity.

"Because Miss Fletcher gave it to me for Christmas." A highly personal gift, from the lady's home shire. She'd blushed when he'd thanked her, another precious rarity. He rose and beheld himself in the cheval mirror. "Will I do?"

"You're merely dining at Aunt Eleanor's," Sylvie said. "You don't have to be fancy for that."

"You look splendid, Papa."

Tyne did not feel splendid, but he felt *alive*. Ready to take on challenges and woo at least one lovely damsel, if she was willing to be wooed. If she wasn't, he'd make a gentlemanly effort to change her mind. Mr. Captain-Come-Lately from Portugal would have to find some other English rose to plant in his Portuguese vineyard.

Or some such rot.

"I'm away to dinner," he said, kissing each daughter on the forehead. "Don't give Miss Fletcher any trouble, and remember: not a word of my marital aspirations. I must conduct this campaign as I see fit, with no helpful interference from the infantry."

"Come, Sylvie," Amanda said, marching to the door. "We must talk."

That sounded ominous, though Sylvie skipped from the room happily enough. Tyne did not skip from the room, but headed down the steps five minutes later, prepared to endure a long evening making up the numbers at his sister's dinner party.

He was plagued by the vision of his Valkyrie waiting alone on the path for a suitor who never arrived, though the image of himself being left in the chilly darkness wasn't any more appealing. Perhaps he'd go to Vauxhall—that was the gentlemanly thing to do—and perhaps he'd leave fairy-tale kisses in the shadows where they belonged.

CHAPTER SEVEN

Giles had been assigned to intelligence work in the army, though army intelligence had often struck him as a contradiction in terms. His tasks were usually no more dangerous than sitting outside a rural inn and counting the number of wheeled conveyances going past in an afternoon, watching to see which farmer was riding too fine a horse for the condition of his acres, or listening at tavern keyholes and interviewing soiled doves.

He'd learned how to follow someone without being obvious, though, and thus he was inconspicuous as he followed Lucy Fletcher from her garden gate late Tuesday evening.

The only explanation for her dismissal of his proposal was that she had another fish on the line, another gentleman panting after her. Why shouldn't she? She was pretty enough—considering her age—she liked children, and she was trapped in the household of a priggish lord. Even a vicar's cottage, where she could be mistress of her own humble world, would appeal by comparison. She'd be a fool to give up such a prospect if the gentleman had nearly come up to scratch.

She'd been so confident in her rejection that Giles concluded his rival must also figure in the lady's immediate schedule.

Clearly, Giles had been correct, for Lucy wore a long, elegant cloak with the hood pulled up. A sleek town coach stopped in the mews for her—no crests showing—and she quickly ascended.

Naughty, naughty lady. But then, Giles knew she had an adventurous streak. He kept up easily with the coach—nobody went galloping through London at night—and hopped onto the boot of a passing carriage to follow the lady across the river.

To Vauxhall. Where else did lovers meet on cool and cozy nights?

Lucy was intent on a specific destination, for she directed her steps straight to the Lovers' Walk, no safe place for a lady. She was, of course, on her way to an assignation. Otherwise, she'd never have gone even a short distance beyond the bright illumination elsewhere in the gardens.

She stopped under a stately oak, one casting deep shadows. The occasional couple, trio, or quartet strolled past, but they seemed to notice neither Lucy nor Giles loitering farther down the walk.

Giles's plan dropped into his head all of a piece, as his best inspirations often did: Lucy was intent on meeting a lover here in the dark, and Giles would oblige her. When she realized that all caps truly were gray in the dark, and one swain could make her as happy as another, he'd have advanced his cause considerably, if not won the day.

LUCY HAD LONG AGO DEDUCED that the Lovers' Walk was not as dangerous a venue as most chaperones wanted their young charges to believe.

In the first place, torches were placed at intervals, albeit wide, shadowy intervals. In the second, the path was frequented by those intent on discretion. Nobody was peering too closely at anybody else, by mutual, tacit agreement. In the third, the path was far from deserted. While not thronged by foot traffic, a lady crying out in distress would be heard and assistance forthcoming.

Of course, that lady's reputation might emerge from the incident irreparably scarred, but her physical safety was at little risk.

Lucy's confidence was further bolstered by the cloak she wore, a loan from Thor and marvelously warm. She'd drawn the hood up before leaving Marianne's coach and had put Mr. DeCoursy's Norse tales in her reticule in case she needed to defend herself from untoward advances.

Not that Thor would make any of those. He was a gentleman, of that Lucy had no doubt.

She was also convinced, however, that he was not *her* gentleman. He was a lovely memory, a very fine kisser, and a man deserving of every happiness, but—

Footsteps along the walkway on the far side of Lucy's oak gave her pause. A man's tread, though soft, even stealthy.

"My dear?" He spoke barely above a whisper. "Is that you?"

If Lucy peered around the tree, she'd give her location away, and yet, she could not be certain that was Thor's voice.

"Madam, I beg you, don't keep me in suspense. This is the appointed time and place, and I'm here, as agreed."

Lucy stepped out from behind the oak. "Punctuality is likely one of your many fine attributes."

She'd recalled Thor as somewhat taller, but perhaps her recollection wasn't accurate. In the darkness, all she could tell for certain was that a man in a top hat and greatcoat stood a few feet away.

"You came," he said, stepping closer.

Without his hammer, he seemed less a god and more a man embarking on a clandestine flirtation.

"As did you, though you must know that my purpose for keeping this appointment was simply to acknow—"

He took her in his arms somewhat roughly. "I've missed you so."

What in blazes? and *This is not Thor* occupied Lucy's mind simultaneously. The scent of this man was wrong, the shape of him wrong.

Giles? "Turn loose of me," Lucy hissed. "Get your paws off me this instant."

"I've thought of nothing but you," he replied. "Of what we both long for."

Good God. The cloak hampered Lucy from using her knee, so she tried to stomp on her assailant's foot, but he was nimble, and she was being bent back off her balance.

One moment Giles—this had to be Giles—was planting wet kisses on her chin, the next he expelled a solid, "Ooof!" against her cheek.

"Get away from her," said a cold voice. "Get your filthy presuming hands off of her, or next time, I'll use this sledgehammer to do something more than poke you in the ribs."

Thor had arrived. Lucy knew that voice, that shape, and even in the shadows, she could see he'd brought his signature fashion accessory.

Giles stood panting beside the tree. "Who the hell are you?"

"I'm a Norse legend, and you are the disgrace who's about to bolt hotfoot up this path, unless you want to be the fool I put period to at dawn."

"Go," Lucy snapped. "I never want to see you again, and don't think your identity is unknown to me. Thank every guardian angel you possess that you survived this encounter and stay far, far away from me in future."

Giles hesitated one instant, while Thor shouldered his sledge-hammer, then Giles did indeed take off at a dead run up the path.

His footsteps faded, though Lucy's heart was still pounding. "Your arrival was timely, sir. Thank you."

"I considered bringing my usual walking stick, but realized you'd have no way of identifying me if I looked like every other strolling swain. Try being inconspicuous while toting a sledgehammer. It's impossible."

He sounded testy, and human, but still formidable. She could not see his features clearly, but she recognized the manner in which he carried his signature accessory.

"I almost didn't come," Lucy said.

"I almost didn't come either. Shall we find a quiet bench?"

Well, that was a relief. Also somewhat lowering. Lucy made sure her hood shaded her face and took Thor's arm. He was considerate, matching his steps to hers, and giving her time to organize her thoughts. They found a bench in the shadows on a side path, and Lucy spared a moment for regret.

Thor was impressive and doubtless a lovely man, but Lucy's heart was spoken for, even if the gentleman did not return her interest in the same way. She had respect in Lord Tyne's house, she had love after a fashion, and friendship.

"Is this an instance when courtesy requires the gentleman to go first?" Thor asked.

"You almost decided not to come," Lucy said, "but changed your mind, for which I am most grateful."

"Gratitude. A fine place to start. When you came upon me at the masquerade..."

"You came upon me, sir. Rescued me from a centurion with wandering hands."

"My name is Darien," he said. "I see no harm in sharing that with you, for I am very much in your debt."

Darien wasn't the most common English name—Lord Tyne was a Darien—but neither was it unheard of. "As I am in your debt, Darien."

"If you'd like me to call that scoundrel out, I'm pleased to oblige. You said you know who he is."

"He's former military. Meaning no disrespect, but he might know his way around a firearm."

"I'm former military and a dead shot, but no matter. I'm also a widower. You knew that much about me."

Lord Tyne had served for a few years in Lower Canada. Why

Lucy should recall that tidbit, she did not know, though people in love tended to hoard details about their beloved.

And she was in love, surprisingly so, though not with Thor.

"I know you lost your wife several years ago, but if you think to court me, Darien, then I fear I cannot encourage you."

He was quiet for a moment, another quality Lucy liked about him. He didn't chatter, didn't need to hear his own voice. Truly, he'd make some woman a lovely spouse.

"Perhaps your affections are elsewhere engaged, as mine are. Two weeks ago, I was content to pine after a worthy young lady and ignore my own longings. You told me that I did the woman a disservice by not declaring myself, and I agree with you. When we conclude our appointment, I will focus my energies on winning her affection, but my resolve in this regard..."

Lucy waited, though he sounded very much like Lord Tyne, in his rhetoric, in his willingness to put aside his own desires to look after the needs of others, in the very timbre of his voice.

He even wore the same scent as Lord Tyne.

Oh.

Dear.

Oh, damn and drat. Of all the painful ironies... Of all the infernal injustices. Of all the heartbreaks.

"You woke me up," he said, giving Lucy's hand a gentle squeeze. "I was bumbling about, watching my children grow older, making brilliant, dull speeches in the Lords, and going slowly mad. Right beneath my nose is a woman whom I esteem greatly, one as ferocious as a goddess on behalf of those she loves, one who can laugh at herself and at life, one I honestly adore."

Lucy managed to speak around the lump in her throat, for that young lady was very, very fortunate. She could not think who the lucky lady was, for Lord Tyne was discreet, and his social calendar his own.

"I'm sure you'll make her quite happy."

"I'm not half so confident of my success as you are."

Hope leaped, the hope that this paragon he'd determined to court might not appreciate the gem life was handing her.

"Then the lady must be a dunderhead, sir. If she fails to appreciate you, she must be the greatest featherbrain ever to float down from on high, for I'm sure—I'm certain—that your esteem would be the most precious treasure that young lady could ever claim."

Another silence stretched, likely relieved on his part, tortured on Lucy's.

"Well, then," he said. "Do I conclude that your circumstances are similar to my own? Have you determined to pursue the distant gentleman who has caught your appreciative eye?"

Must he sound so brisk, so cheerful? "You conclude correctly. I harbor little hope that he'll ever hold me in the same regard I do him, but we respect and care for one another within the limits of our situation. I am content with that."

Or I will learn to be. A tear trickled hotly against Lucy's cheek. She didn't dare raise her hand to brush it away.

"Then we can part friends and wish each other well," his lordship said, "if you so choose, but I'd like to share with you one other aspect of my evening, before I escort you to your coach."

Lucy nodded, all she could manage in the way of communication.

"My children accosted me as I prepared to go out for an evening at a relative's house. They are delightful girls and blessed with the courage of their convictions. They counseled me regarding my future, in no uncertain terms, and then went giggling and conspiring on their way. I thought to be about my appointed rounds, when the children stopped me again at the foot of the stairs."

What could the girls have been about?

"They faced a moral dilemma," Tyne said. "Somebody about whom they care enormously had apparently made free with a possession given to me years ago. They'd seen it laid out on the lady's bed as they'd come to my apartment to assist me with my toilette. The girls didn't know whether to tattle, confront the thief, or hope a misunderstanding was afoot. I told them a misunderstanding was afoot."

His voice had become painfully gentle. "I know you, Lucy Fletcher, and I know you would never, ever steal a fur-lined velvet cloak from your employer."

Lucy Fletcher.

Mortification surged over Lucy, heating her neck and face. "I didn't want to go to that damned masquerade, I vow this. I only went to appease a friend, and I rue... I don't rue the decision, but I never want you to think—"

"Lucy, I know you," he said, drawing her to her feet. "I know you are ferocious in defense of those you love. I know your integrity is bottomless. I know you have more kindness in your smallest finger than most people have in both hands. I know that if I can merely convince you to stay on as governess, then my heart and my household will be the richer for your generosity, but I also know that you kiss splendidly, and I am determined to court you."

"COURT ME?"

Tyne took Lucy in his arms, though that overture required courage on his part. In the night shadows, he couldn't tell consternation from disbelief from horror, and a man in love was capable of tremendous blunders.

"Yes, court you. I told myself as I made my way here that I could be the distant gentleman who'd caught your fancy—or it might be some other lucky soul. If I am not that man, I want to be him, Lucy. I want your kisses, your scolds, your future. I want to read fairy tales to you and live them with you, complete with the messy parts—the lost and sick children, the gossiping domestics, the ever-multiplying nieces and nephews. I've made enough grand speeches to last a lifetime, but this is the only speech that matters. May I court you?"

She put her arms around him as if weary. "You seek to court me, and you think I'm fierce."

Her crown fit perfectly beneath his chin. "You have dragged me grumbling and fussing into being a proper father to my children. You have ensured I am not a stranger to my own siblings. You listen to the upper servants when they would drive me barking mad with their petty complaints, though they aren't petty, of course. You have rescued me from becoming that worst affliction known to society, a speechifying politician. I'd be aiming for a Cabinet post..."

She bundled closer, and Tyne forgot all about Cabinets and posts, though the image of a bed popped into his head. His bed, with himself and Lucy beneath the covers.

"You are awful," she said. "Why didn't you simply reveal yourself after you'd run Giles off with your sledgehammer?"

"I thought that was Throckmorton. If he's that easily routed, no wonder his children rule his roost."

Lucy tipped her head up so the cloak fell back. Tyne could not make out her expression, but she remained in his embrace, from which familiarity, he took a certain degree of—

She kissed him, gently—an invitation to trust.

"I did not reveal myself," he said, "because you might have chosen to content yourself with some other man. In that event, I would have encouraged you to wake the poor nodcock up with the sort of direct speech you serve to me regularly. You might have been mortified to think you'd kissed your employer by mistake—not once but twice—and I didn't want the sweetest, loveliest kisses I've ever... oh hell."

He kissed her back and found the lady was smiling. Then she got a fistful of Tyne's hair, and then *he* was smiling, and then he had her up against the nearest oak tree—or she had him—and all manner of public indecencies nearly occurred, except Lucy's feet got tangled up with the handle of the sledgehammer.

She grabbed Tyne for balance, and they both ended up laughing so hard they nearly went top over teapot into the hedge.

While Lucy tried to compose herself, Tyne located his hat and the offending sledgehammer, then offered her his arm and escorted her back to the coach.

Where she promptly went off into whoops again, pausing only long enough to agree to marry him.

EPILOGUE

"I do believe that the lack of a blue unicorn with a sparkly purple horn will forever live in Sylvie's heart as the only imperfection in our wedding ceremony." To the casual ear, Tyne doubtless sounded his usual self: calm, self-possessed, articulate. The typical English lord offering his opinion on the weather.

Lucy's was not the casual ear, and her new husband was smiling like a Viking with a longship full of plunder.

The coach rattled away from the wedding breakfast, Sylvie and Amanda tossing rose petals at the boot, the crowd of family waving and cheering in the midday sun. Lucy's brothers had brought their families to Town for the event, as had Tyne's many siblings, and talk of a house party had already started.

Tyne took Lucy's hand and kissed her gloved knuckles, then began undoing the pearl buttons that ran from her wrist to her elbow.

"The wedding was perfect," she said, "because you were my groom. I still say we ought to have wed by special license."

Tyne had refused her request, insisting on every propriety—while anybody was looking. Behind closed doors, he'd subjected Lucy to diabolically skilled kisses, whispered promises, and caresses of shocking intimacy. On every occasion, though, he'd stopped short of anticipating the vows.

He paused with her glove half unbuttoned. "Our siblings would not have had time to assemble had the ceremony been performed on short notice, and you deserved to meet my family before you became part of it. They're a loud, opinionated, rumgumptious lot of—"

"Of wonderful people. Much like my own family." She switched arms, so he could start on her other glove. "You did not want our first-born to arrive too soon."

He held her palm against his cheek, and through the thin kid of her glove, Lucy felt the heat of his skin.

"How can I focus on these thousands of buttons, how can I attend to anything, when you tempt me with talk of progeny?"

"Get used to it, my lord. You are married now, and you have tempted me without mercy for the last month." She patted his thigh —*not* his knee—and he drew down the window shade. A week before the wedding, Lady Eleanor had whisked Lucy and the girls to her ladyship's household, which had been wise but irksome.

The girls had needed some time to sort out Lucy's transition from governess to step-mother. A new governess had to be interviewed— Tyne had ceded that decision to Lucy—and fittings without number had to be endured.

"I nearly stole into your bed more times than I could count," Tyne said. "With my valet sleeping in the dressing closet, I did not want to start talk below stairs."

"Did you ask Eleanor to open her home to me?" Tyne would do that, would be that discreet and considerate—also that dunderheaded.

"No, I did not, though my valet will be sleeping elsewhere hence-forth." He had both of Lucy's gloves half undone, loose enough that he could draw them off. "That veil business next."

"All you need do is remove some of the hairpins," Lucy said, "but be careful. I hope our daughters might wear that veil someday."

He paused, leaning his forehead against Lucy's shoulder. "*Our* daughters. Have I told you that I love you? Have I told you that *our* daughters love you? The damned pantry mouser had better love you, or I'll banish him to the stables."

This demonstrativeness was either a benefit of marrying a widower, or simply Tyne's way of being conscientious. He *told* Lucy he loved her, *told* her he loved to look at her, to touch her. He was surprisingly affectionate, taking her into his lap, sitting beside her of an evening in the parlor, holding her hand when they walked into church services on Sunday mornings.

His fingers searched gently through her hair for pins, though he found rather too many, and before Lucy could tell him to stop, not only her veil, but the chignon fashioned at the nape of her neck had come undone. He drew the veil away and piled it atop the gloves on the opposite bench.

"You'll arrive to Boxhaven's estate looking ravished. I like that idea."

"If I'm to look ravished," Lucy said, "hadn't you ought to look ravished as well?"

"Valid point." He took Lucy in his arms, and for the few miles they had to travel before breaking their journey, she did her best to kiss, caress, and tease him into a nearly ravished state. When they alighted from the coach in the estate's forecourt, Tyne's cravat sported two entire wrinkles, his hair was a trifle mussed, and he was missing one glove.

Nonetheless, he was every inch the polite guest when he addressed the housekeeper. "Her ladyship and I will take dinner in the library after we change out of our wedding attire. We will ring for assistance if we require it."

The housekeeper beamed at them, Lucy beamed back. Tyne had prevailed on the Marquess of Boxhaven for use of one of his rural properties to break their journey. The marquess, the same fellow who'd hosted the masquerade ball, had cordially obliged.

"I'm not used to being a ladyship," she said, taking Tyne's arm as they ascended a curving staircase. "I'm not used to being a mama, not used to being a wife."

Tyne knew where he was going, for he'd visited Boxhaven at this property in years past. "We will learn together, my dear. I have been a husband before, but I haven't been *your* husband. Nobody would call me a quick study, though I'm diligent and motivated to excel in my new role. I'm also motivated to get all that damned frippery off of you."

"Language, my lord."

He bowed her through a doorway to an elegant parlor that adjoined a sizable bedroom. A bed of enormous proportions sat under green velvet hangings, and trays holding tea and sandwiches were on the sideboard.

"Right now," Tyne said, "I am entirely yours, and not a lord at all. Would you think me very forward if I suggested we put that bed to use in the near future?"

How polite. How aggravatingly self-disciplined. "I'd think you completely backward if you so much as reached for a sandwich, when all I want is to reach for you."

Tyne came to her, wrapped his arms around her, and all the kissing and teasing in the coach was so much dithering compared to the passion he unleashed on Lucy. His embrace was possessive rather than polite—as was hers. His kisses were plundering, his patience with her clothing nonexistent. He growled—Darien, Lord Tyne— growled—and buttons hit the carpet. Fabric tore, and Lucy tossed his beautiful morning coat in the general direction of a chair.

"We must—" He tried to step back, but Lucy was having none of that. "We must repair to neutral corners."

Like pugilists. "You must undo my buttons." Lucy swept her hair off of her nape and gave him her back.

"I have grown to loathe buttons." Nonetheless, his fingers were swift and competent, and he was equally proficient with her stays. He insisted on removing her shoes, kneeling before her, but Lucy insisted on undressing him too.

She took her time with his sleeve buttons, his cravat, his watch, all the trappings of the lord that covered up the reality of the man: fit, muscular, and endlessly desirable. When she had him down to his breeches, he tugged on her braid to draw her near.

"If you touch me even once more, I will have you on your back on the rug, Lady Tyne."

She pressed her hand over his heart, loving the slow tattoo beneath her palm. "Do you promise?"

Ah, that smile. The Viking smile that assured her, yes, he promised. He promised to love her thoroughly and often, to make all the waiting worth the wonder to follow.

"I have married a goddess," he said, scooping her into his arms and striding into the bedroom. "May I be worthy of that honor."

Oh, to be plundered by a god who knew how to wield his hammer. Tyne gently set Lucy on the bed, stepped out of his breeches, and settled over her without once taking his gaze from her.

She wiggled beneath him, wrapping her legs around him. "My shift?"

"Is the only thing holding my dignity together," Tyne replied, kissing down the side of Lucy's face, from her temple, to her cheek, to her neck. "Though that won't last long. I'll make it up to you, Lucy. For the next three decades, I'll make it up to you if you'll excuse my haste on our wedding day."

She did not excuse his haste. She abetted it, with slow caresses and long kisses, with wandering hands and well-aimed shifts of her hips. When Tyne had eased inside of her, and Lucy was nearly weeping with frustrated desire, he stilled.

"I have dreamed..." he whispered. "I have longed for this moment with you."

"For all the moments," Lucy replied. "To hold you as physically close as I hold your love in my heart." He'd been right to have the banns cried, right to give her weeks to anticipate this joy, but she'd have to tell him that later, for he'd begun to move.

His loving was relentlessly controlled, his tempo escalating by maddeningly deliberate degrees, no matter how Lucy urged him on. She surrendered to his superior command of strategy—for now—and nigh unbearable pleasure was her reward. When she was drifting down from torrents of marital bliss, Tyne let go of his ferocious self-restraint, and the pleasure cascaded through her again.

They were both panting when he eventually stilled over her. The covers had been kicked halfway off the bed, and Lucy's shift was hanging from one corner of the cheval mirror.

Ye gods, ye Norse, Greek, and Roman gods and goddesses.

"I like that," Tyne said as Lucy's hand smoothed over his backside. "I think you left claw marks there."

How smug he sounded. "Don't gloat." Lucy pinched him in the same location, and he laughed. "What a wonderful sound," she said. "My lover's laughter."

He eased from her and crouched on all fours, passing her a handkerchief from the night table. When had he thought to put that there?

"You'll need sustenance now," he said, climbing from the bed and strutting into the sitting room. "I'll need sustenance. I am her ladyship's devoted lover."

He was also—yet another surprise—unselfconscious about his nakedness. What a delightful quality in a husband and lover.

The smile he wore as he brought Lucy the tray from the other room was frequently in evidence in the ensuing weeks, months, and years, the smile of a happy, much-loved Viking. He wore an even more tender smile when—forty weeks to the day after the wedding—she presented him with little Thor.

And little Freya.

And all the rest of the Tyne pantheon who came after the twins. The first time Sylvie was permitted to hold her baby siblings, she declared them even better than a blue unicorn, in which opinion, even her older sister (who had begun to put up her hair) concurred.

HIS GRACE OF LESSER PUDDLEBURY

Previously Published in
Dukes in Disguise

*Dedicated to the late
Jeanne McCarthy
(My everlovin' godmother)*

CHAPTER ONE

Over the clip-clop of the coach horses' hooves and the incessant throbbing of his arse, Coinneach Callum Amadour Ives St. Bellan, ninth Duke of Mowne, endured that form of affection which—among grown men at least—traveled under the sobriquet of *teasing*.

More honest company would call it making sport of a fellow in a misguided attempt to cheer him up.

"Mowed down, they'll say, like so much wheat," Starlingham quipped. "One stray bullet and the great duke is *hors de combat*."

Lucere was not to be outdone. "The moon sets, as it were."

They went off into whoops, endlessly entertained, as always, by a play on the title Mowne, which was an old Scottish term for the lunar satellite... and thus a cognate for a reference to the human fundament.

"If the Sun and Stars had not tarried with a pair of tavern maids, we would have reached the dueling ground sooner," Con groused. "This whole imbroglio is your fault, you two."

There was simply no getting comfortable in a coach after being shot in the arse. No getting comfortable *anywhere*.

"I would be spared my present indignity," Con went on, "but for the flirtatious excesses of my oldest and dearest friends. Bear in mind, if the wound festers, the pair of you will be consoling my mother on the loss of her darling baby boy, and Freddy will become the next Duke of Mowne."

Mention of Mama sobered the Duke of Starlingham and the Duke of Lucere faster than facing a ballroom full of unbetrothed debutantes in the last week of the Season. Confronting such a prospect, the Sun, Moon, and Stars, as Con and his friends were collectively known, would have closed ranks. They'd often stood figuratively shoulder to shoulder, defending their bachelor freedoms against all perils, most especially the artillery fire of the matchmakers.

In the present situation, Con and his friends would have to split up.

"Where did you say we were going?" Lucere asked.

"Outer Perdition," Starlingham muttered. "We're in Yorkshire. Nothing civilized goes on in Yorkshire, where the winters are long and the sheep are notoriously friendly."

"Starlingham, you will take up residence at your hunting box," Con said, assuming that handy dwelling yet stood. "Lucere, you and your manservant, should you refuse to part with that worthy, will have to bide at a local inn or boarding house. Send word to either me or Starlingham regarding your choice of accommodations. I can stay with my third cousin, Jules St. Bellan."

Dear old cousin Jules was one of Mama's many faithful correspondents, though the relationship was so attenuated as to be more nominal than biological. Nominal and fiscal, for Con had been sending a stipend north to Lesser Puddlebury for years.

"Maybe we're doing this all a bit too brown," Lucere said. "Your Uncle Leo might never get word of the duel."

"Maybe you're still cup-shot," Starlingham countered, grabbing for the strap dangling above his head as the coach lumbered through a curve. "If Leo learns we're taking a week's repairing lease in Greater Goosepuddle, he'll suspect Freddy got into another scrape, and then Mowne won't be allowed so much as a spare farthing."

Freddy, next in line for the Mowne ducal title, was *always* getting into scrapes, as were Quinton and Hector, and—not to be outdone by her older brothers—Antigone.

Uncle Leo had decided that Freddy must be taken in hand—*by Con*—or Con would lose control of the family finances, of which Leo was trustee.

"Which of you will marry Antigone if Leo cuts off my funds?" Con asked, for somebody would have to marry her if she was to be kept in reasonable style. Leo's idea of a wardrobe allowance was parsimonious on a good day.

Only two paths circumnavigated Leo's threatened penny-pinching when it came to the family finances. The first was for Con to turn five-and-thirty, which fate would not befall him for another six years—assuming he could avoid further incidents of bloodshed. The second means of prying Leo's fingers off the St. Bellan money pots was to marry. If the Deity were merciful, that duty lay at least a decade in the future.

Con shifted on his pillow. The laudanum was wearing off, and the dilemma caused by Freddy's dueling loomed ever larger.

"Hearing no volunteers for the honor of marrying my darling sister," Con said, "we must deceive Uncle Leo in hopes he never learns of Freddy's latest mis-step. In the alternative, I could take a vow of poverty, which would lead perforce to the cheering vistas of unmitigated chastity and limitless sobriety."

"It might not be so bad," Lucere said, an odd comment for a man rumored to be facing an engagement to a German princess.

"Poverty, chastity, *and* sobriety?" Starlingham asked.

"No, spending a week in Lower Dingleberry. How many times have these people seen three dukes in the neighborhood at once?"

"They must *never* see three dukes in the neighborhood at once," Con retorted. "I shall be Mr. Connor Amadour and swear my cousin to eternal secrecy. He's a mercenary old soul, and his silence can be bought. You two will not trade on your ducal consequence whatso-ever. Be wealthy, be charming, be handsome, but keep your titles to yourselves. The greatest commodity traded up and down the Great North Road is gossip, and three dukes dropping coin and consequence all over some rural bog would reach Leo's notice by the next full moon, as it were."

Three young, healthy, *single* dukes could do nothing without observation and comment by all of society. Freddy enjoyed a little more privacy, but Leo somehow learned of the boy's every stupid wager and bungled prank nonetheless.

"So... we're not to be dukes," Lucere said.

"We're not to have even a country manor for our accommodations," Starlingham added.

"But if we can pull this off," Con said, "I'll retain control over my portion of the family money, which means nobody need marry Antigone, and I won't have to call either of you out for landing me in this contretemps. All we're missing are cold Scottish mornings spent tramping about the grouse moors."

And the gorgeous scenery, and the fresh air, and a chance to get the stink and noise of London out of a man's soul.

"Two weeks, then, but we're also missing good Scottish whisky," Lucere noted.

"And the Scottish lasses," Starlingham said, saluting with an imaginary glass.

Con would miss both of those comforts, but in truth, his allowance also paid for Mama's occasional gambling debt, Antigone's excesses at the milliner's, Hector's charities, Quinton's experiments, and Freddy's scrapes.

Con financed it all out of his own allotment, a delicately balanced enterprise that Uncle Leo could easily upset. Leo never interfered with Con's decisions affecting the *ducal* finances. With the *personal* finances, only Con's funds stood between his immediate family and utter mortification.

Though what could be more mortifying than getting shot in the arse?

"When you do see the Scottish lasses again," Lucere said, "you'll have a fetching scar."

"Would you like one of your own?" Con drawled. "All you need do is attempt to interrupt Freddy's next duel, for he's sure to have another. Stand well clear of the opponents, but position yourself such that Freddy's bullet bounces just so off a rock and grazes your ducal assets. Along with your fetching scar, you'll enjoy a significant mess and no little discomfort. I was wearing my favorite riding breeches, for which Freddy will pay."

"Hurts, does it?" Starlingham asked quietly.

These were Con's friends. He dared not answer honestly, or they'd pound Freddy to flinders when the poor lad had been trying to delope.

"I did fancy those breeches. Their destruction pains me." The truth, when Bond Street tailors could beggar a man in a single season.

Lucere passed Con a silver flask. "We'll drink a toast then, to two weeks of happy ruralizing in Upper Lesser Middle Bog-dingle-shire."

Con took a swallow of mellow comfort and passed the flask to Starlingham, who did likewise.

"To being a plain mister, and not Your Perishing Grace every moment of the infernal day," Starlingham said, raising the flask.

Lucere accepted the silver vessel back and studied the unicorn embossed amid the laurel leaves on the side.

"Good-bye to the Sun, Moon, and Stars, and for the next two weeks, here's to the dukes in disguise." He tipped up the flask, then tipped it higher, shaking the last drops into his open mouth.

Con's arse hurt, but to have such friends, well, that made a man's heart ache a little too. He raised his arm, as they'd been doing since one of them had suffered an adolescent infatuation with the paintings of Jacques-Louis David.

His friends did likewise—the most inane rituals never died—and bumping fists, as one they chanted, "To the dukes in disguise!"

~

"THIS IS NOT A TUMBLEDOWN COTTAGE," Con muttered as the groom and coachman wrestled his trunks from the boot. "I could swear Her Grace said Cousin Jules resides in a tumbledown cottage, barely more than a shack."

The dwelling was pretty, in a rural sort of way. Three stories of soft gray fieldstone topped with standing seam tin, the whole flanked with stately oaks and fronted with a wide, covered terrace the width of the house. Red and white roses vined from trellises up onto the terrace roof.

The place gave off a disconcerting air of bucolic welcome, such as a duke in demand by every London hostess ought not to find appealing.

"Will that be all, *sir?*" John Coachman asked with an exaggerated wink.

"Thank you, yes. I'll see you again in two weeks, and until then, I expect utmost discretion from you and the grooms. Ut. Most."

John wasn't prone to drunkenness, but his groom was young and new to a duke's service.

"Right, Your Worship. Mind that injury, or Her—*your mama* will have me out on me *arse.*" More winking, and then the coach creaked down the drive, kicking up a plume of dust as Starlingham's gloved hand fluttered a farewell from the window. Nobody came forth from the cottage to carry in bags, greet the visitor, or otherwise acknowledge company.

"I'm not a stupid man," Con said, gaze on the bright red front door.

But what did one do without a footman to knock on the door, pass over a card, and ensure the civilities were observed? How did luggage find its way above stairs before the next rain shower?

The knocker was the sort that never came down, so how did one tell if the family was receiving?

Mysteries upon puzzles. How would... Mr. Connor Amadour *go on?*

Insight struck as thunder rumbled off to the south. This was Yorkshire, and thunder rumbled about a good deal, even when the sun shone brightly.

Also five minutes before a downpour turned the shire to mud. Con marched—unevenly, given the increasing pain of his wound — up the steps and *rapped on the door*.

Nothing happened. Why hadn't Con asked John Coachman and the grooms to pile the luggage under the terrace roof? The roses grew in such profusion as to make the porch cozy. A wide swing hung near one end, a worn rug beneath it, embroidered pillows in each corner of the swing.

Con had recently become an ardent if silent admirer of the comfy pillow.

He banged the knocker again, rather louder than gentility allowed. Perhaps the help was hard of hearing. Perhaps they were all down in the kitchen, scrambling to tuck in their livery because it was half day. Even the legendarily hardworking denizens of Yorkshire would observe the custom of half day.

More thunder, more rapping. Life as Mr. Amadour looked decidedly unappealing. A wind began to tease at the surrounding oaks, while Con's trunks sat several yards from the foot of the steps, apparently incapable of levitating into the house.

Mr. Amadour was a resourceful fellow, Con decided, and fit, despite his injuries. He fenced, he boxed, he rode great distances in the normal course. He gave a good account of himself on any cricket pitch and was a reputable oarsman.

Apparently, he had latent skills as a porter too, for it took Con a mere fifteen minutes to wrestle three trunks up the steps and pile them beside the door. Even wearing gloves, though, he acquired a scraped knuckle, two bruised fingers, and a squashed toe.

And he'd started the wound on his backside to throbbing. He couldn't very well check to see if it was bleeding again, though he suspected it was. The surgeon had told him to apply pressure directly to the injury to stop any renewed bleeding.

Applying pressure to a bullet wound amounted to self-torture.

Con reconnoitered. He was a duke, a single, wealthy-on-paper, not-bad-looking duke—not that single, wealthy dukes could be bad-looking in the eyes of most. He'd bested matchmakers, debutantes, card sharps, and Uncle Leo. He'd learned the knack of looking pious while napping through a Sunday sermon.

Cousin Jules would come home, for Cousin Jules never traveled to speak of. He was too busy writing to Mama in an endless correspondence of gossip, gratitude for the last bank draft, and importuning for the next one. Perhaps Jules was on a constitutional out among the lovely scenery.

Con determined that he would admire the scenery too, from the comfort of the pillowed swing at the end of the porch. All would remain cozy and dry on the porch despite the fickle weather, Cousin Jules would ramble home, and within the hour, Con would be tucked up before a fire, a glass of brandy in hand. He'd be a welcome, if unexpected, guest whose worst problem would be all the fussing and cooing from the help.

As it should be.

"I AM GROWING to hate market days," Julianna said.

"You hate that Maurice Warren is becoming bolder," MacTavish replied, casting a scowl at the lowering sky. If anybody's scowl could have chased off the clouds, it should have been his.

"I hate that my coin doesn't go as far as it used to," Julianna said. "You can take the cart straight around back, Mac. I'll help you unload."

That magnificent scowl swung in Julianna's direction. "You'll do no such thing, miss. Bad enough you must haggle with the thieves and rogues at the market. Bad enough that lazy bag-of-sass housekeeper had to take herself off visiting. Bad enough—somebody has come to call, or driven a coach up our lane by misdirection."

MacTavish would have brought the cart to a halt, but Julianna appropriated the whip and brushed it over the mule's quarters.

"You can study the tracks later. We need to unload the goods before the heavens open up, and if you let Hortensia stop now, we might not get her moving until Yuletide."

Because Hortensia, like Julianna, was mortally tired. Unlike Julianna, the mule could make her wishes known, and frequently did. As mules went, she was a good sort. Worked hard, lived on nothing but decent pasture much of the year, and asked for little besides the occasional carrot from the children. But she was the last young mule on the property, and ploughing heavy Yorkshire soil was best undertaken with four stout draft horses, not one overworked mule.

Mr. Warren owned a literal herd of mules, of course. The cart rattled along to the back of the cottage, and Hortensia halted at the door without any prompting from Mac.

"Good mule," Mac said, climbing down. He came around to assist Julianna, but she hopped down on her own.

"Let's hurry. If the rain doesn't start in the next two minutes, the children will come pelting up the lane, and their help isn't to be endured."

"Children, bah. Locusts, sent from the devil to plague adults and innocent mules. Horty agrees with me."

Julianna grabbed a pair of coarse sacks from the back of the cart. "Sometimes, I agree with you, but we'll let that be our little secret."

In the course of "assisting" to bring in the weekly haul from market, the children could drop, misplace, sample, hide, and damage half the goods Julianna had haggled away her morning procuring. Thank the gods of Yorkshire weather, or the charms of Mr. Hucklebee's summer natural sciences academy, Julianna managed to get the produce properly stored in the pantries and larders before any little feet thundered through the back doorway.

The rain was almost as accommodating, though on the last trip to the cart, Julianna felt the cold slap of an impending downpour against her nape. She paused for a moment, face turned to the sky. If the children were out of doors, downpours could mean colds, colds meant sitting up with a sick child, and sitting up with a sick child meant...

"Please take Hortensia around to the stable," Julianna told Mac. "She's earned a few oats for her efforts."

"Oats, in summer? You're daft Julianna Marie MacKinnon St. Bellan." Then, more gently as he grabbed the mule's bridle, "C'mon along, princess. The mule, I'm allowed to spoil. The lady of the house must work herself to exhaustion."

As must the man of all work, muttering all the while. "You can cut some fresh roses when you're done with Horty," Julianna said, for Mac was getting on, and Julianna had to find ways to make him rest occasionally. He'd been getting on for as long as Julianna could recall, but like the sturdy stones that formed her home, his looks never changed. He and Hortensia were the twin pillars of Julianna's independence, and without them...

Maurice Warren's self-satisfied smile rose in Julianna's imagination.

So she sent Mac to pluck roses rather than let him work all afternoon in the barn. Instead of sitting down herself, she started on the stew that would have to do for dinner that night. The meat—a brace of lean hares Mac had caught the previous day—was sizzling in the pan, vegetables chopped and ready for the pot, when Mac tromped into the kitchen, a bouquet of thorny roses in his hand.

His expression promised that, as usual, he had bad news. "Miss, there's a set of fancy travelin' trunks on the front porch. Doubtless, they're full of goods we can sell over in York. Every cloud always has a silver lining, my ma used to say."

Trunks? "We're not expecting guests."

They never expected guests, thank God. Guests ate, they required bed linens, they interfered with household routines. How many times had dear Cousin Marie threatened to visit, and how many times had Julianna put her off?

"The trunks are mighty fine, miss. Shiny brass hinges, stout locks, though a bullet or two judiciously aimed at the—"

"You will not assassinate trunks belonging to somebody else," Julianna said, trading her apron for a plain brown wool shawl. "Nor will you sell goods we cannot claim as ours, lest the king's man take you up and my entire property fall into ruin."

"Not stolen," MacTavish said, crowding after Julianna as she mounted the stairs. "More like inherited, miss. Anybody can inherit or find abandoned goods."

"Mac, have you been at the whisky again?"

"I'm never far from my flask, but that's the rest of it, ye see. The good news is we have trunks on the porch, fancy trunks such as a nob might stash out of the rain. The bad news is..."

Julianna marched to the front door, Mac on her heels. "Out with it, Mac. If the duchess has finally made good on her threats to visit, we'll simply have to endure the expense."

And the shame. Julianna hated taking charity, and for her wealthy relation, Julianna had painted a rosy picture of life in Yorkshire. According to her letters, she thrived on embroidery, she went for long walks in the beautiful countryside, enjoyed the regular company of friends, and was sliding into the cheerful embrace of spinsterhood amid a cloud of contentment and genteel, well-read solitude.

"The trunks are right lovely," MacTavish said, darting around to stop Julianna from passing through the front doorway. Mac could move faster than a guilty eight-year-old boy when motivated. "Did I mention there's bad news too?"

Julianna put her hands on her hips. "There's always bad news too."

Mac peered at the bouquet he still held. "As to that, seems that in addition to a set of fancy trunks on your porch, somebody came by and left a dead man on your swing."

～

"HE'S GOOD-SIZED," a man growled in a Border Scots accent. "His clothing will fetch a pretty penny, though bloodstains are the very devil to get out."

Con's brain refused to function. Impressions came to him in a disjointed and curiously pleasant mosaic. The fragrance of roses in the rain, the sensation of embroidery pressed against his cheek, the scent of hearty fare simmering over a nearby fire.

"He's not dead, MacTavish. Shame on you, and I'll hear no talk of selling his clothing."

"Likes of him won't miss the occasional waistcoat, miss."

A gentle hand brushed the hair back from Con's brow, though the fingers were callused. "Please return to the kitchen, MacTavish. The children are due back any moment, and I'll want them at the table, cramming their bellies with bread and butter while I deal with this... this gentleman."

The vowels were broad and lilting, the register feminine. Heavy boots stomped off. A door closed.

Another gentle caress to his brow. "Sir, can you open your eyes?"

Con wasn't a sir, he was a Your Grace, though something told him that wasn't important right now. His eyes did not want to open. For the lady with the soft voice and the soothing touch, he made the effort.

She was pretty and her face was near his. Hair a lustrous red—not carroty, not quite auburn. Eyes the blue of a summer sky on a still, sunny day. Features... strong, sharp-drawn, a few years past the dimples and softness of girlhood.

Mouth... Con was not exactly a candles-out, bayonet-at-the-ready sort of fellow between the sheets, and yet, a young, single duke consorted only with women who knew what they were about. They didn't expect much bedroom flummery from him, but this woman's mouth was... flummerous in the extreme. Full, rosy, eminently kissable.

He'd linger over the pleasure of acquainting himself with those lips, though at present the mouth they belonged to was also... worried.

"Are you ill?" she asked, ruffling Con's hair.

He shook off the pleasure of that touch and the longing for more of it. "Flummerous is not a word." Con's mouth was dry, which reminded him that he'd been dosed with the poppy. "A mouth cannot look worried."

She withdrew her hand. "Perhaps you've suffered a blow to the head? Can you sit up?"

Her question alerted Con to the fact that he was toppled over on his side, on a porch swing, in the wilds of York-Godsaveme-shire.

Reality came galloping at him from several sides, though, of course, he could sit up. "Almighty, perishing, benighted devils," he said as fire lanced up from his wounded buttock. "I have not been struck on the head."

"It's only your manners that have been injured?" the lady asked, sitting back on her heels. "Then explain the bloodstain at your hip."

Not his hip, his arse, though in this position... the pain was substantial, which hardly signified. What did signify was that a duke did not offer explanations, much less produce them on demand for housekeepers or servants of any stripe.

"I'm looking for Jules MacKinnon. I'd appreciate it if you would please alert him to the arrival of a kinsman."

The woman—who might herself be slightly deficient in the brainbox—plunked herself down beside Con.

"What business have you with Jules MacKinnon?" she asked.

Servants could be more protective than siblings. Con had had occasion to appreciate this very quality. Moreover, he was in the countryside—deep in the countryside—where households were a good deal less formal.

"I am a cousin," Con said. "MacKinnon and I have never met that I can recall, but our households have corresponded for years. I was in the area, my coach developed a problem, and I am at my cousin's mercy for hospitality over the next two weeks."

That was rather good, if Con did say so himself. Having the coachman kicking his heels elsewhere qualified as a problem, and the rest was pure fact.

"You're lying," the woman said, though she sounded as if she often heard lies. Weary, half-amused, half-disappointed. "Polite lies, probably well intended even, but you have no direct acquaintance with Jules MacKinnon, even by letter."

"What I am, madam, is in pain from an injury that could well become infected, and unless you want me expiring on your porch, you will inform Mr. MacKinnon that a relative needs the favor of the household's hospitality for the next fortnight. Tell him... tell him Connor Amadour has come to call."

The name apparently meant little to her. That full, rosy mouth firmed. "What is the nature of your injury? Were you set upon by highwaymen?"

"Yes."

"You're lying again. I cannot have you—"

An aging kilted giant stepped onto the porch from the front door. "Beg pardon, miss. Children are home and at their bread and butter. Where shall I put the trunks?"

The fellow struck Con as a specimen of human geology, all craggy jaw, white eyebrows like flying rowans on a cliff face of a profile, a raptor's gaze peering from faded blue eyes. That face was inhospitable country, with plenty of muscle and meanness as well.

Con rose, though moving after inactivity made his injury scream. The courtesy of offering his hand to the lady was instinctive—to him.

Not to her.

His gloves had come off at some point and lay on the worn carpet. She gazed at his hand, then peered at his face.

"The trunks go in the blue bedroom, Mac. Thank you, and tell the children I'll be along shortly. They are to fold the towels before they come upstairs."

With no more effort than if the trunk had been a sack of feathers, the old fellow hoisted the largest of the three to his shoulder and disappeared into the house.

The lady rose without taking Con's hand. "I cannot abide dishonesty, dissembling, prevarication, or any of their *cousins*. Every member of this household eschews mendacity, or he's not welcome. Tell me the truth: Why are you here, and how were you injured, *Your Grace?*"

CHAPTER TWO

If Cousin Marie's sketches hadn't given him away, if the signet ring fitted to his smallest finger hadn't given him away, his choice of pseudonym would have. No less person than Coinneach Callum Amadour Ives St. Bellan, ninth Duke of Mowne, stood in wrinkled finery on Julianna's porch.

Bloody, wrinkled finery.

"I was injured when the highwaymen fired upon my party," he said, looking exactly like Harold when the boy told a great bouncer. All bravery about the posture, but uncertainty in his green eyes.

"Do dukes typically flee the scene when set upon by brigands, such that injury is suffered to the posterior? Your mother claims you never travel with fewer than two armed grooms, two footmen, a coachman, and two outriders."

Julianna could not imagine this arrogant beast fleeing anything, except perhaps an honest day's work. His very bearing shouted privilege, while his features invited lingering study. Dark red hair—a coincidence, for he and Julianna were not blood kin—height, military bearing, and features that could define male beauty for the angels of portraiture.

His looks made Julianna both angry and unaccountably sad. She wanted to sketch him. She must get rid of him.

The rain intensified, and thunder shattered the heavens immediately overhead.

"Come inside," Julianna said, for Roberta was terrified of storms, and the boys teased her when on their bad behavior. Folding laundry often provoked bad behavior.

"That is how you greet a guest? *Come inside?*"

Julianna marched to the door and held it open. "Come inside, Your Grace. *Now,* before you develop a lung fever to go with your injured nether parts."

He was probably trying to strut, but his injury—he'd bled a narrow, dark streak through his breeches—doubtless accounted for an uneven stride. Handsome breeches they were too. Mac could tell Julianna to the penny what they were worth.

The duke—for this was Mowne, no mistake about it—paused before the open door and peered down at Julianna. Most men other than Mac were not tall enough to peer down at her. She met their gazes eye to eye and made sure the fellow was the first to look way.

"How is it you know of the title?" He had the effrontery to even smell like a duke, all sandalwood and spice, clean soap, and fresh laundered linen. His lashes were as long as a new calf's, and Julianna knew how soft that dark hair was.

"Your mother is ever so proud of you. She's sent dozens of sketches, described the longing glances of hundreds of debutantes and legions of their scheming mamas. Artists beg for the favor of your annual portrait, and any self-respecting rose drops its petals in your path."

He glanced around at the roses embowering the porch, as if botany had abruptly become his true calling. "You are Cousin Jules."

This revelation did not please him, and in that moment, Julianna hated all those debutantes. "Those are my roses, Your Grace. You will note each rose petal remaining affixed to its blossom, despite your uninvited presence." That the duke, the nominal head of Julianna's family, should see what a once gracious country manor had become in her care stung bitterly.

He plucked a white blossom poised to fade and shook it before Julianna, so the petals fell on the dusty toes of her half boots.

"I need a place to convalesce in peace and quiet, *cousin*, a place where nobody will hear of His Grace of Mowne being shot in the backside, and bruit the news about in every ballroom and men's club in the realm. Will you allow me that sanctuary under your roof?"

Several of the rose petals had fallen on his lace-edged cravat. Nobody but a duke could get away with that much delicacy about his dress. Julianna brushed the petals away.

"I cannot afford to turn you away. Your mother's pin money provides necessary cash to support my household, though her charity—"

Another crash of thunder sounded, suggesting God himself was trying to blast the farmhouse to pebbles.

"Let's take our squabbling inside," Mowne said, gesturing as if the premises belonged to him, which they nearly did. "You may scold me for my mother's charity at length, and while you are, of course, impervious to the elements and disease both, I am not dealing well with the ruin of another pair of my breeches."

That wet, dark streak on his flank had grown longer. Something in his gaze had shifted too. Julianna could read little boys as accurately as she could recite her Book of Common Prayer, but she could not read the man bleeding on her porch.

He'd find neither peace nor quiet under this roof, though Julianna refused to be ashamed of the racket healthy children made. She swept into the house and let the duke close the door.

"We need to get you out of those breeches." A fresh stain had a prayer of coming out, even from soft leather. A dried stain was a more difficult proposition, though little Roberta had a miraculous way with a gum eraser.

"Have you any idea how imperious you sound?" the duke asked, limping after Julianna. "My mother would envy you the angle you achieve with those marvelous eyebrows. The headmaster at Eton needed your skill with an eyebrow."

"Don't flatter my eyebrows," Julianna snapped at the foot of the steps. "You are indirectly family, and one cannot turn away family. Even if you are not family to me by blood, you are kin to the duchess, and her generosity is all that stands between the children and the poorhouse. We'll provide this sanctuary from gossip that your pride requires, but don't expect London hospitality."

He braced himself against the newel post, which came off in his hand because too many small children had slid down the banister, their little bums smacking into the polished maple orb with gleeful velocity. Julianna snatched it from him and set it on the sideboard, though it rolled right off and hit the faded carpet with a thud.

"All I need," Mowne said, "is discretion from you, dry sheets, and a bit of toast with my morning tea. In two weeks, I'll be on my way, and you can forget I ever darkened your door. You will please introduce me as Mr. Connor Amadour, distant cousin on the St. Bellan side of the family, if you must introduce me at all. My coach has suffered a mishap, and I'm biding here while the repairs are made, also catching up with my kinfolk and enjoying the fresh country air."

"Such a busy fellow." While he would, in fact, do nothing but stand about ruining his breeches and flattering Julianna's eyebrows. "As it happens, we have a spare bedroom, and I'm competent with minor wounds. Your tea will be weak, and you'll come downstairs to dine in the morning. I simply haven't the help to accommodate a duke."

"Not a duke," he said, following Julianna up the stairs. "A distant cousin, late of... Kent, on the way north to do some shooting. Who is your pet Highlander?"

"MacTavish is our man of all work, and you cross him at your peril. He's the reason this farm hasn't fallen to wrack and ruin, and I treasure him beyond words. Between him and Hortensia, we have a crop, we have gardens, we have stout walls to keep in the sheep and shelter our fruit trees. You malign MacTavish—"

"Yes, yes," the duke said, twirling a lace-cuffed wrist. A hint of lace, a peek of lace, a mere gesture of lace. "Death by eyebrow at thirty paces. This house is lovely."

Julianna almost snapped at him not to admire the house, except... he wasn't wrong, and she was exhausted. Market days had become increasingly fraught, with Maurice trying to escort her everywhere while, to a person, the merchants and tinkers charged her daylight robbery prices for every necessity.

"The house used to be lovely," she said. "The place has grown weary in recent years, faded and worn. The winters are long and bitter, the summers endless work."

They'd reached the blue bedroom, the only other furnished room in Julianna's wing of the house. His Grace's lips had acquired a whitish cast, even in the gloom of the corridor.

The streak on his breeches had grown another alarming inch.

"I'll fetch water, clean bandages, and my medicinals," Julianna said, opening the door to the bedroom. "You will get out of those breeches, and I'll deal with them as soon as I've seen to your wound."

"You are a woman," the duke replied, this time bracing himself on the doorjamb in an elegant, casual pose. "Can't this MacWondrous fellow do a bit of doctoring? A surgeon has already seen to the injury once. I'm sure all it wants is a change of dressing."

In the kitchen, the children were probably begging second and third helpings of bread and butter from MacTavish, or even inveigling him into breaking out the jam. Mrs. Periwinkle would have stood firm against such maneuvers, but she was off visiting her sister in York.

"I have seen more bare male hindquarters than you can imagine," Julianna said. They all conform to a common design, and yours is no different. Your pride is the greater affliction, would be my guess. If it's any consolation, I can likely salvage your breeches, which MacTavish claims are worth a pretty penny."

The duke tried for a smile and came up... short. Oh, the expression was engaging, a practiced blend of charming, arrogant, handsome, and self-deprecating. He'd likely had that one well in hand by the age of three, and his old nanny was still recalling it fondly from some snug pensioner's cottage.

And yet, the angle of Mowne's lean body against the doorjamb suggested not a casual pose, but a desperate facsimile of one. He was injured, bleeding, and... in pain.

Worse, he wanted nobody to see his suffering.

Pride was not the exclusive province of dukes.

"The breeches are ruined," His Grace said, shoving away from the door and sauntering—crookedly—into the room. MacTavish had cracked a window, so the air was fresh, if a bit chilly. "You may toss them in the rag bin."

"They are far from ruined. The stain is still wet, and a good blotting cloth will get out most of the blood. Once it dries, we can take a gum eraser at just the right angle—"

Lace fluttered as he waved his hand. "The breeches are ruined, I say. I never want to see them again, but tell me, where does a fellow sit when he's a hazard to the upholstery and must get his boots off?"

"On the raised hearth," Julianna said, following him into the bedroom and closing the door. "I'll get your boots off. You'll only tear the wound worse if you try, and you're making enough of a mess as it is."

He sat, gingerly, and Julianna resisted the urge to help him. He was pale, and the only thing worse than a duke expecting free hospitality without notice was a duke expiring from loss of blood on Julianna's very hearth.

Though maybe having Mowne underfoot wouldn't be all bad.

MacTavish would take the discarded ducal breeches to the shops in York and come back with nothing less than Sunday roast, a laundry tub that didn't leak, new shoes for Horty, and heaven knew what other necessities.

Julianna took the heel of the duke's right boot in her hand and tugged as gently as she could, for she had the suspicion His lacy, drawling, arrogant Grace knew exactly what the fate of his fine breeches would be.

~

REVELATION FOLLOWED upon insight crowded closely by surprise, very little of it good as far as Con was concerned.

One truly could see spots before one's eyes, for example. When dear Cousin Jules tugged upon the heel of Con's boot, the protest from his backside was painful enough that, in addition to black spots, his vision contracted, and the lady's murmured apology seemed to come from across the surf of an angry invisible ocean.

The second boot wasn't as bad, though Con could feel his life's blood soaking into the wound's dressing.

"Why does nobody warn a fellow that most activities involve the fundament in some way? I dread to sneeze, for example, and rising right now..." He was babbling. Worse, he was whining and babbling. A tanned, callused female hand appeared in his line of sight as the pain in his arse faded to a roar.

"You can remain there until autumn remarking the wonders of your anatomical functions, or I'll help you to the dressing screen," said his angel of dubious mercy. She waggled her fingers. "I haven't all day, Mr. Amadour."

Perhaps she had other arses to insult elsewhere in the house, but —give the woman credit—she pulled Con, fifteen stone of fit adult male, to his feet easily, then kept hold of his hand while another shower of spots faded.

"When did you last eat?" she asked, as if inquiring of a suspect regarding his whereabouts on the night of the triple murder.

"Yesterday."

"You drank your sustenance," she said, leading him to a dressing screen painted the same shade of blue as her eyes.

Quite pretty, that blue, and yes, now that she'd graciously reminded him, Con had passed famished hours ago.

"And you likely got no rest because of your injury," she went on. "What would your mother say?"

Ah, delightful. A compassionate Deity had placed a sturdy wash-stand behind the privacy screen. A great mercy, that, because Con's body chose then to recall that laudanum often gave him the dry heaves.

"My mother would tell me a duke does not bleed in public. If you'll excuse me, I will see about disrobing while you fetch your medicinals."

Being sick might figure on the agenda somewhere as well, but so would being... grateful. The room was pleasant and airy, with roses climbing about the windowsills. The storm was rumbling on its way, leaving the scent of cool rain and lavender sachets in its wake. The herbal fragrance soothed Con's belly, the pattering rain on the roses eased his soul.

Cousin Jules was a tartar, though apparently, she'd had to be. Con had been remiss not to investigate her circumstances himself—Cousin Jules, indeed—even if she'd welcome his prying about as much he welcomed the thought of her probing at his wound.

The wound on his arse, which hurt like nineteen devils were applying their pitchforks in unison. Con waited for the lady to go scowling and muttering on her way before bracing himself against the washstand and forcing the pain down to ignorable proportions.

The pain refused his ducal command. Another revelation. By slow degrees, he peeled himself out of his clothing. Contrary to his valet's conceits, Con was capable of dressing and undressing himself. The valet was a bequest from Con's father, and Con hadn't the heart to pension off a fellow whose greatest joy in life was a perfectly starched length of linen.

The dressing was affixed to his flank by long strips wound about his hips and thigh. He was loath to dislodge his bandages, for the wound was indeed bleeding. One did not, however, want to unnecessarily offend a lady's modesty, regardless of how many arses she claimed to have inspected—nor to affront a duke's already tattered, hungry, weary, and thirsty (come to think of it) dignity either.

From his trunk, Con unearthed a dressing gown. Blue silk, not his favorite, but sufficient unto the present need. By the time Cousin Jules returned, he'd helped himself to a glass of water and was affecting a lounge against the window frame, studying green country-side that seemed to go on forever.

"How shall we do this?" he asked.

"Carefully," she retorted, setting down a basin and a sack on the night table. "And quickly. I've a stew on the stove, and if MacTavish gets distracted, dinner will burn and the pot will be ruined. Can you lie facedown on the bed?"

Facedown was an excellent notion, for another revelation had befallen Con: His cock was in excellent working order, despite fatigue, hunger, humiliation, pain, and volition to the contrary. The notion of Julianna ogling his nearly naked self, her hands on him in highly personal locations, and those hands being no stranger to the male anatomy, had worked a dark alchemy on his male imagination.

Con got himself onto the bed and managed to stretch out without revealing anything untoward. Mere stirrings, but bothersome, highly ungentlemanly stirrings.

He moved pillows aside and got as comfortable as he could. "Tell me about all these naked fellows you've seen. Are you a widow?"

"I am a widow, and there haven't been that many fellows. Modesty in the male of the species is rare in my—oh, you poor man."

She'd twitched his dressing gown aside and peeled away bandages far enough to expose only what needed exposing, a flank more than a cheek, as it were. Her compassion did what Con's conscience could not, and un-stirred the mischief his cock had been brewing.

He said what pain-crazed men had likely been saying since the first spear had creased the first male behind.

"It's only a flesh wound."

A cool cloth was laid over the wound, not shoved at it, as the surgeon had done, but gently pressed against Con's skin.

"Did some half-sober barber-surgeon tell you that? Superficial wounds hurt awfully because they tear through flesh and muscle. You won't bleed to death as you might if an artery were pierced, but this is..."

She wrung out the cloth and brought more relief. This went on for some minutes, until Con was nearly asleep and prepared to sign over his entire wardrobe for MacMiraculous to pawn in York.

"The wound looks clean," Cousin Jules said after a final, careful dabbing at the injury. "Infection can strike any time, though, so we'll want to change the dressing regularly."

Four times a day at least. Considering the article at risk was a duke, and the next in line for the title was Freddy, tending to the wound six times a day might be—

Shame upon me.

"How long have you lived here?" Con had been sending bank drafts for at least... five years?

"Since I married Mr. St. Bellan when I turned eighteen. This might sting a bit."

Whatever minty decoction she'd applied to the wound stung far more than a bit. Then the stinging faded, and for the first time in more than a day, the pain subsided without recourse to the poppy.

"I gather Mr. St. Bellan was not well-fixed?" Con asked.

"John worked very hard. Had he lived, the farm would doubtless have thrived, but as it is, we struggle. Your mother's generosity is necessary, and even with that—" Cloth was torn smartly asunder.

Who was this *we*? Cousin and her pet Highlander, a maid of all work, and a few obese cats? The sheep and goats? But, no.

She had mentioned children.

"As it is, you are the one left working very hard," Con said. "I can re-bandage myself, if you'll leave me the supplies."

"Some fresh air wouldn't hurt the wound," she said. "Fresh air will help it heal more quickly, in fact. I have a bit of laudanum, though we try to save it for when it's truly needed."

We again, and hoarding the medical supplies.

"See to your stew," Con said, remaining on the bed, breathing lavender and relief. "Thank you, for your kindness and for your hospitality. You will be careful not to mention my identity below stairs?"

She gave Con's silk-clad bum a little pat, or maybe she'd accidentally touched him in passing—on his aching backside. So gently.

"We don't have a below stairs or an above stairs, Mr. Amadour. We have only hard work, liberal affection, fresh air, and good, simple fare. I'll bring you a tray now, though don't expect me to make a habit of it. The bandages are on the night table."

Fatigue was crashing down on Con like an overturned coach. "You needn't bring a tray. I'll find my way to your kitchen easily enough. Don't forget to take the ruined breeches."

Con had been in perhaps six kitchens in his life, and none in recent years, but he knew they were typically ground-floor establishments at the back of the house, where tradesmen could come and go without disturbing anybody.... Without disturbing *him*, rather.

"Rest," she said. "Your wound will appreciate a day or two of complete rest."

An hour, perhaps. An hour to nap would be a novel departure from Con's unceasing schedule of responsibilities and recreations. He ought to write to Starlingham and Lucere, make sure they were comfortably ensconced in their temporary identities.

He should also write to his mother, asking what in blazes she was about, expecting a St. Bellan widow's household *with children* to eke by on a pittance. Write to his solicitors, and... Paper would also be hoarded in this household. Quill pens, ink, everything would be hoarded, except hard work, which would be available in endless quantities.

Con pulled his thoughts back from a near drowse. "Do you go by Jules?"

"Julianna."

"Then in a household without an above stairs or a below stairs, Julianna, you must call me Connor." Though the notion was odd. How could anybody function without a proper sense of where they fit in and where they were unwelcome?

She withdrew silently, leaving Con to wonder, as sleep stole over him, and his injured parts were soothed by fresh Yorkshire air, about all those naked backsides Julianna St. Bellan had seen, and how his would have compared to the others if she'd been less considerate of his modesty.

JULIANNA GAVE herself two minutes to lean on the bedroom door and worry.

Also to miss her husband. "Honest John" St. Bellan had been well-liked, good-humored, a tireless worker, and shrewd. When everybody in the neighborhood had been succumbing to the coal developer's promises of riches, John had smiled and kept his hand on the figurative plough.

Old John, Julianna's father-in-law, had accurately predicted that England would become a wheat-importing country in his son's life-time, and John had bet his livelihood on that prediction. The gamble should have paid off. For others who'd not died of a virulent flu, it had paid off handsomely.

Coal was important, at least part of the year. Bread was necessary nearly every day. That thought had Julianna heading for the stairs, because when it came to bread and butter, the children put biblical plagues to shame.

"Seconds, MacTavish?" Julianna asked as she put the medicinals on a high shelf. "And did we wash our hands before we sat down?"

Four little pairs of legs stopped kicking at the worktable bench, four pairs of eyes found anywhere to look but at Julianna. Three blond heads and one brunette—Roberta was their changeling—all bent as if bread and butter required relentless study. John would have known how to remind them without scolding, but Julianna had lost the knack of a cheerful reminder a year ago, when the last plough horse had come up lame.

"I should be flattered," she said, tousling each blond mop and winking at Roberta. "My bread is so delicious, my butter so wonderful, you cannot resist a second serving. I might have to have some myself."

Relief shone from the children's eyes, while MacTavish gave the stew a stir. "How's the patient?"

"Resting," Julianna said, cutting herself a thin slice of bread. How she longed to slather jam on it, to eat sitting down, and ask the children how their studies had gone that morning. "Children, I have some news. Harold, please stop crossing your eyes."

He'd been crossing them at Roberta, which was better than when he took a notion to tease her.

"Yes, missus," they chorused.

Julianna took out her handkerchief and wiped a spot of jam —jam?—from Ralph's chin. "This is good news, for we have a visitor. Mr. Connor Amadour, a distant cousin, is paying a call. He'll bide with us for a short time."

"Can he fold towels?" Ralph asked.

"Guests don't work," Harold shot back. As the oldest, he was often obnoxious, but he was also a hard worker. In the Yorkshire countryside, much—almost everything—was forgiven a hard worker of either gender and any species.

"A guest can grow bored," Julianna said, "and if he'd like to help fold towels to pass the time, as Cousin Connor's hosts, we'll allow him to help." Though how the poor man would sit still for long was a mystery. The wound he'd suffered was no mere scratch.

"I hope he's bored all the time," Ralph said. "I hope he's so bored, he'll like to churn the butter, shell the peas—"

"Beat the rugs," Harold sang out.

"Get the eggs *and* wash the chicken poo off them," Lucas shouted.

"And read to us," Roberta whispered.

Her brothers rolled their eyes, and Ralph shoved at her little shoulder. "We don't need anybody to read to us. We're not babies."

Not any longer they weren't. John had gone off to York one day to buy seed and come back with four children collected from the poorhouse.

We have love to give and none of our own to give it to. They'll die there, or soon wish they were dead. Fresh air, family, a sense of belonging, and an opportunity to make a contribution commensurate with their abilities ... A farm needs children, and the children need the farm.

He had loved them, and they'd loved him, and that winter, he'd died with the children gathered about his bed and worry in his eyes.

"You are my babies," Julianna said. "And I love reading to you."

"So why don't you do it anymore?" Lucas was blessed with a logical mind, according to the curate, Mr. Hucklebee. The boy had not yet learned that logic could sound disrespectful.

MacTavish wrapped up the bread in a towel and put the lid on the butter crock. "Summer is the busy time. Come winter, the evenings will be so long we'll read every book in the house."

Which were fewer and fewer. Julianna passed the last of her bread to MacTavish and gave the stew another stir.

"I will make a trade with you, children. While you fold the towels, I'll read to you. First, I must bring our guest some bread and butter."

"Has he washed his hands?" Ralph asked.

"Why can't he eat with us?" Harold chorused. "There's room at the table."

"He's quite tired from his travels," Julianna said—not a lie. "I'm being hospitable, but you'll get to meet Cousin Connor soon. For now, you will sweep your crumbs for the chickens, wash your hands, and start on the towels, please."

Groans, sighs, the sound of the bench scraping back, but for all that, compliance with Julianna's directions. For now. The boys listened to MacTavish for now too, but they also teased Roberta without mercy some days, tested Julianna's authority, and lately had taken to using their fists with each other.

"MacTavish, if you'd start the children on the laundry and regale them with some of Mr. Burns's offerings, I'll be along shortly to take over."

Over the last of his slice of bread, Mac sent her a look worthy of Ralph in a rebellious mood. The rain was still coming down though, and for Mac to spend the afternoon repairing harness in the carriage house, mucking Horty's stall, and otherwise out in the damp would not do.

Or perhaps Julianna simply wanted Mac to keep an eye on the children while she tended to Connor.

As the children jostled each other at the wash basin and fought over the hand towel, Mac put the bread in the bread box along with the butter.

"So who is this *cousin*, Julianna, and why must you be his Samaritan? He can well afford to stay at an inn."

"Why must you sneak the children jam, Rory MacTavish? You undermine my authority and waste our supplies. Come February, you'll wish you'd saved a bit more of the jam."

Mac had the grace to look sheepish, for about two seconds, then he took up a rag and began scrubbing at the counter. "I'll bring up the other two trunks, but I know what I saw, miss. You've welcomed trouble to this household."

Julianna had had nearly the same thought when John had come home with a squirming lot of dirty, hungry, unruly children. She'd been right, but she'd also been wrong. John had loved the children, and the children were growing to love the farm.

"Mr. Amadour honestly is a cousin, of sorts. His coach has suffered a mishap, and he was injured in the process. There's a pair of fine gentleman's breeches in the laundry that you're welcome to take to the pawnbroker's as soon as I work the stain out."

Which Julianna ought to be doing that instant.

"Roberta can get out the stain. The wee girl's a wonder in the laundry. My granddam had the same knack. That doesn't change the fact that this cousin of yours will meddle, upset the children, and cause talk. Mr. Warren will not approve of talk."

"Who was the first Baptist?!" Harold yelled, flicking water in Ralph's face. "John the Baptist!"

"I'll baptize you, you runt," Ralph shouted back, elbowing Roberta aside. Ralph cuffed the water in the basin so it slapped over the side and splashed on Lucas's and Harold's sleeves. Roberta shrank back, looking worried, while Lucas snatched up the basin.

"Enough!" Julianna snapped before Lucas could dash the remaining water in the other boys' faces. "You will please clean up the mess you've made and meet MacTavish in the laundry. One more such outburst and no dessert for whoever's involved."

Now she'd have to make a dessert, of course. But the riot subsided, and the children did a credible job of mopping at the floor.

"Mr. Warren has caused talk," Julianna said, keeping her voice down. A raspberry cobbler would do, but she'd promised her guest some bread and butter first. "He was glued to my side all morning and blathering about how well his mines are doing."

John and Maurice Warren had been friends, of a sort, but Maurice was convinced coal was the salvation of Yorkshire, when in fact, coal had been the salvation of the Warren family fortunes and the ruin of their tenants' dreams. The men who went down into the mines were a rough lot, not particularly prone to showing up at Sunday services, or to seeing their children educated when those same children could earn coin beside their fathers.

"Maurice Warren is the answer to your troubles," MacTavish muttered. "Honest John would agree with me."

Honest John was dead, God rest his soul. "Please start Roberta on blotting the stained breeches. Read the children a bit of Tam o' Shanter, and I'll be along shortly."

Tam o' Shanter was a sop to the males of the household. Drunkenness, lurking devils, mad storms, beautiful witches, wild dancing, all rendered in Mac's best broad Scots.

"Julianna..." Mac hung the drying towel just so over the back of a chair. "The trunks bear a crest. The Mowne crest. It's a Scottish dukedom, but a dukedom nonetheless. Is this fellow related to your duchess cousin?"

"Yes."

Mac was angling toward some point, one Julianna would not like. She got out the bread and butter again and cut two slices about twice the thickness she normally served herself. She buttered both slices, then she carved off a strip of ham from the joint hanging by the larder.

"How close a relation?" Mac asked.

He probably already knew, though how he knew, Julianna could not have said.

"We have the Duke of Mowne himself under our roof. He is injured in a delicate location and seeks to convalesce quietly rather than be an object of gossip. I've promised him hospitality and discretion in equal measure. For the duration of his visit, he's Cousin Connor Amadour, late of Kent, waiting for his coach to be repaired."

MacTavish swore in Gaelic. Something about when a mule gave birth, which was all but impossible, mules being sterile.

"Language, Mac. Connor is family, and he's hurt."

"He's trouble. If I noticed the ducal crest on his luggage, Mr. Warren will notice a great deal more than that. Then too, dukes have a way of sticking their noses into anybody's business, particularly the business of their family members."

Some cheese wouldn't go amiss, and Yorkshire cheddars were excellent. "This duke has been happy to ignore us for years. His mother's charitable impulses are no business of his. Have you been consorting with many dukes, Mac, that you can vouch for their habits?"

The cheese wheel was heavy, and Julianna couldn't resist a nibble for herself. She passed Mac a bite, which he did not decline.

"You've got it all wrong, lass. Now that Mowne has realized he has a poor relation whose household is going threadbare, his pride will require him to take matters in hand."

Unease joined the cheese in Julianna's belly. "He'll be on his way and forget he ever tarried here. He nearly promised me that."

And Julianna had been both relieved and resentful to have those assurances.

"You've never told the duchess about the children, or about how bare the larder has grown trying to feed them. Yon duke will soon realize you could not have had three boys who look nothing like you within the space of a year, much less well before you married John St. Bellan. His Grace will meddle, all right. He'll send the boys to public school if they're lucky, or send them to the parish if they're not."

Maurice had hinted that Julianna ought to do the latter. Reduce the number of mouths she had to feed and enjoy herself as a "lady of the manor" ought.

"I was arguably gentry when I married John," she said, ladling stew into a bowl. "I'm barely a landowner now. You will cease conjuring worries from simple hospitality. Cousin Connor will not bother with the situation of a rural nobody to whom he's not even related by blood."

Mac spared a glance for the plate before Julianna: bread and butter, cheese, ham, a steamy bowl of stew. Closer to a feast than a snack, by the standards of the household.

"He's trouble," Mac said again. "Expensive, meddling, titled trouble, and you've nothing with which to combat the mischief he'll cause. Go carefully, miss, and don't let his stew get cold."

CHAPTER THREE

The stew was cold. Con ate it anyway, and contrary to the dire predictions of every nanny, mother, and governess in the realm, he did not expire as a result. Who knew? The bread, butter, ham, and cheese met the same fate, as did a glass of cold milk.

He could not recall the last time he'd drunk milk as a beverage, but consuming every drop and crumb on the tray seemed only polite. The stew had lacked delicacy—no hint of tarragon, suggestion of oregano, or trace of pepper, but had been adequately salted.

A stout knock sounded on the door, followed by the Scotsman hauling the second of Con's trunks into the room. Clan MacTavish was an impecunious lot by reputation, but they'd not turned on their own when clearing the land to make way for sheep had become popular, and they'd played their politics adroitly through the whole Jacobite mess.

"My thanks," Con said. "I have the sense if I offered you a vail, you'd scowl me to perdition."

MacTavish dusted enormous hands. "You'd not be worth the bother. Make trouble for Julianna St. Bellan, though, and I'll kill you properly dead."

Con remained seated rather than stand and reveal that he'd added a pillow to the padding on his armchair.

"Nothing like Highland hospitality to make a traveler feel welcome, MacTavish."

"Nothing like deception, added expense, and imposing relations to make an old man feel out of charity with the Quality."

Lucere and Starlingham would like this fellow quite well, as did Con. "How bad are things?"

MacTavish lumbered into the corridor and returned with the final trunk. "What business are the doings of this household of yours, Your Grace?"

"I have a responsibility to every member of my family," Con said, shoving to his feet. "If Julianna St. Bellan is in difficulties, she need only apply to me, and the matter will be taken in hand." How it would be taken in hand, Con did not know, because every penny—every damned farthing—was spoken for.

"She did apply to you," MacTavish said, hands on kilted hips. "Three months later, your mother answered, with a small bank draft. Very small. Four children can eat a lot in three months. They can outgrow shoes, destroy clothing, require a blessed lot of coal to keep warm too. You did nothing in those months, while Julianna grieved a husband gone too soon, and dealt with a spring crop that wouldn't plant itself."

Con added a letter to Mama among the correspondence he'd draft—by his own hand. His secretary would be leaving London for Scotland any day.

"I'm here now," he said, rather than explain himself to that patron saint of mental intransigence, a Scotsman who'd made up his mind. "I'll not shirk responsibility when it stares me in the face, MacTavish."

MacTavish took a step closer. He smelled of wool, equine, and, oddly, of fresh bread. "You'll not meddle, *Cousin Connor*. Maurice Warren will offer for Julianna the instant she looks favorably on his suit, and he'll take adequate care of her."

Con felt an immediate dislike for this Warren fellow. A man didn't wait for optimal market conditions before making a commitment of resources to a cause he believed in. Even Uncle Leo, whose grasp on a found penny rivaled John Coachman's grip on his flask, admitted that investment should be guided by principles other than unfettered greed.

"Spare me the household's petty dramas," Con said, "and I'll spare you my meddling. My thanks again for bringing up the trunks."

The thanks—which were sincere—caused bushy brows to lower. "Can you get your backside properly trussed up, or must I help you with that too?"

"I've managed for now," Con said. "I will bring my tray down as soon as I've finished dressing. I'm not your enemy, MacTavish."

"You're not Julianna's friend." He stalked out, closing the door quietly.

Con managed to shove his feet into his boots without reopening his wound, piled his dirty dishes on his tray, and set out to find the kitchen. The tray was heavier than it looked, the kitchen farther away. Servants' stairs would probably have shortened the journey, but Con had no idea how to locate them, for a well-built servants' stair was usually well disguised too.

As he opened yet another wrong door, insight struck. The Duke of Mowne expected his staff to know how to get him where he needed to be. He also expected them to ascertain the route, reserve accommodations, see to the horses, and otherwise handle the details that, upon reflection, weren't details at all.

The duke himself would never, ever ask for directions. Connor Amadour, though, was just a lowly fellow having a spot of difficulty and biding with family for the nonce. He might have asked directions of MacTavish and been ensconced in the kitchen before a hot cup of tea by now.

Asking directions, dressing himself in half the time his valet took, napping when he was exhausted... life as a distant relation to the duke had much to recommend it. *Much*.

FROM THE CORNER of her eye, Julianna saw the duke march past in the corridor beyond the laundry. He was having a good look around, apparently, though he'd remembered to bring his tray with him to the kitchen. She wanted to chase after him and make sure the door to every empty larder and pantry was closed, and that folded linen sat on shelves bare of provisions.

"Then what happened?" Roberta asked, leaning all her weight on the blotting cloth pressed to the bloodstain on His Grace's breeches.

"You know what happens," Harold said, snapping a towel within inches of Ralph's arm. "The evil witch snatches up the stupid children, because the little girl can't travel as fast as the little boy, who'd find his way home in no time, except his stupid sister is tagging along, as usual, and—"

"Am I interrupting?"

The duke, minus his tray, stood in the doorway, looking somewhat rested, if a bit wrinkled. The children fell silent at the sight of a fine gentleman in country attire, or perhaps simply because a stranger had intruded into their very laundry.

"Cousin Connor," Juliana said, closing her book of fairy tales around her finger. "Welcome. Children, please greet Mr. Connor Amador as I introduce you."

Please recall the manners Julianna hadn't drilled them on in too long, in other words. She started with Roberta, the best bet when decorum and civility were wanted. Harold, Ralph, and Lucas managed floppy, boyish bows, and His Grace returned each child's gesture with a bow of his own.

Elegant, correct, deferential bows that nonetheless trumpeted good breeding and consequence.

"I'm almost done," Roberta said, holding up the breeches. "It's nearly gone, but the rest must be brushed free of the cloth after it completely dries."

The duke appropriated the breeches before Julianna could intervene. The stain was still visible, but Roberta had the right of it. Blotting damp fabric was only a first step. A duke couldn't know that, of course, but Roberta had tried her best, and for her brothers to hear her being chided—

"You have worked a miracle," the duke said, brushing his fingers over the stain. "A miracle, I tell you. I have despaired of these breeches, and they were my favorite pair. Miss Roberta, I am in awe."

The child had very likely never been called Miss Roberta before, nor had she smiled quite that smile. Sweet, bashful, and brimming with the suppressed glee of a girl complimented before her usual tormenters.

Roberta would be made to pay, of course. When Julianna's back was turned, Lucas would taunt, Harold would deride. Ralph might try to distract the other two, but he wouldn't take on both of them at the same time. They weren't bad boys, but they were approaching a bad age.

"Was that the story of the clever children who bested the old witch?" the duke asked. "I haven't heard it since I was a boy myself. Might I join you for the rest of the tale?"

He gathered up a clean, folded towel and arranged it on a stool, then arranged himself on top of the towel.

The children looked to Julianna, for one didn't sit on clean laundry. "Cousin was in a coaching mishap," Julianna said. "He's injured."

"Too injured to fold towels?" Ralph asked.

"Perhaps Miss Roberta could show me how it's done?" Connor asked, hoisting the girl onto his lap. "Or perhaps I might take over the job of reading the story. Anybody who's nasty to a pair of orphaned children deserves to come to a bad end, don't you think?"

More glances were exchanged, and Julianna felt the currents of the children's bewilderment swirling about her. In his manners, his conversation, his cordial demeanor, the duke was turning the laundry room into something of a family parlor.

"Please do read to us," Julianna said, passing over the book and reaching for a towel from the mountain on the worktable.

"Miss Roberta, where shall I start?" Roberta pointed to the page.

"Roberta isn't very good at folding towels," Lucas said. "Her arms are too short."

"She's just a girl," Harold added, for once charitably.

His Grace lowered the book slowly. "*Just* a girl? You're Master Harold, correct?"

"Yes, sir."

"Master Harold, if you'd oblige me by closing the door? We're family, indirectly, and some discussions are meant only for the ears of our trusted relations."

This was nonsense, but Harold was off the bench and across the laundry without a word of protest. When the boy was back between his brothers, Connor brushed a hand over Roberta's crown.

"I ask you fellows," Connor began, "who makes the best biscuits? Is it the butler? The steward? The haughty duke? No, it's the cook, who began life as a girl paying attention to her elders in the kitchen. What would life be without the occasional biscuit?"

Julianna would have a lot less to bribe the boys with if she gave up baking biscuits.

"Who's the most important sailor on the ship?" Connor asked. "The navigator? Bah, he's only reading charts and maps, or the stars God put overhead for all to see. The captain struts about giving orders any swabbie could anticipate, the bosun is always tweeting on some infernally stupid whistle that knows only two notes."

"Then who's the most important sailor?" Lucas asked. "They don't let ladies onto sailing ships."

Oh yes, they did. Julianna kept her peace, though, because most of the women who sailed with the Royal Navy were not considered at all respectable.

"What's the first thing you notice about a great ship of the line?" Connor asked. "Those enormous billowing sails, am I right? They rise up over the horizon, and everyone stops to look. Another ship coming into port, one laden with exotic silks, grain, cotton, wondrous goods from all over the world. A ship bringing more sailors home safely to hug their loved ones once again—because of those magnificent sails. Who keeps those sails in good repair?"

"A sailor," Ralph said.

"A sailor who sat among his sisters as a mere lad and paid attention to how carefully they stitched. When all the other louts at his dame school were ignoring the ladies, the sailmaker was learning a valuable skill from them. Nobody's ship comes safely to harbor on tattered sails, but how many of you can sew as well as Roberta?"

Roberta was sitting quite tall on Connor's lap, and positively... *preening*.

"This girl, this mere girl," Connor said, dropping his voice to an awed quiet, "is the secret to your success in life. I'm sure you've noticed that Roberta has preserved me from the indignity of going about in stained breeches, and she's not done working her magic. A fellow can get into worse scrapes, though, let me tell you."

What followed was a tale worthy of the brothers Grimm, about a young boy feigning sick to dodge lessons and meet friends for a day spent stealing pie, fishing, napping, and enjoying the summer weather.

All went awry, of course, and not a stain but, instead, a great tear in the hapless boy's trousers resulted.

"What was I to do?" Connor lamented when the pile of unfolded towels had been significantly reduced. "I'm not much of a tailor, more fool I, and right upon my person was the proof that I'd disobeyed, told falsehoods, led my friends into mischief, and ruined a new set of trousers. My dignity was flapping in the wind, as it were. I was in for it, and my tutors were not shy with the birch rod."

"I don't care for the birch rod," Harold said, to the assent of his brothers.

"All appeared lost," Connor went on, lowering his voice. "My fate sealed, my future dire, when my younger sister stuck her head out of the window and whispered to me to meet her in the gardener's shed. She'd seen me sneaking out and had watched for my return."

"Was she about to peach on you?" Ralph asked, reaching for another towel.

"My *sister*? My own *younger sister*? Peach on me? How could you think that? I'd let her have a turn on my pony from the time she could walk, routinely saved her a biscuit off my own tray, and always chose her for my archery team. She is *my younger sister*, after all."

"You can shoot arrows?" Harold marveled.

"Not as well as Antigone can," Connor said. "She's a little bit of a thing, but a right terror with a bow. She's handy with a needle too, and that's how she rescued me. Sewed up the torn seam so nobody detected a thing.

"I ask you," Connor went on, "who but a sister could have saved the day like that, and never once breathed a word of my stupidity to anybody? It's the ladies of the family who often have the best solutions to our difficulties, witness my situation now—tossed into the ditch, far from home, breeches a wreck. Cousin Julianna and Miss Roberta are putting me to rights, aren't they? I don't know when I've filled up on such a hearty stew, or had such a nice nap, and now my favorite breeches have been rescued too."

Awful, horrible man. He was thanking Julianna in public, before the boys. He was praising Roberta's cleverness, he was... getting the towels folded without an hour of grumbling and bother from the boys.

Or folding a single towel himself. Julianna would have hated him for his charm, except she was too grateful.

She rose when she ought to have been thanking him. "Cousin Connor, perhaps you could finish reading to the children, while I make us a cobbler for tonight's dessert?"

"I would be happy to," he said, opening the book. "Though I'll have to read quickly. You have the fastest towel-folding crew I've ever seen, and they do such a tidy, careful job too."

Oh bother. He'd never seen a towel folded before in his pampered, ducal life.

"The children are a marvel," Julianna said, "when they put their minds to something."

Julianna endured another marvel: Connor Amadour, duke of the most perilous ditch in Yorkshire, smiling at her. His smile held the conspiratorial pleasure of an adult who'd managed children without generating ill will, but also the glee of a man who'd shown himself to good advantage before a lady. Worse yet, his devilment was simply that—not flirtation, not innuendo, for all his eyes conveyed warmth and merriment shared exclusively with Julianna.

Hunger—or something—went skipping around in Julianna's middle. According to the duchess's letters, the duke did have a younger sister named Antigone, and she was a noted markswoman with her arrows.

Julianna resolved to make a double batch of cobbler.

Convalescing required strength, and His Grace could doubtless put away a deal of sweets. The sooner he was on his way, the better for her ledgers and her larders.

THAT SOMEBODY WOULD READ to Con had been a foregone conclusion in his childhood. Read to him, fold his towels, make his meals, pat him on the head for being a good boy, chide him for being naughty.

He did not much recall the towels or the meals, though some of the stories had stuck with him, and the rare missed meals had been enormous inspiration for martyrdom, despite that he'd doubtless deserved the discipline.

He recalled his parents' disappointment in him keenly, and the pats on his head too. Also the rare hugs and the sense of conspiracy shared with his siblings on occasions such as Antigone's daring rescue by needle and thread. She'd sewn a terrible seam, but spared Con the horror of being marched through the house with his underlinen on display.

For two whole days thereafter, he and Tiger hadn't fought.

"I adore cobbler," Lucas said. "MacTavish says he'd kiss Horty's nose for a bite of Miss Julianna's cobbler. Papa loved her cobbler too."

"MacTavish gets two servings," the boy named Harold explained. "He works the hardest, though sometimes he can't finish his second portion, so we each get an extra bite if we're good about helping to clean up."

"Cobbler does that," Con said. "You think you could eat the whole business yourself, and then your belly contradicts you when it's too late." Starlingham had a tale of woe involving a cobbler made with whisky, though Con suspected the story was part fairy tale.

"Miss Julianna says she doesn't care for cobbler," Lucas observed.

The children referred to the lady of the house as Miss Julianna, but to her late husband as *Papa*. Interesting.

"Do you suspect she's being diplomatic?" Con asked.

"She's telling a fib," Roberta replied from her perch in Con's lap. "She wants to leave more for us."

Three boys became fascinated with the fine art of towel folding. Con hugged the girl, who was the perfect size for hugging, though maybe all children were.

"You're probably right, Miss Roberta, but we needn't let Miss Julianna get away with her falsehoods. Nor MacTavish, if you catch him being less than truthful."

"How do you catch a grown-up in a lie and not come out the worse for it?" Lucas muttered, setting one frayed seam to another. "Miss Julianna works too hard, she never eats much, and she hardly ever sits down. Even now, we can get her to read to us only when we're doing chores, and except for Bertie, we're too old for anybody to read to us."

"*Miss* Bertie," the girl said, sticking out her tongue.

"You're our sister," Harold said. "Our secret weapon against torn breeches. We don't have to call you miss."

"You have to share your biscuits with me," Roberta countered. "Cousin said."

The wonders of the sibling barter economy were likely pondered behind youthful brows, while Con considered the problem the children had so carefully confided in him.

"The next time you must fold laundry," Con said, "you declare a contest. Roberta will referee, and you three boys set the rules. *No adults allowed.* The boy with the largest pile of neatly folded laundry wins."

Ralph smiled, a diabolically angelic grin. "We can declare contests in anything, right?"

"You must first decide the rules," Con said, which had been the best training his tutor could have devised for dealing with the idiots in the House of Lords. By the time he, Lucere, Starlingham, and their friends had determined the rules for their impromptu games and challenges, half the day had gone by, and the occasional nose had been bloodied.

"You can have a race to see who brings in the peat the most quickly," Roberta suggested. "I can keep count."

"I'll bring two buckets at once." Harold was a good-sized lad, maybe a year older than the other two.

"If I use a stout pole across my shoulders, I could bring in four," Ralph countered, "and get it done in half the time."

"You'd have sore shoulders," Lucas said. "Peat is beastly heavy."

"He'd have sore shoulders," Con said, tousling Ralph's hair, "until the exercise had built up his muscles to the point where he could do it easily. Like racing into the village to pick up the post. The first few days, you'll not make the whole way at even a trot. By the end of the summer, you'll be quick as the wind and barely breaking a sweat."

The last of the towels were folded as Con delivered the evil witch to her well-deserved fate. Roberta scrambled off his lap and went to inspect the stained breeches, and Con's backside began to throb.

"What's your first contest?" Con asked the boys across a sea of folded linen.

"We'll bring in the peat, though we rarely have fires in summer," Harold said. "Miss Julianna has asked us to see to it."

She'd probably threatened them within an inch of their little lives for putting it off so long. "Bringing in the peat makes the cobbler taste sweeter, I always say."

"You can't bring in peat, Cousin Connor," Harold said. "You hurt your arse, and Miss Julianna says you're to rest."

"Best do as she says," Lucas added. "She gets to looking at a fellow like he doesn't smell very good when you don't do as she says once too often."

"Then she crosses her arms and taps her foot," Ralph said. "Three times. It's awful."

"I can imagine." Or she'd lift that russet eyebrow and make a man want to trace its arch with his thumb. "What comes after bringing in the peat?"

"We could make a list," Ralph said. "Three things, three contests, a chance for everybody to win at least once. A list and a schedule."

"Spoken like a born man of business, Master Ralph."

Lucas's gaze went to Roberta. "What about Bertie?"

Harold stood and pushed a mop of blond hair from his eyes. "She already won at getting out stains and sewing. She wins at turning pages. She wins at staying out of trouble. I'd say Bertie's way ahead already." The very grudging nature of the admission probably echoed its sincerity.

"Off to the peat pile with you," Con said. "Don't forget to wash your hands when you're done. Dirty business, hauling in the peat."

"I like the smell of it burning," Harold said, refolding a towel given haphazard treatment. "Better than that stinky old coal."

On this the children seemed agreed, as was Connor. "Miss Bertie, perhaps you can teach me how to put the towels away?"

"I'll put them away," Roberta said. "Then I'll finish with the stain. You're to *rest*." She folded her arms, and damned if the little minx didn't lift an eyebrow.

"I will heed your guidance," Con said as the children filed out the door, Bertie with a load of towels in her arms.

Con brought up the rear, but unlike the children, who turned left in the corridor, Con went to the right. No rule, law, list, or schedule prevented a fellow from resting in the kitchen, or learning how to help a busy woman make a fresh cobbler.

THE WEEPS HIT as Julianna cut the butter into the flour. The milch cow, Henrietta, had freshened in May, but already her output had dropped considerably. Winter without butter was an awful prospect, but buying a late heifer would be entirely beyond—

"The boys are bringing in the peat. Roberta is putting away the towels," said a voice at Julianna's right elbow. Connor peered into her crockery bowl, bringing with him a hint of sandalwood. "So this is how cobbler is made? I confess I am amazed. That doesn't look anything like a cobbler."

"It won't look much like cobbler when I'm done either," Julianna said, mashing the butter with two forks. "A proper cobbler, according to my grandmother's recipe, has preserves on the bottom and in the middle, not simply dabbed about to add a dash of color."

Connor leaned across Julianna and dipped a finger in the raspberry jam sitting to her left. When she would have chided him for snitching, he touched that finger to her lips.

"So whose children are they?" he asked. "Was John St. Bellan married previously?"

In a fit of optimism, Julianna had liberally sugared the last batch of raspberry preserves. The flavor was exquisite, all summery abundance and tart luxury. Connor's touch on her mouth was casual and incendiary at the same time.

"I was Mr. St. Bellan's only wife. We took the children in shortly before he died. This is their home. Don't do that again."

This time, Connor helped himself to a dab of jam, his expression suggesting he was tasting the first sip of a suggested vintage at some gentleman's club.

"Took them in from where? You're in the middle of nowhere, barely eking by."

Gone was the spinner of fairy tales and in his place a man who'd probably eat far too much.

"How I eke is none of your affair, sir. John fetched them from a poorhouse in York. They say they're siblings, but I have my doubts. The boys wouldn't come without Roberta. Here, they can *be* siblings."

Connor turned and leaned his hips against the counter. A slight bunching beneath the fabric of his breeches gave away the location of the bandages, but other than that, he appeared hale.

"You told me that you wrote to me when your husband died, and then several months later, my mother returned your letter. Are you quite sure your letter was addressed to me?"

Julianna left off hacking the butter into smaller bits, for Connor would not leave her in peace until he'd got whatever he'd come for.

"Yes, I am certain. It's the only letter I've ever sent to a duke, and I did not enjoy writing it."

"Because you asked for help?" Connor apparently grasped the difficulty of swallowing pride, of admitting fear.

"Because I asked for *your* help," Julianna said, staring at the jumble of ingredients in the bowl. The recipe called for a dash of orange juice, though she hadn't had that ingredient on hand for several years. "I had never met you, and to presume..."

"You comprehend some of my dilemma," Connor said. "Here I am, a duke, a peer of the realm, seventy-third in line for the throne, or some such rot, and I must rely on a struggling widow to keep my secrets."

True enough. "You are concerned with your pride. I'm concerned with what will happen to my children. I did write to you. You did not write back."

He studied her, though Julianna refused to give him more than her profile. He took the towel from her shoulder and dabbed at her chin.

"You've a dash of flour," he said. "Or batter, or whatever one calls a cobbler in its un-cobbled state. You can't blame me for... Julianna?"

One tear, one damned, hot, miserable tear, trickled down Julianna's cheek and splashed onto the towel.

"Go away," Julianna said, sounding very much like Bertie in a taking. "Please go away, I mean. You don't have to leave the house, but if you'd just get out of my—"

Oh hell and damnation, Connor took her in his arms. His embrace was gentle but implacable, and worse, it was the embrace of an adult male who knew how to hold a woman. No fumbling, no awkward distance, nervous patting or brushing.

A snug, lovely embrace such as Julianna hadn't enjoyed for years.

"They are wonderful children," he said. "I suspect most children are wonderful, though one can't know. I was certainly wonderful. I'm sure you were too. MacTavish might not have been."

What came out of Julianna's mouth? What brave, dignified pronouncement did she offer from the depths of a wrinkly, lavender-scented cravat?

"The cow will go dry too s-soon. I haven't the juice of an orange. I'm skimping on the sugar. I hate to skimp, and you'll eat too much, and I'm so tired of being ashamed."

And afraid.

Connor shifted so he leaned against the counter between Julianna and her cobbler, and she leaned against... him.

"You have nothing to be ashamed of," he said. "Not one damned thing."

"I can barely feed the children. If Horty goes lame, I'll not be able to bring in my crops. If the cow dies, we'll not even have cheese. If the blight comes through again, the potatoes are a loss. Each year, I'm planting more potatoes, and that is not what my husband worked his entire life to see happen with this farm."

Potatoes were the crop of the nearly destitute, capable of being tended by children and producing more food per acre than corn, but humble fare it was.

Especially without butter.

"My mother has apparently been reading my mail," Connor said. "For years, she has surreptitiously been reading my mail. Your story confirms it and makes sense of many odd looks, contradictions, and strange coincidences. I don't know why I didn't see it sooner."

The pleasure of his embrace was heartrending, inviting Julianna to rest, to be still and sheltered, to repose in the emotional safety created when somebody cared enough to offer physical comfort.

"I miss my husband."

"I know, love. I'm sure John St. Bellan was a man well worth missing. He chose you, after all, and all of his efforts, all of his resources were devoted to creating a home for you and the children. Of course you miss him and probably always will."

Julianna sniffled, but did not step back. "I'm furious with him too. After five years, you'd think I'd get over that part." She'd never get over the sheer loveliness of a husband's physical company. John had been a quiet fellow, but affectionate.

And lusty. She very much feared Maurice would be lusty too, and that... that would not be lovely.

Connor's fingers made slow, sweet circles against her nape. "Perhaps if you had an orange in the house, or my mother weren't snooping through my mail, we wouldn't be so angry."

Julianna ought to get back to her cobbler, but a certain duke stood between her and the counter. When she rested her cheek against his chest, she could feel the anger in him, now that he'd mentioned it. Hear that edge in his voice, sense it in his posture. A woman who'd been married apparently never lost the ability to read a man.

"What will you do?" she asked.

He was quiet for a few interesting moments. In those moments, fatigue dragged at Julianna, made her eyes heavy, her breathing slow.

"You need to sleep at the club," Connor said.

"You're not making sense." Neither was he sliding away, shooting his lacy cuffs, and snitching more jam.

"When a fellow has stayed too late, drunk too much, lost too much, instead of stumbling home and ending up in the gutter, or worse, he gets a room at the club for the night. Often he keeps rooms there, for a fee. Will you take a nap while I finish making this cobbler?"

Julianna pulled back to peer at him—a mistake. He still had lashes worthy of a newborn calf, was still tall enough that she had to look up at him, but now she knew what his smile looked like and exactly how warm his embrace could be.

She pushed dark hair back from his brow. "You'll ruin my cobbler, and it's a double batch. The children would be so disappointed I'd never live it down."

He might have kissed her—she was certainly tarrying in kissing range for no discernible reason.

"I wish I had an orange to give you, Mrs. St. Bellan. An entire basket, in fact. I'd like to help."

Now she stepped aside. "You're in my way, sir."

He moved not one inch. "Here's the problem. If I let on to my ducal solicitors where I am, they'll tell Uncle Leo, who will effectively shut the purse strings for years and cause the equivalent of riot and mayhem in the Mowne dukedom. At least fourteen scandals will follow, and I'll have no peace. I have a very limited budget myself, despite being the head of your family. Nonetheless, but for my mother's meddling, your circumstances might admit of an orange or two."

"You feel guilty," Julianna said, her anger directing itself at him, not at a husband long dead.

"I feel *responsible*, and you will chastise me for it. How do I make this cobbler?"

She pushed him one step to the left, and after resisting for a moment, he obliged. "How is your backside, sir?"

"A mild throb that threatens to descend to an undignified itch. Can you spare me some paper?"

"Yes. Without paper, I could not write to your mother, so I'm careful not to run out. If you're truly intent on learning some culinary skills, then I'll brew a pot of tea."

Because at the rate she was going, Julianna would never remain standing until the children were tucked in for the night. She explained where the writing supplies were as she made tea, allowing herself to use fresh leaves for the first time in three days.

While Julianna sat at the worktable and swilled a lovely, strong, hot, sweet cup of tea, she instructed the duke on how to make a creditable cobbler, even without the dash of orange juice. He took direction surprisingly well, though Julianna spent her entire tea break wondering what sort of kisser he'd be.

CHAPTER FOUR

Dear Tiger,

I have need of some coin for reasons I'm not at liberty to disclose. Please post what you can comfortably spare to the Yorkshire inn named below. UDR. *Enforce same on Her Grace BAMS. Freddy is well but has taxed my resources. Uncle threatening utter ruin, as usual. Moon and Stars send love, as do I, to you, Hector, and Quint. Mama must bear my ire, for now. SNM. C.*

THE NOTE WAS TINY, as befit one carried by a pigeon, but for all that, it was the most precious communication Antigone had received from her older brother in years.

"Antigone! Antigone Charlotte Dardanella Josephine Marie! Open this door or have your mother's complete collapse on your conscience."

Antigone's cat yawned, for even the pets were inured to Mama's histrionics. How Mowne stood Her Grace's daily dramas was a mystery.

"Coming, Mama!" Antigone tucked her brother's note into her

skirt pocket, for Mama could read upside down in far too many languages.

"That boy!" Mama said, sweeping into the library. "That awful, mean boy. I try to help him, try to guide in him in the ways his sainted father no longer can, and what do I get? Read this!"

Another tiny note was shoved at Antigone. Pity the poor pigeon who'd carried double the load.

Your Grace,

For the remainder of the Season, your allowance has been cut in half. If you ever read my mail again, your funds will be cut off entirely. Kirkwood has been asked for his resignation by post for having accommodated your meddling. Drummond's livelihood hangs by a thread. I am very disappointed in you, madam.

Complain to Uncle Leo of this development, and you will do so from the permanent comfort of the dower house. Mowne

"YOU MUST WRITE TO HIM," Mama said, stalking back and forth before the fire. She'd begun to apply henna to her flaming hair even before Antigone's come out, but she was still an impressive figure. "He's met some woman, and she's put him up to this, I vow it. That Culpeper girl was the determined sort."

No woman in her right mind would take on Mama for an in-law, which fact probably accounted for Mowne's continued bachelor status.

"Mama, please have a seat, and I'll ring for tea."

"Tea will not return my funds to me! Helen Gibbersley expects vowels to be paid immediately, as if we were officers on leave with nothing better to do than shoot at each other on foggy mornings. I will have my funds of that boy, or else."

UDR. The initials were a long-forgotten relic of the code developed among the ducal siblings and stood for Utmost Discretion Required. No whining to adults allowed, no turning to sympathetic servants. Sibling bonds alone would have to resolve the difficulty.

Antigone had wondered in recent years if Mowne even recalled that among his dependents and responsibilities remained a trio of siblings in addition to Feckless Freddy.

"Mama, how much do you owe and to whom?" Antigone asked.

Her Grace named an appalling figure, though Antigone suspected it was accurate to the penny.

"How much is owed to you?" Antigone asked.

Mama's hems swished to stillness around her slippers. "A duchess doesn't bother with those amounts. I can't very well ask for the sums to be paid, can I?"

Mama meant well, most of the time, but she could become invested in her own consequence to the exclusion of common sense. Antigone, on the other hand, loved puzzles, her brothers, and haggling with milliners. Freddy, Hector, and Quint all but ignored her, while Mowne paid her bills, admired her frocks, and escorted her when escort was needed.

He also never, ever let her help with anything.

"Mama, you will bring me your vowels, both those owed and those owing. You will not breathe a word of this to Uncle Leo, or he'll applaud Mowne for cutting you off, and then where will you be? You recall how Leo was with Aunt Lillian?"

Mama seated herself on a delicate gilt armchair, though for a woman of her statuesque proportions, the effect was not to enthrone a duchess so much as to put the penitent on the sinner's stool.

"Lillian was a flighty, nonsensical, interfering woman," Mama said, twitching back her skirts the better to reveal intricate embroidery about the underskirt. "Leo chose poorly."

According to Con, Leo had married the love of his life and lost her too soon. An excess of concern for remaining family members had turned Leo penny-pinching and sour.

"Mama, have you been reading Mowne's mail?"

Much sniffing ensued, and twitching of skirts, and shifting about on the chair. "A mother worries."

This mother worried mostly about gossip, tattle, and maintaining her position as the Duchess of Mowne—a *dowager* duchess being a far less powerful and interesting creature.

The next acronyms in Con's note had been equally intriguing: BAMS—By Any Means Suitable—and SNM.

Show No Mercy, as when Lucere or Starlingham had committed some childhood offense that generated the sort of animosity of great moment to small boys. For the space of entire hours, the Sun, Moon, and Stars might stop talking to one another when in the grip of a childish pique.

"You won't read his mail again, will you?" Antigone pressed as the cat hopped onto the sofa beside her. King James was a grand specimen, all feline dignity and magnificent orange coat. "When Mowne makes up his mind, he cannot be reasoned with, and you have offended him beyond bearing."

Antigone had learned years ago not to leave her mail where Mama could even see it, coming or going. Why hadn't Antigone warned Con about Mama's snooping?

"I have tried to assist your brother to step into his papa's shoes. This is the thanks I get, when all I've done is sort through a few bits of correspondence."

Meaning Mama was reading nearly every letter to find its way to the ducal address.

"You have cost Kirkwood his post," Antigone said. "What would Papa think of that?"

Kirkwood, the Mowne town house butler, had been old when Antigone had been born. He was a relic not of the former duke, but of Antigone's grandfather—and was the duchess's familiar among the staff.

Mama withdrew an ornate double-ended scent bottle from her skirt pocket. "I'll tell Kirkwood not to resign. Mowne is being dramatic. It's a very unattractive trait in a person of high station. *Very* unattractive." She took a significant whiff from one end of the bottle —more posturing, for lavender graced the library air, not the reviving spirits of ammonia the bottle likely also held.

"What's unattractive," Antigone said, "is a mother undermining her own son's authority under his very roof. Fortunately, the dower house at Mowne is lovely. I'm sure you'll be very comfortable there, and your friends will visit you often."

Showing no mercy was downright enjoyable, even more enjoyable than haggling with milliners.

Mama jammed her scent bottle back in its pocket. "Teasing your own mother is beneath you, Antigone Charlotte. I'll not have it."

"You're right. I shouldn't tease, and you should never have read Mowne's correspondence. Your friends won't visit you, unless they're pockets to let and need a repairing lease. Given the way your set gambles, that will be a frequent occasion for a few of them."

Mama rose to yank the bellpull. "I have raised a brood of vipers. Sharper than the serpent's tooth, and whatever the rest of that quote is." She appropriated the seat behind the estate desk in another artful rustle of skirts. "I must indulge your brother's queer start for the nonce, nonetheless. I'm not about to hare off to Scotland to argue sense into his misguided head. I'm done trying to help, do you hear me? Done exerting myself to the utmost to ease his burdens every day in every way I can. What can we do about those vowels?"

Drummond, the conscientious solicitor who handled disbursement of the family funds, would doubtless be relieved to hear of Mama's latest sacrifice.

"You'll no longer have time to meddle with Mowne's mail," Antigone said. "I'll tell you what to do about your vowels, and you will follow my directions to the letter." Lucere and Starlingham had warned Antigone years ago about the perils of the casual IOU. "If you owe Helen Gibbersley fifty pounds, you send her Penelope Framingham's note of hand for sixty, along with an apology for not being able to make an exact exchange. You thank Helen for her willingness to be a bit flexible, and trust your own note will come back from Helen by return post."

Mama left off poking through the desk drawers, closing the last with a bang. "One does this? One trades the vowels about? Are you sure? Do your brothers know how this is done?"

The cat hopped off the sofa and strutted across the library. "One does so at a discount, so to speak, which is part of the danger of even making a note of hand. Your obligation can travel anywhere in Mayfair—or beyond—and the unscrupulous gambler can find herself owing an enormous sum to a party whom she'd rather not recognize in the street."

Mama's horror was probably entirely genuine. "*Anybody* can collect on my notes?"

Well, no. IOUs were not enforceable contracts, for they did not represent an exchange of consideration. They were a mere promise to pay, unsupported by legal weight. A debt of honor, in other words, which concept might tax Mama's tenuous grasp of personal integrity.

"Anybody can hold you accountable for the sums you owe, and Mowne has apparently already directed Drummond to reduce your pin money by half. Perhaps it's time you did enjoy some Highland scenery, Mama."

Mama was a Lowlander, her people hailing from the Borders, though she seldom acknowledged those antecedents.

"Scotland is relentlessly cold, young lady. The men are always flaunting their knees in those ridiculous kilts, and nobody sleeps properly during a Scottish summer. I'll enjoy a few weeks' respite at Mowne, and you may tell Drummond to direct my few remaining funds there."

Having ensured Mama would not inflict herself on Mowne in person, Antigone spent the next hour sorting out her mother's finances, and then penning notes to Hector and Quint. Utmost Discretion Required meant only the St. Bellan siblings were to know of an epistle's contents.

The time had come to remind Hector and Quint that their older brother was more than simply the fellow who signed bank drafts, managed Mama, placated Uncle Leo, and kept Freddy from ruining them all.

CON WAITED NEARLY a week for Antigone's reply, and during that week he felt shot in the arse all over again.

Julianna worked without ceasing, an education in itself for a man who'd thought running a dukedom demanding. The household had a cook/housekeeper, but Con could not decide if that good woman had been let go, sent on an unpaid visit to relatives in York, or had chosen to take a summer holiday.

Julianna, meanwhile, didn't merely give orders, review draft correspondence, and stay out waltzing until all hours. She swept, washed, cooked, totaled ledgers, stitched, cooked some more, beat the rugs, cooked yet more...

While Con tried to keep the children productively occupied and his hands to himself.

His wound itched, his conscience positively tormented him, and his cock... became an increasing bother as well.

"Make me a list, and I will go to market for you tomorrow," Con said when the children had been put to bed with another story of Con's misspent youth.

"You cannot," Julianna replied, drawing her needle through the hem of Harold's trousers.

"MacTavish goes in to York to fetch your mail and bring Mrs. Periwinkle home to us tomorrow, and Maurice will escort me about at market. I consider that preferable to having him take me to services."

Between MacTavish's silences, Julianna's haunted gaze, and the children's declarations that peat was better than coal, Con had concluded that nobody in the household liked Maurice Warren, but they dared not say so.

"Julianna, if you don't want this fellow sniffing about your skirts, you tell him his attentions are flattering, but you cannot in good conscience encourage them. He expresses his regret that he's misread the situation, begs your pardon, and asks that you let him know if you'd ever reconsider. This is how it's done, and there's an end to it."

In the alternative, Connor could simply strut about in his ducal finery, wave the signet ring conspicuously, and let it be known Julianna was a valued relation of the Duke of Mowne. Even for a widow of independent means, Warren would be bound to reckon with her family before imposing his addresses on her.

"It's not that simple," Julianna said, drawing the thread snug against the fabric. "Mr. Warren has been a friend to me and to this farm."

While Connor had been his mother's dupe, kicking his heels two hundred miles to the south. To reveal his identity outside this household would invite Uncle Leo's worst interference, though, and then where would Antigone, Hector, and Quint be? Where would the charities be that Connor supported from his own funds? The notes of hand he'd quietly bought for his friends until their own finances came right? The small pensions, and not so small, that Uncle Leo would never have approved?

"Mr. Warren has lent you a few mules he can easily spare," Connor said. "Any neighbor should do the same for a widow trying to make a go of good land. I've wondered where your neighbors have been, in fact."

Julianna's needle paused. She sat back in her rocking chair, her eyes tired, but curious. "What do you mean?"

How to put this? "I don't think farmers in Kent are that different from farmers in Yorkshire, and as to that, I own farms in the East Riding. Won them from Northumberland, and God knows he has land to spare."

She let her sewing fall to her lap. "You win farms in card games?"

Connor took the trousers from her and resumed stitching. He'd learned to stitch hems in the past week, make bread, sweep, scrub pots with sand and a tough rag, and more.

All manner of useful activities were within the grasp of an injured duke. He'd put the boys up on Hortensia one by one and passed along some rudimentary equitation, taught them how to

groom her properly, and how to tie a simple neckcloth. They'd
watched him shave, and joined him in a nightly hand of whist.

In another week he'd be gone, but while he was here, he'd make
up for five years of neglect as best he could. Then too, all this activity
had meant he'd slept well, when dreams of Julianna hadn't plagued
him.

"Northumberland has farms coming out his... his ears," Con said.
"He's a good farmer too, unlike some dukes I could name. I'm not a
bad farmer, for a duke, and I know that neighbors in a district cooperate. They schedule their shearing, haying, and harvesting together.
They confer about who's growing wheat and who's growing barley,
whether the year will be wet or dry, and when to trade their breeding
rams, and so forth. Your neighbors all but ignore you, apparently."

Julianna rose and brought the tallow candle closer to Con's
elbow. They were in her parlor, which five years ago had likely been a
pretty room. Now, the carpet was worn, the space over the mantel
vacant, and the curtains tattered about the hems.

"When John was alive, it was different," she said, dropping back
into her rocker. "You're right about that, but at first I thought the
neighbors were simply respecting the privacy owed a widow during
mourning, and then I was too tired to think. You sew a fine seam, Mr.
Amadour."

Her smile had become Con's reward for jobs well done. To
glimpse that smile, he had read a dozen fairy tales, swung the children about by their wrists until he was dizzy, and groomed the mule
until she'd fallen asleep.

"Are you ashamed to be seen with me, Julianna?"

The question had cost him, but needed to be dealt with. Con
hadn't left the farm in the past week. He'd healed for the most part,
though sitting a horse was still out of the question, and he'd rested
and pondered life in a way not possible for a duke. MacTavish had
brought word of two other swells biding in the area—Lucere and
Starlingham, of course—and Con hadn't wanted to add to the talk.

"I am not ashamed of you," Julianna said, "but a widow must be careful. Mr. Warren will not like to hear of me keeping company with a young single fellow under my own roof, regardless that he's a distant relation of my late husband. I cannot afford to court Mr. Warren's disfavor."

Mr. Warren could not afford to court the disfavor of Julianna's ducal relation, did he but know it.

"I have means, Julianna. I simply need time to redirect them. Once the Little Season ends in the autumn, my mother and sister leave Town, my brothers go off flirting to the house parties, and my friends often pay their vowels. I can put this farm to rights by harvest, if you'll allow it."

Her expression went from tired to bleak. "Thank you for those good intentions, Connor. Thank you from the bottom of my heart, but I hope it won't come to that."

She rose and kissed his cheek, a gentle, lingering kiss that bore more resignation than gratitude, and between one flicker of the candle and the next, Con hit the limit of his damned ducal gallantry.

He kissed her back, on the mouth. Set the sewing aside, cupped her chin, and informed the lady—lip to lip—that distant relation of a long-departed spouse or not, this was a kiss between a healthy, if arse-shot, man and a healthy, if exhausted, woman.

Julianna made a soft, yielding murmur, and Con rose to envelop her in his arms. In the past week, he'd sneaked the occasional arm around her shoulders or her waist, a half hug, a pat on the shoulder, and each time Julianna had reciprocated with a shy, bewildered smile.

Once, she'd let her head rest on his shoulder, and Con had nearly danced a jig, despite any repercussions to his wound. Twice, he'd felt a surreptitious pat to his bum that might have been his imagination or sheer accident.

"We shouldn't—" Julianna muttered, twining her arms around Con's neck. "I can't—"

"You are the most independent, selfless, hardworking woman I've met. A damned duchess of the dales, and if you want to kiss me, you should be free to kiss me. God knows, I want your kisses."

His compliment was genuine, and another testament to the degree to which Con's family situation had drifted from its proper course. A duchess should be generous and kind, gracious and dignified, while Con had allowed his mother's widowhood to lapse into—

He lost track of that thought as Julianna pressed closer. Hers was not the rounded, pampered form of a London beauty, but rather, a strong, fit, womanly shape that could match a man passion for passion.

And heaven defend him, the lady could kiss. She went a-plundering with her tongue, delicately at first, then more enthusiastically as Con returned her overtures and shaped her waist and hips with his hands.

He loved the feel of her beneath his palms. Loved all that vitality and strength, femininity and eagerness, responding to his touch.

Kissing Julianna, he sorted out what had been distracting him for the past week.

At this humble farm, as Connor Amadour, he'd come alive. He'd felt what it was to work hard physically and see the immediate results. Not make investments by means of three intermediaries, but make bread and slice it still warm from the hearth.

He'd not trimmed expenses from the gardening budget for his town house, but trimmed the hair of a young fellow still in the grip of boyhood, and seen a bit of the young man emerge.

And he'd fallen in love.

Con shaped a luscious, full breast, and Julianna's hands on his back went still.

Her forehead dropped to his shoulder. "Connor, I have missed—"

She'd missed her husband. Con kissed her—a quick buss—rather than hear that sentiment, understandable though it was. He wasn't missing anything, for he was exploring completely new terrain.

"I have missed the passion," she said. "The sense of being cast away and relieved of all thought, all cares, breath even. I've missed feeling desired, and I shouldn't be telling you any of this."

Who else could she tell? From what Con had seen, not even the other widows in the neighborhood, the pastor, or the families on the nearest farms took notice of her. If they'd known she counted a duke among her allies, they would never have dared to neglect her so.

"I'm coming to market with you tomorrow," Con said. "Let them all wonder about your haughty relation, let them speculate that you have friends in high places of which they knew nothing. John St. Bellan had to have mentioned a duke on the family tree at some point."

Her arms fell away, and she stepped back. "You cannot come to market with me, Connor. My neighbors will think the worst of us both. Any mention John might have made of you will be forgotten when I flaunt your wealth and good looks before the whole village. Puddlebury *is* a village at heart. We're lucky to have a market day we're so small, and nobody will believe such as you is simply my visiting relation after all these years."

In other words, his past neglect would cost her his present consequence, even were he free to flaunt it. In the space of a morning, all her hard work and proper living, her charity to the children and hymn-singing in church would mean nothing as she fell from genteel widowed neighbor to rural disgrace.

Con took her in his arms again, but remained silent. For years he'd brushed aside the odd looks from servants and solicitors, the peculiar non sequiturs in correspondence or conversation that should have caused him to suspect his mother's meddling.

For all he knew, his brothers were reading his correspondence, and Antigone was borrowing his new stallion in Con's absence.

He'd not paid attention.

The Bible in the Mowne library included a family tree, and Con had never truly studied it to learn who Cousin Jules was.

Mama had gambling debts, and Con had never chided her for

them. Hector was a soft touch for charities that Con suspected were little more than swindles.

Something about Julianna's circumstances—and Mr. Maurice Warren's role in them—wasn't adding up. Con had learned his lesson, though. He was here, he was the Duke of Mowne, however disguised, and for the next week, he would pay very close attention.

Julianna sighed, then slipped from his grasp, and when she wrapped her shawl about her and withdrew, Con let her go and resumed his mending.

JOHN WOULD HAVE UNDERSTOOD what Julianna was about to do, maybe better than she understood it herself. He'd been kind and practical, both, and had told Julianna never to deny herself happiness for the sake of his memory.

Happiness was nowhere to be found these days, but pleasure... pleasure might be as close as the bedroom across the hall.

John had been a generous man too, though not as close to perfect as Julianna had once thought. John had disdained *women's work* even through the long winter when the land was fallow and the housework unceasing, he'd dreamed too ambitiously most years, and he'd trusted Maurice Warren.

Not well done of John, that last part.

Julianna looked in on the children, changed into her nightclothes, got ready for bed, and brushed and rebraided her hair. Saying her prayers would have to wait for another time. Julianna's tap on Connor's door met with a moment of silence, then the door opened, and there stood the Duke of Mowne, naked from the waist up, his chest and the hair at his temples damp.

"Are the children well?" He held a towel in one hand, his feet were bare, his features were etched with concern.

"The children are fast asleep. May I come in?"

His expression became unreadable, but he stepped back and held the door for her. His room was the best guest room on the premises, the only one still entirely furnished, and yet... it had become shabby.

"Are *you* well, Julianna?"

The grate held no fire, though the night was cool. Connor had brought up a single tallow candle from the parlor, and thus shadows flickered about him. The house was so profoundly quiet, Julianna could nearly hear her heart hammering against her ribs.

"Make love with me, please." She wouldn't beg, but she'd ask. Invite, something in between. "I'm a widow. I can bestow my favors where I wish, as long as I'm discreet."

Connor pulled a shirt down over his head, the muscles of his arms, belly, and chest bunching and rippling, but he didn't do up any of the buttons.

"You can't be seen with me at the market, but you invite my intimate attentions now. What am I to make of this, Julianna?"

"You are to make nothing of it," she said. "A week from now, you'll go on about your ducal business, and I'll have a farm to run. We're adults free for the present of other encumbrances. I like you. You seem favorably disposed toward me."

He folded the towel over the top of the privacy screen, seams matching precisely, no hurry at all. "You want a dalliance of me?"

Julianna longed to give him her heart, but what a paltry offering that would be, mortgaged to a farm, four children, and very likely a future with Maurice Warren.

Though apparently, even dukes could be cash-poor. "I want an hour with you," she said. "A special hour."

She'd asked to see his wound the previous day and confirmed it was healing well. He'd have a scar, but the bandage was more a safeguard now than a necessity. The sight of his exposed muscular flank, though, would remain emblazoned on Julianna's memory for the rest of her days.

Connor took a step closer. "You would have *one hour* of pleasure with me, and then we rise in the morning, please pass the eggs, Harold get your elbows off the table?"

"The boys no longer need reminding, thanks to you."

He grasped Julianna's braid and tugged her closer. "One hour? If that's the best St. Bellan could do with his lawfully wedded wife, I must reduce the esteem in which I hold him. A *single hour*, Julianna?"

Fifteen minutes, if she and John had been tired, but that wasn't the point Connor was making.

"I'll settle for an hour," Julianna said.

"I won't," Connor murmured, closing the distance between them. "You are warned, madam, I will not settle for an hour, when you deserve so much more."

For long minutes, he expounded on that point, kissing Julianna anywhere except her mouth and touching her only with his lips. She endured that pleasure as best as she could, vaguely aware Connor was issuing a challenge.

One hour from now, she would not be stealing out the door, ready for a night of dreamless slumber before getting up to make the bread in the morning. Perhaps she'd not leave in two hours, or even three.

She wouldn't *want* to leave ever. Julianna slid her arms around Connor's lean waist, hugging his warmth close. Connor was aroused, truly, unmistakably aroused. By *her*, in her threadbare robe, with her freckled hands, her tired eyes, and unremarkable figure.

"How I have longed..." he whispered, arms closing about her.

Julianna craved his embrace, craved the strength and caring in it, craved the fit of their bodies seamed together. She stood in the circle of Connor's arms, kissing him, nuzzling at the male contours of his neck and shoulders. He'd used the lavender soap she'd made last summer, and his flesh was still cool from his ablutions.

"Into bed with us," Connor said, patting Julianna's bum. "Before I have you against the wall."

Relief coursed through her. He was a duke. Of course he'd understand dalliance. Some helpful soul probably wrote treatises for ducal heirs about how to accommodate the intimate demands of widows without getting entangled in expectations.

Julianna turned back the bedcovers and started to climb between the sheets.

"Are you that modest?" Connor asked, undoing the buttons of his falls. "I'm not particularly modest. Hard to be when there's always a valet about who lives to fuss one into clothing."

"I usually wear my nightgown to bed because the sheets are cool."

"The sheets will soon be quite warm," Connor said, shoving his breeches down. His arousal arrowed up along his belly, a testament to both desire and his lack of modesty.

Julianna turned away. One didn't want to compare, but joyous, heavenly days and celestial nights. The term *merry widow* abruptly made more sense to her.

Connor came up behind her. Julianna could feel his heat along her back and his breath on her shoulder.

"Last chance to change your mind, Julianna. I do not share my favors lightly, nor do I hold you in casual esteem."

He'd learned that people took advantage, in other words. "I esteem you greatly," Julianna said as he slid his arms about her waist and pulled her back against him.

She did esteem him greatly, for taking the boys in hand, for complimenting her cooking, for setting an example—of helpfulness, good manners, good humor, and cooperation—that the boys were inspired to follow.

She esteemed him for doing what Maurice Warren could have done so easily and hadn't—for simply being decent.

Connor kissed his way from the top of her shoulder to the shivery spot below her ear, gently pushing aside her nightclothes, setting a tone of leisurely seduction.

"I've never been... enticed before," Julianna said. "I like it."

"You are the impetuous sort?" Connor murmured, gently cupping a breast. "A little impetuosity can be marvelous."

A little pressure was marvelous-er. A little gentle exploration of this touch and that caress, on both breasts at once, and Julianna's nightclothes became an impediment to pleasure. Connor helped her

out of them—his assistance was practiced without being presuming—
and then Julianna was naked with a man for the first time in years.

Why, oh why, hadn't she told him to blow out the candle first?
Summer nights in Yorkshire took forever to grow truly dark, even
when the hour was late.

"I'm not... I'm not young," Julianna said. "I'm not what I once—"

Connor wore only the bandage about his waist and flank. "Thank
God you're not a silly, blushing girl, unsure of herself and incapable
of knowing what she wants and deserves. This might have escaped
your notice, but I'm not a boy myself."

His smile was far too wicked to belong on any mere boy, and
abruptly, everything inside Julianna came right. Tomorrow would be
an awful day, mincing around the market with Maurice fawning at
her side, while Julianna spent far too much coin for far too little
merchandise. She'd come home frustrated, worried, and trying to put
a good face on matters for the children and MacTavish, probably
fooling none of them.

Tonight, she was desired, and her every wish was about to be
indulged.

LUCERE MAINTAINED that success with a new lover was all about
tempo, about being able to read how aroused the lady was, and
knowing when to get down to the business of pleasure, as it were.
Starlingham maintained that being a good lover required lingering
afterward, and that much would be forgiven a fellow who'd been too
hasty or too dilatory, if he indulged the lady's whims when the fire-
works had concluded.

Especially her whims where fine jewelry or good seats at the
opera were concerned.

Connor might have said—before—both of his friends had valid
points. Now, he knew they were both wrong.

The essence of loving a woman well was simply that—loving her.

Putting her first, listening for her responses, attending to her needs and wishes. *Paying attention.*

Julianna liked having her breasts touched, for example, a happy discovery because Con enjoyed touching them. He laid her on the bed, came down over her, and took a moment to admire how candlelight created shadows of the curves and hollows of her body.

"You taste good," he said, kissing his way down the center of her chest. "Of roses and fresh bread. Maybe a hint of basil. Delicious."

Her hands landed in his hair, holding him close. "You are ridiculous."

What Con was, was determined. Determined to look after this household that he'd neglected for the past several years. Determined that the sense of usefulness and mutual caring he'd found here wouldn't be left behind when he departed from Lesser Puddlebury.

And determined that Julianna would at least consider coming with him.

She grasped intuitively something Con was only beginning to realize: Infatuation and desire were but the immature and frolicsome impersonators of love. True love got up early to make the bread, taught a little girl her letters by the light of a tallow candle, and asked an old man to sharpen the knives, simply so he'd have an excuse to sit by the warmth of the kitchen hearth.

True love was a lot like being a duke: endless helpings of duty, hard work, and honor, mostly in the name of aiding others to thrive or preserving them from folly. Con had spent days marveling at Julianna's discipline and self-restraint, and nights wondering if she was as passionate about her pleasures as she was about caring for the children.

The notion enthralled him as no mere passing encounter ever had. Ridiculous, to be nigh thirty years old and never truly have made love.

Con put his ridiculous mouth to Julianna's nipples and made her wiggle and sigh for a good five minutes, long enough to convince him that being enticed did, indeed, agree with her.

"Do you know," he murmured, "how lovely you look to me when you're sewing up Harold's breeches? How much I want to kiss you when you're kneading the hell out of the bread? How much I resent that you send MacTavish and the boys to replace your roses, but never send me?"

Julianna traced the contour of his right ear, an oddly pleasurable caress. "If MacTavish and the boys are off cutting roses, then you are in the kitchen, reciting poetry and scrubbing the pots for me, aren't you?"

"Strategy," Con whispered. "How I adore a woman with firm command of strategy, but Julianna, now isn't the time for subtlety."

She ran a toe up his calf. "It's not the time for ducal proclamations, Connor. You do know how to go on in bed?"

He retaliated by sitting back enough to ruffle the curls between her legs. "Right now, I barely know my name. I know only that I want to be inside you."

She stretched, she arched, she let him play for a few minutes, or perhaps she was learning a little bit how to play herself.

"I know your name, Connor," she said when Con had her moving restlessly against his hand. Her sex was wonderfully damp, and Con's cockstand rivaled a drover's staff. "I know I want you inside me."

"Do you want me inside you *now*?" He would expire if she said anything other than *yes*.

Julianna grasped him by the shaft, the first time she'd put her hands on that part of him, and drew him right against her.

A *yes*, by God.

Con braced himself on his arms and kissed the woman he hoped would become his duchess. The joining was easy and sweet, also profoundly tender. He knew by watching Julianna's face, that in accepting him this way, she also said yet another good-bye to her late husband and to the young woman who'd married years ago with such hopes and innocence.

He kissed her as they joined, kissed the passion and the welcome, the grief and the approaching glory. When Con was hilted inside her, he lowered himself to his forearms.

"Julianna, I will not fail you."

She undulated sumptuously, and words became superfluous.

Con did not fail her. He sent her into pleasure's maelstrom easily and often, until consideration alone made him pause.

"I could love you all night," he whispered. She might be making up for lost time, appeasing years of unsatisfied desire while he was learning to love a woman, truly love her, for the first time. Fresh bread came into it, folded towels, the boys, washing the eggs with Roberta, and reading stories.

Asking his siblings for help was part of it, as was trusting that Lucere and Starlingham could manage without him too.

Loving Julianna involved all of Con, and the joy of that, the odd, unexpected passion of it, was like coming home to himself in a way that being just another duke could never accomplish.

Julianna's fingers brushed over his derriere. *Enough.*

Never enough. Con sent her over the edge one more time, then withdrew and allowed himself the consolatory bliss of spending on her belly.

The damned towel was hanging over the privacy screen across the room, but even that—even forgetting to tidily fold a handkerchief on the night table—pleased Con. A fellow in love was allowed to be a bit disorganized about his passionate encounters.

He tended to his lady, then to himself, and left the towel on the night table when he climbed back into bed.

"I do believe, Julianna St. Bellan, that recourse to a timekeeping device would suggest, more than an hour has elapsed. Come here."

She curled close, her head pillowed on Con's shoulder. "I don't want to get up. My own bed feels miles away, across an arctic plain, down miles of lonely corridor."

Her bed was probably four yards from Con's. "I'll tuck you in when it's time to placate appearances." Con kissed her brow and started mentally composing a letter to Uncle Leo. "Sleep now."

She murmured something and did that thing with her toes that made Con's heart purr.

"What time do we leave for market?" Con would make sure she slept in. Fortunately, eggs and toast were among the fare he'd learned to cook.

Her eyes opened, the butterfly kiss of her lashes sweeping upward against Con's shoulder.

"Connor, you cannot come to market with me. We've been through this."

Perhaps Starlingham had a point. Perhaps the cuddling part mattered rather a lot. "When you become intimate with a man, then his escort is yours to claim, Julianna. I don't indulge in an amour and then pretend a woman who has granted me the greatest liberties means nothing to me." Connor wouldn't allow such a callous lout among his distant acquaintances.

Julianna hiked herself up on an elbow to peer at him. Con had forgotten to blow the candle out, but it would soon gutter on its own.

"Connor, I must tolerate Maurice Warren's escort at market, at the very least. He'll see me from shop to shop and merchant to merchant as he always does, ensuring I get the best bargains. Then he'll bow me on my way, if I'm lucky. Lately he's had a look in his eye I haven't found at all comforting."

Julianna brushed Connor's hair back from his brow. He'd come to love that casual touch from her, for she did it even before the children.

"What sort of look, Julianna?"

She flopped to her back so they no longer touched. "Like he's about to propose. I strongly suspect he's about to propose. Either that, or he'll call the mortgage due that John signed with him five years ago. Possibly both. Both is my worst nightmare, but it makes the most sense."

CHAPTER FIVE

Julianna had forgotten how an argument with a man could sour everything, though that probably explained why John had never told her of the mortgage he'd signed with Maurice Warren.

She would have sold her wedding ring, her dresses, her grand-mother's cameo—anything to avoid relying on Maurice Warren's good offices to see the farm through a bad year.

Now, she would have sold her soul not to feel the nagging tension between her and Connor across the breakfast table. She'd wanted an hour of passion last night, a respite from her cares, an interlude of simple adult pleasure.

Not too much to ask, but so much less than Connor had offered her.

Tenderness, passion, caring, *ferocious* cherishing, such as even Julianna's late husband had never quite conveyed in years of marriage.

And then questions she could not answer: Had she ever seen this mortgage document? Was it a mortgage or a promissory note? What were its actual terms? Was forfeiture of the farm required by the note, or had Warren merely implied as much? Where had the money gone that John St. Bellan had supposedly borrowed so shortly before his death?

Julianna could answer none of it, but neither could she afford to provoke Maurice into foreclosing. Months ago, Maurice had begun implying payment was overdue, and this morning, Julianna could hardly keep her tea and toast down, she was so unsettled.

"May we have a turn on Mr. Yoder's mare before you go into York?" Harold asked MacTavish.

"Best not," MacTavish said. "When you borrow a horse, you don't go lending it around to others. You lot behave yourselves, and I'll be back from York with our Mrs. Periwinkle as soon as I can."

"I'd like to see this mare," Con said. "Perhaps you might stop back this way after you've picked her up?"

A look passed between the two men. Bertie used the moment to take another piece of toast from the plate in the middle of the table. Con plucked it from her grasp and added butter—not too much, but not skimping either.

"I'll pass by here on my way to York," MacTavish said, pushing back from the table. "My thanks for an excellent omelet, Miss Julianna."

"Take Mrs. Yoder some roses, please," Julianna said. "And thank the Yoders profusely for the loan of the mare."

Connor had asked MacTavish to fetch the mail from York, today of all days, so Julianna would take the children with her to market. Maurice was not fond of the boys, though neither was he rude to them, nor they to him—overtly.

All too soon, the boys were on the front porch, faces scrubbed, hair combed back, and Connor was leading Horty around, the cart rattling behind her.

"Where's Bertie?" Harold asked. "She's never late."

"Miss Roberta tarried arranging the flowers in my room," Connor said. "I account myself most privileged."

He was up to something, but at least he wasn't sulking. Last night, he'd argued, he'd fumed, he'd argued some more, but then he'd grown quiet, wrapped himself around Julianna, and rubbed her back until she'd fallen asleep.

"What will you do to pass the time?" Julianna asked, pulling on her driving gloves. These were gardening gloves in truth, but they protected her hands well enough.

Con scratched Horty's hairy neck. "I'll get some weeding done, beat a few rugs, maybe make a cobbler."

"Cobbler for dessert!" Lucas yelled, which caused Hortensia to startle.

"Into the gig," Connor said. "I'll hand your mother up."

Did he know he referred to Julianna as their mother? The children didn't seem to mind... and neither did Julianna, really. Con kissed her on the cheek in parting and tousled each boy's hair.

"Best behavior, gents. Spend your tuppence well."

Julianna unwrapped the reins from the brake. "What tuppence?"

"For many jobs well done," Connor said. "I've asked the boys to help Miss Roberta choose some hair ribbons. She said she'd prefer green, because it's MacTavish's favorite color."

Damn him for his thoughtfulness. Sixpence was nothing to most households, but to these boys... Julianna could not recall when she'd ever given them money of their own. She simply hadn't any money to give.

Roberta dashed onto the porch, her hair in lopsided braids courtesy of Ralph's attempt to be helpful. Practicing for if he ever had to braid up a mane or a tail, he'd said. Con tucked tuppence into Roberta's hand, and lifted her into the back with the boys, though he hugged the girl conspicuously in the process and been hugged in return too.

Julianna searched Connor's gaze for something—ire, reassurance, clues—but he was very much the duke this morning, not the lover, not the amiable relation.

"Horty, walk on," Julianna said, giving the reins a shake. Hortensia obliged with a mule's version of alacrity.

When Julianna glanced over her shoulder at the foot of the drive,

Connor stood before the house, merely watching, while she drove off to meet a man she didn't like or trust, but would probably marry.

CON HAD PURPOSELY NOT CLEANED his boots very well, and he'd borrowed a too-large, dusty coat from MacTavish. Because Con wouldn't put anybody to the bother of ironing his clothing, his attire was wrinkled, if presentable by village market standards.

The two-mile walk into the village set Con's wound to itching, and also gave him time to think.

He'd sent MacTavish into York's pawnshops with two trunks of London finery, including watches, cravat pins, a spare pair of brand new Hoby boots, cuff links, fobs, and assorted whatnot. More trunks had of course gone north with Freddy, and yet still more clothing hung in cedar-lined wardrobes at Mowne.

None of which Con could retrieve without risking Uncle Leo's notice, or unacceptable delay.

"Well, if it isn't yet another genteel stranger lounging about trying to look inconspicuous and mostly failing." Starlingham took up a lean next to Con outside the posting inn. Across the street, the market day merchants were doing a brisk business on the Puddlebury village green.

Con had warned the boys to ignore him and had also given them tasks more specific than that.

Starlingham blew the foam off a tankard of ale. "How's the, er, injury?"

"Healing. How do you find your accommodations?" Con was also holding a tankard of summer ale, as were various others loitering outside the inn. The day was sunny, noisy, and not a duke's usual summer diversion.

"My accommodations are... interesting. I've never been to a village market before. Puts one in mind of a London ballroom with livestock."

Starlingham had a point. Across the green, a pair of fiddlers busked for pennies. The tavern had set up a keg to draw custom on the front terrace, much like a crystal punch bowl drew thirsty debutantes. Business was being transacted, of course—much business occurred at Mayfair's social gatherings too—but the general air was convivial.

"We're not so different," Con said as a sizable ewe darted away from the green and a small boy pelted after her.

Starlingham stuck out a booted foot, stopping the ewe for the instant the boy needed to grab two handfuls of fleece.

"Thank 'ee, sir!"

Starlingham lifted his mug and smiled. "You mean people the world over aren't so different from one another? Do you feel a poem coming on? I'm told the Lakes will bring out the poet in anybody."

The Lake District lay farther west. Perhaps Con and Julianna would honeymoon there. "I mean dukes aren't so different from the farmers in the dales. How fares Lucere?"

"Can't say, which suggests he hasn't shot anybody—or been shot. Which one is Cousin Jules?"

Con had spotted Julianna before he'd ordered his ale. She'd worn a straw hat without so much as a ribbon to dress it up, and that very plainness made her easy to track.

"She's with the gent in green."

"Blond fellow going a bit portly amidships? Squire Lumpkin? Why isn't *she* with you? If I had a *Cousin Jules* who looked like that, she'd have my devoted escort."

She did have Con's devoted escort. "Squire Lumpkin is Maurice Warren, who has both farming and mining interests in the area. Wealthy gentry."

"Mines," Starlingham said, taking a sip of his ale and wiping his mouth on his sleeve with the practiced indelicacy of any yeoman. "Don't care for them. My papa refused to own them. He said he couldn't trust the factors not to employ children. Nasty business when children are hacking themselves to death on coal dust before they're properly grown. The gent in green is sticking quite close to your cousin."

And Julianna was tolerating Warren's presumption. Letting him lean close and attend every word of her conversations with the merchants, though Warren didn't even carry the lady's basket.

"If I asked you for all the coin you have with you, would you lend it to me, Starlingham?"

"Don't be daft. I'd give it to you if you promise not to thrash me for implying you need the charity. Pity I haven't much coin, though. My valet or coachman usually carries the purse. This is the best ale I can recall having."

Well, damn. "Fresh air and the good Yorkshire sunshine give a man an appreciation for the simpler joys. How dare that presuming buffoon?"

Warren had just doubled the amount of honey Julianna had placed in her basket. Reached right past her and dropped a second sizable jar next to the first, then stood by while Julianna parted with coin she could not spare.

"Are we still leaving next week?" Starlingham asked, a bit too casually.

"You'd rather tarry here?" Con certainly would. For the rest of his life.

"Uncle Leo would grow suspicious," Starlingham said. "Can't have him playing skittles with your pin money."

"Spoken like a true friend who occasionally owes me blunt." Con bumped his tankard against Starlingham's. "Until we do leave, I'll pass the time folding linens and stitching hems. If you see the Sun come out, pass along my best regards."

Starlingham gave a minute bow, and Con set his half-full tankard on the nearest table for some enterprising child to enjoy... or sheep, or stray duke in disguise without much coin. Ralph came sauntering across the road, hands in his pockets, a gleam in his eye. He sidled right past Con, as if the abandoned ale were his goal, but spoke loudly enough for Con to hear.

"You were correct, sir. Mr. Warren's a right bastard, and I'm not sorry I've used bad language."

"Save it for when we get home," Con said, shading his eyes to admire the very modest church steeple. "Tell Harold and Lucas to do likewise. Good work."

Good work, but bad news. Con made his way to the vendor selling lemons, limes, and oranges, bought the best two on offer, and tucked them into his pockets. He tugged his hat brim down and found a handy patch of shade near the smithy, from which he could watch Mr. Warren work his wiles on an unsuspecting widow.

Con relished the opportunity to study an adversary he would not underestimate. A promissory note signed by a man who'd departed this earth five years ago was easy to forge, though proving the forgery would be nearly impossible.

The Duke of Mowne could have swarmed Warren with solicitors, inquiries, and intimidation. With a little time, His Grace could sell a farm in the East Riding to rescue a farm in Lesser Puddlebury.

Connor Amadour could not call upon the resources of the Duke of Mowne, and based on the increasing worry in Julianna's eyes, even if Con did reveal himself as the duke, he had no time—no time at all—to bring the duke's resources to bear on Julianna's situation.

"PLEASE STOP PACING," Antigone muttered. "You're attracting notice again."

Hector flopped down beside her with a loud sigh. Quint flipped out his tails and took a more decorous seat on her other side.

"This is one of the finest posting inns in York," Quint said, withdrawing a deck of playing cards from a pocket, "but a lady of your quality loitering about in the common can't help but earn stares."

"With such handsome escorts, the stares aren't all directed at me." Antigone was accustomed to being overshadowed by her brothers, to being teased and flirted with by their friends. She was not accustomed to harebrained journeys half the length of the realm, but Quint and Hector had both leaped at the notion.

While Mama had packed for Kent, thank heavens.

"That fellow does not belong here," Hector said, sitting up straight.

Sir Walter Scott's novels had imbued all things Highland with dashing romanticism, and kilts were not unheard of even in London ballrooms. The closer to Scotland one traveled, though, the more in evidence clan dress became. Usually, the kilts were patterned in bright plaids, neatly folded, all tucked up with jeweled pins, silver brooches, and the like.

This fellow's kilt had seen better days, and the pleats had gone soft for want of pressing.

"Big lout," Quint said, shuffling the cards. "Wouldn't want to tangle with him when he's put away a wee dram too many." Quinton always traveled with cards, a chess set, and dice, all of which had helped to pass the hours in the inn's common.

The Scot in question was tall, muscular, and into the ageless years. He might be fifty, he might be seventy. Cold blue eyes said he would not be trifled with.

For the second day in a row, Antigone and her brothers had come down from their rooms early, intent on spending the day appearing to pass the time in the common. All manner of people had come in to pick up mail.

When the Scot stepped up to the bar, the publican took the towel from his own shoulder, refolded it twice, and passed across a single letter—presumably Antigone's reply to Con.

"That's him," she said, the refolded towel being the agreed-upon signal. "Of all the urchins, footmen, dandies, and dowagers, that... that representative of Clan MacMuscle is Con's emissary. Quickly, you two, or we'll never catch him. I own I am intrigued."

"I'm alarmed," Quint said, stuffing the cards back in his pocket.

"I'm having the time of my life," Hector retorted, springing to his feet. "Haven't had this much fun since Tiger threatened to turn her archery skills on Lucere's horse."

"She would have hit the poor creature too," Quint muttered, escorting Antigone to the common's side entrance. "Quite the markswoman, is our Tiger."

Antigone loved it when her brothers used the nickname Con had given her in infancy. Nonetheless, as they gained the street, and the Scotsman climbed into a farm cart that bore two trunks bearing the Mowne ducal crest, Antigone had to admit Quint and Hector were both right.

The adventure of rescuing Con had been a lark thus far, but this development—an enormous Scottish ruffian in possession of Con's personal luggage—was purely alarming.

"MAURICE WANTS A FORTUNE FROM ME," Julianna said, skirts swishing. "He tried to dodge and deceive, as you said he would, but I pressed him for answers." She paced the length of her porch while Connor sat on the swing—on a pillow on the swing—exuding a damnable calm.

"You asked him about both the principal sum borrowed and the rate of interest on the loan?"

Connor had been very insistent last night, very clear. Whether a mortgage or a promissory note or something else entirely, whatever John had signed—Connor had had doubts that John had signed anything—the document would state a sum borrowed and terms of repayment.

"Maurice didn't want to tell me even that much. Why bother my pretty head—he used those words, my *pretty head*—when settlement discussions would obviate the need to mention such unpleasant details?"

Marriage settlement discussions, of course. Maurice had taken the gloves off, to use language the boys would understand. Julianna was to marry him, and all monies owed him would be "worked out" in the settlement discussions pertaining to "disposition of the real estate."

Stealing the farm that Julianna was determined should go to the children.

"Come sit beside me, Julianna, and tell me what he said."

Such calm, reasonable words. "Not even you, Connor, not even with such a harmless suggestion as that, should tell me what to do right now. I am in a taking. I have never been in a taking before." A taking meant Julianna wanted to throw herself into Connor's lap and weep on his shoulder, also apply her broom repeatedly to Maurice Warren's backside.

Connor stood, plucked a white rose, and passed it to her. "You should be in a taking. Shall I tell you the rest of it?"

The rose had thorns. Julianna held it carefully. "Yes. The whole of it, and then I can find apprenticeships for the boys, write MacTavish a character, give him Horty, and—"

And what? Send Roberta back to the poorhouse? Maurice had hinted that he might find an apprenticeship for Roberta, because she was such a *biddable child.*

"You will visit Maurice Warren in jail," Connor said, taking Julianna's rose from her grasp and gently batting her on the nose with it. "I asked the boys to watch you at market today, and they did."

"I saw them." All on their own, enjoying their freedom. Julianna would soon need to let down trouser hems for Lucas and Ralph too. "That rose should be in water."

Connor tucked the rose into a half-full vase Julianna had brought out. He leaned a hip against the porch railing, silhouetting himself against the rioting roses and the afternoon sun.

"Warren has apparently directed the merchants to bilk you at every turn. They are all, every one of them who can, charging you double what they charge anybody else. Warren stands beside you to enforce this behavior. Two of the merchants pulled the boys aside and told them you ought to buy your goods in York if you want better prices."

"York is half a day's journey coming and going, assuming the roads are passable."

"And Warren knows you can't leave the children that long. Did he mention that the sum you owe him is subject to late penalties, delinquent fees, anything like that?"

Everything like that, and Maurice had been so sad, so reluctant to tell Julianna the true state of her indebtedness.

"He named a total." Julianna collapsed onto the swing, muttering the amount loudly enough for Connor to hear. "I'm ashamed. I hate being ashamed. Why haven't I forced an accounting from him sooner? Now, he won't even give me until harvest to make a payment and says he owes it to John's memory to attend to matters now."

Attend to *matters*. Holy matrimony should mean years of shared dreams, work, laughter, loving... And Maurice Warren might as well be buying another mule at auction.

"I think the matter he wants to attend to is a fortune in coal," Connor said. "MacTavish told me a surveyor came down from Northumberland earlier in the summer, and there's talk in the village that Warren's mines are playing out. That could be why Maurice is forcing your hand. He is desperate to impress investors, and yet, he has no capital of his own. Your property is the asset he needs to lure them into turning over their coin."

The children were across the lane, playing in the apple orchard. Even Roberta was up a tree, impersonating a pirate or a highwayman. Why did children never play at being farmers, shepherds, blacksmiths, or publicans?

"He wants to turn one of the best farms in the shire into a coal pit," Julianna said. "A fitting metaphor for what my life will become. I can resign myself to such a fate, but for the children..." For the children... Maurice would make her beg, plead, bargain, and agree to anything, and she'd do it, to keep the children playing in their trees, grumbling about their chores, squabbling over the last bite of cobbler.

Connor prowled away from the railing and drew Julianna to her feet. "I cannot resign myself to such a fate—not for you, *and not for us*. Where is your fight, Julianna St. Bellan? Do you know the family motto?"

"*Faciemus proelio*," Julianna quoted. "We make war, or battle, or something grand. All very well for dukes and coal nabobs, but I make bread. I make beds, and I make children do their sums."

His arms came around her. "Only a duke can recognize a duchess in disguise. You make a home out of hard work and love. You make children feel safe. You make a farm successful despite a knave trying to bring you down. You make me so proud of you, if I had a sword, I'd cheerfully run Maurice Warren through for you."

"You don't have a sword," Julianna said, heart breaking. "You have kindness and honor. You have patience with the children and with me. You have a fortune you cannot command as you ought. You have a scar on your backside, and you have such kisses..."

Connor gave her some of those kisses. Sweet, soft, fierce kisses that tempted Julianna to take him upstairs that instant.

"If I marry you, I gain control of my fortune shortly thereafter," Connor said, his hand going to Julianna's nape. He knew exactly how to touch her, how to squeeze and caress and muddle her...

"You cannot marry me," she said, burrowing closer. "You are a duke. I am the widow of a distant relation and even poorer than I thought I was."

"I can marry you, but not in time to keep Maurice from snatching away your farm, and this farm matters, this legacy that John St. Bellan wanted for you and the children. A ducal marriage is a complicated, drawn-out business, done properly. If we marry simply to foil Maurice, you'll be doubting forever after that I chose you for love and no other reason. Then too, Leo might prove difficult, and I'm not in the mood to humor anybody's crotchets where you're concerned."

Julianna's insides had gone from unsettled to fluttery, and her anger was slipping away on a rose-scented tide of wishes and hopes.

"What are you saying, Connor?"

"I'm saying, please marry me, Julianna. Me, your Connor, who isn't very quick with a needle, but he tries hard to keep his stitches straight. He'll put his shoulder to the plough if need be. He'll read to the children at night so you can have an extra hour of sleep. I have no confidence I'll ever be able to direct my own fortune—Leo is stubborn and contrary and tiresome. I should have told him to stop interfering years ago, regardless of my papa's damned will. I should have taken my family's excesses and my mother's meddling in hand. I was too busy being a dupe instead of a duke."

How fierce he was. Julianna spared some pity for this Uncle Leo fellow if he thought to turn up tiresome now.

"I wish my late husband had explained this loan to me," she said, pushing Connor's hair off his brow. He was proposing to her, offering her marriage, and yet, he would always be the duke too. "I know nothing of being a duchess."

"I knew nothing of being *myself*," Connor said, leading her back to the swing. "I waved a gloved hand, and a coach-and-four appeared before my mansion. I don't need that to be happy. I'd rather hitch up your mule and put her away for you when you come home. I'd rather read to four rapt children in this farmhouse than make speeches nobody listens to in the House of Lords. I'd rather love you than be a duke to the rest of the world. This farm, you, the children... that's duchy enough for me, and if Leo doesn't like it, he can spend my fortune himself. Please marry me."

Everything in Julianna wanted to say yes, of course, yes. She was a mother four times over, though. MacTavish, even Horty, depended on her to be wiser now than she had been in the past.

She took a seat, and Con came down beside her. "What about Maurice, Connor? You're willing to spend the rest of your days as the duke farming in the dales, but we might not even have a farm. Your uncle could disdain to recognize your marriage to a nobody, and then the children would have nothing. Once the mining starts here—and it could start literally overnight—the farm is gone forever."

Con took her hand and kissed her fingers. "I asked a few questions in the village today. Maurice fancies himself quite the gentle-man, even to the point of assembling a weekly card game for the gentry in the area. They lounge about the posting inn's best parlor and think they're playing for lordly sums while they over-imbibe and run the serving maids ragged. I'll win your farm back before Maurice can start crying banns on Sunday. See if I don't."

"Our future comes down to a wager? What have you to wager with?"

"A duke might not know how to stack hay, wield a scythe, or brew ale, but he can handle a deck of cards the way you knead bread, my love. He can loll about, swilling spirits, wagering, and looking useless by the hour. He can pay far better attention than most people know. I'll be a duke in disguise, and Maurice Warren will be much lighter in the pocket for my efforts."

Five years of widowhood took a toll on a woman's ability to trust anything to chance. "We could elope to Scotland."

"Which would take a good ten days of planning and travel, at least. While our backs are turned, Maurice Warren could buy himself a judgment of foreclosure from a friendly judge and dig up half your pastures."

In the middle of a summer afternoon, Julianna shivered. "I hate Maurice Warren."

Con's arm came around her shoulders. "He deserves your hatred, but I also have to wonder who else's, Julianna. If he has every merchant on the green cowed, if he's talked your neighbors into ignoring you, if he can threaten everybody in the shire... somebody needs to put him in his place. Not only for you and the children, but for all the widows and all the children. For the farms he'll go after next, the children he'll send down his mines. This shire needs a duke or two, and I know one who happens to have time on his hands."

This was not the Connor Amadour whom Julianna had found asleep on her swing last week. This was a different fellow, a different sort of duke, a different man.

The children were right across the lane, making a racket in the trees. At any moment, MacTavish could rattle up the drive in the Yoders' cart, or worse, Maurice might presume to pay a call.

Life was short. Life was sometimes tragically short, and five years of working hard and hoping had got Julianna a tired back and a powerful, unscrupulous enemy. She shifted so she was sitting in Con's lap and put her head on his shoulder as his arms came around her.

"Best Maurice Warren, Connor. Trounce him, shame him, humiliate him. Take back from him what he's stolen and make sure the entire shire knows you've done it. Put him in his place, because I have every confidence, if Maurice had to groom a mule, cook up a pot of porridge, or make a tired fairy tale exciting for good, innocent children, he'd fail miserably. See Maurice put in his place, and I'll marry you gladly."

She'd marry Connor on any terms at all, but he'd set a task for himself that went beyond her, the children, and even the farm. He'd had the title for years, but in a way Julianna didn't entirely grasp, Connor had only now decided *how* to be the Duke of Mowne.

"It shall be as my future duchess commands," he said, kissing her temple and setting the swing to rocking.

Julianna fell asleep in his embrace. She ought to have been plagued by nightmares and worries, but stealing a nap on the swing with Connor was the best, most refreshing rest she'd had in years.

DUKES MIGHT EXCEL at playing cards, lolling about, and looking bored, but they did not excel at waiting. Con, at least, did not.

MacTavish did not come home from York on market day. He did not come home the following day either, and while Julianna made cheerful excuses in response to Mrs. Yoder's polite inquiries—the housekeeper's sister had asked her to tarry another day, perhaps—worry crowded the entire household close.

Duke or not, no stranger could join a card game without some demonstration of his ability to handle the stakes. In increasingly wrinkled finery, with a single watch chain and ring to his name, Connor would pass for gentry, or even a lord's younger son, but little more.

"MacTavish will return," Julianna said when they'd tucked the children in. "This time tomorrow, you'll have full pockets and look every inch the duke. You'll be sitting about the inn's best parlor, winning great sums, swilling excellent brandy, and looking bored."

"How can you be so calm? I've half a notion to ride Horty into York tomorrow and search through every hostelry and livery. Horse thievery is a hanging offense."

Julianna took Con by the hand. "You aren't concerned that Mac might have stolen your clothes? Your jewels? Your trunks?"

Even the feel of her hand in Con's had a rightness about it. "Of course not. But for tomorrow's card game, I wouldn't miss them. They'd be little enough recompense to MacTavish for standing by you when everybody else has fallen under Warren's sway. I'm more concerned that your only ally has lost his nerve."

Or worse, attracted the notice of thieves. Here in the country, crime was seldom an issue. In a bustling place like York... Con knew city life, knew its temptations and pitfalls. MacTavish was one man, laden with relative treasure, and no longer young.

Julianna led Con into his bedroom, then closed and locked the door.

"Rains might come tomorrow," she said, "and ruin what promises to be a good harvest of wheat. The blight can show up on the potatoes. Harold could come down with a lung fever. Roberta might step on a nail, for she does love to go barefoot in the grass. Horty could turn up lame. The roof might leak, the chickens all die."

"Hush," Con said, putting a finger to her lips. Eggs were a major staple at breakfast and a significant part of other meals as well. "You are frightening me, and I'd flattered myself that I possessed some modicum of courage. I have four siblings who test that courage regularly."

Siblings whom he... missed. Quint had surprising reserves of discretion. Hector brought good humor with him nearly everywhere. Tiger had a practical streak not often seen in a duke's daughter, and Freddy... Freddy had an enviable store of derring-do.

"Family tests our courage," Julianna said, kissing Con gently. "They die, blast them. Your papa left you too soon. John should be sitting out on the porch this instant, watching the moon rise over a lovely farm. The land tests my courage, the children test everything in me... MacTavish will come home."

Nobody reassured a duke, and yet, Julianna's embrace was not only reassuring, but fortifying. Whether MacTavish came in time or not, Julianna's affection and loyalty would not waver. Her kisses said as much. Her hands, stealing little caresses as she helped Con disrobe, made the same promise. Con provided reciprocal courtesies, unhooking this, untying that, until they were both under the covers, her head resting on his shoulder, her bare knee tucked across his thighs.

"Your wound has healed quickly," Julianna said.

Everything in Con had healed during this interlude in Lesser Puddlebury. "I'm worried." He could say this to her, in the dark, under the covers. He could say it to her anywhere, and she'd not judge him for it.

"So am I. Let's distract each other, shall we?" She slid her hand slowly down, down, to grip Connor snugly by something much more interesting than his worries. Her touch was gentle but sure, and quite... inventive.

Inspiring, even. When Con would have retaliated, Julianna rose over him instead.

"Not tonight, Connor. Tonight you let me love you. You have exhausted yourself these past two days, doing MacTavish's work. Tonight, you enjoy your rest."

Con should protest. He should remonstrate, and review options, and think up contingencies. He should go downstairs and pen an imperious epistle to Uncle Leo and pawn the last set of fine clothes he possessed to hire a messenger to gallop to Scotland...

Though in which direction Scotland lay, Con could not have said just then.

Julianna's idea of distraction included using her mouth in ways Con, with all his London experience, would never have expected of a woman. Her attentions proceeded at a luxurious pace, as if she enjoyed driving Con to incoherent sighs.

"You excel at distraction."

"Mmmm." Followed by a swirl of her tongue, left then right, then right, right...

Con gathered her braid at her nape, though whether he was bent on encouraging her or dissuading her, even he could not have said.

"Julianna, please..."

She nuzzled him in the most lovely, indelicate location, then sat up. "I was never so daring as a younger woman, never so selfish or indulgent of my curiosity. I hope you're convinced of your own fortitude, sir."

Con hauled her over him as gently as madness allowed. "*Fiend.* Lovely, luscious, delectable, sweet—for the love of God, *Julianna.*"

With no ado whatsoever, she'd swooped down on him, joining them in one glorious descent. She was ready—she was wonderfully, enthusiastically ready—and yet, a small corner of Con's awareness, the part not praying for restraint to match his supposed fortitude, was admiring more than Julianna's naked form.

To love like this in the face of possible ruin took courage. To know that tomorrow might bring more uncertainty and worse options, and yet love tonight with unfettered passion, that took... that took a degree of faith and strength that stole a man's breath.

Julianna was loving Connor with all the hope in her, all the faith she had in herself, laid before him like a feast of optimism, resilience, and loyalty. *We'll manage,* she said with every kiss and caress. *We're in this together.*

And she was right.

This was what it felt like to be loved, for himself, unconditionally, come what may.

Con returned her passion, cherishing her every curve and callus, her every sigh and whimper. He couldn't sustain nearly as much restraint as he wanted to, but that was part of loving, too—the surrendering, to passion, to hope, and to pleasure. They soon lay in a tangled, panting heap of warmth and wonder, the only sounds their breathing and the rustle of the covers.

"I love you," Con said, mustering the energy for one last, lovely kiss to the lady's lips. "I love you."

"Then I am already your duchess, and you are my duke, for I love you too. Come what may. Blow out the candle, Your Grace, and dream with me."

CHAPTER SIX

Never, ever would Julianna regret the nights she'd spent in Connor's arms. His reserves of tenderness and passion—and his displays of imagination—would keep her memories warm into great old age, even through Yorkshire winters, destitution, and the possible heartbreak of failing the children who in the past week had taken to calling her Mama.

"Where's MacTavish?" Roberta asked over the last of her cobbler.

"Probably on his way home right this instant," Julianna replied. "We gave him much to do in York, and Mrs. Periwinkle might have been reluctant to leave her sister. Would you care for another serving of dessert, Bertie? You didn't take very much to begin with."

To give away MacTavish's portion of the cobbler had been a slip. The boys exchanged looks that said they well knew Julianna was anxious.

"Let's save the last of the cobbler," Connor said. "MacTavish will be hungry after days away from home cooking. Children, if you'd help with the dishes, your mother can assist me to don my finery."

Con had called them all together on the porch after luncheon and explained exactly what was afoot. He'd used simple language, nothing alarming, and yet, the children seemed to grasp the gravity of the situation.

Without a word of protest, the boys rose and took their dishes to the slop bucket.

Roberta turned huge blue eyes on Connor. "Mr. Warren pinched me once. On my arm. I didn't do anything wrong either. I don't like him, and he's not nice."

"Where did he pinch you?" Connor asked.

Roberta pointed to the muscle near her shoulder, which Con kissed. "I will make him pay dearly for treating one of my ladies ill, Roberta. He should not have done that. If anybody else *ever* behaves similarly, you tell your mama, your brothers, or me."

Roberta studied Connor with a seriousness that tore at Julianna's heart, while the boys silently cleared the table. "Will you be my papa?"

Oh God. Oh God. Oh God.

Con's smile was sweet and grave. "If your mama will have me, and I hope she will, I would be honored to be a parent to all of you."

The children were safe, in other words. Whatever else happened to the farm, the children would be safe. Connor would find the coin, the determination, the way forward, regardless of his family's foolishness, or the already strained ducal exchequer.

"I'll shine your boots," Harold said, "as soon as the dishes are clean."

"I can brush your hat and jacket," Ralph added.

"I'll start pressing your shirt," Lucas chimed in. "And don't worry, I won't scorch it. Roberta will make sure I'm careful."

While Julianna would help Connor dress as she tried not to panic. For the sun was setting, and even a duke could not win back a farm without the means to first invite himself into the requisite game of chance.

～

THE DUCAL FINERY felt the same—pressed, starched, exquisitely fitted—and yet, it felt different to Con too. A costume, chosen for his purposes, not simply the outfit handed to him by his fussing, fawning valet. Another exquisitely embroidered waistcoat, another perfectly starched cravat.

They were his battle dress, now.

"Will I do?" Con asked, turning slowly, arms outstretched before the children. Julianna had pronounced him ready for the evening before they'd come downstairs. She'd refused to kiss him, saying she must not wrinkle his cravat, but Con sensed the worry in her.

Four equally fretful little faces surveyed him from the sofa. "You're very fancy," Ralph said. "Mr. Warren won't like that you're fancier than he is."

"Good." Harold passed Connor a spotless top hat. "The more Mr. Warren doesn't like it, the happier I am. He pinched Roberta, he wants to steal from Mama. He deserves to land in Horty's manure pit."

"He *has* been stealing from Mama," Lucas said. "Mr. Greenower and Mr. Plumley said as much."

"Where's MacTavish?" Roberta whispered.

Con was out of excuses for MacTavish, and Julianna had given up an hour ago. The summer sun was sinking inexorably toward the green horizon, and Con's hopes were sinking with it.

Julianna met his gaze over the children's heads, the look in her eyes resolute. "MacTavish will come. He's never let us down, never shirked, and he'll not—"

Roberta bolted to the window. "I hear wheels! He's home!"

The children thundered onto the porch, waving and yelling uproariously as a bay mare trotted up the lane, MacTavish at the reins, a plump, graying woman beside him. The trunks were gone, a good sign, and MacTavish wasn't scowling any more than usual. He pulled the gig up before the house and swung the housekeeper down.

"What's all this racket? You'll spook the poor mare, and she's had a long, tiring week."

MacTavish apparently had too, but he was back, and Julianna and the children were swarming about him, all smiles and hugs. Con came down the porch steps, waiting, because MacTavish obviously had something to report.

When the children had dragged Mrs. Periwinkle into the house with Julianna in tow, Con offered MacTavish a hand. "Welcome home. You had me worried."

MacTavish watched the others depart, his expression hard to read. "I am sorry for going a bit off schedule. I got engaged."

Ah, hence the slight daze in MacTavish's blue eyes. "Congratulations. So did I."

"Maud said we should give you lovebirds some privacy. I told her she was daft. Never knew how much sense a daft woman could make when she's determined to celebrate her engagement. Then there were the pickpockets."

Not pickpockets, please God, not pickpockets now. Much less pickpockets, *plural.*

"How much did they get?"

"You lot, with your fancy airs... They get every groat from you every time, because you expect some grimy boy to be fumbling at your watch chain. That's not how they operate."

"MacTavish, my fist will operate on your newly engaged face if you don't get on with the telling. My family—and our mule—are depending on me to save the farm on the turn of a card tonight. For that, I need money, not a parable."

MacTavish's grin was a work of benevolence. "*And the mule?* That's the last time I argue with Maud Periwinkle MacTavish. The pickpockets got nothing, for all their trying. A good pickpocket dresses like quality and works with two accomplices. The finest of the three lifts the goods from your pocket so lightly you never feel but a bump and jostle. Quick as a wink, he hands off the goods to the second, often a lady, the prettier the better. The third fellow, looking a bit down on his luck, takes off at a conspicuous run, but has no contraband on him, while the lady slips quietly away."

Well, yes, that was how it was done. "You were followed by pick-pockets for days?"

"Most tenacious and best-dressed criminals I've ever seen. I had to take some of your goods to every pawnbroker in York to get the best price. If I'd left them all with one, he wouldn't have been as inclined to bargain."

MacTavish passed over a reassuringly heavy bag of coins. "You're set, lad. I'll mind the farm, you catch a rascal. The whole shire will be in your debt, and you'll never want for cobbler again."

Julianna had come out on the porch and stood at the top of the steps, her shawl clutched about her. Con took one instant to imprint the image of her there among her vining roses, then blew her a kiss.

"I'm off to battle. Wish me luck."

"*Faciemus proelio,*" Julianna said, blowing him a kiss in return. "Failing that, knock Maurice Warren into the dirtiest manure pit you can find and blacken both of his eyes. Roberta asked me to tell you that. She said manure stains never come out."

"Remind me not to cross our daughter," Con said, bowing. "Mac-Tavish, if you could drop me outside the village before returning the mare, I'd appreciate it."

"I can do better than that," MacTavish said, passing over a silver flask. "I can tell you who plays in this card game and how they play, how much they already owe Warren, and how many daughters they have to dower."

"All the better," Con said, climbing into the cart and taking a seat on the hard bench. They were all the way to the edge of the village before he realized something else that had changed for the better.

His wound no longer pained him. Didn't even itch, in fact, not in the slightest.

~

GETTING into the game had been the work of a moment, for apparently, every baronet's son and squire was tired of losing to Maurice

Warren. Con had introduced himself as Connor Amadour, then smiled, bowed, dropped a few innuendos about needing to avoid some London matchmakers, and easily gained himself a seat at the table.

Warren sported a prosperous figure, thinning blond hair, and three gold watch chains stretching across his paunch. His manner was gracious if a bit obsequious. A sennight ago, Con would not have noticed the fawning. Warren also won steadily, which any damned fool would have noticed.

Winning streaks happened—very, very rarely. Long winning streaks tended to happen before the odds, or the machinations of a particular card sharp, were about to knock a foolish man on his arse. One by one, the others at the table dropped out, while Con's resources dwindled.

He saw Julianna losing one pasture after another. Her orchard, her crops, her home farm, her home wood...

Panic tried to take root, but Con batted it aside. Dukes did not panic, and neither did competent farmers.

"Let's order another bottle, shall we?" Warren suggested. "Celebration of my windfall, consolation for your losses. A fancy London gent like you can stand to lose a bit, eh? The evening is young, after all. You might win back a bit of your own before we call it a night."

That sop to Con's dignity, thrown across a table from which all others had departed, brought with it an alarming realization.

Warren was cheating. Sitting directly across from him, Con could observe him from only one vantage point. Had Lucere or Starlingham been on hand to take the flanking chairs, Warren's perfidy might have been checked. Con was without his allies and was not himself adept at cheating, nor did he wish to be.

"If I wanted to invest some real money," Con said as Warren signaled for yet more brandy, "are there opportunities in this area?"

Warren passed the deck over for Con to cut, but instead of cutting, Con picked up the cards and shuffled them. The markings were subtle, barely discernible unless a player was paying attention.

"Real money?" Warren echoed. "Investment sums," Con said. "The cent-per-cents are all very well for a sister's dowry or a widow's portion, but to hold a man's attention, something more adventurous is required, don't you think?"

"A canal would be—"

Con waved a hand, his signet ring winking in the candlelight. "Canals were fine for our fathers' day, but steam will soon make the rails a viable alternative. My brother is something of an inventor, and he assures me this is so."

The markings weren't falling into a pattern Con could detect with casual handling, and Warren's gaze had gone calculating.

"Mining in this region is quite lucrative," he said. "One needs a sound grasp of the local terrain, such as a lifelong resident of the area has, and familiarity with the mining industry, which accomplishment I can also boast, Mr. Amadour. My own modest wealth owes much to a certain perspicacity where mining ventures are concerned."

Oh, right. Which was why every fellow who'd left the table had likely lost a good portion of his savings to Warren and now could not risk offending him over even a hand of cards or a jar of honey in the market.

Inspiration came to Con as the serving maid set a fresh bottle on the table along with clean glasses.

The deck was marked with minute pinpricks and nicks along the edges of the cards. Con set to subtly adding to the wear and irregularity of the surfaces while Warren blathered on about the potential riches a man of vision might find if he were patient and daring, shrewd and well connected, brilliant but willing to trust those who'd trod the path to riches before him.

Warren ought to be making speeches in the Lords, so impressed was he with his own elocution. Con kept him going with questions and with brandy, and all the while, Con worked the deck.

And yet, when play resumed, an hour went by with Con barely winning back the sum he'd brought with him.

"Are you tiring, Mr. Amadour? I confess wagering against somebody other than my neighbors is a refreshing change. Suppose we raise the stakes to something a man of your consequence might find interesting?"

In other words, enough of the markings on the cards remained that Warren was confident he could still read them. Con felt a sense of floodwaters rising, crops withering, and fate closing a fist around Julianna's hopes and dreams.

He hadn't lost ground tonight, and he'd learned a great deal about his opponent. Retreat might be the wisest course, a chance to regroup...? Lucere and Starlingham could travel on without him, perhaps?

And have Leo sending pigeons in all directions. "What do you have in mind?" Con asked.

"Congratulations are in order, Mr. Amadour. I'm about to announce my engagement to a certain young lady, and as it happens, the dowry she'll bring to the union is the jewel in the crown of a potential mining empire. Mineral rights are the true wealth of Yorkshire, sir, and by combining my marital good fortune with a certain—"

Con casually worked his thumbnail under the label on the brandy bottle, when he wanted to bash his opponent over the head instead. Warren hadn't even bothered to propose to Julianna. He'd simply made threats and taken advantage of her grief and lack of business acumen.

And now here was Julianna's great ducal champion, without means, without allies, without a plan—

Con had Julianna's love, though, and that was all he'd ever need.

"You're seeking investors," Con said. "I need a place to invest my coin. Most interesting."

"I thought you'd agree. Let's call for a fresh deck, shall we? Our play is about to get interesting."

Their play would turn disastrous if Con allowed a "fresh" deck of Warren's choosing to be brought to the table. Calling Warren out abruptly loomed as a wonderful solution. The bastard was a cheating, lying disgrace who took advantage of widows, children, neighbors, and merchants.

Lucere and Starlingham might not approve, but they'd serve as Con's seconds. Freddy would approve, as would Hector, Tiger, Quint, and even Mama.

"Warren, I don't think a fresh deck will serve, not in the sense you mean."

Something in Con's voice, in the sheer menace of his tone, must have communicated itself to his opponent. Warren left off shuffling—or reacquainting himself with the tools of the immediate swindle.

"Perhaps we should just get on with the wagering, Mr. Amadour? I do admire a man of dispatch."

"Dispatch, excellent choice of words." For Con would love to dispatch this scoundrel.

"Or we can resume our discussions at another time," Warren said, downing his brandy all at once. "If you've been traveling, you might want to seek your bed and consider the day's developments. I could meet with you, say, Tuesday next, if you're tarrying in the area?"

By Tuesday next, Con needed to be on his way to Scotland—or announcing his engagement. "That won't serve either."

Impatience flickered across Warren's brow.

Con was reaching for his gloves, about to call a man out for the first time, when the door opened.

"Ah, exactly what a fellow hopes to find at the end of a long day's journey." Hector strutted in, followed by Quinton. "Good company, some fine spirits, and a bit of diversion over a deck of cards.

Gentlemen, Lord Hector St. Bellan at your service."

Hector?

And Quinton?

Warren was on his feet faster than Harold settled to his cobbler. "Lord Hector, good evening. Mr. Maurice Warren at your service, and this is Mr. Connor Amadour. Who would your companion be?"

Quint bowed. "Lord Quinton St. Bellan. We had distant family in the area once upon a time and, on a lark, thought we'd pass through on our way to the grouse moors. Very pretty country, but... sheep and dales and dales and sheep, you know, followed by more dales and sheep. A hand of cards can look quite attractive by comparison. May we join you gentlemen?"

"You had family in the area?" Warren inquired carefully.

"A generation or two back," Quint said, taking the seat to Warren's right. "Farmers, from the distaff side of the family. Every ducal family has a distaff side or three. What are we playing?"

They were playing... some game, but Connor had never been happier to see his siblings. Bless Tiger, bless his brothers, bless all family who came to one another's aid unasked.

"Whist," Con said, "and I'm happy to partner you, Lord Quinton or Lord Hector. I've had the advantage of several hours' play with Mr. Warren, so it seems only sporting that each pair include one of you, rather than allow familiars to side against you. I don't suppose either of you travels with a deck of cards? Mr. Warren and I were about to call for a fresh set."

For Quinton always traveled with his own cards, both to pass the time, and to prevent... mischief.

"My brother gifted me with a deck from France," Quinton said. "Freddy's the artistic sort, but it's not a deck one can display before the ladies. While Lord Hector and I wash the dust of the road from our throats, I'll have my man fetch it down to us."

And just like that, the tables turned. Left to skill rather than cheating, Maurice Warren was soon losing badly. Hector didn't help, for which Con was grateful. The cards were honest, and Con and Quint made an excellent team.

They did not cheat, they cooperated.

And they won... and won, and won... until Hector frowned at the scribblings made on a sheet of foolscap.

"I don't mind telling you, Warren, we've about exhausted my immediate cash stores. Doesn't do to keep much of the ready on one's person when traveling the provinces. What say we get serious?"

Quinton sat back. "Your credit is good with me, Mr. Warren.

One hears ceaselessly about the trustworthiness of the English gentry. Backbone of the nation, lifeblood of our economy, and all that. A note of hand is common between gentlemen of means where we come from."

Con remained silent. His brothers had done a brilliant job of being themselves—young lords at loose ends, not as idle as they appeared, but hardly astute businessmen.

They were the best of brothers, though.

"As it happens," Con said, "Mr. Warren and I were discussing an interesting situation before you gentlemen joined us. He has investment opportunities, and lo and behold, I have substantially more cash before me than when I started the evening."

"Give Mr. Warren a chance to win it back," Hector said. "Only sporting thing to do. Besides, these chairs are hard on a man's backside, and the serving maids are glowering at us. I don't fancy a glowering serving maid."

More to the point, Julianna would be worrying.

"Win it back?" Quint scoffed. "Are we schoolboys playing for farthing points? My brother is a duke. I'd love to be able to tell him I won an interest in a mining venture at some rural outpost. What is the name of this town?"

This town was Connor's new home.

"Lesser Puddlebury," Warren said, eyes darting from Quinton to Hector to the calculations on Hector's paper. Warren picked up the paper and studied the column of figures thereon.

"I own a mortgage," he said slowly. "Badly overdue, ripe for collection, tenants barely scraping by. We'd be doing them a kindness to turn them out, in fact. And regardless of which of us foreclosed on this property, it would be a useful addition to my own mineral rights. Mr. Amadour and I were discussing such a venture earlier in the evening."

In other words, Warren would allow even strangers to turn Julianna and the children out in hopes of keeping his mining prospects alive.

A manure pit was too good for such a man.

"I'll wager you," Con said. "My winnings for your mortgage. If the farm is failing as you say, then you're the one being done a kindness, Warren. Nothing says there's coal to be had, and legal proceedings can take forever if the judges are feeling contrary. I daresay their lordships might charm the law into signing a judgment of foreclosure more effectively than either you or I could."

"Mining?" Hector mused, taking the sheet of figures from Warren. "I know many a younger son who's done well with mining investments. Lord Quinton, shall we?"

"Another hand, but then I must seek my bed. This brandy is not quite up to standards, and we'll want to be on our way early. I've seen enough sheep and dales to last me into my dotage."

But they hadn't seen Con's beloved, met the children, or admired the endless beauty of Julianna's farm. Con looked forward to sharing all of that wealth with his brothers, and with Tiger, assuming she lurked above stairs in the inn's best rooms.

The end of the evening was a work of ducal dispatch.

All Con needed to win the mortgage on Julianna's farm was a steady focus on the cards. Con was lying about his identity, of course. He had played both with and against his brothers, but he was also telling the truth.

He was new to the area, had no expertise with mining, and did routinely make business investments on a much larger scale than Warren envisioned. Time to point that out to Uncle Leo, among other things. And had Warren *paid attention*, he might have noticed the evidence of Con's identity glinting on Con's smallest finger all evening.

Con sat back as Hector gathered up the cards and tidied them into a stack. "An evening well spent, Mr. Warren, I thank you. You're out one mortgage, but probably not much of a loss from where you're sitting."

"Perhaps not," Warren said, helping himself to the last of the brandy. "I still have many fine ventures in train."

Quint and Hector muttered good nights, though Hector paused at the door to wink at Con over Warren's head. Con ignored him, lest he offer applause on an excellent and well-timed performance of fraternal loyalty.

Exquisitely timed, in fact.

"And in addition to all of your fine business opportunities," Con said, "you're in anticipation of holy matrimony. A man can't contemplate a more worthy and rewarding venture than that."

Warren grimaced. "She's pretty, I'll give her that, or she used to be. Going a bit... mature around the edges, though. Might have to look elsewhere, in fact."

That grimace, even more than Warren's lying, cheating, and stealing, offended Con on Julianna's behalf. She'd worked damned hard for years, far harder than she ought, because Warren had been stealing from her.

"If you're discussing Julianna St. Bellan," Con said, gathering up his funds and Warren's note of hand, "which would be extremely ill-bred of you, then please be informed that the lady would under no circumstances accept a proposal of marriage from you, for she has already accepted my suit."

He rose, needing to put distance between him and Warren before he did violence to the man.

"Your suit?" Warren peered up at Con. "Who the devil are you to be proposing to Yorkshire farm widows?"

"I'm the man who just prevented you from making good on a despicable swindle," Con said. "Mrs. St. Bellan will anticipate receipt of any and all documents purporting to be notes, mortgages, or encumbrances on her property not later than noon tomorrow. Those documents had best withstand the closest scrutiny by the best solicitors at the command of her ducal relations, some of whom joined you at cards in this very room.

"I noticed," Con went on, "you did not call her situation to their attention when you had the chance, though the lady is much in need of her family's support. You are a disgrace, Warren, and if I were you,

I'd take a repairing lease on the Continent before the mine's creditors get word you're rolled up."

Which they would as soon as Con could put pen and ducal seal to paper.

The bottle hit the table with a thunk as Warren pushed to his feet. "You can't know my financial situation, Mr. Amadour. I'm not rolled up. I have prospects, and my associates understand that business means risk, not like farm crops that come in year after another. Business partners will see a fellow over a bad patch, extend him a bit of credit. Nobody turns his back on Maurice Warren without regretting it."

Righteous certainty backed Warren's statement, as if seven hundred years of breeding and reputation stood behind him, or seven hundred years of arrogance, rather than fortunate birth, greed, and lack of honor.

Con picked up his hat and gloves. "I am relieved to say, Mr. Warren, and I will happily report to my fiancée, that I pity you. Miss Roberta wanted me to knock you into the manure pit, and well you deserve it. I've learned something, though."

"Begone, sir, and have the wench bring me a fresh bottle on your way out."

"I do not take orders from felons, Warren, and Horty's manure pit is pure gold compared to your company. Manure makes the crops grow, while you are a pestilence who'd best make travel plans while he still can."

Con sauntered out, tired but jubilant, only to find Hector and Quint waiting for him in the common.

"I love you," Con said before either brother could set down his drink. "Thank you from the bottom of my heart, and I love you both. I love Tiger, and Freddy too. I love Horty, MacTavish, and the children, of course—very much. Please do not leave the area without paying a call on Julianna St. Bellan. I warn you, you will be stuffed with the best cobbler you've ever eaten."

He hugged his brothers, kissed each one on the cheek, then

dashed into the cool night air and half ran the entire distance back to the farm.

"DAMNED THING IS A FORGERY," Lord Hector said, passing Maurice Warren's so-called promissory note over to Lord Quinton. "That's the sloppiest description of a piece of agricultural property I've ever seen."

"Uncle Hector said damned," Roberta bellowed from that same fellow's lap.

"Sometimes," Julianna replied, "the word takes on its literary meaning." Such as when the signature on the note bore no resemblance to John St. Bellan's handwriting. "Would anybody like more lemonade?"

Connor's siblings had come out to the farm bearing gifts. Lady Antigone traveled with her own stores of fresh fruit, Lord Quinton had already performed a few card tricks for the children, and Lord Hector had brought a colorful picture book of exotic birds that the boys were paging through in a rapt huddle on the porch steps.

"Stay where you are, Julianna," Lady Antigone said, rising from the chair Connor had brought out for her. "I'll fetch the pitcher."

This gathering had started in Julianna's guest parlor, a space in which she'd set foot only to dust in recent years, then moved out to the porch. The children were looking as dazed and pleased with life as MacTavish and Maud did, albeit for different reasons.

"This is a da—right pretty patch of ground." Lord Quinton sat tailor fashion on the floor, his lemonade balanced on his knee. "A pretty part of the world."

"The winters can be a challenge," Julianna said. And how odd to think she might not spend the winter here.

"I'll keep you warm," Connor murmured, but not quietly enough to escape the notice of his siblings. He sat beside Julianna on the swing, the cushions having been given up to his brothers.

With his family looking on, he'd taken a firm hold of Julianna's hand.

She wore Connor's signet ring in place of another token to be chosen when they had access to Edinburgh's jewelers, though Julianna would always treasure this simple ornament the most. For several hours last evening, in the privacy of the best guest room, that ring had been all she'd worn.

And a smile too, of course. She was still smiling, and might never stop. "I don't understand something," she said, over the general merriment. "How did you three discern Connor's location in Lesser Puddlebury?"

"Antigone got the idea of seeing who picked up her reply to Con's letter," Hector said, brushing a hand over Roberta's crown. "We hared about York, following MacTavish as he visited every pawnshop in the city, until Hector simply asked a shop owner if he knew the direction of the big Scot who'd parted with some lovely clothing. The shop owner knew MacTavish from some darts tournament or other, and so out to the countryside, we came."

"We asked about at the Puddlebury Inn," Quinton said. "Heard there was a regular game of cards in progress in the best parlor, and the players included a swell answering to Con's description, though the fellow hadn't even taken a room at the inn. The rest was the best lark I've had in ages."

"The best timing you've had in ages," Connor said. "I cannot thank you all enough for coming to my rescue. I was ready to call Warren out."

Lords Quinton and Hector found it necessary to study the roses, which were in particularly good form on this lovely summer morning. Lady Antigone studied her oldest brother.

"You've done nothing but look after us, Connor. We've been spoiling for a chance to return the gesture, but you never ask for anything. You manage Uncle Leo, mitigate Mama's excesses, keep Freddy from jail, dance with the wallflowers... we've been remiss, not looking after you."

Con stroked his fingers over Julianna's knuckles. "I've been remiss then too, but having seen the error of my ways, I will impose on all of you regularly. I can promise you this as well: When Leo and I are done rearranging the ducal finances, you will have your own funds, and I want neither to hear nor speak of what you do with them, unless you invite my opinion."

"Even Freddy?" Antigone asked.

"Especially Freddy," Con said. "I strongly suspect half his adventures were an effort to keep me from growing too much like Uncle Leo."

The talk wandered on, the boys getting into an argument about the plumage of peafowl, into which debate Connor's siblings entered with high spirits.

"They are pleased for you," Julianna said, beneath Lord Quinton's fanciful insults to Lord Hector's judgment.

"They are relieved, as am I. I think this is what my father would have wanted me to see to first, the protection of my family's heart, and yet, I let it slip from my view."

"John St. Bellan would thank you for seeing to the protection of his family's heart too," Julianna said, laying her head on Connor's shoulder. Foiling Maurice Warren's greed had settled some aspect of Julianna's grief at last—the guilt perhaps, the sense of having been let down by her late husband and wanting to resent him for it.

John had never borrowed a penny against the farm, Julianna was now certain of that.

"We'll visit often," Connor said. "Your first love is buried here, the children adore their farm, and somebody will need to listen to MacTavish fret about the crops and the sheep and Horty's moods."

MacTavish would have the tenancy on generous terms until the children were of age to decide what to do with their legacy. Julianna had suggested this, and Connor had been delighted with the idea.

Connor seemed delighted generally, a veritable Duke of Delight. "I'll be sorry to leave this place," Connor said as the argument shifted from peafowl to the best route up the hill for viewing the farmstead.

"I'm not at all sorry I came. In fact, I don't think that was a bullet that creased my fundament after all. I think it was Cupid's arrow."

Antigone's head came up. "You were *shot* in the... the... *nether parts* with a *bullet*, Mowne?"

Con abruptly looked very much the duke. "Did I say that? I must have misspoken, for a duke would never tolerate such an indignity. Shot in the hindquarters? Never. I was felled by the arrow of true love and intend to remain in that blessed state for all the rest of my days and night."

As it happened, he did just that, and so did his duchess of the dales.

DUCHESS IN THE WILD

Previously published in
Duchesses in Disguise

Dedicated to those with the courage to go exploring,
and to those who sustain the explorers

PROLOGUE

"Avoid the London Season, you said. Enjoy the peace and quiet of the beautiful dales." Sir Greyville Trenton fell silent as his gelding slipped, then righted itself—again.

"The dales are beautiful," Colonel Nathaniel Stratton replied over the huffing of the horses and *slip-slop* of hooves on the wet road.

"If you like varying degrees of wet as far as the eye can see," Kit Stirling added. "Or if you've a penchant for cold. I haven't felt my toes since the first mile out of Lesser Puddlebury."

Grey brought Zeus to a halt as they crested yet another rise and were smacked in the face with yet another wet, frigid breeze. Early spring in Yorkshire left much to be desired.

"What the devil is that?"

"It's a coach wheel," Stratton said, extracting a flask from the folds of his greatcoat.

Twenty yards ahead, the wheel protruded above the grassy swale at the side of the road like a dark flag of surrender. The ruts gouged in the roadway indicated a recent accident.

"Save your brandy, Nathaniel," Stirling suggested. "The survivors might need it."

The coach lay on its side, an enormous traveling vehicle that had apparently taken a curve too hastily. The mud-spattered horses were held by a young groom at the head of the leaders. The lad was soaked to the skin, and looked as if the next gust of wind might blow him down the lane.

The door popped open, and a head swathed in a scarf emerged.

"Halloo!" Stratton called. "Have you need of assistance?"

"Ever the gallant soldier," Grey muttered. "At least we'll die of exposure in company."

"Your sunny nature will prevent that tragedy," Stirling replied.

A long-barreled horse pistol appeared in the hand of the person trapped in the coach. "Stay back."

"*Women*," Grey said. "Worse, we've found a damsel in distress— an armed damsel." The lady had a slight accent, something Continental.

"My favorite kind," Stirling replied, riding forward. "Madam!" he called. "If you're in difficulties, we'd like to render aid."

The lady's head disappeared like a hedgehog popping down into its burrow. She emerged a moment later, still brandishing her pistol.

"Come no closer."

"Female logic at its finest," Grey said. "We're to render gentle-manly aid by freezing our arses off at gunpoint. This damsel has no proper notion of how to be in distress."

"Who are they?" the lady asked, wiggling her pistol in the direction of Grey and Stirling.

"Those good fellows are my guests at Rose Heath manor, my home."

"Perhaps the introductions might wait," Stirling suggested. "We're two miles from safety, the rain shows no signs of letting up, and it's growing colder by the moment."

The lady once again dodged down into her coach-burrow, then emerged *sans* pistol, a second scarved head beside her.

"Our coachman should return at any moment," the second lady

said. She spoke with great—utterly irrational—certainty regarding the prodigal coachman's impending arrival.

"That is at least a baroness," Grey observed. "A woman who expects a man in service to defy the very gods of weather when her comfort is at issue was to the manor born."

"Then let's get her and her friend to the manor posthaste," Stirling said, "before we all freeze for want of somebody to make proper introductions."

I miss the jungle, where welcome was either an honest threat of death or immediate and genuine hospitality.

The thought went wafting away on a sideways gust of rain. Or possibly sleet.

Stratton rode forth and touched a gloved finger to his hat brim. "Ladies, pleased to meet you. We three gentlemen are at your service. Your good coachman might well return, but that he'd leave you here while a storm howls down from Scotland, does not speak well for his judgment. We offer you a cozy hearth not two miles away and assurances of our gentlemanly conduct."

Exactly what a trio of highwaymen would say. Grey rode forward to join his friends at the lip of the ditch. "Ladies, we'll all soon succumb to the elements, making your understandable caution an exercise in futility. Take your chances in the ditch or with us. In the ditch you will drown. With us, you will merely endure bad company, but do so in the midst of adequate creature comforts."

"He makes sense," said a third woman.

Good God, how many of them were in there?

Grey nodded. "Thank you for that observation." He wasn't about to take off his hat in this weather. "Perhaps you'd allow us to make haste as well as sense?"

Some sort of silent conference ensued, with the ladies exchanging glances among themselves. The first one, the pistol-wielding woman, hoisted herself from the vehicle with a nimbleness that surprised, given her voluminous cloak and skirts.

"You," she said, gesturing at Grey. "I'll ride with you."

"If you can contain your enthusiasm for my company," Grey said, riding as close to the coach as he could, "I shall endeavor to do likewise regarding your own. Sir Greyville Trenton, at your service."

She was a youngish woman, and yet, her posture as she stood on her upturned coach was regal, despite the dirty weather pouring down around her. Grey waited—patience was another of his few gifts —until he realized the lady was trying not to smile.

At him.

"Madam, you are welcome to enjoy the invigorating weather at your leisure once my horse is safely ensconced in his stall. That objective remains two miles distant, so I must ask you, for the sake of all concerned, to consider getting into this saddle with all due haste."

She put a hand on his shoulder, adopted an approximate side-saddle perch before him, and tucked her skirts about her.

"You may proceed, sir, and please inform this good beast that one ditch per day is my limit."

That was an Italian accent. An *imperious* Italian accent, something of an oxymoron in Grey's experience.

"Of course, madam. Zeus, take heed."

Grey's mount shuffled back onto the muddy road, while Grey— for the first time since returning to England—also tried not to smile.

CHAPTER ONE

Francesca Maria Lucia Theresa Amadora Heppledorn Pomponio Pergolesi, dowager Duchess of San Mercato, sat as properly as she could, given that she was in the wrong kind of saddle, on the wrong sort of horse, in the wrong country, in the wrong season.

Also with the wrong man, but the concept of a *right* man defied definition in any of the languages with which she was familiar.

Her English was in good repair, but she'd forgotten so much about the land of her parents' birth. The cold, of course, but also how bleak the light was, what little light England had in early spring. How relentless the wind, how cheerless the landscape.

She missed Italy, where being a widow of rank was a fine status; where sunlight, hearty food, excellent wine, and warmth had been hers in abundance.

"Madam will please remain awake," the gentleman sharing the saddle said. "If you fall asleep, the cold can steal over you and create injuries you'll never recall receiving. The ensuing infections can end your life."

His voice would give her a permanent chill before the elements did. "I'm not likely to fall asleep in such charming company, Sir Greyville."

"I beg your pardon?"

He was a big man, and he moved with his horse easily. When Francesca had spoken, he'd tipped his head down to put his ear nearer her mouth. The fool hadn't even a scarf to protect those ears.

"I'm awake," she said more loudly. If nothing else, proximity to Sir Greyville would ensure she remained conscious. With a hand on each rein, he was all but embracing her, and because of the motion of the horse's walk, she was hard put not to bump against him.

"You will have a more secure seat if you permit yourself to lean against me, and you'll make Zeus's job easier as well."

"You're very solicitous of your—"

The dratted animal chose that moment to put a foot wrong and slip in the mud. The jostling tossed Francesca against Sir Greyville, who remained relaxed, steady, and calm behind her.

The horse plodded on, and Francesca gave up the battle for dignity in favor of greater safety.

"Take my scarf," she said. "If I turn up my collar, I'll stay warm enough."

"Take the reins."

Very odd, to converse with a man in imperatives, but for the present situation, expedient. Sir Greyville soon had her scarf wrapped about his neck and ears, while Francesca bundled into his chest and missed Italy.

"What brings three women out to the dales at this time of year?" Sir Greyville asked.

Well, perdition. Englishmen thought they ruled the world—the parts they wanted to plunder—and thus the world was supposed to answer to them.

"A coach, Sir Greyville. A coach brought us out to the dales."

"If we're both to impose on Colonel Stratton's hospitality for the foreseeable future, I had best warn you now. I am a scientist, madam. I study flora and fauna in exotic locations when funds permit. My mind is prone to questioning, to assembling cause and effect from observed data, the way some men must wager or ride to hounds."

He used the word *scientist* as if it were a lofty title—cherubim, seraphim, archbishop, scientist. Francesca had agreed with Olivia and Mary Alice that none of the ladies should disclose her true identity for the duration of this holiday—the roads were doubly unsafe for women of wealth—and yet, she had the sense Sir Greyville wouldn't care that he rode with a duchess.

He wasn't a fortune hunter then. Thank God for small mercies.

"I see neither flora nor fauna to speak of," Francesca replied. She saw green and wet, wet and green, with a topping of slate-gray clouds. Perhaps the epithet Merry Olde England was intended to be ironic.

"In this environment, my objective is to organize and edit the notes gathered from more than three years' investigation into the Amazonian jungles. A lack of biological distractions serves that goal. You have yet to explain what brings you to this corner of Yorkshire."

Weariness brought her here, along with despair, boredom, and—Pietro would laugh heartily at the notion—even some lingering grief, five years after losing her husband.

"Like you, I seek peace and quiet. London at this time of year becomes crowded and pestilentially social."

Widowhood had allowed Francesca to retreat from the worst of the entertainments for a few years, but she was in England now, where the London Season was an orgy of matchmaking in the guise of a social whirl. Execrable English cuisine didn't help one bit, and the chilly reserve of the typical Englishman tempted a sane woman to leave the realm. The impecunious English bachelor, by contrast, was the social equivalent of a barnacle.

The horse started up another incline, leaning into the wind, and the weariness that Sir Greyville had warned Francesca of threatened to overtake her. This was her life now, varying degrees of uphill, bad footing, and bleak terrain.

How had this happened? How had a lively, good-humored, young girl, appreciative of all the privileges of her station, become a creature to whom a muddy ditch did not look nearly as perilous as it should?

"That's our destination," Sir Greyville said as they topped the rise some moments later. "We'll be at the gates within a mile, and the going will be easier after that."

Across the dreary landscape, nestled at the foot of a great hill, sat a manor house. From this distance, details were obscured by rain and mist. Lamps lit on the front terrace and along the drive gave the edifice a fairy-tale quality in the afternoon's deepening gloom.

"I have it on the best authority that we admire the view at the risk of imperiling your dear horse," she said. "Onward, Sir Greyville."

He sent the horse forward without comment. Perhaps Sir Greyville was the kind of man who made a mistress of his work. The Italians understood passion, whether aimed at a vocation, a pastime, or another person. No cold reserve for them.

Sometimes not much sense either, though.

Francesca had plenty of sense, which was why, purely for the sake of conserving warmth, she tucked nearer to Sir Greyville and closed her eyes.

WHAT SORT of woman brought the scent of jasmine with her even in the midst of a pounding deluge?

The lady's hair tickled Grey's chin, the same way her scent tickled his awareness. Pleasing, soothing, enticing—jasmine had a mischief all its own when a man had lived in the tropics for years at a time.

The lady nestled closer, and purely to secure her more safely in the saddle, Grey switched his reins to one hand and wrapped an arm about her middle.

Somewhere in the jungles, he'd been freed of the bothersome longing for female company. Other biologists on the expedition had taken pleasure when the opportunity had arisen, but how was a fellow to explain that the relationship was one of mutual convenience rather than something more permanent when that fellow spoke very little of the lady's language?

And then there was the matter of children. A man who'd leave his own progeny behind when he returned to his homeland was no sort of gentleman, in Grey's opinion, and thus he'd earned all manner of nicknames.

Saint Greyville.

His Holiness.

Sir Monk.

Deprivation had come to his rescue just as the taunts, in combination with the heat, bugs, poisonous plants, jungle predators, and bickering biologists, had plucked his last nerve. Somebody had made off with all of the expedition's rations and two of their boats. The simple challenge of preserving his life had taken precedence over the urge to procreate, an observation Grey would document for the greater scientific community, just as soon as he could deposit—

Who the devil was this woman, anyhow?

"I don't know your name, madam."

"Francesca... Heppledorn... Pomponio."

She spoke as if selecting names from a list, and it occurred to Grey he might have a courtesan in his arms, or a thief, or one of those Italian wives given to poisoning inconvenient husbands.

He took another surreptitious whiff of jasmine before launching his investigation. "My guess is Amalfi Coast, or thereabouts, but you're either not native to Italy, or you were educated at a very young age by people not native to Italy."

She lifted her head from his shoulder. "You can tell that simply by listening to me?"

"I am a scientist and well-traveled, and have met many of your countrymen in pursuit of my investigations." Intrepid lot, the Italians, if prone to contention.

"My father was an English diplomat in an Italian court. I was born and raised in Italy, and Papa thought it prudent to educate me in keeping with the local culture. My mother demanded that I have some exposure to England, so I was sent here occasionally for summers with my grandparents and for a year of finishing school where I met the other ladies in our party. What's your excuse?"

Her story was plausible. Italy was a collection of courts, states, duchies, and shifting alliances—enough to provide employment for an army of English diplomats who preferred good wine and ample sunshine with their diplomatic intrigue and exotic mistresses.

"My excuse?"

"For abandoning the shores of Merry Olde England? You are not a Captain Sir Greyville, or a Colonel Sir Greyville, so you chose to turn your back on your homeland and go larking about in the tropics."

"I wanted to explore the world beyond Kent and Mayfair, of which there is more than most English boys can dream."

Not the whole truth—he'd wanted to get free of his father's expectations and get on with the thankless business of being an earl's spare.

"You don't think English *girls* dream, Sir Greyville?"

Contentious, indeed, though she wasn't strictly Italian. "It's adequately documented that female children of many nationalities dream, but in the normal course, one expects they dream of a home of their own, some babies, a good tisane for a megrim, or a safe lying in. I haven't gathered data on the subject of an English girl's dreams, so I ought not to speculate."

"Perhaps you have noted in your vast observations that the *normal course* is typically the course that benefits men."

"Benefits men? If it does, that's because to the male falls the duty of providing and protecting," Grey countered. "Without his good efforts, which society justifiably supports, the female, given her weaker physical attributes and burdened by the duty to produce young, would soon find herself at the mercy of predators and unkind elements."

Let her argue with that from the comfort of his saddle.

"If the blighted male could keep his breeches buttoned, the

burden of producing young would not become one of the most regular threats to the lady's life. Moreover, the reckless incompetence of a male coachman must be considered when assigning responsibility for my current predicament. Then too, I have yet to see women take up arms for twenty years and leave a continent in ruins."

Her arguments were not without a scintilla of logic, but that was the trouble with amateurs playing at science. They could concoct fancies from anecdotes, casual reasoning, and passionate convictions that bore only a passing relation to rational discourse.

The gates of Rose Heath manor house came into view, and because Stratton ran a proper establishment, the gatehouse was occupied, and a welcome light shone from its windows. As the horses descended the final declivity, a signal light also appeared on the roof of the gatehouse.

"Well?" the lady demanded. "Do you admit that ordering the universe to suit the whims of men rests not on a scientific foundation but a selfish one?"

"Mrs. Pomponio, a gentleman does not argue with a lady."

"He who refuses to fight cannot lose the battle, though he can lose the war." In perfect Latin. "Who said that?"

"*I did*, and I can say it in six other languages."

She had Grey by two languages, and that included the native dialect he'd picked up in the jungle.

He would not ask her how many of her instructors had been men. "The manor house has been alerted to our arrival. You'll have a hot bath, sustenance, and a warm bed within the hour."

The household would not know to heat enough water for six baths, so the gentlemen—coach-wrecking, rutting, war-mongering incompetents though they might be—would have to wait for their comforts until the ladies had been accommodated.

"I am not normally so combative," Mrs. Pomponio said. "I apologize for my lack of graciousness. You are being most gallant."

"Gallant? That's doing it a bit brown, don't you think? It wasn't my decision to rescue you, but rather our mutual host's, and we haven't gone so much as ten yards out of our way to bring you to safety."

Though Stratton and his lady had turned off at some point. Stirling was bringing up the rear with his sodden damsel, who looked none too pleased to be in the company of a notorious London rakehell.

Mrs. Pomponio shifted, tucking her scarf more securely about Grey's neck. This inflicted another whiff of jasmine on him, as well as the novel experience of being *fussed*.

"I would rather you were full of manly drivel and flirtation, Sir Greyville. If you continue being so blunt and honest, I might begin to like you."

"Can't have that, can we?" For then Grey might find himself liking her, with her odd notions, lively mind, imperious speech, and sweet scents.

"I am a Continental widow of comfortable means, Sir Greyville. For the most part, I can *have* whoever and whatever I please. Consider yourself warned." Mrs. Pomponio settled into his arms and closed her eyes, as if napping the last few hundred yards was what she pleased at that moment, and bedamned to sleet, logic, cold, and Grey himself.

Grey let her have the last word, despite all temptation to the contrary.

He hadn't held a woman in years, and her last assertion—that a Continental widow of means was free to dally at will—was true enough, provided the parties were discreet. Fortunately, his own inclination to dally—his potential, possible, *hypothetical* inclination to dally after three endless years of abstinence—would be entirely subsumed by the burning need to get his notes into publishable form.

Thank the everlasting powers for science, yet again.

TO BE HELD in a masculine embrace that sought nothing other than to provide security was lovely.

Also bothersome.

Francesca resented Sir Greyville's gallantry even as she admitted she was starved for proof that *homo gentlemanliness* was not an extinct species. The men who fared best at the ducal court in San Mercato were handsome, flattering, utterly selfish, and as randy as boar hogs in spring. Her father had fit right in, as had her husband.

Francesca had no reason to believe Englishmen in Yorkshire were any different, and yet, Sir Greyville's hands hadn't once wandered where they ought not, his conversation had borne no sly innuendos, and his smiles...

He hadn't smiled. Not once. *How dare he be so genuine?*

Very likely he'd thought Francesca's warning about dallying where she pleased a sophisticated jest. In fact, she hadn't had the nerve to dally anywhere, not with half the court plotting her ruin and the other half trying to propose to her.

Sir Greyville smelled good, of fine wool, cedar soap, leather. Masculine, English scents that put Francesca in mind of girlhood summers in Dorset.

Worse, Sir Greyville Trenton *felt* good. He was solid and warm, a bulwark of masculine confidence and competence. In bed, he'd know what he was about—provided he didn't lapse into biology lectures between rounds of frolic.

As the horse slogged up the drive, the manor house loomed larger and larger. This was not a quaint country cottage, but rather, a substantial and well-maintained dwelling.

A fountain in the middle of the circular drive boasted a sculpture of three swans that would have been a convincing addition to the *Palazzo Ducale* in Venice. Numerous windows marched along the building's front.

Wealth—old, understated wealth—stood before Francesca, and she respected that. A man who commanded resources of this magnitude could have ridden past a toppled coach without a backward glance.

She shivered, despite Sir Greyville's sheltering presence at her back.

"Almost there," he said. "You will be cosseted and pampered within an inch of your reason. Only by virtue of unrelenting self-discipline do I make any progress with my work at all."

"Couldn't you be self-disciplined later?" Francesca asked. "You've endured privations without number, for years. A little cosseting might put you to rights."

"I assure you, madam, I am as much to rights as I care to be put. Science is a competitive undertaking, and findings that remain unpublished do nothing to fund future expeditions. Time waits for no man, particularly not the man of science."

Francesca was growing to hate the word *science*.

"Well, I hope a hot bath waits for this woman of limited patience and frozen toes. I could eat a banquet about now as well, provided the menu included something other than boiled beef, boiled cabbage, and brown bread. If the English could devise a way to boil bread, they'd probably do that as well."

The horse came to a halt beside the mounting block without any apparent guidance from his owner.

"I believe you describe the dumpling, more or less. Feel free to argue with me, however, for the dumpling has no leavening and you seem to enjoy airing your opinions. Lean forward, that I might dismount."

Francesca complied, though she was impressed that Sir Greyville knew how to make dumplings, and would admit as much.

He got off the horse and immediately the cold was worse. The wind cut like so many blades of ice, the sleet came down with more force. Grooms had scurried forth to take the horses, and Francesca had to consciously review the process for getting out of the saddle.

Sir Greyville put his hands at her waist. Francesca braced her hands against his shoulders and prepared for a graceful descent to *terra firma.*

Her boots hit the ground, pain shot up both legs, and the *terra* refused to hold *firma.* She slipped, slid, sloshed, and would have gone down into the mud except for Sir Greyville's steadying hold.

"It's the damned cold," he said. "It steals into the limbs like a fever, only worse. I spent three years longing for the English country-side. I must have been demented to miss this place."

He scooped Francesca up against his chest and strode toward the house. A footman scampered beside them, an enormous umbrella doing nothing to hold the elements at bay.

"I am capable of walking," Francesca said, though her dratted teeth chattered.

"I am *not* capable of providing a decorous escort when the sooner we're out of this blighted weather, the less likely we'll be to die from exposure. If your extremities are numb, you are already at risk of harm."

He could lecture while he hauled her about, though Francesca stifled further protest when being hauled about was such a lovely experience. Whatever else might be true of men of science, their expeditions made them fit and surefooted.

When Sir Greyville reached the front door, Francesca expected him to set her down, but he simply kept moving past the liveried foot-man, pausing only long enough for the aging butler to whisk off Sir Greyville's dripping hat.

Francesca had a vague impression of soaring ceilings, acres of oak paneling, and sparkling pier glasses before Sir Greyville carried her into what looked like a small library.

He deposited her on a sofa before a roaring fire, then tossed two bricks of peat on the flames.

"This is the estate office, and the fire is always kept blazing in here at my request. My notes are arrayed about. Don't touch them. I have a system. Disturb it at your mortal peril."

"You rescue me from the elements only to threaten me with your wrath?" The heat was heavenly, the scent of peat delightful.

"You're a quick study." He went down on one knee and began fussing with the laces of Francesca's boot. "I like that in a woman. So many ladies feign a lack of wits, thinking it attractive. It's not. Nothing could be more tiresome to the typical Englishman than dull-wittedness in a lady."

"You've courted many Englishmen that you've gathered data regarding their preferences?"

Sir Greyville paused between boots. "Have you courted many Englishmen?"

The scarf lay loosely about his shoulders, and Francesca got her first good look at him. His hair would probably be auburn when dry, possibly Titian. His nose belonged on an emperor, and the rest of his features lived up to that nose. Strong, masculine, by no means pretty, but hopelessly attractive.

He was a man in his prime, his complexion darker than most Englishmen's, and he'd age wonderfully.

Unless one of those tropical fevers carried him off prematurely, or some woman delivered him a mortal blow he'd never see coming.

"What are you doing with my boots, sir?"

"Getting them off of you. I assume your fingers are stiff with cold, and the last thing Stratton needs is a sick woman malingering under his roof or passing along an ague to his small daughter. Do you drink tea, coffee, or chocolate? Perhaps you'd rather a toddy or a medicinal glass of brandy?"

"I am perfectly capable of removing my own footwear." Francesca ran her fingers through his hair, flicking the dampness from it. "Your gallantry is appreciated, but unnecessary. Perhaps you'd best get your own boots off, lest the colonel have a sick Englishman under his roof, hmm?"

Sir Greyville's hair was marvelously soft. For a moment, they remained in a tableau, with Francesca engaging in some retaliatory cosseting—he'd presumed to unlace her boots—and Sir Greyville oddly docile on his knees before her, his lashes lowered.

He rose in one motion. "I'll send a maid to you. Don't touch my notes."

Francesca let him have the last word.

Why on earth would she bother touching his notes when touching him was so much more interesting?

CHAPTER TWO

Because Grey had misrepresented his publication schedule as pressing to both Stratton and Stirling, he was not expected to take meals with the rest of the household. He was permitted as eccentric a routine as he pleased, which was very eccentric indeed.

And yet, nothing much was getting accomplished. A lassitude had afflicted Grey ever since arriving here at Rose Heath, and while his mind toyed with ideas—and worries—his work did not progress.

That relative inactivity might explain why he'd taken such notice of Mrs. Pomponio's boots when he'd unlaced them for her two hours ago. Her footwear was beautiful, if impractical. Soft, tooled leather with a ridiculous number of hooks and buttons. Restoring those boots would cost some servant a significant effort.

"You there," Grey said to a maid passing by as he emerged from his bedchamber. "If you'd please fetch a substantial tray to the estate office, I'll take my evening meal while I work."

The maid looked like she wanted to say something, or ask him something, but she merely bobbed a curtsey and scurried off. The help at Rose Heath manor was blessedly well trained, and thus Grey had enjoyed a hot bath despite the presence of the stranded ladies.

He'd enjoyed carrying Mrs. Pomponio inside from the drive too, male brute that he was. He'd claimed to her that his show of strength had been for pragmatic reasons, but in fact, he'd simply wanted to be a gentleman—a useful, helpful creature worthy of a lady's notice.

Elsewhere in the house, Stratton was probably presiding over a delightful meal with the three lady guests and the flirtatious Stirling. The witticisms would flow along with the wine, and the company would be as merry as it was tedious.

"Everything bores me of late," he muttered, sailing into the estate office. The heat hit him with a welcome impact, as did the sight of his notes, all exactly where he'd left them.

Mrs. Pomponio was where he'd left her too, though she was wrapped in a man's night robe and a small hot air balloon's worth of silk nightgown. She looked quintessentially English, with golden hair cascading over her shoulder in a thick plait and the elegant height of the Saxon aristocrat.

At present, that height was curled on the sofa before the fire, and the lady was softly snoring. Completing this picture of feminine contentment were thick wool stockings on her feet—men's stockings, if Grey weren't mistaken.

"Madam."

Her breathing continued in the slow, relaxed rhythm of restful sleep.

She was a widow, and she'd had a trying day. Grey decided to leave her to her slumbers, rather than rouse her. Not strictly proper, but then, neither was ending up in a muddy ditch at the mercy of the elements.

He sat at the desk and resumed transcribing where he'd left off. If he contemplated the magnitude of his task, he'd never complete it. The sheer variety of life in the Amazon jungle was staggering, as was the quantity of rain, the mass of insects, and the array of potentially fatal mistakes a biologist might make.

How long he sat scribbling away, he did not know, but he eventually became aware of Mrs. Pomponio watching him.

"Madam is awake."

"My eyes are open," she said. "Not quite the same thing. What time is it?"

"Going on nine."

She rose and stretched with her back to Grey, and damned if he didn't find her unselfconscious maneuver attractive. Cats stretched with that thorough, unapologetic sensuality. She put him in mind not of the nimble little ocelot, but of the sleek jaguar—the cat that kills with one leap, according to the guides.

"I'm sorry I fell asleep in your sanctum sanctorum," she said, rustling over to the desk, "but for the first time in ages, I'm not cold. You have an interesting collection of notes."

Grey rose, torn between outrage that she'd trespass on his notes and the temptation to invite her to stay warm as long as she pleased.

"I asked you not to disturb my documentation. Was my request in any way unclear?"

She patted his cravat. "You didn't ask. You ordered me not to touch your notes. More than once. A man giving me orders is novel enough in my life that I remark such occasions. Because you have all these papers arranged in piles by date, I didn't need to touch them to read those pages plainly on display. Have you considered arranging them by topic instead of date? I assume that's what the symbols in the right-hand corner are for."

"They are."

She'd bathed, and the scent of dear old English lavender soap clung to her person along with a hint of that damnable jasmine. The nerve of the woman, smelling so luscious.

Her eyes were gray—he'd wondered—and without boots she was a good six inches shorter than he. In bed, the fit would be exquisite.

Grey was wondering if she might caress his hair again—because he was daft, of course—when a knock sounded on the door.

"Come in," he yelled.

A footman and a maid brought substantial trays into the room and set them on the low table before the hearth. The maid built up the fire, the footman lit an extra sconce, and the pair of them withdrew with a murmured, "G'night, ma'am. Sir."

"Did you order dinner for me?" Mrs. Pomponio asked, taking a seat before the tray. "Most considerate of you. I hadn't anything suitable to put on after my bath and couldn't possibly dine in company as I'm presently attired. Doubtless, our trunks should be here sometime tomorrow, but until then, I'm a monument to purloined clothing."

That was *his dinner* she was about to consume. Grey sat beside her, prepared to tell her as much, but she picked up a roll and tore it open with her fingers.

"Is there anything on earth more delightful than fresh bread?" she murmured.

"I can think of a few things."

She gave him a look, steam wafting from the roll along with the fragrance of yeasty sustenance. "Such as?"

Thick wool stockings on a pair of slim, feminine feet. Delicate, contented snoring from the couch while Grey finally made some progress on the section of his treatise that dealt with plant poisons.

"Sunshine, in moderation," Grey said. "Healthy children and how they can laugh at almost anything. Old women telling stories around the fire at night. A sharp razor against the whiskers, safe passage home. Shall I butter that roll for you?"

"I can't possibly eat all of this by myself. You must join me, or I'll earn the enmity of the cook. Never a good idea, to disappoint the cook."

She passed him a butter knife, and Grey nearly forgave her for reading his notes. Her diplomatic upbringing had given her the gift of convivial conversation, and before Grey knew it, he'd eaten two sandwiches, finished a bowl of soup she'd claimed was too bland for her palate, and consumed a sizable plum tart.

The soup *was* bland, though it was hot and hearty, and the conversation was charming. Mrs. Pomponio told him of spilling punch on her own bodice to get away from a presuming ambassador, "pulling a swoon" to earn freedom from another state dinner, and pretending an ignorance of French to avoid the flirtatious advances of a young colonel.

The food disappeared, the fire burned down, and half the bottle of merlot was consumed as well. Despite her outlandish attire, Mrs. Pomponio had shared a meal with Grey as graciously as any grand hostess, and she'd eased some of his restlessness too.

"May I assume your French is as facile as your English and your Italian?" he asked, topping up her wine glass.

"French isn't difficult if your Latin and Italian are on firm footing, and in Italy, we heard French all the time. Why?"

Grey ranged an arm along the back of the sofa and prepared to humble himself—or give the lady something to do besides snoop through his notes.

"One of the pressing tasks before me is to solicit funds from those who support the sciences and have the means to finance expeditions. As much as I must organize my notes and publish my findings, I must also attract the support of a worthy sponsor for my next venture."

"Always, we must be practical," she said. "I take it you have potential sponsors in France?"

"One can't know until one asks, as difficult as it is to request anything of anybody. My family would offer some support for my endeavors, but they tend to confuse support and control."

At every turn.

She took a considering sip of wine. "How can they control you when you're thousands of miles away, beyond the reach of civilization?"

Insightful question. "They will offer funds, provided I marry the bride of their choice. I'll capitulate to that scheme, thinking that one must marry, and if doing so enlarges society's grasp of the known world, it's an acceptable compromise."

"One wonders why the lady would find it acceptable, for she'd be essentially widowed for years at a time while you were off doing all of this commendable enlarging, and she wouldn't be able to remarry or even frolic."

That had troubled Grey as well. What sort of woman married with the expectation that her husband would cheerfully abandon her for the company of insects, poisonous plants, and deadly snakes?

"The scheme has many flaws."

"I gather you are as yet unmarried."

"With the assurances of the young lady involved, I was willing, but my brother took me aside weeks before the nuptials and informed me that, well, yes, the funds were promised, though not at the level initially proffered. The settlements had been drafted, all was in readiness, but a man new to the institution of holy matrimony would be better off exploring, say, the standing stones no farther away than Orkney, preferably in summer. I was to content myself with the study of rocks, for God's sake. Rocks that had been sitting plainly in evidence when Gilgamesh was a lad. No wonder the young lady had had no qualms."

"You were to study rocks indefinitely?"

"Until two male children were thriving in my nursery, and I know what would have come next."

She set down the wine glass. "You would be exhorted not to leave your children without a father figure, or to deny their grandmother's fondest wish for a granddaughter, and of course the granddaughter would desperately need her papa and at least one sister. Family can be most vexing. What did you do?"

"Wrote the young lady an apology, marshaled what private resources I had on hand, and took off for South America. That was nearly four years ago. The young lady married another and has two sons. My brother apologized and said the entire situation was all Mama's fault. She is a countess. If you've not met many titled women, they are a species unto themselves."

She curled her feet up onto the cushions. "Oh?"

"I admire my mother without limit, but I draw the line at studying damned rocks for years on end. In any case, my French is good, not perfect. If I'm to correspond with potential funding sources in France, a review of my prose would be appreciated."

He was asking for Mrs. Pomponio's help, but resorting to that handy fig leaf of English syntax, passive voice.

She bounced about on the cushion, tucking her hems over her toes, her braid inadvertently brushing against Grey's arm.

"I will edit your French," Mrs. Pomponio said. "You have shared your cozy office with me, though I do think your work would be easier if you let me organize your notes by subject."

He liked looking at her, he liked talking with her, he liked *arguing* with her. Some part of his rational mind was strongly admonishing him that this way lay much trouble, but the wanderer who'd finally come home—to a cold, dreary welcome—ignored the warning.

"You might be departing on the morrow," he said. "You'd get partway through the job and leave all in disarray. I have little tolerance for disarray, else I'd never survive my explorations."

"We'll work on your tolerance," she said, patting his hand. "Surely Colonel Stratton would not begrudge three ladies a few days to recover from an accident and repair our coach?"

Why hadn't Grey done a more thorough inspection of the vehicle when he'd had the chance?

Because he'd been too preoccupied with the lady atop it.

"I'll draft my correspondence this evening, and in the morning you can start with my French letters—"

Oh God. He hadn't said that, had he? Yes, he had. He'd referred to contraceptive sheaths by their most common vernacular appellation and set the lady's eyes to dancing.

"I'm sure your French letters will be all that a lady could wish for," she replied, rising. "The meal and your good company have made me quite relaxed. I can hope my bedroom has been adequately warmed by now, and I'll see you—and your letters—in the morning."

"Shall I light you up?"

"Please. I am certain I know where my bedroom is—the Peacock Room, if I recall—but I was certain I'd arrive safely to my destination when I set out this morning."

Grey took a taper from the mantel and used it to light the

carrying candle on the sideboard. "Had your expectations been met, my evening would have been impoverished."

That specimen of gentlemanly drivel happened to be the truth, which might be why Mrs. Pomponio merely smiled and took his arm.

She was not a giggling girl, or a countess who regarded her family as so many chess pieces.

And she'd not touched his notes, not in the strictest sense of the words.

Grey led her upstairs in silence, their footsteps muffled by thick carpets. The house was too big to be anything but frigid in the midst of an early spring storm, and yet, for Grey, a little warmth lingered. He'd spent an enjoyable evening with a lady who didn't expect brilliant wit or boring small talk from him, and she'd agreed to read his French letters.

He almost burst out laughing halfway up the steps, but instead settled for kissing Mrs. Pomponio's cheek when he bid her good night.

If she was to read his letters, he'd best spend the rest of the evening writing the damned things, hadn't he?

HOW COULD a man who was so clearly brilliant at his calling be an utter dunderhead about asking for funds?

Francesca sat at Sir Greyville's desk, reading letters that swung from abject pleading, to exhortation, to flights of biological hypothesis, to claims of grand medical contributions (and profits), back to scolding.

As a professor, Sir Greyville would be magnificent. His ability to advocate on behalf of science was touchingly inept.

"Ah, Mrs. Pomponio, you are an early riser."

The great scientist stood in the doorway to the estate office, a cup of something steaming in one hand, a slice of buttered toast in the other.

"Good morning, Sir Greyville. I trust you slept well?"

He closed the door with his foot. "You may trust no such thing. I have yet to acclimate to this dreary latitude, and everything from the quality of the daylight, to the cold, to the texture of the sheets against my skin, conspires to keep me from the arms of Morpheus."

Even in a royal pet he exuded energy and rationality.

"I slept wonderfully, thank you," Francesca said. "To be safe and warm and in the company of good people with hot chocolate and shortbread to break my fast was a much rosier fate than I courted yesterday."

He wrinkled his lordly proboscis. "Quite. How bad are the letters?"

So that's what had him worried?

"Awful. Your French is good, with just enough minor imperfections that the recipient can feel superior to yet another hopeless Englishman, but your technique is sadly wanting."

He slouched into a chair on the other side of the desk. "I know. I haven't the knack of cajoling, which puts me at a sore disadvantage. I had a devil of a time at public school. Can't say the young ladies thought much of me either. No charm."

On that signal understatement, he bit off a corner of his toast with good, straight, white teeth.

"You have integrity and brains," Francesca said, passing over the first of the letters. "I took a few liberties with your prose."

He set aside his coffee—the scent was wonderful—but not his toast and munched his way through the letter.

Francesca enjoyed watching him, enjoyed watching his gaze move across the page as he demolished his toast slice. That he would approve of her efforts mattered more than it should.

"You're a damned genius," he said, springing to his feet. "This is brilliant. A touch of flattery, a bit of regret for the loss to the world should its wonders remain needlessly unexplored, a casual disparaging of those squandering means on idle pleasures... You're very, very good, Mrs. Pomponio."

His praise was precious, not only for its sincerity, but also for its uniqueness. Men complimented duchesses incessantly. Francesca had endured odes to her eyes, her hair, her wit, her hands, her grace, her eyebrows, for God's sake.

The men offering all of this praise did not bother to ascertain whether the compliment bore any relation to the woman at whom the words were flung.

"I'm glad the letter meets with your approval. I was raised by diplomats, and delicacy of expression was served at every meal. I was also my father's secretary and amanuensis after my mother died. I revised a few more of your letters, but have several yet to read."

Francesca had been eager for something useful to do, something interesting. After peeking at Sir Greyville's notes yesterday—but not touching them—she'd gained an impression of a restless mind as insightful as it was observant as it was imaginative.

God forbid this man should be shackled to some dreary old ring of stones for the rest of his days.

He peered down at her, his expression quite severe. "Madam, I do not approve of this letter, I damn near venerate it. Show me the others."

Another order. A woman whose letters were worthy of veneration could make a few rules.

"Say please."

He aimed another glower at her over the last of his toast. "Everlasting goddamned please, I beg you, won't you please, I entreat you, may it please madam to look favorably upon my humble treaty—and for good measure, because I am a man smitten by the talent I see on this page—if you'd be so endlessly kind, may I *please* see the other letters?"

Francesca handed over two more letters. "Smitten lacks credibility coming from you, but you did say please."

Smitten was lovely, as was the ferocity in his dark eyes. They were brown, with agate rims that put Francesca in mind of winter seas.

"I am as smite-able as the next man, and I tell you sincerely..."

He trailed off, the second letter in his hand. He wasn't like some Englishmen who had to move his lips to read French. He could drink coffee and read at the same time, unerringly grasping the cup, bringing it to his mouth, and setting it down without taking his gaze from the page.

"Shall I do the rest of them?"

"A moment."

His concentration was absolute. What would it be like to have that concentration turned on *her*? And did the texture of English sheets offend his skin because he slept without benefit of a nightshirt?

Francesca hoped so.

"This one is as magnificent as the last," he said, setting the second letter down. "Your penmanship, your turn of phrase, your salutation —every detail—is rendered to encourage a favorable reply. I am in your debt."

His penmanship was legible, but like him. No soft curves, no graceful details. Communication in its most utilitarian form.

"Nonsense. You pulled me from a muddy ditch, Sir Greyville, and lectured me to safety, then fed me dinner and kissed me good night. I will have to write many letters to repay your kindness."

"I did kiss you good night," he said, peering down at his mug of coffee. "I hope you took no offense."

She'd been surprised, pleased, and slightly disconcerted.

Duchesses were not allowed to be disconcerted, poor dears.

Though scientists were apparently allowed to be shy.

"My name is Francesca," she said. "You have my leave to use it."

"My friends call me Grey."

A nice moment blossomed, with morning sun streaming in the windows, the peat fire blazing in the hearth, and Sir Greyville smiling at his coffee cup.

His smile was sweet, devilish, subtle, and unexpected. Francesca was surprised to discover that the man was gorgeous, but for the toast crumbs on his cravat.

"Do you need to work at this desk?" she asked. "I can manage at the table."

"That would suit. Shall I ring for a tray?"

"Nothing for me, thank you." She rose, pleased to have more work to occupy her. All of her personal effects—her embroidery hoop, her flute, her lap desk—was lashed to the boot of the upended coach. This situation had proven something of a challenge when it came time to dress.

The Rose Heath attics had been raided though, and Francesca was attired in a marvelously warm wool day dress ten years out of date.

She organized herself at the worktable, Sir Greyville settled in at the desk, and soon the sound of two pens scratching across foolscap joined the ticking of the clock and soft roar of the fire.

"I'm happy."

Sir Greyville looked up. "Beg pardon?"

"I didn't mean to say that aloud, but it's true. I'm happy. I have nothing of my own with me, I'm far from home, in very unexpected surroundings, but I'm happy."

"Then you're on a successful expedition. Carefully study the terrain, weather, flora, and fauna and take copious notes."

He went back to his transcribing, and Francesca to her letters. One went to a lady, a French comtesse who was visiting friends in York. Currying her favor required a slightly different approach. Francesca took a break between letters to look in on Mary Alice, who'd suffered a few injuries when the coach had overturned.

When Francesca returned to the estate office, she finished the letters and stacked them on the sideboard. She then indulged in the temptation to study the fauna sitting behind the massive desk.

Sir Greyville had hooked a pair of wire-rimmed spectacles about his ears and propped his boots on a corner of the desk. Very likely, he'd forgotten Francesca was in the room, much less in the same country. From time to time, he'd mutter something in Latin, or brush the quill feather with the fingertips of his right hand.

"You're left-handed," Francesca said. "That explains part of your difficulty drafting pretty correspondence."

"So it does, but not all. I simply haven't your gift."

She brought the letters over to the desk, and he stood, as if realizing that a gentleman doesn't prop his boots on the furniture in a lady's presence.

He took the letters and set them aside. "I will read them word for word, not to assure myself that you accurately conveyed my sentiments, but rather, to learn from your example."

"If one of the Frenchmen funds your next expedition, you must write to me. I would be pleased to know I was of aid to modern science."

She brushed the crumbs from his cravat and kept smoothing her hand over the froth of lace and linen when not a single crumb remained.

"Madam?"

"You asked me a question earlier."

"I am a font of curiosity. You'll have to be more specific."

He smelled good, he looked good, and Francesca abruptly felt both bold and vulnerable. "You didn't ask, exactly. You said, 'I hope you took no offense.'"

He caught her hand in his. "Because I kissed you. On the cheek."

"I took no offense. I haven't been kissed, on the cheek or anywhere, for a very long time."

Then she kissed him. Not on the cheek.

CHAPTER THREE

The last person to kiss Sir Greyville Trenton had been Professor Hiram Angelo van Ostermann, a Belgian with a passion for orchids. Grey had brought him several intact, healthy specimens from Mexico and had been treated to that Continental effusion, the triple kiss—left cheek, right cheek, and left cheek again. They'd been parting after a long evening of wine and science, and the professor was the sentimental sort when it came to orchids.

Sentiment was too tame a word for the response Mrs. Pomponio —Francesca—evoked with her kiss. She was no blushing girl to ambush a fellow then go giggling on her way. She remained in the vicinity, her lips moving on his, tenderly, sweetly, intimately.

Not a good-night buss, not thanks for orchids safely delivered. She offered a kiss as lovely, intriguing, and varied as the densest forests and loftiest mountain peaks, and *by God*, every sense Grey possessed begged her to continue her explorations with him.

As her arms stole around his waist, and the soft, full female shape of her swamped his awareness, he could admit that he'd been starving for human touch and parched for sexual joy.

Not mere erotic pleasure—pleasure was as close as his left hand.

Joy. The delight of reveling in animal spirits with another, the glory of being a human creature in the full flood of shared biological imperatives.

Grey took Francesca in his arms and settled her on the desk. A pile of notes went cascading to the floor, and he jolly damned didn't care.

She broke the kiss and rested her forehead against his shoulder. "Mother of God, Sir Greyville."

He stroked her hair and marveled at the arousal coursing through him. "Was that a happy Mother of God or a dismayed one?"

She lifted her head enough to meet his gaze. "Both, or more accurately, impressed. Have you made a study of kisses, gathered data on many continents, compared findings?"

Grey rummaged about for the pretty way to say what he felt, then gave up, because if he bungled his answer, this would be their first and last passionate kiss.

"If I were to undertake such a study of kisses, I'd have to start in Italy, among the daughters of English diplomats." He was distracted for a moment by the scent of Francesca's hair, which bore the fragrances of lavender and jasmine.

"To narrow the sample population further," he went on, "I'd focus on the blond ladies with fine gray eyes, who have put the foolishness of youth behind them and yet gained impressive skill with the kiss. Ideally, my investigation would be limited to those subjects named Francesca Pomponio. If the subject were willing, I'd make a very thorough study of the topic."

She gave him her weight. "You are a very silly man."

"Yes."

Silly and, to use her word, happy. At that moment, with his notes littered across the carpet and Francesca in his arms, he was happy.

He and she remained thus, arms entwined, while Grey wallowed in the pleasure of holding a willing woman, one who returned his embrace and enjoyed his kisses.

"I'm distracting you from your work," Francesca said.

She was asking a question, exercising the delicacy of expression that preserved Grey from being the one to inquire.

"You have distracted me from everything. I think perhaps I needed a distraction. What news do we have of your coach?"

She eased away, and Grey let her go, only because he could console himself with the sight of her. Her lips were a touch rosier, and a single pearl-tipped hairpin was dangling from her chignon.

"Our host says that righting the coach will take some effort, and then at least two wheels will require repair, and he suspects an axle has been cracked as well. He predicts, between spring storms, the Yorkshire roads, and the extent of the damage, we will be cast on his hospitality for at least two weeks."

Thank God for Yorkshire mud. "Are you disappointed?"

She went to her knees and began picking up Grey's notes. He assisted, passing them to her so she could restore them to order.

"You will think me one of those forward, pathetic, Continental widows, but no, I am not disappointed. I am *interested*, Sir Greyville, in making a study of you."

They were on the rug, both of them kneeling, several pages still lying about.

Her admission troubled her, while it delighted Grey. "I would like to be studied. I have so little to offer any woman, that my opportunities for... What I mean to say is, that in so many words, I rarely find myself... Bloody hell. I want to kiss you for the next two weeks straight."

She regarded him as if he'd lapsed into the native dialect of the upper Amazon basin.

"I gather you neglected your kissing while you were so attentive to your science."

"I neglect everything when I'm absorbed with a project. I get crumbs on my cravat, forget where I put the glasses sitting on my very nose, and have been known to write on my cuffs rather than go in search of more paper, but for the next two weeks, I would very much enjoy getting to know you better."

That was as delicate as he could be, and damn anybody who intimated that a short mutual indulgence in pleasurable intimacies with Francesca Pomponio would put him behind on his work.

Further behind.

"You are bound to return to your jungles?" she asked.

The jungle belonged to the Almighty or to the Fiend, depending on the day. Grey couldn't tell whether Francesca wanted reassurances that he wouldn't plague her with expectations, or wished he had more to offer her.

So he gave her the facts. "I doubt I'll return to the Amazon, but I will return to the field. I'm suited to investigation, and it makes me feel alive."

So did her kisses. Interesting coincidence.

She cupped his cheek with her palm, soft female warmth to freshly shaven male angles. "I have been a widow for five years, and I do not undertake an intimate friendship with you lightly. I barely know you, and you know even less of me. Maybe that is what allows us to wander into this jungle together, the knowledge that we'll part, and fondly, but we will part."

Englishwomen didn't make speeches like that. They also didn't seem a very happy lot.

"We'll part very fondly if our first kiss is any indication."

"That was our second."

Grey crawled to her side of the rug. "This will be our third."

FRANCESCA HAD WATCHED all of the intrigue, drama, and influence-trading in the Italian courts with a certain dispassion. When affairs of the heart had entangled with political machinations, as they often did, she'd been honestly baffled.

What could possibly be worth enduring such a *mess*? Such inconvenience and potential loss of dignity? Horrendously public marital discord, needless violence, lavish gestures, and plots behind every

marble column had seemed like so much farce to her, much to her
father's amusement.

"Someday, you'll understand," he'd said.

Pietro, nearly twenty years her senior, had said much the same
thing.

Well, the great insight was at last befalling her. As Sir Greyville
Trenton prowled on all fours across the carpet, Francesca gloried in
the sense that nothing, not his science, not a servant banging on the
door, not a promise of funds for his next expedition, would have
stopped him from initiating their third kiss.

Better still, he wasn't embarking on this frolic in the dales
because he wanted political favor, or access to the family wing of the
palace, or the cachet of having enjoyed the intimate favors from the
ducal widow.

Sir Greyville wanted *her*.

In her plain, borrowed dress, with her hair in a bun worthy of a
retired governess, and not a jewel in sight, Sir Greyville wanted her.

He touched her hair and leaned very close. "I need to lock the
damned door." He kissed her nose and got up in one lithe move, then
locked the door.

Francesca remained on the carpet, not trusting her knees to
support her should she stand.

"Madam, if you continue to gaze up at me like that... On second
thought, I wish you'd always look at me like that." He extended a
hand down to her and pulled her to her feet. "When you regard me
thus, I feel like one of those sinfully delectable cream cakes devised
by the Italian chefs. All I desire is for you to consume me, and you are
happily intent on that very goal. I have never been anybody's cream
cake. The sensation is rather like being addled by fever."

He was fearless, if a bit eccentric in his choice of comparisons.

"When you look at me," Francesca said, "I want to kiss you. I
can't believe I said that. I'm not normally... That is... The Italian court
culture is interesting. The men can be hounds, but then, with whom
are they hounds, if not with the women? Some men prefer the

company of other men, of course, but on the whole, between wives, mistresses, ladies of easy virtue, and affairs, a great deal of..."

In no language could Francesca finish the thought she'd been bumbling toward.

"A great deal of mating behavior takes place?" Sir Greyville suggested, kneeling to pick up the last of the papers.

"Yes, exactly. Mating behavior. I did not participate in it. I didn't want to compromise my privacy, or allow anybody undue influence over me."

"You flatter me," he said, rising, "though I gather flattery is not your intent. I've been similarly unwilling to embroil myself in any situation that could prove inconvenient when it came time to embark on another expedition. One must avoid creating expectations, on the one hand, and subjecting oneself to the risk of disease, on the other. One must be prudent, and that is a bloody nuisance I am happy to temporarily depart from."

He stacked the papers, tapping the edges of the pages against the desk until the lot was tidy, if no longer in exact date order.

"We must exercise discretion," Francesca said. "My friends are ladies, as am I."

"And you are in the company of gentlemen. Have no fear that what transpires between us will become grist for the London gossip mill. I can't stand Town, myself, and if I didn't have to periodically give papers or meet with potential sponsors, I'd never set foot south of Oxford."

Well, thank heavens. Francesca was in the wilds of Yorkshire precisely because she too had no use for the London Season. A wealthy widow with a title was bachelor-bait, and she'd had enough of that in Rome, Paris, Milan, and Berlin.

"How do we do this?" she asked.

"You aren't asking for a biology lecture, I trust?"

He'd launch into one if she were. And if he did, she'd find it arousing. Ye gods and little fishes.

"I was married for five years," Francesca said. "My husband was thirty-six when we married and assured me he was quite competent in the bedroom. He was considerate and... considerate."

With his mistresses, he'd doubtless been passionate, but with a wife, his attentions had become downright boring. That hypocrisy was an aspect of Italy that Francesca didn't miss at all.

"Then he was a dunderhead," Sir Greyville said, shaking a drop of coffee from his empty cup into his open mouth. "Meaning no disrespect to the departed, but he ought to have been passionate, wild, demanding, playful, inventive, tender, adventurous, accommodating, and—why are you looking at me like that?"

"You are an authority on marital intimacies?" Pietro had accounted himself such, though Francesca had had her doubts. What woman would tell a ducal lover that he lacked playfulness?

Though he certainly had.

Sir Greyville set down his mug. "The institution of marriage is a uniquely human invention. In the wild, animals mate at will and, in many species, un-mate at will. In varying degrees, they cooperate to raise the young, but just as often, the union is based on mutual protection or passing whim. One cannot escape biology, and if the male of the species doesn't want his mate growing bored, uninterested, or quarrelsome, he'd damned well better show some willingness to contribute to her contentment."

"I'm in the presence of a radical," Francesca said, but then, Sir Greyville was likely passionate in all his opinions.

"Marriage," he said, "has no counterpart in nature, unless you allow for a few species that pair for life to raise young, though their sexual fidelity is far from assured. The human parties, by contrast, speak their vows and are stuck with one another. If the lady plays a man false, he is compelled by law to support the resulting offspring. What is radical about taking steps to ensure those offspring are his? If he is the most attractive source of intimate pleasures, those odds increase. I'm considering writing a paper along these lines, but Stratton says he'll disown me if I publish it."

Sir Greyville had taken to pacing, as if his mental energy was so abundant, it even moved his body.

"I suspect the Church of England would ex-communicate me," he went on, "which means my mother would have an apoplexy. Over a simple theory supported by common sense and abundant observation. You see the frustrations a man of science endures on every hand?"

His friends probably told him he'd been in the jungle too long and had no idea how their teasing bewildered him.

"Galileo was threatened with death for propounding a theory," Francesca said, "one that has been proved true."

If she'd kissed him, he could not have looked more pleased. He took her by the wrist and led her to the sofa.

"You asked a question earlier," he said, waiting for her to be seated, "about how we go on with this intimate friendship. How would you like to go on with it?"

Ten minutes ago, with kiss number three a heartbeat away—kisses to the nose didn't count—Francesca would have said she wanted to *go on* immediately, on any handy surface that wasn't too far from the fire.

"May I have a day to think about that?" she asked, feeling very bold—also stupid. What woman delays eating a cream cake after five years of going without?

"That is an excellent notion," he replied. "My best experiments have all been the result of focused contemplation. If I might make a suggestion, though, I'd like our first encounter to be in a bed."

Good heavens. "Not too much to ask."

"I am easily chilled in this climate and in this house, and cold is not conducive to optimal reproductive functioning for the human male. Beds are not cold when occupied by an enthusiastic couple."

Sir Greyville Trenton was not cold either. He was brilliant, unusual, fearless, and unique, and even before Francesca had become his lover, she knew one other thing about him: When she climbed into the repaired coach with her friends and left the Yorkshire Dales behind her, she'd miss Sir Greyville Trenton for the rest of her life.

"Beds are cozy," she said. "I will look forward to embarking on this adventure with you in a warm, cozy bed. Shall we get back to work now? I'll start on that stack of notes that was knocked asunder by our... that was knocked asunder."

By their mating behavior.

"A fine plan, though given your skill with a pen, I might have word of funding in less than our allotted two weeks."

He didn't seem entirely pleased with that prospect, and Francesca took what comfort she could from the briskness of his observation.

CONTRARY TO COMMON PERCEPTION, the scientific mind was driven as much by imagination as by ratiocination, at least Grey's was. The prospect of an intimate liaison with an intelligent, lovely, learned, and discerning lady—and no messy entanglement to follow— ought to have distracted him from his work.

To his surprise, the opposite was true.

With Francesca rustling about in the office, Grey could finally settle to his writing. He could let his mind roam over hypotheses, data, and conclusions, over descriptions of specimens he'd not seen for more than two years, but must bring to life on the page for his scientific brethren.

And sisters. The occasional woman plied her hand at science, usually side by side with a spouse, father, brother, or uncle. Intrepid lot, though none of them had ever stirred Grey's mating fancies.

"Your lunch," Francesca said, causing him nearly to jump from his chair. "Which you will please eat."

She stood beside Grey's desk, arms crossed, looking like a delectable governess—a contradiction in terms, based on his child-hood acquaintance with the species.

"Is it noon already?"

"One of the clock. You ordered a tea tray at ten and then didn't touch a thing on it. I was compelled to help myself lest the staff be offended."

"What is this staff you speak of?" Grey lifted the lid from a bowl of soup. The scent of beef and potatoes alerted him to the fact that he was hungry—famished, in fact. "I don't recall seeing evidence of any staff."

"I refer to the footmen who came in twice to build up the fire, once to deliver the tea tray, and once more to inquire regarding our wishes for the midday repast. I'm off to assure my friends I yet draw breath, while you, I suspect, must remain in the wilds of Peru."

"Brazil, actually. I won't reach Peru for a week at least." Grey's desk was littered with paper, most of it covered with writing and sketches, a few pages bearing a single heading.

The tray at his elbow included sandwiches and a bowl of stewed apples. He adored stewed apples, had dreamed of them in the jungle, which was probably a sign of mental imbalance.

"Sir Greyville." Francesca leaned closer. "Eat. Put the pen down. Pick up the spoon, or the butter knife, or a sandwich, but eat. You'll be nodding off over your notes an hour from now if you don't take sustenance."

He did that—fell asleep at his desk.

"You and my mother would get on famously," he said, buttering a roll and dipping one corner in the soup. "She is a formidable woman, and I respect her greatly. None can stand before her version of hospitality. At the conclusion of her house parties, guests are rolled out to their coaches in wheelbarrows, felled by an excess of Mama's hospitality. Have you grown weary of my scintillating company already that you must flee our literary laboratory?"

Francesca wandered off to toss more peat onto the fire. "Some of us must get up and move occasionally. I'll take a turn in the garden while the sun is out. I suggest you leave the room as well. Inspect the fountains, visit your horse, lose a game of billiards to yourself. Get out of that chair."

Grey considered lifting the bowl of soup to slurp the contents jungle-style—he was that hungry and the soup that good—but he was in the presence of a lady, one spouting daft notions.

"If I leave my desk, the work, which is going well for once, ceases to progress."

"If you fall asleep over your soup," she retorted, "the work ceases to progress, and your linen is the worse for your lack of moderation. I should be back in an hour or two."

"Francesca." He didn't want her to leave, which was silly. Perhaps he was a very silly man, after all.

"Sir Greyville?"

"Grey will do. Thank you for your company this morning."

He'd flustered her. He rose, because a little flustering was good for the soul. Possibly. The hypothesis wanted testing.

"My father was much like you," she said, rearranging the peat over the coals. "When he had a pen in his hand, all else ceased to have meaning for him. He wrote books on diplomacy, memoirs, travel guides. He loved to write, to listen to other people's stories, to document his observations. He had a marvelous wit, which was half the key to his diplomatic success."

Had that worthy diplomat ever listened to his own daughter?

Grey took the wrought-iron poker from Francesca's hand, set it aside, and wrapped his arms around her. "I will miss you." He referred to the general case, commencing two weeks hence, but when Francesca said nothing, he retrenched. "I made great progress this morning. If you tarry among your friends, I will pine for your quiet presence. How are the notes coming?"

She'd begun the reorganization of his notes, from chronological order to grouped by subject. The task was tedious, thankless, and detailed. Grey would have put it off for years, but Francesca was not only ploughin through it, she was making cross indexes, so any topic or date could be found easily.

"My greatest difficulty," she said, reciprocating his embrace, "is that I start to read what's on the pages. You have a gift for accurate description, for connecting stray bits into a coherent whole. I'm learning a lot."

She was probably learning a lot about the man who'd written the notes, which bothered Grey not at all.

He held her for a moment, gathering her warmth. Lions sat close to one another while watching the moonrise, and Grey understood a little better why. In Francesca's embrace, he found peace, and also sadness. They'd part as she'd reminded him.

Fondly, but they would part.

"Off to lunch with you," he said, easing away. "The jungle calls me."

She kissed his cheek and was gone on a soft click of the door latch.

In fact, the jungle no longer called to Grey. He'd been so bloody sick of the place after the first year, he'd known he'd never return. With that conclusion in mind, he'd made his one expedition count, staying until the last possible month. He respected the jungle, appreciated its beauty and its great variety, but he'd not make a career of braving its dangers.

He'd earned the right to describe himself as "an explorer of the Amazonian jungles," a coveted credential, but at present, he was more interested in exploring his friendship with Francesca Pomponio.

They had only the next two weeks for that adventure, after all.

CHAPTER FOUR

Francesca had spent the morning peeking inside the mind of a man who was part poet, part artist, part logician, and part healthy male animal. Sir Greyville had delighted in exertion of the body as well as of the mind and had covered thousands of miles in the time some of his colleagues could barely cover hundreds.

He noticed everything, from insects, to rock formations, to tiny blooms, to wildcats that outweighed most grown men. His sketches included smiling native women—not a stitch of clothing to be seen— and a fearsome fellow who had worn a necklace of enormous teeth and little else.

Francesca had told her friends that she was delighted to assist Sir Greyville with his work—which she was—and that she'd be equally delighted to depart when the coach was repaired.

Which she would not be.

Oddly enough, she suspected her friends might also be reluctant to resume the journey, which made no sense, for they had to be bored. If they'd sought boredom, they would have endured yet another London Season.

Francesca detoured to her room to fetch a shawl, for even on a sunny day, a turn in the garden had left her slightly chilled.

The lunch tray sat outside the estate office door, not a morsel of food remaining. She opened the door without knocking, lest she disturb Sir Greyville's concentration.

At first, she didn't see him, but a soft snore alerted her to his presence on the sofa. He didn't fit, so one knee was bent, and the other foot was on the floor. His arms were crossed, and his neck was at an awkward angle against the armrest. His battered tall boots stood side by side at the end of the sofa, like a pair of grizzled, loyal hounds waiting for the return of their master.

In sleep, Sir Greyville looked younger, also more tired. His English complexion had been darkened by the sun, and even in repose, he had crow's feet at the corners of his eyes. Francesca eased the earpieces of his spectacles free and draped her shawl over him.

He craned his neck and muttered something, possibly the Latin words for cooked apples.

Francesca lifted his head, tucked a pillow against the armrest, and left him to his slumbers—despite the temptation to run her fingers through his hair a few more times. She'd been back working at the notes for some time, developing an index of maps and sketches, when the sofa creaked.

"I am brought low by beef stew," came from the sofa. "Why doesn't anybody make a damned sofa sufficiently commodious that a short respite after the midday meal need not occasion a crick in the neck and cramp in the shoulders?"

"Why doesn't anybody think to leave the office and use a bed for such a respite?" Francesca replied.

He sat up abruptly, a crease bisecting his left cheek. "You have finished your luncheon. What time is it?"

"Going on three. The mail has arrived and is sitting on your desk."

He rose, folded the shawl over his arm, picked up his boots, and came to the table to lean over Francesca's shoulder.

"I dreamed of you. You were swimming in some damned grotto, attired as nature made you. Shall I come to you tonight, Francesca?"

In his notes, he'd referred to a jungle cat that killed with a single leap. Francesca felt the opposite, as if she'd been quickened, brought to life, by that one question. Sir Greyville's breath fanned across her neck, followed by a sensation so tender, so warm and unexpected, she closed her eyes the better to withstand it.

His fingers pushed aside the fabric of Francesca's dress, followed by his lips, right at the join of her neck and shoulder. He cradled her jaw against his palm, traced her ear with gentle touches, and in the space of a minute melted every coherent thought from her mind.

"This will not do," he said, resting his forehead against her shoulder. "I grow aroused simply touching you. Tell me to sit at my desk, Francesca, and say it as if you mean it."

"Grey."

His lips again, so soft, and the barest scrape of his teeth. "Hmm."

"Yes. Now go sit at your desk. This instant."

He tarried another moment, then straightened and ever-so-cherishingly draped the shawl around her shoulders. Francesca nearly asked him to do it again, so precious was his casual consideration.

"Yes, I should come to you tonight?"

"Must I draw you a diagram?" Francesca took up a penknife and pared a finer point onto her goose quill. "You asked a question, and I answered it. Now answer your mail, or grouse about your neck, or put your boots back on. Your spectacles are in your pocket."

He sauntered off. "I hope you're as assertive in bed as you are in the office, for I am not shy when it comes to carnal joys—as best I recall. I like to approach such occasions with an agenda, a list, if you will, of activities and the order in which I'll undertake them."

"The mail, Sir Greyville. Correspondence. Sci-ence."

"In our case," he said, settling into the chair, "my agenda will be succinct." He pulled on both boots and sat back. "*Make Francesca scream with pleasure.* Best to stick to simple imperatives when a situation is likely to become fraught, don't you agree?"

"Heartily. Shut your naughty mouth, or I will revise my agenda for the evening."

He donned his glasses and shut his naughty mouth, and Francesca did not revise her agenda.

She hoped he wouldn't either.

AS THE AFTERNOON WORE ON, the weather continued unabatingly English, which was to say, cold, wet, windy, and disobliging for two minutes, then achingly lovely for five. If Grey had been able to take a turn in the garden with Francesca, he might have abandoned his increasingly discommodious chair. If he'd been able to go for a hack and put her up on a guest horse beside him, he might have even left the estate grounds.

Perhaps tomorrow, after they'd become lovers in fact.

He set aside a page full of detailed observations and never-before-published theories to take a moment to behold Francesca Pomponio. Surely the mating urge was affecting his brain, for the picture she made tempted him toward maudlin phrases and impossible hopes.

Firelight gilded her hair.

The curve of her jaw begged to be cradled against his palm.

That sort of maudlin tripe.

Grey consoled himself with the knowledge that maudlin tripe contributed substantially to perpetuation of the species. He'd simply never been afflicted with such a bad case of the mating urge before, and that had to be a consequence of prolonged deprivation.

A good scientist put his faith in the simplest hypothesis that explained all the data.

He did not "tear his gaze" from the sight of Francesca brushing the quill feather across her lips, but rather, resumed reading his correspondence.

Scientists did their part to keep the royal mail in business, and Grey was no exception. He debated theories and experimental design with dozens of colleagues, congratulated them on their triumphs, and commiserated with their frustrations.

The third letter had him out of his chair. "May the Fiend seize that rabid, two-faced weaseling disgrace of a poseur and inflict on him a lifelong case of the quartan ague."

Francesca put down her pen. "I beg your pardon?"

Grey waved the letter at her. "Harford, the ruddy bastard. He stole my idea."

"How can one steal an idea?"

"He assured me at great length that he was done with fieldwork, had had enough of its savagery and deprivations. He vowed he was ready for a professor's chair, pipe, and slippers. Too many damned biologists, he said, as if the botanists aren't overrunning the jungles at a great rate. I maundered on about the vanilla orchid and the insect that must be responsible for its pollination."

Francesca rose and took the letter from him, scanning its contents. "He's off to search for this moth or bee or whatever, and thanks you heartily for encouraging him to pursue the idea."

"I never encouraged him, not in the least, and I should have known he was inviting me to unburden myself of a lucrative theory. Harford is by no means a pure scientist, but then, neither am I."

She folded the letter and set it aside. To Grey, the correspondence should have come banded in black, so bitter was his sense of betrayal. He'd liked Harford, had enjoyed arguing plant morphology with him, and had considered collaborating with him on some future expedition.

"What is a pure scientist?" Francesca asked, leaning back against the desk. "You make it sound as if there's some sort of chastity at stake."

"Not chastity, but nobility of purpose." She'd moved enough stacks of Grey's notes that he had room to sit on the desk, so he perched beside her. "One can pursue new knowledge for its own sake, because knowledge in itself has virtue, or one can take a more applied approach."

She took off her shawl and folded it over her arm. "You refer to money, though you resort to typical English roundaboutation to do it. A pure scientist has a rich papa or wife. The fellow who takes a more applied approach might turn his discoveries into coin."

Grey would forever associate the scent of jasmine with the soothing balm of honest, common sense.

"More or less, but even among the more pragmatic men of science, we don't steal each other's ideas."

"*You* don't steal other people's ideas, Sir Greyville. Of that, I am convinced. Moreover, your close associates well know where this theory originated, because they know you. If this Harford person goes off on his bee quest, your colleagues will all know where he got his inspiration. I cannot but think that a profession dedicated to accurate observation and clear understanding will ostracize such a charlatan."

Grey took off his glasses, folded them into a pocket, and kissed Francesca's cheek. "Thank you. I would have taken two weeks to talk myself around to such wisdom. You're right, of course, and my colleagues will all be very circumspect in their discourse with Harford henceforth. The problem is, this was one of my ideas most likely to attract a wealthy sponsor. Vanilla is valuable, but hard to propagate outside its native environment. The issue is pollination, which refers to that process by which, from season to season, the plant propagates—"

"Copulation, you mean, for the vanilla plant."

"It's an orchid, technically. I do seem fixated on certain activities, don't I?"

She leaned into him and slipped an arm about his waist. "You're a biologist. Of course you're fascinated with propagation. You'd be reduced to studying rocks, otherwise. Rocks needn't propagate, poor darlings."

They remained for a moment in that half-embrace, for Grey's arm had found its way about Francesca's shoulders.

"When I was nine," he said, "my older brother decided he preferred my pony to his. He'd been given a pony a year before I had, being the elder and the heir, and thus my pony was a particular joy to me. I'd trained the little beast in all manner of tricks and told him all my sorrows. His name was Tiger. I was informed by my father that one pony was as good as another, and I was to surrender my mount out of filial loyalty. My brother was taller than me and thus deserved the larger equine."

"I hope Tiger tossed your brother into the ditch on his spoiled little head."

"Tiger was a perfect gentleman, and so was I, but I've taken a dim view of thievery and dishonesty ever since—a dimmer view. My brother was not taller than me. I'd already gained nearly an inch on him, though my father had failed to notice. I take infantile delight in the fact that I'm two inches taller than his lordship now."

"Good. Did your brother ever apologize? Stealing a horse is a grave offense under English law."

A capital crime, as a matter of fact. The realization gave Grey's childhood memory of betrayal a better sense of proportion.

"I'm not sure he knows an apology is necessary. I yielded what was mine and pretended I'd rather enjoy the countryside on foot anyway. Thus was a biologist born, at least in part."

Francesca shifted so she stood between Grey's knees, her arms about his waist. "I pretended I didn't mind my husband's endless procession of mistresses. I yielded what was mine too."

A SMALL BOY'S pony was of great importance to that boy, whether he was English, Italian, or Persian. Francesca stood in the circle of Grey's embrace and admitted that at least Pietro had not set his sons against each other intentionally.

Just the opposite. With the children of his first marriage, he'd been generous, but fair and even-handed. He'd also been a model duke, and—if Francesca were honest—a disappointing spouse.

"If your husband was variously unfaithful, he was an ass," Grey said. "I hope you told him as much. Men are not beasts, entirely at the mercy of their procreative urges."

Was a duke more or less of a beast than other men? "The wealthy, well-born Italian male is a privileged creature from the moment of his birth, rather like your brother. Pietro was simply an exponent of his upbringing."

Grey rested his cheek against the slope of her breast. "I don't believe that, else my brother should have turned out to be a tyrannical, selfish, philandering terror. Sebastian is actually a decent fellow. Your husband made choices, and one of them was to wed you and recite public vows of fidelity. I gather he was somewhat older than you?"

To hold on to Grey, and to be held, fortified Francesca. She did not normally dwell on her marriage, but Grey saw the situation with a logical mind and, apparently, no particular loyalty to his gender.

Refreshing, that.

"I was eighteen, he was thirty-six and so very dashing. He flattered, he flirted, he charmed as only an Italian man at the height of his powers can charm. My father encouraged the match for diplomatic reasons, and I was desperate for a household of my own. The wedding night was sweet, magical, enchanting, and I convinced myself I'd found a fairy-tale prince."

Why did the grand old fairy tales never feature dukes as their heroes?

Grey sat back and brushed his thumbs over Francesca's cheeks. "Francesca, I'm sorry. If a man will break his vows to his God, his community, and his wife, he has no honor. I realize my views are quaint, laughable even, but I cannot abide a hypocrite."

Francesca turned so she could lean into Grey's embrace. She'd rather be closeted in a dreary office with this quaint man than share the splendor of a ducal court with her late husband. She hadn't realized she'd needed a man—a man whom she esteemed—to confirm her instincts, but Grey's apology helped ease a grief that had started within two weeks of her wedding.

"To appearances, Pietro was attentive, and that was the extent of the fidelity he believed was required. He found my histrionics juvenile and even touching, but really, what was the problem? He'd always be available to *accommodate me* when I had need of him. His mistresses in no way diminished his regard for me, or his willingness to tend to me in bed. I simply made no sense to him. I was a toy he could not figure out, though a pretty enough toy."

Grey stood, which put the length of him smack up against Francesca. He was quite tall up close, a good six inches taller than Pietro had been.

And yet, to an eighteen-year-old bride, Pietro had been imposing indeed.

"If that was your husband's view of his marital obligations," Grey said, "then he was nothing more than an orangutan with powers of speech, meaning no disrespect to the orangutan. I have argued this point with many a colleague. We cannot as a species claim the Almighty awarded us dominion over the earth and then act among ourselves with no more civility than stray dogs. Even in the most remote wilderness, predator and prey manage to share the water holes without descending into outright interspecies warfare."

Francesca kissed him. "And at that point in the discussion, somebody changes the subject, for your logic is irrefutable while their arguments rely on an interpretation of Scripture uniquely supportive of their vices."

"They change the subject or mutter about how poor Sir Greyville was in the tropics for too long. Kiss me again, please."

Francesca obliged Grey with a spree of kissing that banished the miseries of the past and reassured her that he desired her honestly and for herself.

"Promise me something," she said, stepping back. "Promise me you won't accommodate me tonight."

Grey took out a prodigiously wrinkled handkerchief. "You will please explain yourself."

The handkerchief was for polishing his spectacles, which Grey held up to the light coming in the window. He might have been asking Francesca to explain her mama's recipe for syllabub, and yet, Francesca knew she had his attention, despite the call of the jungle.

"Don't insinuate yourself beneath the covers without uttering a word," Francesca said. "Don't kiss me on the cheek, climb aboard, and start thumping at me until you collapse two minutes later as if you're Pheidippides after running from Marathon to Athens. One wants some communication about the business, a certain mutuality of participation, not... not thumping."

She could never have said that to her husband, because after the first two weeks of marriage, she'd mostly wanted his thumping over with. From his mistresses, the duke had expected passion; from his duchess, duty was all he'd sought.

The rotter.

Grey stuffed his handkerchief back into his pocket, all willy-nilly. "Francesca, if I begin to thump, however you define the term, you tell me to stop, describe how you'd like us to proceed, and I'll make appropriate adjustments. You are not the subordinate on this expedition, and I have no more of a map or compass than you do. That said, my bed is the larger, so I'd rather you insinuated yourself beneath my covers than the other way around."

"That makes sense." And also allowed her to arrive and depart as she pleased. "Are we expected to join the others for dinner?"

"I am forgiven my eccentricities when it comes to attending meals, in the interests of science, or perhaps because my dearest friends need only a little of my company to remind them why they allow me to disappear into the jungle for years at a time. It's threatening rain again."

The office had become cooler as the afternoon had progressed. For a man acclimated to the tropics, the chill would be significant.

Francesca wrapped her shawl about Grey's shoulders and returned to the table, which was closer to the fire. "I'll order us trays, and the others will have to manage without us."

Grey resumed his place at the desk, her cream wool shawl about his shoulders like an ermine cape. He made an eccentric picture, but as he read, he occasionally paused, sniffed at the wool, and smiled.

Francesca got back to work—the ocelot was an interesting crea-ture—but her view of the upcoming days and nights had changed. She wasn't merely addressing lingering disappointment over her marriage, or taking advantage of an opportunity for some discreet pleasure.

She was falling in love, and with a man who longed to disappear into the jungle once again.

GREY'S PRIDE had not let him share with Francesca the full brunt of his dismay at Harford's betrayal.

Dismay being a euphemism for utter, roaring, wall-kicking, head-banging rage with generous helpings of profanity in at least three languages.

Harford had not only charmed Grey's theories about the vanilla orchid from him, he'd spent an entire bottle of wine listening to Grey debate which widowed countess, beer baron, or coal nabob would likely support an expedition to test that theory.

And one of Grey's carefully cultivated wealthy contacts had apparently decided to fund Harford's expedition.

"Damn and blast." Sebastian had introduced Grey to most of those wealthy contacts, and this turn of events would disappoint the earl mightily.

"Did you say something?" Francesca asked.

"The time has got away from me," Grey said, rising stiffly. Good God, his arse hurt. "One would think I had nothing to look forward to this evening, when in fact my anticipation knows no bounds."

So his acquaintance with Harford was a failed experiment in resisting the lure of professional charm. Francesca's hand in marriage had been surrendered on the strength of some randy Italian's charm, and that loss had been far greater.

And yet, she had arrived to widowhood with dignity, humor, and self-respect intact.

"I wanted to get through an entire year of your notes," she replied —*primly*. "You've been in that chair for the past ten hours, more or less. I don't know how you endure it."

Grey had taken a short break when the call of nature had become imperative, as best he recalled. "I'm the determined type, though my detractors call me stubborn. Shall you seek your bed now?"

The clock had chimed eleven, and the house had acquired the quiet stillness of nighttime deep in the country.

"I will seek *your* bed," she said. "Do we go up together, or exercise some discretion?"

"We go up together, and I bid you good night at your door, so you might enjoy some privacy as you prepare for your slumbers. You dismiss the maid and then come to me."

She peered at him over his glasses, which she'd purloined after they'd eaten supper. "You've thought about this."

"I've thought about little else." And yet, Grey had been productive. Not only in the sense of having scrawled words onto pages, but also on a deeper level. Francesca's occasional questions, her counterexamples, and pragmatic retorts were his guides in a jungle of words and theories, did she but know it. As the afternoon had worn on, Grey had grasped theoretical interrelationships, sequences of ideas, and narrative connections that would make his summary both lucid and interesting to non-scientific readers.

"You've thought about little else?" she asked, taking her shawl from his shoulders. "Then what were you writing the livelong day?"

Without her shawl, the room was colder, though Grey could ignore cold. He'd liked having the scent of jasmine all around him and knowing he wore something of hers.

Perhaps he truly had been in the tropics too long.

"I was writing about adventures," he said, plucking his glasses from her nose. "And now, instead of writing about adventures, I'd like to embark on one. With you."

She sailed out the door ahead of him, but he suspected he'd pleased her. Grey snatched up a candle from the mantel and followed her into the frigid dark of the corridor.

"Where exactly will your next expedition take you?" she asked.

"India, I hope." Provided somebody put a small fortune at his disposal.

"To do what?"

He took her hand as they gained the stairs. "Set up a tea plantation, if I'm lucky. Before I went to South America, I had a chance to tour parts of China in the company of some Dutchmen. When I left China, I found that somebody had used my luggage to smuggle a quantity of tea seeds and slips out of the country."

"Another one of your high-minded men of science at work?"

"Not bloody likely. The Chinese guard their tea more closely than we do the crown jewels, and with good reason. But for tea, in my opinion, we'd still be a nation of gin sots. Had the contraband been discovered before I left China, I'd be the late, disgraced Sir Greyville Trenton. I'm hopeful the plants can thrive in parts of India, but must undertake further experimentation."

"You've waited four years to make these experiments?"

"For the past four years, while I've been bumbling about in the jungle, those plants have been carefully propagated by a trusted friend in the far western reaches of India. I hope that habitat closely approximates the growing conditions in China. Ceylon might do as well and is more accessible by sea. I simply have more investigation to do."

To talk with Francesca about his dreams was precious, as was watching her spin his notes from straw into gold, as was seeing her bustling about with his glasses on her nose.

If this was a manifestation of the mating urge, Grey had never seen or heard the symptom described by any biologist. Poets had probably maundered on about such sentiments, but little poetry had found its way into Grey's hands.

"India is very, very far away," Francesca said, pausing outside her door. "I'm glad, for the present, that our bedrooms are only across the corridor."

"So am I."

Grey was also glad that the windfall of tea had shown up in his baggage, though doubtless, somebody else had been very un-glad not to recover their stolen goods, and yet, Francesca was right. India was so very, very far away.

"Take your time," he said, bowing over her hand. "Take as long as you need, and join me if, and only if, you truly wish to do so."

She went up on her toes and kissed his cheek. "I won't be long."

And then she was gone.

INDIA WAS NOT DARKEST PERU, but it was still half a world away, and as Francesca took down her hair and tended to her ablutions, she hated India.

For good measure, she hated China too, and ocelots, and those larger exotic cats with the name she wasn't sure how to pronounce. She hated biology, and botany, and that Harford weasel—she hoped the Mexican jungles gave him a bad rash in an inconvenient location or two—and she hated desperately that coach wheels and axles could be repaired in a mere fortnight.

"I have landed in a very muddy ditch, indeed," she informed her bedroom. The maid had built up the fire, bid Francesca pleasant dreams, and quietly withdrawn.

If the staff or any of the other residents of Rose Heath suspected that Francesca and Sir Greyville were embarking on a liaison, they'd given no indication, and yet, Francesca hesitated.

She'd never done this sort of thing before—of all the pathetic clichés—though she'd also never encountered a man like Sir Greyville Trenton, and probably never would again. On that thought, she charged across the corridor and entered Grey's room without knocking.

"I'm nervous," she said, remaining by the door.

The room at first appeared empty, then Grey's head appeared over the top of a privacy screen in the corner. Half his face was covered with lather, and he had a razor in his hand.

"I am unsettled as well," he said, scraping lather from one cheek. "This is not my typical excursion into uncharted territory. Do I shave, or will that make me too much the fussy Englishman? Italian males tend to be hirsute. Perhaps the lady likes a fellow sporting some evening plumage. Will my English pallor and relatively light hair coat be unappealing to her? Do I turn the covers down, or is that presumptuous? Cold sheets are damned unromantic, if you take my meaning. You will note I've turned down the quilts and built up the fire. Give me a moment, and I'll pour you a glass of wine."

He could shave himself and prattle at the same time. Francesca had never seen her husband shaving—being shaven, rather.

Francesca came around behind the privacy screen and treated herself to a view of a long, trim back, shoulders and arms wrapped with muscle, and damp hair curling at Grey's nape. Even at twenty years old, Pietro would not have exuded this much fitness and vitality.

Watching Grey complete his toilette, his movements unselfconscious even when half-naked, Francesca was abruptly angry all over again.

Two weeks? All she was allotted with this considerate, handsome, brilliant, plain-spoken, hardworking man was *two weeks?*

Then she'd damned well make them count.

"Take as long as you need," she said, going to the bed, "and join me if, and only if, you truly wish to do so."

She was unbelting her robe when Grey embraced her from behind. "Don't be nervous, Francesca. Be honest, and for the next little while, be mine."

His words gave her a bad moment, because she hadn't been entirely honest. To him, she was merely Francesca Pomponio, widow of some wealthy Italian. Would Grey, who was English to his bones despite his world travels, be upset to learn she was a dowager duchess, and not simply well-off, but disgracefully rich?

Francesca decided to ponder that issue later, when Grey's lips weren't tracing the line of her shoulder and his arousal wasn't increasingly evident at her back. She turned, wrapped her arms around him, and kissed him as if he were departing for India in the morning.

And merciful angels, did he ever kiss her back.

He could have plundered, but instead he investigated. His kisses were by turns stealthy, sweet, tender, and devious. He sipped, tasted, teased, and all the while, his hands wandered over Francesca's nightclothes. He shaped her hips, then her waist, then cupped her derriere and urged her closer.

"Bed," she muttered against his mouth. "We embark on this adventure in a bed. Now."

"That's honest. Also an excellent suggestion." He stepped out of his breeches and tossed them in the direction of the privacy screen. "If you need assistance disrobing, I'm happy to oblige."

Happy, was he? His *felicity* was magnificent, and he was utterly unselfconscious about that too. More Englishmen should spend time exploring the jungle, if Sir Greyville Trenton was any example.

"What is the scientific term for that particular variety of happiness?" Francesca asked, handing him her robe.

He sent it sailing to the privacy screen as well.

"The *membrum virile*, aroused," he said. "Erect, rampant, engorged. Happy applies as well, while you are shy."

Francesca was, but Grey had not only seen all manner of women unclothed, he'd sketched them.

In detail.

"I need assistance." And time. Francesca wanted years and eternities with Grey, and not two dreary little weeks on the Yorkshire Dales.

He started at the top of her nightgown, untying bow after bow with deft, competent fingers. With each bow, Francesca felt her past and all its disappointments and frustrations falling away. She wasn't a dewy, innocent bride and was glad, for once, that inexperience and ignorance no longer plagued her.

Grey stepped back when all the bows had been undone and nakedness was a single gesture away.

"Only if you want to, Francesca."

He meant that. He would take nothing from her as a matter of right or assumption—not her time, not her trust, not her intimate affection.

She drew back the sides of the nightgown, let it fall from her shoulders, and handed it to him. "Tell me what you see."

He folded her nightgown and tucked it under the pillows, then walked a slow circle around her.

"Female," he said. "Age between twenty-five and thirty. Caucasian, blond hair, gray eyes, heritage predominantly Saxon, possibly by way of the Danes or the Norsemen. Height about five and a half feet. No obvious deformities or significant scars. In good weight, with good muscle tone. No evidence of parturition."

He was asking a question. They'd avoided the topic of children until now.

"Two miscarriages," Francesca said. "One somewhat bruised heart, though time has mended most of the damage." Then she was back in his arms, skin to skin, the scent of cedar blending with his body heat.

"Francesca, when I look at you, I see heaven. I see every good thing. Every human, wonderful, pleasurable joy, and I want to share them with you, right now."

He scooped her off her feet and laid her on the bed.

SOMEDAY, Grey wanted to ask Francesca about the miscarriages, about how she came to be widowed, about any family she still had in Italy. He wanted to know about growing up at an Italian court and if her heart would again be bruised when they parted.

He wanted to know everything about her, and not as a scientist examines a specimen.

"I promise not to thump," he said, which caused Francesca to smile against his shoulder. He'd come down over her when he should have taken a moment to admire the picture she made naked on his bed. She was the mature female goddess, rounded in ways the typical Englishwoman was not—thanks be to Italy—and both sturdier and more feminine as a result.

"Aren't you cold?" Francesca asked.

Grey had neglected to draw the covers up, and yes, his backside was cold. She was warm, though, and soft, and fragrant, and naked.

"How am I to think of covers when your abundant charms are resplendent in my very bed?" he groused, sitting back to yank the quilts up. He took the place beside her on the mattress and drew her into his arms.

Now that the moment was upon them, any pretense of finesse had deserted him. "You mentioned communication and mutuality of participation, madam. This would be an ideal time to elucidate your meaning."

She sighed and snuggled closer, and Grey relaxed. They were to talk, apparently, and of all people, Francesca was the person with whom he'd never wanted for conversation.

"Tell me about your home," Francesca said. "About your dragon of a mama and your decent brother. I was an only child, and both of my parents are dead. I have two aunts, whom I dutifully visited in Sussex before coming north."

His home? A fine place to start. "I haven't a home, exactly. I have some means thanks to one of my grandmothers, and I own a lovely estate in Kent, which I rent out. Property close to London is in demand, and I'm seldom in England for long periods."

"Do you want a home?"

She asked the most peculiar questions, but they bore the insight of a colleague at a distance from the subject.

"I haven't given it much thought." *Until now.* "There are

nomadic peoples who thrive, but their wanderings are driven by the
need for food, fresh grazing, fuel, or other necessities. As an Englishman, I was raised with an attachment to the land—king and country,
et cetera—but my livelihood and my contribution have rested on
exploring wildernesses. What about you?"

He'd dodged the question. Spouted off knowledgeably on irrele-
vant tangents in the best scientific tradition. Though how was a man
to ponder imponderables when delicate female fingers were stroking
over his chest and belly?

"I own property in Italy and England," Francesca said, "also
lands in France, though I'm thinking of deeding the French land to
my tenants. It's difficult to manage an agricultural holding at a
distance, and the wars left so many in France with so little."

"Keep a portion of that land," Grey said. "French vineyards are a
lucrative proposition, though they take time to become profitable. I
have an associate who can advise you in detail. The man is mad about
grapes."

Francesca's caresses were driving Grey mad, and she still hadn't
ventured below his waist.

Time to do some exploring of the treasures at hand. Grey drew
Francesca close, close enough that he could stroke her neck and
shoulders.

"I would not have thought you'd be mad about tea," she said,
leaning over to kiss his chest. "I've become fascinated with the scent
you're wearing."

"A colleague sent it to me. It's made from a bunchgrass native to
India. *Khus* is drought resistant, and can also withstand submersion
for weeks if the root system is developed. Generally noninvasive—
God in heaven, Francesca."

She'd scraped her teeth across his nipple. "Perhaps you can grow
this grass in your tea garden."

Grey endured in silence while she explored his chest, his ribs,
and eventually—three eternities and four ground molars later—the
contours of his arousal. Her touch was more curious than bold,

suggesting her late husband had failed utterly to indulge his lady's scientific inclinations.

"You desire me," she said.

"Madam has a talent for understatement. One hopes my sentiment is reciprocated."

She arranged herself over him and pinned him at the wrists as the end of her braid hit his chest. Her next experiment involved letting just the tips of her breasts touch him as she fit herself over his arousal.

Grey tried to catalog impressions, but got no further than *heat*, *dampness*, and *madness* as Francesca began to rock.

"I have investigations to make too," she said, "and experiments I've longed to perform, but I was never in the right company, never properly provisioned. Move with me, please."

He became her private wilderness as she kissed, tasted, caressed, and undulated. By the time Francesca took Grey into her body, he was a welter of need and delight, longing and jubilation. This was erotic intimacy in the ideal, a joining so profound it eclipsed awareness of any other reality. Grey might have been back in Brazil or on a ship to India, for all his surroundings had fallen from his notice.

There was only Francesca, pleasure, and wonder.

"Up," he said, patting her bum. "I want to touch you." Needed to, and not only for his own satisfaction. He was in bed with a woman glorying in the wonders of her body, and he was determined that no pleasure should be denied her.

"You are touching me," she retorted, complying nonetheless. "You are most assuredly... I like that."

He'd covered each full, rosy breast with a hand and counterpointed thrusts and caresses. Francesca's nipples were wonderfully sensitive, and when her head fell back, and she surrendered to sensation, Grey made a vow to get her damned braid undone before the next time they coupled.

Because there would be a next time, and as many times as he could manage between now and when she left him.

Francesca's breathing quickened, and she pitched forward, her movements becoming greedy.

Grey held her, and held on to his self-restraint, while she thrashed her way to completion on a soft, sweet murmur of his name. For long moments, she remained panting in his arms, and his own satisfaction surprised him.

He hadn't spent, and didn't intend to when it would risk conception, and yet, he was happy, proud, and content, despite the clamoring of desire.

Francesca's breathing slowed. She kissed Grey's cheek and whispered in his ear. "I bring news from Marathon. The Persian invaders have been routed by our brave forces. Let the celebration begin."

CHAPTER FIVE

Reason, the enemy of passion and adventure, tried to dim Francesca's joy not three hours after she'd left Sir Greyville's bed, and bedeviled her over the next sennight.

She was not a giddy girl, to be falling in love after five years of widowhood. In one week, she'd be leaving, and then this interlude on the stormy dales would be nothing but a memory. She had been overdue for some pleasure, long, long overdue, and Sir Greyville Trenton had happened into her life at the right time under the right circumstances.

"Balderdash," she muttered.

Grey peered at her from the chair behind the desk. "Beg pardon?"

He looked delectable, with his spare pair of spectacles perched on his nose, his cuffs turned back, and his jacket hung over the back of the chair. His eyebrows would grow more fierce as he aged, but Francesca couldn't imagine his heart growing any more fierce than it already was.

Perhaps Pietro had been a selfish dullard, but Francesca suspected the boot was on the other foot: Sir Greyville Trenton was a force of nature in bed, on the page, and everywhere in between.

"Creating these indexes will be my undoing," she said. "You refer to the same plant or insect by its English name, its local name, and its Latin name, if it has one. I often don't grasp that you're referring to the same bug or flower until the tenth time I see it. You're just as bad with landmarks, and that's before Spanish and Portuguese get involved."

"I hadn't realized I'd created such a muddle."

He'd created the muddle to end all muddles, and not only in his notes.

"I've decided to use English as the unifying reference," Francesca said. "The glossary will be in English, with all foreign language terms listed after the English definition. If that doesn't suit, you can devise some other system on the voyage to India."

He rose and came around the desk. "If I get to India. I've had nothing but rejections and silence in response to my letters."

They'd developed a system in this regard as well. The mail came in, Grey opened it, and he stacked the rejections on the corner of the desk. When Francesca wanted a break from ocelots, jaguars, and indexes, she wrote a gracious response to the rejection. She begged leave to keep the esteemed party informed regarding future developments and thanked them for their continued interest, with all good wishes, et cetera and so forth.

Grey signed the letters and off to the post they went, to be replaced by more disappointment the next day.

Each night, Grey made love with her more passionately and tenderly. Each afternoon, he opened the mail and became quieter and more pensive.

"Your friends seem well-off," Francesca said. "Colonel Stratton and Mr. Stirling, I mean. I realize asking for their support might be awkward, but needs must."

Grey drew her to her feet and wrapped his arms around her. "They both supported the last expedition generously. I have hopes that some of the samples I brought back can be developed for medical or horticultural purposes, but so far, it seems I've discovered more poisons, of which the world already has enough. My memoirs will bring in some revenue, and I did find four new species of orchid that will catch the interest of the bromeliad enthusiasts. Even so, I can't ask for more money without showing a return on the investments already made."

He would not accept support without giving something in return, damn him.

"What about your brother?" Francesca asked. "You gave him your pony. If he's an earl, surely he has some coin to spare."

Grey drew away, went to the sofa, and patted the place beside him. "I'll tell you a secret, one unknown even to my friends."

Francesca knew much about Sir Greyville Trenton that she suspected nobody else knew: what a mare's nest he made of the covers when he was dreaming, that he missed England for all his talk of thriving on exploration, that he was an accomplished artist with an eye for natural beauty, that he was both affectionate and playful.

And that she would miss him for the rest of her days.

"As a diplomat's daughter, I learned to be wary of secrets," she said, coming down beside him. "They can be more trouble than they're worth."

He wrapped an arm around her shoulders, and Francesca cuddled close. They'd taken to working like this in the evenings, she reading over his writing for the day, and he reviewing her work. The closer the time to part came, the more constantly Francesca craved Grey's touch.

"Here's the Trenton family secret: Earldoms cost a perishing lot of money. If anybody ever offers you one, politely decline, lest you end up bankrupt. I suspect this is why peers cannot be jailed for debt, because a need for coin goes with the lofty title."

Francesca's late husband would not have argued. On the rare occasions when Pietro lost his temper, it was in response to one of his sons overspending, or one of his ministers failing to manage within the budgetary means allotted.

"Your brother is pockets to let," Francesca said. "That's why you rent out your estate in Kent, because your family needs the money."

Grey let his head fall back against the cushions. "I made the suggestion that Sebastian and my mother use my estate as their residence and rent out the family seat. This sort of thing is done fairly often, though I know it causes talk. The scheme was eminently sensible, the family seat being huge, commodious, and well maintained. Mama threatened to disown me. Sebastian's wife would rather plague visit the house than become an object of pity."

Francesca scooted about, wiggling down to rest her head against Grey's thigh. "They refuse to practice economies, so you go hat in hand to strangers, hoping to find a means of supporting your family while risking your life, braving all manner of hardship, and having no home of your own."

His hand paused mid-stroke over her hair. "You sound like Stratton and Stirling, though they aren't half so blunt and at least wait until we've done some justice to the brandy."

"I loved my husband, Grey. He was a good man, though far from perfect. When he became ill, and his mistresses took up with his wealthy friends, he apologized to me. He began to make promises, all of which began with, 'When I'm back in good health...' He never regained his health, and our marriage never blossomed into what it might have been. I want you to blossom."

She used the edge of her sleeve to wipe at her eyes. "Two years in China, four years in the jungle, you mentioned a voyage to Greenland when you were twenty. Is that what you want for the rest of your life? Do you really owe your family that much risk and deprivation, year after year?"

He lifted her into his lap, when Francesca had feared he might leave the room.

"I cannot abide your tears," he said, mopping at her face with a wrinkled handkerchief. "Francesca, you must not cry. Please stop."

"I c-can't," she wailed. "I don't want you to go. I know you love the adventure, and I know you make a great contribution, but I want you to be safe and happy, and I want—"

He kissed her, which was fortunate, because she'd been about to confess to wanting to sleep beside him every night, whether in a bed, a hammock, or on the bare, hard earth.

"This is why I must go to India," he said. "Because there, if I can learn to cultivate tea, I will have a commodity of great value, and I'll be able to produce it within the British empire. I can also teach others how to grow it and use my plantation to start more tea gardens. The venture could be enormously lucrative, and while India is far away, it's not the Amazon jungle. I can see no other way to justify the faith my friends and the scientific community have shown me, Francesca. Fortune for once smiled upon me, and I owe it to my country and my family to seize the opportunity with both hands."

Grey grabbed the afghan from the back of the couch and wrapped her in it. Francesca closed her eyes and reveled in his embrace, even as she resented his devotion to honor.

All too soon, one of those dratted wealthy sponsors would realize what an opportunity Grey's next adventure posed, and he'd be away again, for years, possibly for the rest of his life.

And yet, she found a reason to be comforted too.

He was no longer spouting lofty platitudes about science, knowledge, and the betterment of mankind. He'd admitted to a very human ambition to look after his family. Francesca had been unable and unwilling to compete with science as Grey's first passion, but she understood the need to care for loved ones.

She understood that need very well and fell asleep pondering how she might assist him to reach his goal, because she cared very much for him indeed.

"ANOTHER ONE," Grey said, putting the letter on the stack for the day. "The comtesse has developed a passion for mummies. I had high hopes for her, but even your skill was insufficient to interest her in my next expedition."

Grey was losing interest in his next expedition. India had seemed perfect—exciting but not a series of unrelenting perils. He'd visited a few of the Indian ports on the voyage to China and liked what he'd seen. In India, he could find a balance between a need for intellectual stimulation and a need for his science to produce some goddamned coin.

He'd lost his balance the moment Francesca Pomponio had joined him in Zeus's saddle. What he needed more than anything was time with her.

Francesca rose from the table and came over to perch in Grey's lap, which she'd occupied for some agreeable time the evening before.

"I'm sorry the comtesse disappointed you. Are there more potential sponsors you'd like me to write to?"

He drew her close, the feel of her in his arms a comfort against all miseries. "I've gone through my old journals, asked my colleagues, and importuned my brother. My resources are exhausted. I will be reduced to taking a professorial chair at Cambridge, while better connected, more charming fellows are getting back out into the field."

He was whining, and Grey detested whiners.

"You're tired," Francesca said. "You haven't taken a break yet today, and the sun is even shining, or it was."

Some considerate soul named Francesca had put a cushion in Grey's chair, and thus his ability to remain seated had improved. His ability to remain optimistic had deserted him utterly.

"Francesca, I am not very good company right now. Perhaps you should dine with your friends."

She rose, when he wanted to cling to her and bury his nose in her hair.

"I will order us trays," she said, "because the dinner hour approaches. I suspect my friends are finding the company of *your* friends very agreeable, though one wonders where Mr. Stirling has got off to. Are you fretting over money?"

"Yes." No money meant no travels to India. No travels to India meant no hope of repairing the family fortunes. No hope of repairing the family fortunes, much less fortifying his own, meant no hope of taking a wife.

Grey had admitted that to himself in the small hours of the morning, as he'd carried a sleeping Francesca back to her bed.

Because Francesca was regarding him with that level, patient look, he told her the rest of it.

"I'm also increasingly resentful of my brother's unwillingness to take what steps he could to put us back on solid footing. It's not as if I'm inviting him to move into a crofter's hut."

"You've made do with much less than that on many occasions."

"I've slept in my canoe and been grateful. Slept in trees, subsisted on coconuts, fished with a knife lashed to a stick, and damned near watched my toes rot off, but my brother cannot make do with a mere thirteen thousand acres of some of the best farmland in the home counties."

"You put me in mind of a duchess I once knew," Francesca said, picking up the letter from the comtesse. "Her life looked like one grand soiree, all jewels and pretty clothes, lavish meals and handsome courtiers. She was terribly lonely, often exhausted, criticized for what she did and for what she failed to do. Court intrigues ranged from affairs with her husband, to plots on her life, to attempted poisonings. I would not wish that life on anybody."

She spoke with quiet vehemence, perhaps about a friend she'd known in Italy.

"In every fairy tale, there's a wolf," Grey said. "In every garden, a serpent or a poison frog. Do you miss Italy?"

He was changing the subject, or trying to.

"I have money, Grey. I have pots and buckets of it, and it's my money, earned enduring years of marriage. I will sponsor your expedition to India."

She flung the offer at him as if she knew he'd refuse it, for he must.

He rose and took the letter from her. "I am more grateful to you than I can say, Francesca, but you are a widow, alone in the world but for two aunts whom I suspect you support. I see how you attire yourself here—no jewels, no costly silks, no ostentation whatsoever. Even your nightgown bespeaks a woman of modest means. You're young, and what funds you have must last the rest of your life. I cannot allow you to do this."

She whirled away. "*Allow?* You cannot *allow?* Who are you to allow me anything, Greyville Trenton?"

He was an idiot. "I misspoke. I cannot ask you to do this. An expedition is exorbitantly costly. Stock all the machetes you please, and if nobody lays in a supply of whetstones to keep them sharp, you're doomed by the fifth day in the jungle. If some idiot accepts a block of sugar instead of salt, more doom. The contingencies and precautions all cost money, and I cannot safeguard my future at the expense of your own."

Francesca was standing before the fire, her arms crossed, and Grey felt as if he were bludgeoning her with a poker.

"You were willing to accept money from the comtesse."

"She is a noblewoman," Grey said. "She has an obligation to do what she can for the greater good with the means entrusted to her. She has taken such risks before and has extensive family to care for her if an expedition comes to naught."

The argument had the barest pretension to logic, but Francesca could not possibly grasp the sums at issue and that the money—an entire fortune—could simply disappear. All Grey had to show for his trip to Greenland was a few papers in scholarly journals and memoirs purchased mostly by his friends.

Also a lung fever that had nearly killed him.

"That's your justification for rejecting my help?" Francesca said. "I'm not a noblewoman?"

"You're oversimplifying. I cannot be responsible for squandering your widow's mite, Francesca. I'll sell my estate in Kent before I'll allow you to put your future at risk for me."

"Don't do that," she said, marching up to him. "Don't part with the only asset you have of your own, the one place you might call home, in a desperate gamble to bring the family finances right. Don't do it, Grey."

Her previous display had been pique, annoyance, or mere anger. This was rage.

"People sell estates all the time, Francesca, and the more London sprawls into the countryside, the more the estate is worth. I will provision a modest expedition, let my brother manage the remaining proceeds in the funds, and content myself with a succession of projects that allow me to do what I do best."

He'd never planned on selling his only property, and the idea made him bilious now.

"Englishmen go home, Grey," Francesca said. "My father told me this, and he was right. An Englishman might spend twenty years in India, Canada, or Cape Town, but he'll come home. If you suffer an injury in the field, where will you retire for the rest of your life? If the title needs an heir, where will that future earl be raised? Under your brother's roof? In a canoe? And you'll entrust your money—the last of your private funds—to a man who can't understand a basic budget?"

She was magnificent in her ire, and her litany was nothing more than Grey's own list of anxieties, though Sebastian and Annabelle had plenty of time to have a son.

"I mention selling the estate as a last resort," Grey said. "I can always sell a farm or two first."

"No, you cannot," Francesca said, pacing before the fire. "You sell a farm or two, and your income from rent drops, and the value of your estate falls too, because you sell off the best tenancies first. You have a bit of cash, but that cash always seems to disappear into necessary repairs, pensions for the elderly retainers, or emergencies. Do not sell your land."

Her husband had been wealthy, and she spoke with the conviction of one who knew her subject well. Still, she wasn't merely lecturing, she was quietly ranting.

"Why are you so upset, Francesca?" She hadn't been this emotional discussing her husband's infidelities or his death.

"Because you are an idiot, Greyville Trenton. You are the most intelligent, dear, principled, hardworking idiot I've ever met. Your brother is the earl, your mother is a countess. They are relying on you to *risk your life*, over and over, to keep them in pearl necklaces, matched teams, and Bond Street tailoring. Forget an obligation to do what they can for the greater good. Where is their obligation to do what they can for *you?*"

She asked a question that Grey had not permitted himself to pose.

"You make a valid point." More than that, Grey could not say. His family had no idea the dangers he'd faced, and he'd left them to their ignorance rather than risk them meddling. They likely pictured the Amazon forest as a dampish place populated with spotted house cats, pond frogs, and the occasional parrot to add a dash of color.

"You mean I'm right," Francesca said. "You're right about something too."

"An increasingly rare occurrence."

"You said you were poor company and advised me to take myself off. I'll oblige you. Leave the letter from the comtesse on the desk. I'll answer her in the morning."

She left without a hug, a kiss, or a touch of the hand, and she didn't even have the decency to slam the door.

AS PIETRO LAY DYING, he'd stopped referring to the time when he'd regain his health and instead resorted to a series of warnings. Each of them had begun with, *You must listen to me, Francesca.*

The man who'd seldom listened to his wife demanded that she listen to him, and Francesca had tried her best to oblige.

He'd told her widows were vulnerable, and she might find pleasure where she chose, but to guard her heart. Always end an affair too
soon, he'd said, end it with a smile and fond kiss. Let no man develop
assumptions where her future was concerned—or her money.

Sir Greyville would have failed spectacularly at Italian court
intrigue. He refused to develop designs on a fortune laid at his booted
feet.

"He'd make a study of an intrigue," Francesca muttered. "Sketch
its parts in the wild."

The maid looked up from banking the fire, but said nothing, for
Francesca had spoken in Italian. Working with Grey's notes, calling
upon Latin, French, Spanish, Portuguese, and even the occasional
reference to Dutch, had revitalized her linguistic facility.

Also her body and, damn the man, her heart.

"Will that be all, ma'am?" the maid asked. Ma'am, not Your
Grace, not even *signora*.

"Yes, thank you."

The maid curtseyed and departed on a soft click of the door latch,
and then Francesca was alone. She had no intention of wasting a
night in solitude when she might spend it with Grey, even though he
was a stubborn, pig-headed, arrogant...

No, not arrogant. Protective, but also presuming.

Francesca could not afford to indulge his gentlemanly sensibili-
ties. She gathered the candles from the mantel, sat down at the
escritoire, and took out paper, ink, sand, and pen. She was halfway
through a letter to her banker in York when the door opened.

"I apologize," Grey said, closing the door. "I'm not very good at it,
and not sure it will do any good when I cannot accept your money,
but I upset you and must make what amends I can."

He was attired in a worn blue velvet dressing gown and his black
cotton pajama pants, though his feet were bare.

"You'll catch your death without slippers," Francesca said. "Give
me a moment to finish this letter, and you can make another try at

soothing my ruffled feathers, though you're right. It won't do any good."

While she signed and sanded her letter, Grey wandered the room like a wild creature in a menagerie—restless, exuding unhappiness, in want of activity. He opened the wardrobe, where pressed gowns hung and slippers were lined up by color. His next investigation led him to the cedar-lined trunk at the foot of the bed, where Francesca kept shawls, pelisses, cloaks, and boots.

He closed the trunk and sat on it. "I must get to India, Francesca, but I'll not bankrupt you to do it."

"You wouldn't bankrupt me." She hadn't the means to prove that to him, though, not here in England, and he'd demand proof.

"You can't know that. The optimal approach is to outfit an entire vessel, hand-choose my subordinates, bring all manner of botanical equipment with me and enough of my personal effects that if I never return to England, I can establish a household, conservatory, and laboratory of my own. The effort is comparable to moving a small, highly specialized army."

And one stubborn Englishman.

"I have resources you do not," she said, capping the ink bottle and pouring the sand back into its container. "By way of compromise, please allow me to contact them on your behalf. You'd be surprised how many princesses and dowager duchesses a diplomat's daughter befriends at an Italian court. Don't let your pride get in the way of your reason."

Grey had great pride, but was also eminently rational.

"You think *women* will fund my next investigation?" He hadn't dismissed the idea out of hand, which was encouraging. "I had considered the comtesse an anomaly, an eccentric."

Whose coin he'd been willing to take.

"You drink tea in England largely because Catherine of Braganza made it a popular court drink, else you men would have hoarded it in your coffee shops. Think of the last time you took tea, Grey, and the

time before that. A lady presided, and she doesn't go through her day
without drinking tea several times."

He was on his feet again, poking his nose into Francesca's effects.
He lifted the lid of her jewelry box, which held only the few decora-
tive pieces Francesca traveled with.

"I will concede that tea is a lady's drink. What would you say to
these women?"

"That I've learned of an investment opportunity full of both risk
and potential reward." *He has dark eyes, dark hair, a brilliant mind,
and a good heart, for all he's sometimes dunderheaded.*

Grey examined a strand of pink pearls that had been Francesca's
first gift to herself as a widow. "All investment opportunities present
those factors. What else?"

"That if this investigation goes well, greater society could benefit
as much as the investors do, eventually, but that scientific snobbery
means this project will likely not receive the attention it deserves
from other sources."

He threaded the pearls through his fingers and sat cross-legged on
the bed. "That's very good, and you're right. Haring about India in
search of optimal conditions for a tea farm is hardly glamorous, not
when compared with orchids in Mexican jungles or emeralds from
darkest Africa. I also can't disclose exactly why I'm looking now, lest I
put my own fledgling operation at risk."

He toyed with the pearls, luminous beads among candlelit shadows. "Send a half-dozen letters, no more. I can't have it said that Sir
Greyville is growing desperate, though I am."

He'd apologized, he'd listened to her, he'd made concessions.
Francesca had by no means made her last argument, but the time had
come for her to compromise as well.

"You're desperate to find funding?" she asked.

He regarded her across the room, his expression unreadable.
"Very nearly. I'm also desperate to see you wearing these pearls and
nothing else."

They had so little time. "If I asked you to leave, would you?"

He was off the bed, the pearls put back where they belonged. "Of course. I'll bid you pleasant dreams and hope to see you in the morning."

Another man would have tried to change her mind, flirt her past her frustrations, or explain to her that his stubbornness was an effort to put her best interests above his own. With Grey, Francesca didn't need to protect her privacy, and maybe because of that, she couldn't protect her heart.

"Stay with me," she said. "For the time we have left, please stay with me."

LADY HESTER STANHOPE was said to be leading an excavation of the ancient city of Ashkelon—leading it, not tagging along after her father, brother, or husband.

After serving as hostess for no less person than the British prime minister, she'd collected a companion, a personal physician, and such other retainers and supplies as she'd needed, before embarking on an adventure that was the envy of half the British scientific community.

Where it would lead, nobody quite knew. The scientific establishment seemed torn between discrediting her as an eccentric and admitting grudging envy for her pluck. Nothing—not shipwreck, not cultural prohibitions against women, not privation or hardship—had deterred her from her objective.

Caroline Herschel, sister to the recently knighted William Herschel, had been his salaried assistant when he'd served as royal astronomer. The woman had discovered no less than eight comets, among her other contributions.

How many anomalous data points could one man's theory of himself as scientist withstand?

Grey set aside the question as imponderable, for science was useful only in situations lending themselves to measurement by the five senses. More complicated questions, such as how to put matters right with Francesca, required tools Grey did not command.

Last night, he'd apologized, but he hadn't agreed to take her money. For the first time, they'd made love silently, no lover's talk, no whispered confidences or spirited arguments. The aftermath had left him wrung out and, in some way, unsatisfied.

He missed Francesca already, though she sat at her customary place across the office, her pen moving steadily. She'd sealed up her letter to the countess before Grey had come down, and now she was occupied writing to her "resources."

"Francesca, might you attend me for a moment?"

"I'll be through here in two minutes."

He took out a clean sheet of paper and let his pencil flow over the blank space. When she'd stormed off last night, he'd sat in his pillowed chair and tried to sketch her. Without a live model, he'd made a bad job of it.

"That's done," she said, setting her correspondence aside. "What would you like to discuss?"

"Join me on the sofa, please."

Francesca took off his best glasses—maybe they were hers by now —folded her arms, and remained in her chair.

He still hadn't the goddamned knack of phrasing his needs as requests. "I meant, would you please join me on the sofa?" Grey said, depositing his own aching backside in the middle of the cushions. She'd have to sit next to him, one way or the other.

"For a brilliant man, you are difficult to educate," she said, taking the place to his right. "But I do see progress."

Grey took her hand, knowing full well she was still unhappy with him. They'd made love, they'd not made peace.

"Stratton informs me that your coach should be repaired by week's end. You'll be free to resume your journey by Monday at the latest. Will you allow me to write to you?"

She stared into the fire rather than at him. "Why?"

Because he'd go mad without knowing how she fared, because his theories would not be as well-reasoned without her questions to test them, because nobody would celebrate with him as sincerely when he'd finished a publishable version of his accounts.

"Because there might be a child."

She withdrew her hand. "But you..."

"I have taken precautions, but conception can occur nonetheless. I have at least two godsons whose existence attests to this fact." Darling little fellows he didn't get to see often enough.

"And if I've conceived?"

What was the right answer, assuming there was one? "I will, of course, take responsibility for the consequences of my actions." Not an outright proposal, which Francesca might well fling in his face, but not a wrong answer, Grey hoped.

And why hadn't he proposed when they'd first become lovers?

Because he had so little to give her. No real home, no income other than what little he set aside from the revenue his estate generated, no solid prospects of a professional nature—*none*. A time of shared pleasure was all he could honestly offer.

That answer didn't satisfy him. He doubted it would satisfy her.

"You are a good man," she said, "and in the grip of circumstances not entirely of your own making. I have ample means to raise a child, Grey, and you needn't fear I'd foster out my own progeny. After two miscarriages, if I have a chance to be a mother, then propriety can go hang, and a loving, joyously devoted mother I shall be."

He should not have been surprised, at either the ferocity of her maternal instinct, or his reaction to her assurances that means were the essence of the discussion. He'd seen many families in far-flung locations whose means would be pitiful by British standards, and yet, their children had been happy and thriving.

"I cannot make demands of you," Grey said, "but I can ask that you inform me if such developments are in the offing."

"I'll think about it."

He also could not insist that he had a right to know. Not even that monument to patriarchal arrogance, the British legal system, gave a man the right to supervise the upbringing of his children unless that man was married to their mother.

Grey rose and for once could not make himself return to the damned chair behind the desk. "Please know that your joy in and devotion to the child would be matched only by my own. If you'll excuse me, I'll catch a breath of fresh air while the sun yet shines."

IN THE FEW DAYS REMAINING, Francesca developed a routine with Grey that ensured they'd not have any more difficult discussions. He took to riding out in the morning, while she worked diligently on the indexes and glossary. In the afternoons, while Grey focused on his manuscript, Francesca napped or tended to correspondence she'd neglected the previous week. A duchess had every bit as much correspondence as a biologist, after all.

What time they spent together was taken up with discussion of poison plants, poison fish, and poison frogs, that being the topic of Grey's current chapter. He did not seem to be making much progress on it, though Francesca suspected she knew why.

To use Grey's terminology, their experiment had yielded unexpected results.

In plain English, they'd surprised each other. A short, spontaneous liaison undertaken in the interests of pleasure and affection had become something altogether different. Friday arrived without Francesca having replied to Grey's request to stay in touch by letter.

Grey had said he'd treasure a child of theirs, and yet, he still waited anxiously for word regarding funding for his expedition to India.

What was she to make of that?

"You have an avalanche of mail today," she said as a footman put the stack on his desk. "If I can work without interruption for the rest of the afternoon, I can finish up your glossary, and you'll have your notes arranged by subject and cross-referenced by date."

The footman—his name really was John—bowed and withdrew, while Grey wrinkled his nose at the mail. "I almost dread reading my correspondence anymore. Do you depart tomorrow, Francesca?"

Their nights had been spent in a silent frenzy of tenderness, and then they'd fall asleep, too exhausted to do more than hold each other in the darkness.

"Monday," she said. "I'll part from my friends in York."

"You'll not spend a holiday with them?" Grey's question was oblique, but at least he was admitting interest in her future.

"My friends appear to be making plans at variance with our original intentions. I have business in York, and it's a lovely city." If one enjoyed a crumbling Roman wall and a minster so old its stone roots sank into antiquity.

Though an Italian duchess had no need of more antiquity.

Rather than inquire directly of her itinerary, or bring up again the fraught notion of a child, Grey went back to his correspondence. He had the ability to soldier on, despite reluctance or difficulties. That came through in his notes and in Francesca's observations of him.

He was a good, honorable man, and she was so frustrated with him that when he opened her door that night, she nearly tackled him.

"I take it today's correspondence held nothing of importance?" she asked.

He closed the door and locked it. "No rejections. I will count that as progress. I finally get a glimpse of you with your hair down."

"My hair? What has hair to do with—?"

He stalked across the room, his dressing gown flapping about his knees. "Your hair is beautiful, and I want to sketch you with it down. We're almost out of time, Francesca. Let me have at least a likeness to recall you by."

Not too much to ask, and yet, Francesca hadn't counted on the fact that when she sat for him, she had nothing to do but watch him sketch her. Grey's focus was singular as his hand moved across a blank page. The gap in his dressing gown, the lock of hair that refused to stay behind his left ear, he took no notice of either, while Francesca was forced to stare at both.

"Will you let me see the finished result?"

"Will you let me write to you?"

His question gratified her on a purely selfish level. "I'll leave you the direction for my aunts in Sussex. They always know how to reach me."

"Thank you."

For another half hour Grey was silent, the only sounds his pencil scratching across the page and the fire burning down. Francesca's shoulders were growing chilled when he finally set his pencil and paper aside.

"Shall I braid my hair now?"

"No," he said, rising and shrugging out of his dressing gown. "You shall not. Do you know I made more progress with my infernal manuscript when you were on hand to distract me in person? This business of disappearing for naps... I'm aware that I deprive you of sleep, Francesca, but I've missed you these past few days."

She would miss him forever, if he had his way. "Grey..."

His trousers went next, tossed over the back of the chair at the escritoire. To her surprise, he was fully aroused.

Simply from looking at her?

"Now," he said, stalking to the bed, "you distract me from within my own mind. I see you on the banks of the Amazon, in the high Andes, in the blinding sunshine on the waves of the Atlantic. I hear you scolding me for inconsistent terminology, and I listen to the soft rustling as you shuffle stacks of chaos into a tidy, rational order."

Some fever had seized him, an anger and a determination Francesca couldn't fathom. "If I don't braid my hair, come morning—"

"Come morning, we will be that much closer to your departure," he said, untying the bows of her nightgown. "Come morning, I will bury myself once more in plants that yield a paralyzing toxin, twenty-foot-long alligators that can swallow a man whole, and schools of pretty fish that make a plundering army seem tame. Right now, I'd like to bury myself in you."

All over again, she was swamped with terror at the risks he'd taken, month after month, and the risks he'd take again.

"No more jungles, Grey, please. Find places to explore that won't try to kill you twice a day."

His answer was an openmouthed kiss, one that sent her sprawling onto her back across the bed. He kept advancing, wrapping his hands in her hair, crouching over her as if he were a wild beast let loose from the pages of his journal.

He was no longer the man of science, confident of his powers, observing and analyzing from the safe distance of intellect and reason. He was the storm in Francesca's heart and the fire in her body. He was hope, misery, rage, and longing, and at least until Monday, he was hers.

Grey had shown her any number of ways to make love—side by side, back to front, on her knees, her back to the wall, and her favorite, him on his back beneath her. For this coupling, Grey remained for once above her, his weight anchoring her to the mattress.

"I have nothing to offer you but this," he said, joining them on one hard thrust.

The words were jarring and the sensation overwhelming. Too soon, Francesca was spiraling upward, desire besieging her from within.

"You have so much—" she managed, before Grey was kissing her again, his passion nearly savage. She went over the edge, bucking against him until she could see, hear, touch, and taste only a pleasure so intense it left her in tears.

CHAPTER SIX

The staff apparently knew not to disturb Mrs. Pomponio of a morning until she was stirring behind her door. In any case, Grey recalled locking Francesca's door the previous evening. In the cool light of approaching dawn, he studied his sketch where it sat on her escritoire, a good effort, if a bit too...

Too passionate, too wishful, and too wistful.

"Grey?"

He tended the fire and climbed back under the covers. "I should have left you two hours ago."

Francesca moved into his embrace easily, for they'd acquired the knack of sleeping together the first night. "It's hard to get back to sleep in a cold bed, isn't it?"

Impossible. "I suppose if one is tired enough, sleep comes eventually. Francesca, will you be all right?"

She turned to her side, so Grey was spooned around her. "I will miss you and be upset with you for some time. Rub my back, please."

He'd learned to do this and wished he could ask her for return of the same favor. He had much to learn about asking for kindnesses and had a sinking suspicion that if he couldn't learn those lessons from Francesca, he'd never master them.

Her back was a wonder of feminine grace, but sturdy too. He'd studied anatomy—what biologist hadn't?—but in the past week, he'd studied *her*. Her right shoulder was a fraction of an inch higher than her left, and that asymmetry was repeated in her hips. The hair at the juncture of her thighs bore a reddish tinge, and her second toe was longer than the first.

She liked chocolate—vanilla was bland by comparison—and a German fruit brandy made from cherries. She sometimes dreamed in Italian, sometimes English, and had a collection of cream cake recipes inherited from her late mother-in-law that she considered a dear treasure.

"You do that so well," she murmured. "Your greatest talents lie in the bedroom, Grey, not the jungle. Will you be all right?"

No, he would not. In the past two weeks, his concepts of family, science, himself, and his place in the world had been upended, thanks to one forthright, passionate widow.

"One expects challenges."

Francesca rolled over and peered at him in the gloom. Her hair was a glorious mess, and desire rose as the covers dipped low across her bosom.

"I meant what I said, Greyville. Please do not consign yourself to the most dangerous, difficult, disease-ridden corners of the earth in an effort to prove you don't want your pony back. You've racketed about for ten years and made both your point and your contribution."

He pushed her hair away from her brow and arranged himself over her. "I adore you when you lecture me." He adored her every waking moment and in half of his dreams.

She ran a toe up the side of his calf. "Somebody needs to lecture you. I will worry about you."

"India is civilized enough." In places. At times.

"India is too far away, and so are you." She urged him closer by virtue of clutching his backside.

Grey retaliated by getting his mouth on her nipple, and for sweet, lovely moments, they teased each other into a fever of desire. He managed not to hurry the joining or the lovemaking, because he needed to hoard impressions against the coming separation.

That effort was hopeless. Memories were not objects, to be cataloged and preserved, and no memory would lessen the pain of sending Francesca on her way Monday morning.

Her breathing took on the rhythm of escalating desire, and Grey needed all of his focus to restrain his own pleasure. He dared not open his eyes to watch as passion claimed her, and he dared not close his eyes lest sensation claim him. He settled for fixing his gaze on the spill of Francesca's hair across the sheets, gold on ivory, silk on cotton.

She shuddered beneath him, and when he was sure she could bear the sensation, he withdrew and spent on her belly.

"I wish..." she said, stroking his hair. "I wish, and wish, and wish, Greyville."

He wished, he dreamed, he racked his brain, and second-guessed himself. "I know, my love. I know."

He held her while she dozed, and wishes lay in silent disarray in his mind, like so much leaf litter on the forest floor after a terrible storm. He could not leave her, he could not offer for her, he could not take her money and risk it all in India, but to India he must go.

Grey awoke to the scents of jasmine and peat—a distinctive combination—and the warmth of the sun on his shoulder. He got out of bed, dressed, and kissed a sleeping Francesca farewell.

How he hated himself for keeping the truth from her.

He'd said the mail contained no more rejections, which was true but not honest. A titled acquaintance of the comtesse had caught wind of his project and made so bold as to express an enthusiasm for his proposal and a desire to invest in it.

Funding had been very nearly promised, and all Grey could think was that he didn't want to leave Francesca, not for all the tea in... not for all the tea, anywhere.

FRANCESCA HAD FOUND the Sabbath observation in England a form of purgatory. Nobody undertook travel unless from most dire necessity, industry of any kind was frowned upon, and even Sir Greyville Trenton limited his activities to reading.

While Francesca packed up her belongings and worried. Grey was keeping something from her, though she wasn't sure what. He'd had no correspondence from family that she'd seen, but then, she didn't go through his correspondence like a snooping wife.

"Have you left already, Francesca, that you disdain to join me in the office this afternoon?" Grey stood in her bedroom doorway, and despite the late hour, he was still dressed.

Just as well.

"I am, as your powers of observation confirm, very much still here. I did not want to burden the maids with tending to my belongings, so I've packed my trunk and will be ready for an early departure tomorrow."

"Damn it, Francesca, I don't know whether to bow and wish you safe journey, or make passionate love to you for the next ten hours."

For all but the last few months of her marriage, Pietro would never have thought to consider Francesca's wishes in either regard. He'd come and gone as he pleased, in her life and in her bedroom. What a miserable lot a duchess endured, if Pietro's example held true across the ducal species.

"Greyville." She stood immediately before him. "You should do what makes you happy, but I cannot... That is..."

He closed the door and took her in his arms. "Tell me, Francesca."

The lump in her throat had grown to the size of an Italian duchy. She shook her head and clung to him. "I'm being silly."

He carried her to the bed—how she would miss his masculine displays of consideration—and sat with her in his lap.

"Do you know," he said, "I have spent more time talking with you than with any other adult woman, save perhaps my mother? One doesn't exactly talk with Mama though. One accepts orders. In all the times we've spoken, Francesca, I've never heard you refer to any friends, save your traveling companions."

What blasted observation was he going on about now? "Olivia and Mary Alice are friends of long standing. Good friends."

He scooted back so he was supported by the headboard. "And did these good friends, in all the years since your come out, ever visit you?"

"My acquaintance with Olivia doesn't go back that far. Mary Alice wrote."

"Twice a year?"

"What is your point, Grey?"

"You have made me ponder my situation, Francesca, and it seems in some ways similar to your own."

She doubted very much he'd been married to a self-important Italian duke. "Explain yourself."

Grey kissed her temple. "There are wildernesses, and wildernesses. Some pose a danger to the body, and some pose a danger to the spirit. I was nearly dragged overboard at one point early in my last exploration by a great, black creature similar in nature to an alligator, but twice as long."

"The caiman. You drew pictures of them."

"Sketches made from a great distance, I can assure you. I think your husband's infidelity nearly dragged you overboard. You mention no friends in Italy, no in-laws with whom you still correspond. I suspect you came to England because your aunts are here and because it holds at least memories of friendship."

Francesca had made that discovery in the past two weeks herself, but memories of friendship were not the same as the living, breathing article.

"Do you have friends, Greyville?"

"I have colleagues and, like you, close associations left over from my youth. I account Stratton and Stirling true friends, and I hope they would say the same of me. Friends tell each other what's amiss, Francesca, and though we part tomorrow, I am your friend."

She snuggled closer and considered his hypothesis. "Do friends typically make passionate love with each other at every opportunity?"

"Friends are kind and honest with each other. They are tolerant of one another's foibles. They offer acceptance, commiseration, and companionship. They share joys and sorrows and often hold each other in great affection. You will have to explain to me how that definition precludes shared intimacies."

It didn't, and worse, Francesca had hoped her marriage would have all of those qualities. In the end, it had, but only in the end.

"There's no baby, Greyville. My courses started this afternoon."

His hand on her back slowed. "And how does this development find you?"

Weepy, angry, bewildered. "It's for the best."

He gathered her close. "That's not your heart talking. What is convenient is not always for the best. Your news leaves me feeling sad, thoughtful, disappointed—also relieved that association with me has not unduly burdened your future."

They remained on the bed while Francesca considered his list. If she'd been carrying his child, he would have married her, and all manner of complications involving money, science, and friendship would have ensued.

She hoped there was another way. "I wish you weren't so noble."

"Noble, I am not. That burden at least remains my brother's. Would you like me to sleep in my own bed tonight, Francesca?"

She sat up enough to peer at him. "What are you asking?"

"You needn't look at me like that. I would not impose on you when you're indisposed, but I would like to stay with you."

Grey so rarely asked for anything for himself, and Francesca very much wanted his arms about her, more than ever.

"Please stay." She couldn't have asked that of any friend, nor did she think it a typical request between lovers, considering her indisposition.

Only a husband would be allowed such intimacy. Before the tears could claim Francesca again, she helped Grey out of his clothes and climbed beneath the covers with him one last time.

SAYING good-bye to Francesca was hell.

Grey insisted on walking her to the coach wherein her friend Mary Alice waited. All the way, Francesca lectured him, about indexes, subheadings, and lists of sketches and figures. Was this how his family had felt when he'd maundered on about curare and caimans as his departure date had approached?

"Francesca, you will please recall that I am acquainted with the notion of an index and that the figures you mention were drawn by my own hand. I might have some insight into their organization."

The Yorkshire breeze blew nearly constantly, and already a strand of her hair was whipping across her lips.

"Insight and action are two different things, Greyville. If you don't start listing the figures separately from the sketches now, you will never do it. Several years of illustrations is an enormous body of work, and unless it's well organized, none of it will be of use to anybody."

One of the coach horses stomped, causing the harness to jingle. Other farewells were in progress several yards away, between Stratton and the woman Mary Alice. Stratton's small daughter looked as woebegone as Grey felt.

"I will be no use to anybody for at least a month after you get into the coach, Francesca."

She glanced back at the house, where no less than six dozen servants were doubtless watching from the windows.

"Then I'd best be on my way, hadn't I? Thank you, Grey, for everything, and please be safe."

She kissed him, and not some tame peck on the cheek. She kissed him as if her kiss would have to last him the whole distance to

India and beyond. He kissed her back as if, more than funding, science, honor, or reason, she was all that would sustain him for the journey.

If he made the journey.

His arms stole around her, and she leaned on him, and to perdition with whoever might be watching.

She was about to climb into that coach and leave him, as if he were a wilderness that had been adequately explored and documented, and he could in good conscience do nothing to stop her.

"Francesca, will you write to me?"

"I need your handkerchief. This shouldn't be so difficult."

He produced the requested item. "I've been considering some options and will write to you, even if you don't write to me. Your welfare will always concern me, and my work matters, but depending on variables outside my control, at some—"

She put two gloved fingers to his lips.

"I love you, Sir Greyville Trenton. Wherever you go, whatever endeavor you undertake, however your fortunes wax and wane, I love you."

Before Grey could respond, before he could form a single word, he had to stand back so Francesca's traveling companions could join her inside.

Then some idiot—Stratton perhaps?—had slammed the coach door closed, and the team trotted off.

Grey raised his hand in farewell and stood in the drive apart from the others long after the coach had disappeared, staring at the drifting plume of dust, waving at nothing.

"Your expression suggests that woman just departed for darkest Peru and will never return."

Stratton walked over to Grey, and from the look in his eyes, the past two weeks hadn't exactly been his idea of a springtime frolic. He'd appeared quite fond of Francesca's friend, and she of him. The child had apparently returned indoors.

"Francesca is bound for York," Grey said.

"And you'll shut yourself up in the damned office and pretend your heart isn't breaking?"

The last of the dust had dissipated, leaving only the wind and the high green hills on all sides. "Two weeks ago, I would have told you that the heart cannot break," Grey said. "The organ can cease to function, but it's not a watch, to stop running as a result of an imagined impact on the emotions."

"That does sound like your typical pontifications, but it's not two weeks ago. What do you say now?"

Grey started marching for the house, his host in step beside him. "Now, I want my pony back. Sebastian has been riding my Tiger long enough."

"Greyville, I have endless respect for your brilliance, but perhaps it's time you took a repairing lease. A short respite never hurt—"

"Don't lecture," Grey said, "or I shall have to strike you. Manifestation of the frustrated mating urge perhaps, or a simple reaction to a surfeit of nonsense."

"My dear friend, I suspect you've been in the tropics too long, and now you're determined to hare off to India, of all the bug-ridden, fever-infested, pestilential purgatories. Stirling and I have often discussed the benefits of an academic—"

"The problem isn't the jungle," Grey said, striding into the manor. "I am the problem."

"Was there ever any doubt of that?"

"Some friend you are. I need to think. Be off with you."

"You've said farewell to the first woman you've noticed as anything other than a specimen in years. I will make allowances, but you're being an idiot. How will you get her back?"

And there was the problem, now that Grey had let her go. "I don't know, but I am the determined sort, and I'm well aware that a machete has little value in the jungle without a whetstone."

"Greyville, I do believe the bonds of friendship require that I get you drunk."

"A reciprocal burden falls upon me, given the mournful expression with which you watched that coach depart. Let's be about it, shall we?"

ITALIAN WOMEN often wore black quite well, while English-women, especially blond, blue-eyed Englishwomen, seldom did.

"Blond, gray-eyed Englishwomen," Francesca corrected herself, pulling off her gloves.

Despite how black washed out her complexion, Francesca had found that traveling in widow's weeds made sense. She need not attire herself as a duchess, and her privacy was respected more than it would have been had she not been heavily veiled in black.

"Good day, Your Grace. I hope your walk was enjoyable?"

MacDuie, her butler, had conveyed with the leased house, like the furnishings and cook. Francesca liked to hear him speak, for his Scottish accent was as unrelenting as his good cheer.

"My walk was peaceful, thank you."

"You have a caller, Your Grace. A gentleman."

She paused, her bonnet ribbons half untied. She'd worn her favorite mourning bonnet, the one with thick black netting that preserved her from prying eyes but still let her see and breathe.

"Has Mr. Arnold come over from the bank?"

"The gentleman's card is on the sideboard, Your Grace. A Sir Greyville Trenton. Quiet fellow, and he has some sort of letter for you. He said he wanted to deliver it in person."

Oh heavens. Oh gracious.

After nearly two weeks of waiting, hoping, and wishing for even a note, Francesca had all but given up. She was certain he'd have written, but being Grey, of course he had not. He was here, in person, ready to observe, collect data, and draw his own conclusions.

She draped her veil over her face. "No tea tray, MacDuie. I don't think the gentleman will be staying long."

Perhaps he wanted to thank her in person. She stopped halfway up the winding front stair, nearly felled by the notion that he'd already made plans to depart for India.

She entered the formal parlor very much on her dignity.

"Your Grace." Grey stood, his bow most proper. He was exquisitely attired for a morning call, not a wrinkle to be seen, and the sight of him left Francesca's knees wobbly. "Thank you for seeing me."

She gestured to the chairs arranged before the hearth. "Please have a seat, Sir Greyville."

His brows knit at the sound of her voice. "Now that is most odd. I am here because your handwriting bore a striking resemblance to that of another, a lady I esteem most highly. Perhaps an Italian education accounts for such a similarity, but you even sound like her. In any case, an offer as generous as yours deserves the courtesy of a reply in person."

Of course he'd recognize her penmanship and voice. Francesca had an Italian accent, but she usually worked to keep it behind her teeth.

"You received my letter?" she asked, putting a hint of Tuscany in the question.

"I did, two weeks ago, and I must thank you from the depths of my being for your proffered generosity."

"Shall we sit, Sir Greyville?"

He was studying her with *that look*, the one that said a quizzing glass was unnecessary, because Sir Greyville Trenton was examining the specimen, and no instrument or measuring device could improve upon his powers of observation.

He waited for Francesca to choose one of the velvet-cushioned seats, flipped out his tails, and settled near enough that she caught a hint of his exotic fragrance—the one from dratted India.

"I have penned my reply to your offer," he said, passing over a letter. "My abilities with spontaneous social discourse are wanting. Perhaps you'll read my letter now?"

Francesca broke the seal and recognized the tidiest sample of Grey's penmanship she'd ever seen. He must have copied the letter several times. And yet, as legible as the words were, Francesca could not make sense of them.

He was *rejecting* her offer. Throwing it aside when she'd delivered his heart's desire on a silver platter. Bewilderment, rage, and a curious frisson of hope had her reading his words three times.

"I don't understand, Sir Greyville. In the space of two weeks, you've decided your passions lie in another direction? I was given to understand that your dedication to science is second to none and your interest in this Indian venture considerable."

He rose and prowled the room, which was about as nondescript as elegant furnishings and good housekeeping could be. The oil painting over the mantel was of some red-coated stag posed just so in an alpine meadow, and the sideboard, chairs, and sofa were all of matched blond oak.

England at its genteel finest, and but for his sense of energy, Grey belonged in this room.

"My interest in the Indian venture will continue unabated, Your Grace, but I find for the present that more pressing concerns keep me in England."

Whatever did that mean? "Should one be concerned for your family, Sir Greyville?"

He left off admiring the stag and looked at her as if he could see right through her veil. He couldn't. Francesca had seen her reflection in enough mirrors to know the veil shielded her from observation.

"My family will be making a remove from our seat in the Midlands to a more modest property in Kent."

"*What?* I mean, I beg your pardon?"

He made a circuit of the room, pausing to study an etching of some flower or other. "The time has come for me to explore a wilderness closer to home. The matter involves a lady, Your Grace, so I will keep my comments oblique, but my mind is made up. I'll not be leaving for India in the immediate future."

He looked very severe, very resolute, also tired and dear.

Francesca folded her veil back and pinned it to her bonnet.

"Grey, what on earth are you going on about? India is your heart's desire, your dream. I can make that happen for you."

He was across the parlor in two strides. "I knew it was you! By damn, Francesca, what are you about? You leave me, and now you're a duchess, and possibly not even English. I can make no sense of this."

She saw in his eyes the same emotions roiling through her—bewilderment, anger, and a small gleam of hope.

"I am the dowager duchess of the Italian duchy of San Mercato, also Francesca Pomponio Pergolesi, widowed these past five years. One travels more safely without a title, and my friends and I had a significant need for privacy."

"You haven't been sleeping," he said, scowling down at her. "And you stole my glasses."

"You stole my heart."

"One can't—you stole mine first."

They glared at each other for a fraught moment, then they were kissing, wrapped in an embrace that brought back memory upon memory, all of them happy.

Francesca broke the kiss, feeling as if she'd taken her first decent breath in days. "Are you traveling to India or not?"

"Not without you," Grey said. "Black does not become you, Francesca. The weeds threw me off, which you probably intended. *Camoufflage*, as the French would say."

"If you start spouting science now, Greyville, I will put you on a boat for India myself."

"You'd save me the trouble of getting you to the docks, for I won't leave without you, Francesca. I've had a brisk exchange of letters with my brother."

"Come," she said, taking his hand and leading him to the sofa. "Tell me."

It wasn't their sofa, but sitting beside Grey anywhere soothed an ache in Francesca that had been building for two weeks.

"I told Sebastian I wanted my pony back. He was the earl, not I, and responsibility for the family finances rested on his shoulders, not mine. My family is welcome to reside with me in Kent, but I'll no longer spend years hacking my way through insects, snakes, and mud to keep him in matched teams."

"You quoted me?"

"You have the better command of persuasive prose, Francesca. We needn't belabor the obvious."

She took his hand, drew off his glove, and laced her fingers through his. "So you'll live in Kent, cheek by jowl with your family? What about your science? What about your tea plantation?"

What about us?

"Francesca, I have more specimens, journals, and drawings than I can organize in a lifetime. I've sent plants to Kew, to the family seat, to my own conservatory, to Cambridge, and to colleagues. I can busy myself with that inventory for the next six decades. I don't need to single-handedly establish the tea industry in India. I need you. Only you."

He kissed her knuckles, while Francesca looked for holes in his theory.

"You were concerned that you'd deplete my means if I financed your voyage to India. I am scandalously wealthy, Grey. My banker will happily meet with you and describe the extent of my holdings. I'll give it all away in a moment if penury is necessary to merit your continued notice."

His arm came around her shoulders. "When I watched your coach roll away, I realized something."

Francesca had realized a few things too. "Tell me."

"Family should look after one another. Sheep know this, dogs know this. My impulse to aid my relations was not wrong, but I domesticated my family instead of allowing them to develop their natural abilities. Sebastian has composed heaps of music he hasn't published because an earl should give away his talent. That's balderdash, to use your term. Mama has jewels she never wears and doesn't even like. She should sell them and invest the proceeds. I could go on."

"You're very good at going on, among other things." Mostly, he was good at being Sir Greyville Trenton, scientist at large and the man Francesca loved.

"Well, my dear family can either accept my hospitality or fend for themselves. A little time in the wilderness is good for us all. Having discovered the obvious, I am now intent on offering you marriage."

"Don't you dare go down on one knee," Francesca said, rising. "Pietro did that, in the greatest display of hypocrisy I've ever endured. I don't want to live in Kent with your dragon of a mother and your spoiled sister-in-law."

He rose and took out his handkerchief, and even that had been neatly folded into his pocket. He produced a pair of spectacles from an inside pocket—the second-best pair.

"Francesca, I would like to support my wife, assuming you'll have me. We can reach an accommodation—my manor house has thirty-six rooms—but you will have to elucidate your reservations."

Thirty-six rooms was nearly the size of the ducal villa Francesca had called home for five years.

"I understand that you want to support your wife and children, Grey, but I want to support science. As it happens, I meant what I said in my letter to you. Establishing a tea industry in India strikes me as a brilliant investment opportunity and a way to contribute significantly to the realm."

If he polished his spectacles any more vigorously, he'd part the lens from the frames. "You *want* me to go to India? Francesca, the voyage can take months, and my destination is the western region of the subcontinent. I could easily be gone for five years."

"We could be gone."

He dropped his spectacles on the carpet and made no move to pick them up. "I'm not sure I heard you correctly."

The handkerchief in his hand shook minutely, as if a small tempest beset it.

"We could be gone. Officer's wives go out to India all the time, Grey. My plan was to follow you out and capture you in the wild. I never anticipated that you'd pounce upon a widowed Italian duchess right here in England."

"You were prepared…? You were prepared to *follow me to India?* Francesca, I hardly know what to say."

She picked up his glasses and handed them to him. "Say what's in your heart. I love you, and I want you to be happy. I want you to make the contributions only you, Sir Greyville Trenton, can make. If that means I sleep with you in a hammock, then I'll sleep with you in a hammock. It's as you said, Grey. Loneliness stalks us, bitterness, regret. Against those predators, the only haven is love. For two weeks with you, I was content, complete, and full of dreams. I want that back. If I have to go to India to get it, that's a small price to pay for a lifetime of happiness."

His arms came around her. "You deliver a very convincing lecture, Francesca, and I cannot hope to equal its eloquence."

She kissed his cheek. "Try."

"Yes, love." He fell silent for a moment, then spoke very softly, right near her ear. "I enjoy science."

"And you are very good at it." Brilliant, in fact.

"And I am very good at it. I love you. I would like to become the best in the world at that undertaking. I would like my expertise in this regard to eclipse all known records and become a species of love unto itself. I can pursue my objective in India, in Kent, and anywhere in between, but only if you are by my side, as my wife, my companion, my lover, and my guide."

"Your skill with a lecture is improving."

"I'm the determined sort. Say yes, Francesca. Please, or I'll make an idiot of myself and start begging."

"Yes, Grey. Yes, I will be your wife, and all those other things, in India, Kent, and everywhere in between. Do you suppose we might remark the occasion by exploring my private apartment in the next ten minutes?"

He resorted to a manly display of consideration and swept her up into his arms. "A logical place to start the expedition, though you will have to give me directions."

"It will be my pleasure."

Francesca directed him up to her bedroom, and from there through the weeks of preparation for their next adventure.

On the way to India—they named the vessel *Tiger*—she frequently directed him in their private cabin, and as the wildly lucrative Trenton tea garden became productive, she remained an invaluable source of guidance.

By the time Francesca, Grey, and their two sons sailed back to England some five years later, the family finances had come gloriously right. When His Lordship—Grey was raised to a barony—wanted a taste of the wild, he had to look no farther than the other side of the bed, where his duchess in disguise was always ready to pounce and, in a single leap, love him as wildly as ever his heart desired.

TO MY DEAR READERS

I hope you enjoyed these little bagatelles, for I certainly had fun writing them. The interplay between aspects of a lover kept hidden by a subterfuge, and the traits and truths revealed by the same disguise fascinates me. Might have to come up with another trio of tales along these lines!

If you're in the mood for more happily ever after lite bites, I've written a number of **novellas**, some of which I'm in the process of republishing as rights revert to me from the original publisher. My next full-length novel, **Miss Delectable**, launches my **Mischief in Mayfair** series, and I've included an excerpt below. These stories take up where the **True Gentlemen** left off, and yes, Sycamore Dorning sticks his oar in whether anybody asks him to or not.

To stay up to date with my new releases, pre-orders, and short-term sales, following me on **Bookbub** is the best bet. I also put out a newsletter just about monthly—when I have something pass along—and I promise if you **sign up,** I will never spam, swap, sell, or trade away your address. (And unsubscribing is easy.) I also have a **Deals** page on my web site, updated around the first of each month, where I announce early releases of new titles on the **web store**, web store exclusives, or vender-specific discounts.

However you choose to keep in touch, I wish you, as always, HAPPY READING!

Grace Burrowes

Read on from an excerpt from. **Miss Delectable**, book one in the **Mischief in Mayfair** series!

EXCERPT—MISS DELECTABLE

Colonel Sir Orion Goddard has raised self-reliance to a high art, but when one of the boys in his household falls ill, and demands that Rye summon Miss Ann Pearson to tend the patient, Rye has no choice but to ask for the lady's help...

~

"She's here!" Louis's shout nearly startled Rye out of his boots. "I brung the lady!"

"Good work," Rye said, going to the top of the ladder and peering down into the shadowed stable. "Miss Pearson if you could join us up here? Louis, fetch the lantern and then see to your supper."

The stable had grown dark while Orion had waited, and memories had crowded in. How many hours had he spent in the infirmary tents, listening to a dying man's final ramblings or writing out the last letter the fellow would send home? How many times had he refused a fallen soldier's entreaty for a single, quick bullet?

"Colonel," Miss Pearson said, arriving at the top of the ladder. "Good evening."

Orion took the basket from her and waited while Miss Pearson dealt with her skirts and climbed from the ladder into the hayloft. Louis passed up the lantern and tried for a gawk. He climbed back down when Orion aimed a glower at him.

Benny clearly did not want an audience.

"Miss Ann has come," Orion said to the boy curled in the straw. "You will do as she says, my lad, and if she says to send for the surgeon, we send for the surgeon." No soldier ever wanted to fall into the surgeon's hands, much less commend another to that torment.

"I ain't 'avin' no bloody sawbones," Benny muttered. "Go away, Colonel."

"You're insubordinate," Orion said, brushing a hand over the boy's brow. "Mind Miss Ann, or you'll be scrubbing pots for a week."

Miss Pearson watched this exchange with an air of puzzlement. "Where is the injury?"

"He won't tell me," Orion said, straightening. "Won't let me move him, won't stir from his nest, but there is a wound or ailment of some sort."

"If you will give us some privacy, I'll see what I can do."

Orion regarded the miserable child. "This boy is dear to me. Please spare no effort to bring him right." He would not embarrass Benny with a closer approximation of the truth: Loss of the child would unman him and send the other five boys into paroxysms of grief.

"We need privacy, Colonel."

"I won't go far." Rye *could* not go far, could not leave a man downed on the battlefield. "Holler if you need anything, and I do mean anything."

"I understand." She made a gesture in the direction of the ladder, her gaze calm and direct. *Be off with you. I have the situation in hand.*

He'd forgotten how petite she was, how serenity wafted about her like a fragrance. "Benny was right to have me send for you, and thank you for coming."

"I will render a full report as soon as I've examined the patient, but I cannot do that until you remove yourself from the immediate surrounds."

Orion made himself descend the ladder and busied himself tidying up the horses' stalls while soft voices drifted down from the hayloft. Benny was holding a conversation, not merely moaning out orders, an encouraging sign.

Darkness fell. Summer had departed and autumn had arrived. Rye's hip told him as much on the chilly evenings and chillier mornings. Still, Miss Pearson remained in the hayloft, speaking quietly. Benny responded, and the cadence was that of a normal chat, though Orion could not make out the words.

"Colonel?"

"Here." Orion left off scratching Scipio's neck and returned to the foot of the ladder.

"The patient will make a full recovery, but I need a set of clean clothes, warm water, and some rags. Also a sewing kit if you have one."

"Stitches?" *The poor lad.* "I have some laudanum if that will help."

"Let's start with the clean clothes."

"But that—" *Made no sense.* Orion's protest died aborning as Miss Pearson's skirts appeared at the edge of the hayloft, followed by her person climbing onto the ladder.

A gentleman did not watch a lady descend a ladder, even in the near darkness of a stable in the evening. Miss Pearson wasn't strictly a lady—she labored hard for her bread—but Orion had at one time considered himself a gentleman.

He turned his back until Miss Pearson was standing before him in the gloom of the barn aisle. She'd taken off her straw hat, and her cuffs were turned back. She smelled good—flowery and fresh—a contrast to the earthy scents of the stable.

"Benny will be well," she said with calm conviction. "Clean clothes are the first priority. Bone broth, chamomile tea, light activity, and the malady will ease its grip in a few days."

"You're sure?" Orion said, peering down at her. "You aren't a physician, and the boy was clearly in misery." *Showed evidence of serious injury.*

"I am as certain of my diagnosis as I am of my name, Colonel. Fetch the patient some clean clothes, and you and I will talk."

Orion's relief was unseemly. He'd worried for his sister Jeanette when food poisoning had brought her low, but Jeanette was an adult, and she'd clearly had Sycamore Dorning to fret for her too. These boys had nobody and nothing, and life had already been brutally unkind to them.

"Thank you," he said, taking the lady's hand and bowing. "Thank you from the bottom of my heart."

Miss Pearson ambushed him with a hug—a swift squeeze, followed by a pat to his shoulder. For a small woman, she hugged fiercely. The embrace was over before Orion could fathom that he was being hugged, and that was fortunate.

He'd sooner have taken another bullet than withstand Ann Pearson's affection.

"The child is lucky to have you," she said, stepping back. "I gather Benny is one of several children in your care."

"They are hardly children anymore. They eat like dragoons and grow out of clothing almost before it's paid for." Orion cupped his hand to his mouth. "Watch the lantern, Benny. I'm off to find you clean togs and scare up the tisanes Miss Pearson has prescribed."

Benny's head appeared over the top of the ladder, bits of hay cascading down. "You won't tell the others?"

Tell them what?

"You are suffering a brief indisposition," Miss Pearson replied. "Perhaps something you ate disagreed with you. The colonel and I will discuss what's to be done."

Some silent communication passed between Miss Pearson and the patient. Benny shrugged and withdrew from sight.

"No more piking off," Rye called up to the loft. "I don't care if you have consumption, the Covent Garden flu, and sooty warts. You don't desert the regiment just because you feel poorly."

"Yes, sir." The resentment Benny packed into the two mumbled syllables was reassuring.

"Come, Colonel." Miss Pearson gathered up her basket and marched down the barn aisle. "I daresay Benny could use some sustenance, and I want a look at your medicinals."

Orion followed reluctantly. "You're sure the lad will come right?"

"Benny will be fine. Have you eaten supper?"

"No, and now that I know we're won't be measuring Benny for a shroud, I admit I am famished. The cook/housekeeper usually leaves me a tray on the hob before she departs for the night. You're welcome to share."

"Your help doesn't live in?"

Rye crossed the alley and escorted Miss Pearson into the garden, where crickets sang a lament to winter's approach. A cat skittered up over the garden wall, and fatigue pressed down on Rye like the darkness itself.

"My housekeeper lives around the corner with her daughter and son-in-law. I believe Mrs. Murphy has a follower and would rather see him on her own turf. My maid-of-all-work and man-of-all-work are a married couple—he also serves as my coachman—and they dwell over the carriage house."

Miss Pearson moved through the night with the same easy assurance Orion associated with her in other contexts. She'd been comfortable in Jeanette's sick room. In the Coventry's kitchens, she'd been thoroughly at home.

"You have married servants, Colonel?"

"My former batman and his wife. I value loyalty over convention."

"I suspect you value loyalty over almost every other consideration. My gracious, your roses are lovely." Miss Pearson made her way down the cobbled path to the overgrown roses along the stone wall.

"These are not damasks, and yet..." She sniffed. "They are marvelous."

"Careful," Orion said, pausing on the path. "That one is French and has serious thorns. A gardener at the Château de Neuilly traded me a pair of bushes for a few bottles of my wine. Said that rose originated on the *Île Bourbon*."

"Perfumiers would pay you a fortune for these roses." She bent closer and took another whiff of pink blooms.

"I traded champagne fit for a king for that specimen. I was trying to sneak my best vintage into the cellars of the Duke of Orléans, but I suspect my wine met its fate in servants' hall."

Miss Pearson made a pretty picture, sniffing the roses by the light of a gibbous moon. Something of poignancy tried to gild the moment, with the crickets offering their slow song and the thorny roses perfuming the night air.

She'd hugged him, was the problem. Nobody hugged Orion Goddard, and he liked it that way. Needed it that way.

"Your champagne was well spent," she said, straightening. "Do your boys maintain this garden?"

His boys. They were his, though he didn't dare think of them in those terms. "They do, with some guidance from me. Shall we go in?"

"I suppose we ought to. Benny can't spend the night in that stable."

"I'm sure he has on many an occasion. Benny's my best sentry. Likes his privacy and thinks deeply as a matter of habit. The other fellows don't quite know what to make of him, but they worried at his absence."

"You worried at his absence," Miss Pearson replied as Orion ushered her into the hallway that led to the pantries and kitchen.

"Nearly panicked," Orion said. "The lads have eaten. If you're hungry, we'll have to forage. Drew!"

The boy trotted across the corridor from the servants' hall. "Sir?"

"Benny ate something that disagreed with him and needs a clean set of togs brought over to the hayloft. A basin of warm water and some rags wouldn't go amiss either, though he'll want privacy if he has to clean up. See to it, please."

"Aye, sir." Drew bowed to Miss Pearson—where had the lad picked up that nicety?—and scampered up the steps.

Miss Pearson began opening the kitchen's cupboards and drawers. She was on reconnaissance, clearly, and because Orion knew only the basics of survival when it came to the kitchen—bread, butter, jam, cheese, that sort of thing—he let her explore.

The tray on the hob held a bowl of lukewarm soup, as well as bread and butter. Many a night, Orion had subsisted on the same, but he was truly hungry and for once wanted something more substantial.

"The chophouse will be open for another hour," he said. "We can manage sandwiches if that will suffice."

Miss Pearson left off pillaging and gave him the oddest look. "Sandwiches will do, and we begin by washing our hands. What is Benny's full name?'

"Benjamin," Rye scrubbed up at the wet sink and moved aside so Miss Pearson could do likewise. "The boys all choose their names when they come to live here. Drew, for example, is Andrew Marvell Goddard. Drew was smitten with the poet's epitaph 'the ornament and example of his age, beloved by good men, feared by bad, admired by all, though imitated by few; and scarce paralleled by any,' or something like that. That Marvell stopped the crown from hanging Milton impressed Drew as well."

Miss Pearson rummaged in her basket and set a tin on the worktable. "And you gave the boys your family name?"

"Goddard is the only name I have to give them." The only name Orion had to defend, and he'd made a bad job of that mission, thus far. With Jeanette safely married and another good harvest all but complete, he'd see his name properly cleared.

"And the rest of Benny's name?"

"Benjamin Hannibal Goddard, his middle name chosen for the famed Carthaginian of old. Why?"

Miss Pearson swung the kettle over the coals on the raised hearth that took up half of the kitchen's outside wall. She'd made a pretty picture in the garden, and she made a different sort of pretty picture in the kitchen.

Rye should have tarried longer in France, where a call upon a certain good-humored and friendly widow in Reims could have figured on his itinerary.

"You had no idea, then?" Miss Pearson asked as she withdrew a loaf from the breadbox and took a knife from a drawer.

"No idea of what?"

She wielded the knife with a mesmerizing sort of competence, the slices perfectly even. "Not Benjamin Hannibal, Colonel. The child's name is Benevolence Hannah."

Orion was hungry enough to risk snitching a slice of bread. He tore a crust off and chewed. Reasonably fresh, probably made that morning.

"Strange names for a lad."

Miss Pearson paused in her artistry and slanted him a look.

The bread abruptly stuck in Orion's throat.

Benny's indisposition that had visited last month and was back again a few weeks later. The use of grime as camouflage for cheeks that would never grow a beard. The reticence around the other boys, the knit cap worn in all weather...

"Rubbishing hell."

Order your copy of **Miss Delectable**!